SUPERNATURAL
DETECTIVES

4

SUPERNATURAL DETECTIVES

4

SHIELA CRERAR

Ella M. Scrymsour

LUNA BARTENDALE &
THE UNDYING MONSTER

Jessie Douglas Kerruish

COACHWHIP PUBLICATIONS

Landisville, Pennsylvania

CONTENTS

INTRODUCTION

TIM PRCHAL
Oklahoma State University

"Oh, you modern women!" Doctor Chisholm scolds Shiela Crerar, Psychic Detective. He then adds, "You dabble in science and medicine, you dabble in politics and law, and now you dabble in the occult. What else is there left for mere man?" In 1920, when Ella M. Scrymsour's stories featuring Crerar were first being published, roles for women were indeed starting to expand—but only slightly for a select few. In actuality, Crerar and Jessie Douglas Kerruish's Luna Bartendale are very likely the only two females among the first wave of fictional supernatural detectives. This wave began as a ripple with Dr. Martin Hesselius, who narrates the stories in Joseph Sheridan LeFanu's *In a Glass Darkly* (1872), and crested with Algernon Blackwood's John Silence and William Hope Hodgson's Carnacki, who appeared in 1908 and 1910 respectively. From Ireland and Britain, the wave reached American shores in the 1920s and 1930s with Seabury Quinn's Jules de Grandin and Manly Wade Wellman's Judge Pursuivant. Amid these and several other male characters investigating the paranormal, Crerar and Bartendale become something distinctive if not a bit radical.

The scarcity of female supernatural detectives in fiction is hard to explain, especially when considering the prominence of women in the spiritualism movement. This movement, after all, coincides with those early paranormal mystery stories and helps to explain some of the original interest in them. Ever since the Fox sisters ignited interest in communication with spirits in the mid-1800s, women regularly fulfilled the role of psychic medium, conducting séances and channeling the voices of those who had crossed to the great beyond. That women should serve as hostesses between the physical and spiritual realms seems very much in keeping with the era's notions about "the sensitive sex." The term "sensitive" was routinely used to denote a person who is able to psychically sense spirits, and Bartendale goes so far as to describe herself as a "Super-sensitive." In addition, when Kerruish includes the name Madame Blavatsky among real-life paranormal investigators such as Arthur Conan Doyle, readers are reminded that women held their own when it came to dealing with spirits.

Another roadblock to explaining the gender imbalance of super-natural detectives appears when considering authors who kept their contributions to the mystery genre separate from Gothic horror. Though certainly in the minority, female crime-solvers were on the rise as competition for Sherlock Holmes and his fellow fellows. By the time Scrymsour and Kerruish came onto the scene, British readers had been introduced to Catherine Louisa Pirkis's Loveday Brooke in 1893 and Baroness Orczy's Lady Molly in 1912. In America, the very popular Anna Katharine Green introduced readers to Amelia Butterworth in 1897 and Violet Strange in 1915. This is only a sampling of precedents by women authors, and male writers had been creating female detectives since the 1860s. So why do Crerar and Bartendale appear so alone in "solving uncanny mysteries or the 'laying of ghosts'," as Crerar's advertisement in *The Times* puts it?

A theory might be constructed by positioning two prominent yet conflicting conventions of fiction in the late nineteenth and early twentieth centuries. Serial heroes of this era tend to be bachelors—sometimes, confirmed bachelors as with Holmesian detectives. This ensures that the characters are free to pursue an endless string of dangerous criminals or supernatural fiends. Imagine, for example, what a *Mrs.* Carnacki might have said about her husband's chums regularly gathering at the house so he could narrate his perilous encounters with the otherworld. Keeping serial heroes unmarried was practical and profitable, but it presented a problem for serial heroines. According to popular sentiment, proper young ladies might be permitted to devote themselves to serving those in need for a limited time; however, their end goal should be to wed. This explains why both Crerar's and Bartendale's stories conclude with the detectives getting married. Bartendale even ends up losing her super-sensitivity to occult phenomenon when it is conquered by love, "that grand passion that sweeps up all powers of soul and brain into itself." Unless they happened to be aging spinsters like Agatha Christie's Miss Marple, this period's young, female detectives tended to have limited life spans.

Despite their following the convention of a woman sacrificing her professional life for wifehood, Crerar and Bartendale exhibit traits that can be admired by feminists and any other readers who like their heroines reasonably heroic. Like her descendent Buffy the Vampire Slayer, Crerar plunges boldly into almost any treacherous situation, be it a terror-inducing room or a werewolf's cave. She endures getting roughed up a good deal for her trouble, too. On the other hand, despite the signature skepticism, Special Agent Dr. Dana Scully inherited the stoic determination that Bartendale uses to carefully discern and infer the facts of her own *X-Files*-style mystery. These grandmothers of later female supernatural detectives are at least as daring and diligent as they are dainty and delicate, and they are probably far better suited for handling problems that are demonic rather than domestic.

Crerar's and Bartendale's stories are well worth reading for reasons other than gender, too. Scrymsour offers us a rare look at an occult detective in training. Crerar is new enough at her job to make embarrassing mistakes, for instance, by jumping to a very wrong conclusion about a foreigner in "The Werewolf of Raunnoch." Kerruish's work is notable in that it is one of the very few examples of a novel-length case found among that first wave of supernatural detectives. Quite possibly, the only other two such novels are Uel Key's *The Yellow Death (A Tale of Occult Mysteries): Recording a Further Experience of Professor Rhymer the "Spook" Specialist* (1921) and, if Van Helsing fits the role, Bram

Stoker's *Dracula* (1897). Rather than novels, this early body of fiction is dominated by short stories that appeared in magazines and, in some cases, hardcover collections.

At the same time, both authors provide insights into how readers—especially British readers—were turning to fictional haunts to help psychologically process the devastatingly real haunts lingering after World War One. More than once, Scrymsour has a character remind Crerar that she lives in a modern age of science and cynicism, not one conducive to believing in kilt-wearing phantoms and wraiths. One senses, though, that the author is trying to counter her original readers' disillusionment, coaxing them to at least entertain the thought that old-fashioned wonders still surround us. Kerruish is much more obvious in evoking the post-war malaise. The recent battle experiences of Oliver and Goddard very much shape the characterization of these two lead figures. Furthermore, the ancient curse that plagues the Hammonds in this novel can be equated to the violent streak that persists in overwhelming humanity regardless of any purported triumph of twentieth-century civilization over the savagery and superstitions of earlier ages.

The cases of Crerar and Bartendale, then, can be read for what they reveal about the Great War, about the genealogy of later fictional women who battle paranormal foes, about genre, or about gender. They stand as important and distinctive works in the body of founding supernatural detective fiction. If read chronologically—Crerar preceded Bartendale by two years—we see the start of one supernatural detective's career and then the finale of another's. The two characters mirror each other nicely, and they certainly would have relished one another's company. It is quite fitting that they now appear together for the first time in a single volume so that you, too, may relish the company of these two ground-breaking, ghost-busting characters.

SHIELA CRERAR

ELLA M. SCRYMSOUR

THE EYES OF DOOM

Shiela Crerar felt very lonely as she sat in her tiny sitting-room in her dreary lodgings. She was tired, too, mentally as well as physically, and she tried to forget the misery of the past six months.

An orphan, she had been brought up by an uncle who idolised her. For twenty-two years she had lived in happiness in their home in the Highlands. She could visualise it now. A smallish house for a laird, built in the true Scottish baronial style, with turreted roof and pepper-box corners and a tiny courtyard. "Kencraig" was built on the top of a high eminence overlooking Loch Lubnaig, and it had been one of her chief delights to sit among the heather and watch the rippling waters of the lake beneath. To her left was Ben Ledi, and she revelled in his rugged beauty. He stood for strength and chivalry in her young mind, and she always thought of him as a rough but courteous Bruce, with shaggy locks and tartan kilts flying in the wind. It was only a girlish fancy, but to her the Ben was a living personality—nature's gentleman—a Highland chief.

For twenty-two years she had bid him good morning and waved him a good night. For twenty-two years she had wandered among the heather, bathed in the Loch, and driven into Callender once a week to do her shopping. And now—she wondered why this sorrow should have come to her. Six months ago she had been out in the woods gathering rowan berries. She had gone home gay and bright, but there was no welcoming figure of Uncle John waiting at the door for her. She went into his study—and, oh, the horror of it! He was sitting at his desk, his eyes open wide, his mouth twisted

sideways, his hands cold. He did not answer her call. She knew he
was dead. "Heart failure," the doctor said, and Shiela felt that the
light had gone out of her world.

The funeral over, she had gone into the library with Mr.
MacArthur, her uncle's attorney. At first Shiela did not understand
what Mr. MacArthur was trying to tell her. She couldn't realise that
she had been left penniless, with only a heavily mortgaged estate
as a legacy. Mr. MacArthur advised her to sell Kencraig, pay off
the mortgage, and with what little remained over fit herself to take
her place among the workers of the great world. But Shiela refused
to sell her home. Every stone was precious to her, every corner
was a dear, living friend.

At last she agreed to let it on a five years' lease to a rich American widow.

"What do you intend doing now?" he asked.

"I shall have about a hundred pounds. I shall go to London,
and try and get something to do there."

She was obstinate. She procured cheap rooms in London in a
road derisively called Air Street. Her hundred pounds did not go
far. In vain she tried for work in the great Metropolis; no one
wanted her. Depressed and silent, she sat in her little room, and
wondered what would happen when her scanty money gave out.
She was a petite maid, with nut-brown hair and grey eyes that
looked all too trustingly at a cruel and heartless world.

She had no money to spend on amusements, and as she walked
the streets of the great city she saw visions of the long ago. She
wandered in Lincoln's Inn, and saw the passing of sedan chairs;
watched gallants, with silken coat and jewelled sword, bend low
before their lady loves. She sought out "old London," and lived
alone in the seventeenth century. Always psychic, her gift seemed
trebled in her sorrow and loneliness, and her only friends now were
the dim ghosts of the past.

She was sitting in the gardens of Lincoln's Inn one day, when
she suddenly became aware of a quaint figure beside her—a
wizened man of perhaps sixty years, in a dark, claret-coloured suit,
with a black three-cornered hat upon his knee. And as she looked,

he took a pinch of snuff from a beautifully enamelled box, and applied it to his nostrils, his little finger delicately poised like a bird on the wing.

"You are sad and lonely, little lady," he said suddenly. "Why not help those that are sad and lonely too? You have a gift—a most wonderful gift of sight. Use that sight for your own benefit and the benefit of mankind. I promise you, you will not fail."

"But how?" she began, but the quaint little figure had gone; and there was only a fat old woman, with an untidy dress and a rusty black bonnet, watching her curiously from the further corner of the seat.

Shiela felt dazed. She rose and looked round. No, she was still in the bustling world of taxis and motor-buses. The picturesque past had vanished. She smiled a little, and went home, but her brain was working hard. She slept well that night, and when morning came her mind was made up.

For the next three days an advertisement appeared in the agony column of *The Times*:

> Lady of gentle birth, Scottish, young, penniless, possessing strong psychic powers, will devote her services to the solving of uncanny mysteries or the "laying of ghosts." Offer quite genuine. Reply, with particulars and remuneration offered, to S. C. c/o Mrs. Barker, 14b Air Street, Regent's Park, London.

And now she was waiting—waiting. Two days had passed since her advertisement had first appeared. A double knock sounded. The postman! A footstep sounded outside, and Mrs. Barker appeared.

"A registered letter for you, my dear," she remarked cheerily. "I'll be bringing yer supper in 'alf a tick. See, it's a bloater tonight, ain't it? A poor man's steak, I calls it."

And Shiela shuddered slightly. The well-meant vulgarity repelled her; the stench of cooking fish nauseated her. She felt nervy, restless, ill. The Highlands were calling her—she longed to feel the springy heather under her feet—to drink in the strong air. It was the call of the hills!

She looked at the thick, crested envelope curiously. It was certainly an answer to her advertisement, for it was addressed to her initials—S. C. Slowly she read it, and a flush of excitement crept into her cheeks.

> Dunfunerie,
> Loch Long, N.B.
>
> If S. C.'s offer is really genuine, will she accept the enclosed £10 on account for immediate expenses, and wire Lady Kildrummie that she is prepared to try to solve, and perhaps lay for ever, the very unpleasant mystery known as the "Kildrummie Weird"? If S. C. states the time she will arrive at Arrochar Station, Lady Kildrummie will see that there is a car sent to meet her.

Shiela's eyes glowed. Arrochar! Scotland! Her luck had turned at last. She was going back to her beloved Highlands. But would she succeed in her undertaking? Then she remembered the "little old man" in Lincoln's Inn. "You will not fail," he had said. Of course, she had heard of the "Kildrummie Weird." Who had not? Was it not as much speculated upon as the hidden mystery of Glamis? Was it not even as mysterious? What was the story—did not some great calamity happen when the Weird appeared?

Next day she wired Lady Kildrummie that she would come at once, and she caught the night train to Glasgow where she changed for the West Highland line. At Arrochar Station, over which Ben Lomond towers, she looked round eagerly.

A tall man in the late thirties came towards her—a handsome man, rugged, strong, in a kilt of the Cameron tartan, his mother's clan.

"Miss Crerar?" he asked, raising his bonnet. "I am Stavordale Hartland. My aunt, Lady Kildrummie, asked me to meet you."

His voice was pleasantly tuneful, and the wholesome admiration in his eyes could do nought but please her. Instantly she compared him to rugged Ben Ledi, and, had the man at her side but known, it was the greatest compliment she could have paid him.

Dunfunerie was situate on the Argyllshire side of Loch Long, nestling under the great shoulder of "The Cobbler" himself. Lady Kildrummie met her with outstretched hands. "How good of you to come, my dear. Are you by any chance related to Crerar of Kencraig?"

"He was my uncle."

"Then you are doubly welcome, for Kencraig was my late husband's greatest friend. Now, Stavordale, you can leave Miss Crerar and me to have tea together."

It was not until they had finished their tea that her hostess commenced her story.

"My dear, I am in great trouble," she said, by way of starting. "Your advertisement interested me, and I wondered if you could 'lay for ever' the Weird that haunts this place. Up to now the story has been kept absurdly secret—I think none of us wanted to believe in it. Since the time of Coinneach the Strong, in the latter part of the sixteenth century, Kildrummie has been cursed by this Weird. Every twenty-three years some terrible calamity has occurred in the family, preceded for about six months by 'The Eyes'."

"The Eyes?"

"Yes, the 'Eyes of Doom' they are called. The Kildrummie Weird takes the form of eyes that appear and disappear, and are mainly seen in the west wing. In recent years calamity has fallen on this house after the Eyes have been seen. In 1874, the year I was married, my husband's two elder brothers died—each by his own hand. One was found drowned in the Loch, the other was shot on the summit of the 'Cobbler' yonder. At both inquests the verdict was 'accidental death,' but we all knew better. It was 'the Eyes' that had driven them mad. My husband became heir to the title, and in 1897 my eldest son poisoned himself. Again it was put down to an accident. He was dabbling in photography, and it was supposed that he took some cyanide by mistake for his medicine. But it was no accident—twenty-three years had passed, and he had seen 'The Eyes.' This is 1920, Miss Crerar; it is twenty-three years since Diarmid died, and I am afraid. My son Duncan, the only one left to me, is now twenty-six years old. Lately he has complained of being kept awake at night by curious creakings. He has seen strange lights, and, oh, he is changed. I can't explain what I mean; you will see for yourself; he is all nerves. I am convinced he has seen 'The Eyes of Doom.' Will you try and solve the mystery for me, Miss Crerar? What the cause is I don't know, but the hideous waiting for some tragedy to fall is terrible."

"I'll do my best, Lady Kildrummie. I can promise you no more."

That evening Shiela met Duncan Kildrummie. Although young, he was a distinguished soldier—had won the D.S.O., and been mentioned several times in despatches, and had the reputation among his friends of being a regular dare-devil. But Shiela had a shock when she saw him. His hands were restless, the flesh under his eyes was puffy and dark, and if he was spoken to suddenly his whole body would respond with nervous twitchings.

"Lady Kildrummie," she said after dinner, "will you put your son into another room to sleep, and leave his empty for me to examine? I can see he is in a state of great mental distress. Can't you get him to go away for a change?"

"It's no use, Miss Crerar. I have begged him to go away, but nothing will induce him to leave."

That night Shiela changed into a dark rest-gown, and when everyone had retired to bed she prowled up and down the long corridors armed only with a tiny flash-lamp. She unlocked the chapel door and went inside. Suddenly she felt an icy blast that seemed to pierce through her, and the heavy door closed silently behind her. She felt startled, and tried to open it, but the catch was down on the other side. She was locked in! The sudden gust of wind was not repeated, yet she found she was shivering with cold from head to foot. Always venturesome, the thought never entered her head to find a way of rousing the household. If she was unable to get out, then she would stay in the chapel till day came.

She sat down in one of the old-fashioned pews and looked about her. The moon was conveniently bright, and she could distinguish objects quite clearly by its light.

As she sat she became aware that someone was looking at her, and she turned sharply round.

A pair of eyes was gazing at her, eyes so mournful, so full of grief that Shiela felt her own fill with tears of sympathy.

And as she met the piteous gaze she became suddenly conscious of the fact that the eyes were not framed by a face! She rose with a startled exclamation of horror, and turned away, but to her right another pair of eyes appeared, eyes this time that were mad with hate; eyes so filled with loathing and malevolence that Shiela backed away from them in fear. But now the whole chapel seemed filled with the ghastly sight. Eyes with expression, eyes without! Eyes kind, eyes cruel! Eyes imbecile, eyes fanatical! Eyes with every expression in them that man could conceive.

Shiela put out her hands to beat the swelling mass away, but even as her arms were extended in front of her they were caught in a ghostly vice, and she was dragged to the vestry door.

She was drawn by unseen hands—hands that possessed an unseen body. All that she could see of her captor was two eyes, eyes that shone in the moonlight and that looked at her with cruel menace.

The vestry door swung silently open, and she was dragged through, followed by the eyes. She had no time to look round, for the door that communicated with the west wing, which was always doubly locked and barred, now stood open wide, and through it Shiela was taken.

The west wing was partly a ruin, and the wind whistled through glassless windows and roofless halls. Then the grip of iron relaxed, and she found she was in a small turret chamber, and around her were twenty-three pairs of eyes—all baleful and cruel, except one, and that one pair seemed as if they might belong to a wounded deer, so plaintive were they, so mournful and sad.

Shiela moved towards the door, but the eyes surrounded her. She tried to dodge them, tried to get away from them, but it was impossible. She was as keenly guarded as if by living bodies. Then she grew really frightened, terrified, her brain seemed to go numb, her teeth chattered, and she cried aloud in her agony of dread. But the eyes grew fiercer and more cruel—they seemed to menace her. With a cry she threw herself at the bodiless terrors, and all became dark.

For awhile she remembered nothing, then she was conscious that she was being carried down long corridors and up steep stairs. There was the sound of a click, and a voice said, "Do you want anything, Miss Crerar? I heard you call out, so I came across to you." It was Lady Kildrummie.

"I'm thirsty," cried Shiela, "and, oh, please, Lady Kildrummie, will you put the light on."

But Lady Kildrummie stared in amazement, for she had switched on the electric light as she entered the room! She bent over the girl. Here eyes were open wide, but they met her gaze with a cold stare. The sight had gone!

"My dear, my dear," she breathed, "what has happened?"

"I—I hardly know. I—I was in the chapel—oh, do please put on the light. It is so dark here."

Tenderly the elder woman put her arms about the girl.

"Tell me first what is the matter," she said gently. "The dark is so peaceful, and I am here with you."

Incoherently Shiela spoke. "I was in the chapel—through the turret room. There were twenty-three eyes—" The girl's voice trailed off. She seemed to be in a stupor, but her eyes were still wide open. Lady Kildrummie rang a bell.

"Tell Doctor Graeme to come here at once," she said to the startled maid. "Miss Crerar is ill."

The genial doctor, a guest in the house, came hurriedly and examined the girl.

"She's had a shock," he said.

"Her eyes! Her eyes!" cried Lady Kildrummie, distractedly.

"My God! Blind! But she was all right at dinner!" said the doctor.

That night a watchful vigil was kept over Shiela, and when the sun rose she awoke from her torpor and looked at Lady Kildrummie in amazement.

"What is the matter?" she asked, curiously. "Why are you here?"

And her hostess realised that she had regained the power of sight. When the doctor saw her he stared at her in amazement.

"My dear young lady, why, I—I—bless my soul—there's nothing wrong with her!"

Shiela told Lady Kildrummie of her experience in the night, but her hostess smiled.

"You have certainly described the turret room, Miss Crerar, but you couldn't have got into it last night, as I hold the key."

"But I did," protested Shiela. "The door was open wide."

"Well, we will go and look at it as soon as you are up, but I assure you it would be quite impossible for anyone to open the door without my key."

"Now," said Lady Kildrummie later, "you see this door is twice bolted and twice locked."

The bolts were stiff and the key turned with great difficulty, but the nail-studded door swung open at last. Shiela gave a little cry of triumph. The floor, thickly coated with the dust of ages, was marked by freshly made footprints—footprints of long, pointed boots that crossed and recrossed each other—and among the old-fashioned prints were some made by a little, light modern shoe.

Shiela took hers off, and bent down to the mark nearest the door. It fitted exactly!

"I was here last night," she whispered, hysterically.

But Lady Kildrummie was almost speechless, and terror shone in her eyes. "The Eyes of Doom," she muttered, hoarsely. "God help us, for our troubles are beginning."

That night as Shiela was preparing for bed again the melancholy eyes appeared. She looked at them fearfully. It was an awe-inspiring sight to watch those expressive eyes move about, propelled by an unseen force. They seemed to float in the air, and she knew their power of locomotion rested in the bodies that were hidden from her sight. And even as she waited the other eyes manifested themselves. She tried to resist, but the ghostly hands were too strong, and again she was taken to the turret room. A circle of eyes was around her—eyes on a level with her own, but only space above them and space below. But they seemed less malignant, less cruel, though terrifying nevertheless. They seemed to be trying to tell her something, but she was unable to read their message. She was nervous, she was on the defensive, and unconsciously she rendered herself out of tune with the Weird. She was not in a fit psychic state to understand them. She was in too material a condition. The eyes seemed to realise this, and they grew menacing again, fretful, impatient. Again there came to the girl a space of forgetfulness, and when she awoke to realities she was back in her room, and she realised she was blind!

She moved uncertainly about the room. Everything seemed unfamiliar to her, unreal. Her eyes hurt her, they seemed inflamed, they were sore. All night long the pain was unbearable, and she sat on a chair, helpless and miserable. But as the dawn came so a veil seemed to be lifted from her eyes, and she could see once more. It was a blindness that came with the darkness and went with the morning light.

During the day Shiela was trying to get into communion with the astral world. She was trying to fit herself to "see" even deeper into the mysteries of the "unknown." It was her first trial alone, and she was gradually becoming fitted for the task she had set herself.

Daily Duncan Kildrummie grew more silent, more morose, more taciturn. The Kildrummie Weird was trying to claim him as its victim, and he realised it and knew he was too weak to hold out against it for long. Soon he, too, would die—and die "accidentally," as so many members of his family had done.

The eyes grew more venturesome. One night a pair hovered over the dinner table, and gazed at Duncan intently. All saw them, and as Lady Kildrummie screamed in terror they disappeared. But Duncan rose, and stumbled blindly out of the room. Stavordale went quickly after him, and found his cousin staring at the cold waters of the Loch. He was staring, staring, and there was a look of madness in his eyes. The next night several pairs circled round him. He tried to beat them off, but they seemed always just out of his reach, and their expression mocked him.

Stavordale Hartland attached himself to Shiela, and she found his strong personality a great help to her in the nerve-racking time she was going through. Night after night when the eyes claimed her she found she was a helpless entity in their grasp. And in the turret room they supplicated, entreated, menaced her, and still she was unable to read their meaning.

And daily the eyes seemed to appear more often. They followed Duncan from room to room, they drove him out of the house, and he would disappear for hours at a time, and his mother's heart would ache with apprehension.

One night Shiela resolved not to go to bed, and Lady Kildrummie and Stavordale agreed to sit up all night with her in the library. For Shiela had come to dread the period of blindness that was forced upon her in so mysterious a way, and she wondered if in company she would be strong enough to resist the ghostly hands.

First one pair of eyes appeared, and then another, until all twenty-three pairs surrounded the trio. As if turned to stone, Lady Kildrummie and Stavordale Hartland watched Shiela forcibly dragged out of the room. They could neither move nor speak, and when Shiela returned to them she found that three helpless people would have to stay in the library until dawn, for this time they were all blind!

Next night Shiela and Stavordale were standing together watching Duncan walking restlessly up and down the terrace.

"Don't you think you had better give all this up, little girl?" said Stavordale Hartland, and his voice held a tender, caressing note.

"I can't," she said, passionately. "Look at him. He is all his mother has. Can't you see the Eyes are driving him mad? The Weird will claim another victim unless I can prevent it." And even as she spoke the evil eyes appeared, phosphorescent in the darkness, and with a wild shriek Duncan Kildrummie fled into the blackness of the night. Until the morning he roamed the country at large, and when he appeared at breakfast he was haggard and worn, and the most inexperienced eye could tell that he was really ill.

Shiela alone seemed to have a soothing effect upon him, and when later in the day Dr. Graeme administered a sleeping draught, he suggested that Shiela should sit by his bedside until it took effect. Lady Kildrummie left her for a moment, and immediately Shiela was conscious that the Eyes were watching her.

Before she realised it she was in the turret room, and she found she was numb from head to foot—she was powerless to move. As she watched, the eyes suddenly materialised into men. Gradually their bodies appeared until twenty-two men in doublet and hose stood before her. Their garments were of silk and velvet—rich, costly, gay. And the twenty-third of that ghostly company was a girl, almost a child of not more than fifteen years. Her hair was unbound and her face distorted with grief, and she clung piteously to a black-bearded man of middle age. A ghostly play began, and all the while Shiela watched with increasing horror. Others appeared on the scene—men in kilt and plaid, with dirks drawn, dirks red with blood. Roughly the girl was torn from the arms of her father and bound with hempen ropes.

The scenes that followed were hideous to behold, and Shiela knew that there was a power at work that compelled her to watch. The captive girl writhed and tore at her bonds, but all to no purpose— they were too cunningly tied. Not a word was said aloud, but the agonised expressions, the black terror spoke louder than words.

Two ghostly figures in black carried in a red-hot brazier; the coal burned and seemed to splutter, yet made no sound. Two long irons were placed in the glowing coals. The prisoners made a desperate effort to overpower their captors; for a few moments the whole place was in confusion, but gradually their efforts were subdued, and one by one they were dragged to the fire. One by one the red-hot iron was plunged into their eyes, one by one they were blinded and flung aside to die.

Shiela watched twenty-two men done to death in this awful way. She watched their agonies of pain, their writhings, their torments, and the scene was all the more horrible because of the deathly silence that accompanied it.

There was but one more victim—the girl. Roughly she was dragged to the brazier, but a merciful Providence intervened, she stumbled and fell, and when a man roughly turned her over with his foot he found the gentle spirit had fled.

The assassins looked round the room at the dead, and even as they did so the scene changed, and Shiela found she was out in the chestnut avenue, standing before the giant tree, the pride of Dunfunerie. The rain poured down in torrents, the wind blew hard, her dress clung to her figure and chilled her, her shoes were covered with mud. A black-cowled monk approached, with beads and breviary. Horror came into his countenance as he stumbled over the still warm bodies. He touched the girl in gentle pity, but he was jostled away rudely. He opened his book, and Shiela could see that he was pleading to be allowed to say a prayer over the bodies. A huge man struck him, and as he picked himself up he silently cursed the murderers. He cursed them on the Holy Book, but they jeered in his face and continued their nefarious work.

There under the spreading chestnut tree a pit was dug, and, with neither prayer nor priest, into it the girl was flung. Then followed the other twenty-three. The hole was small—the bodies protruded above the sides. With a ribald smile on his cruel face, the menacing figure in black forced the ground to receive them. The pit was covered in with earth, the murdered ones were safely hidden away, and Shiela realised she had witnessed a scene that had taken place some three hundred years before, a scene that had been re-enacted for her benefit. At last she knew what "the Eyes" had tried to tell her.

The figures died away, they seemed to be absorbed into the atmosphere itself, and once more only twenty-three pairs of eyes were left, but they were eyes that looked at her with gratitude. They knew she understood.

And as she watched them, too, fade away she was conscious that her limbs were once more warm. She looked round in bewilderment—there on the bed lay the sleeping form of Duncan Kildrummie. She was back in his room. She felt her dress—it was quite dry. Her shoes had no trace of mud upon them. Lady Kildrummie entered.

"My dear, I'm sorry," she said, "I am afraid I have been rather a long time. Why—" she broke off, "what's the matter?" For Shiela was gazing at the open door, and her expression was soft and pitiful. But Lady Kildrummie could not see the figure of a frail young girl, dressed in a soft homespun with a white kerchief round her shoulders, a girl who looked at Shiela with thanks in her soft brown eyes.

"I think I shall be able to help you lay your 'Weird' successfully, Lady Kildrummie," said Shiela. "I'll tell you later, after I have had time to think." Next day a small party gathered underneath the chestnut tree. The turf was smooth and velvety—it had grown undisturbed for many centuries, but now it was being removed.

"Ah!" said Shiela, suddenly, for as the spade dug deep into the rich brown earth a skeleton arm appeared. Reverently the mould was moved. Twenty-two skeletons were unearthed, twenty-two skeletons of full-grown men, but at the bottom of the pit was a tiny skeleton, a skeleton crushed and broken. And Shiela knew it was the last remains of the girl—the Weird with the mournful eyes!

Reverently the bones were placed in an empty stone sarcophagus in the little chapel, and reverently the minister spoke the prayers for the dead. And as the last amen was said, Shiela heard an unseen choir burst out in song. It was the *Gloria in Excelsis Deo*.

Lady Kildrummie drew her cloak about her shoulders. "Do you hear the wind whistling?" she asked. Shiela smiled. She knew.

Six weeks later Duncan Kildrummie was up for the first time, after a serious attack of brain fever, during which for some days his life had been in the balance. But now the nervous twitchings were entirely gone, and his eye was clear and steady.

"And you think we are free of the 'Weird' at last?" asked Lady Kildrummie, as she was bidding Shiela goodbye.

"I hope so. I don't know the history of the turret room, but I should say the twenty-three were trapped there, and perhaps for religious reasons were foully murdered by some of your forebears. They were refused a Christian burial, and that accounted for their hatred and their hauntings. Their poor spirits were unable to rest in peace. Every twenty-three years—their number—they returned, but they could not make themselves understood."

Stavordale accompanied Shiela to Glasgow. He was very silent during the journey, but as the train was drawing into the city he suddenly took one of her hands.

"Miss Crerar—Shiela—I—I—won't you give all this up?" he urged.

"I—I can't, Mr. Hartland."

"But why? Shiela, won't you be my wife?"

"I—I can't explain, but I have a mission to fulfil. I have set myself a task, and I must complete it." She smiled at him. "Won't you wait a little?"

"Then you do care," he said, triumphantly, as he sought to draw her towards him, but the train had already stopped at the platform of the Glasgow terminus. Then all was bustle and rush, and it was not until he had said goodbye to her as she left for Edinburgh, where she had engaged rooms, that he realised she had not replied to his question!

Well, perhaps the time was not yet ripe for his love-making, but he realised whate'er might befall he had met his fate. And, like a knight in the "days of long ago," the wish of his lady was his law. He would bide her time, impatient though he might be.

THE DEATH VAPOUR

The telephone bell rang. Shiela Crerar picked up the receiver. "Yes, Hullo!" Her eyes brightened, but her voice remained cool and sedate. "Mr. Stavordale Hartland? Yes? What? Oh, dear! Yes, come round at once, and tell me all about it. Goodbye."

Half an hour later Mr. Hartland was ushered into Shiela's pretty little sitting-room in Edinburgh. He held her outstretched hand in both his, and looked hungrily into her eyes; but she deftly freed herself, and sat down in an armchair by the window.

"Now tell me all about it," she said, motioning him to a seat opposite her.

"Very strange things have been happening at my sister's home," he began. "First we heard curious groanings about the place, but took no notice of them, putting it down to the wind under the eaves. Then the groanings changed to terrible cries, and now a peculiar vapour has manifested itself, which leaves a most unpleasant odour behind it."

"What is it like?"

"I can only describe it as a volume of steam. It has appeared in all parts of the house, and at all times. It hovers about for a few seconds and then disappears. I can't describe what it is, but there is something so horribly evil about it that my sister is frightened to death."

"Why doesn't she go away?"

"She can't, Miss Crerar. Her husband, who died quite recently, left a most eccentric will. He bequeathed all his money and property to her on one condition."

"And that is?"

"That until her son marries, she spends nine consecutive months each year at her house—Duroch Lodge."

"And how old is her son now?"

"Kenneth is just ten, so, of course, for his sake, she must obey the condition of the will. She knows all about you, and begged me to ask you to help her. Will you?"

"Of course I will," said Shiela. "Where is Duroch Lodge?"

"Quite near Benderloch. I suppose you couldn't come today?" he went on, hesitatingly. "A train leaves just after twelve."

Shiela looked round the room thoughtfully, and then consulted her wrist watch. "Call for me with a taxi at a quarter to twelve," she said, briskly. "I'll be ready."

"Thank you so much, Shi—Miss Crerar," but with a gay little laugh, she was gone.

They caught their train easily, and when they reached Duroch Lodge Lady Morven was waiting for them.

She was a matronly figure of forty, pleasant and motherly.

"My dear, can you help us?" she cried. "You are so young—so feminine. I expected a bespectacled young woman—sexless—who would tackle the problem from a purely scientific point of view."

Shiela laughed.

"I'm not very old—twenty-three," she said, naively. "I'll do my best." A vague, dreamy look came into her eyes. "I'm Highland, you know, and I've the second sight. I feel sure I can help you."

"Thank you, dear," and the elder woman kissed her impulsively.

After lunch Lady Morven took Shiela all over the house, to make her familiar with every nook and cranny, every hole and corner in it.

"I don't want you to tell me any more," said Shiela. "I just want you to treat me as an ordinary guest."

Three days passed, which Shiela enjoyed immensely. She played golf, rode, walked, and, in the evenings, sang Highland folk songs. There was no sign of anything uncanny happening, and Shiela wondered if it was simply mind pictures that had been conjured up by a hyper-sensitive woman, and if there was really no mystery at all. It was March, and the wind was very cold, and the glow of the fire in her bedroom cheered her enormously. She curled herself up in a big armchair in front of it, and prepared for a delightful read before she finally got into bed.

Eleven had just struck—the whole house was still. There was nothing to be heard but the rustling of the trees outside, and the sharp gusts of the wind.

Suddenly there came the sound of a most terrible cry, a cry so full of poignant horror—of unutterable misery—of despair that it made her blood run cold. As it died away, it seemed to leave the place even more quiet than it had been before.

Shiela rose and opened her door softly. Now that her blood was stirred she had no sense of fear. She knew she was coming to grips at last with the unknown, and every nerve in her body thrilled at the thought. The long corridor was empty, but through a circular window at the end the moon sent her pale beams; and the scudding clouds made them appear and disappear in a weird fashion. As she stood, watching and listening, Lady Morven's door opened.

"Did you hear it?" she cried. "Oh, it was terrible."

"Go back," said Shiela sternly. "Leave me."

The door clicked, and once more Shiela was alone. Quiet as a mouse she waited, but no cry came again to startle the stillness of the night. After a couple of hours of watchful vigil she returned to bed, and wondered in her heart if some cruel practical joke was being perpetrated by an unknown enemy.

Next morning Lady Morven greeted her guest with awestruck eyes.

"You aren't afraid?" she asked, curiously.

"Let me watch with you," suggested Stavordale Hartland. "I don't think it is wise to leave you alone. You might have a fright that would upset you for life."

"Please," said Shiela. "I came to help Lady Morven. I must do it my own way."

"Will you call on me, if you want any help?"

Shiela smiled into the earnest eyes that were watching her so closely. "I promise," she said, but she thrilled at the look of gratitude he gave her.

"Oh, it's terrible," moaned Lady Morven. "I must stay here. If I do not I lose my entire income, and everything not entailed is left to charity, so that my little son would suffer too."

"Did your husband know of these—these hauntings?" asked Shiela.

"I don't see how he could have done. They only started since his death—five months ago."

"It was an extraordinary will to make."

"I think it was done to feel he could tie me down, even when he was dead. It curtailed my freedom. He always hated me"—she smiled wanly. "It was a *mariage de convenance*, my dear, and sometimes he was really cruel to me. The only consolation I had then was little Ken."

That night as Shiela was playing the piano in the drawing-room, she heard a smothered cry from Lady Morven; she looked round, and her hands involuntarily clashed on the notes, which resulted in a crashing discord.

Close by the fireplace rose a misty vapour—like the steam from a kettle, but of yellowish tint; just a thin spiral column that rose from floor to ceiling, and writhed and twisted in serpentine coils.

Shiela rushed towards it, but even as she drew near, it vanished from sight, leaving a slight sulphurous odour behind.

Later the dreaded cry came twice in quick succession, and even Shicla felt a cold shudder go down her spine as she heard the blood-curdling sound. But though she waited throughout the night, nothing else happened.

Next day she examined the walls and floors where she had seen the mist rise, but there was nothing to account for its appearance. As she went up the stairs to her room that night she saw the vapour at the end of the passage, and she noticed that it was in the full light of the moon's rays.

"Deduction number one," she said to herself. "It must have light. Yesterday it was between the fire and the electric light, tonight it is basking in the light of the moon."

She went towards it fearlessly, but the smell was stronger, and nearly stifled her. But as she reached the evil-looking column, it disappeared.

For the next few days the phenomenon was more pronounced. Almost every hour it could be seen in some part of the house; but the baleful vapour always kept in the direct rays of some light, artificial or otherwise.

Shiela's eyes grew bright. She spent nearly all her time alone-rummaging round the old world passages—investigating the little family chapel—even hunting among the ruins of the tiny Priory that had once flourished, and was now a mere handful of bricks and stone by the rose-garden.

"Have you a copy of Sir John Tadson's *History of Historical Scottish Houses*?" she asked one day.

"I think so," said Stavordale, and he went with her into the big, old-fashioned library, where they discovered the musty old volume, that had probably not been opened since it was first purchased in 1823.

"Have you found anything out, dear?" asked Lady Morven at dinner that night.

"I think so," she replied. "At any rate, I want to try an experiment. The moon will be at the full tomorrow at nine. The beams will fall right across the corridor to your door, Mr. Hartland. Now, if the 'Death Vapour' appears tomorrow night, it seems within the bounds of possibility to presume it will appear where the moon-beams will fall directly on it. Don't you think so?"

"Yes, of course, judging by past experience."

"Well, I want you both to help me."

"How?"

"I will hide in the shadow of your room, Lady Morven, close to where the beams will be at their brightest. I want you to stand behind the curtains over my door, and just watch. If I need any help, you will be there to give it, if not, well, I think the ghost will have been 'laid' successfully." She wouldn't explain what she intended doing, and Stavordale felt very anxious. The little "nut-brown" maid had grown very dear to him, and the experiments in which she had engaged herself were none to his liking. He knew little about the occult, but he had a wholesome dread of interfering in things supernatural.

That night, at a little before nine, three human beings took up the positions allotted to them in the corridor. Gradually the moonbeams crept nearer and nearer. The night was clear—there was not a cloud in the sky, and there was only the faintest breath of wind, which hardly stirred the leaves on the trees.

There was a feeling of death in the air. Shiela alone was calm and restful. In her gown of white she looked almost like an angel.

No one spoke—the stillness could be felt. Suddenly the vapour appeared, the evil vapour which filled them all with dread. And even as they watched they saw Shiela suddenly throw herself, with a half-articulate cry, at the writhing mass. Stavordale saw the dress mingled with the foggy matter, and instinctively he rushed forward, but even as he did so, there came from the vapour that terrible cry. Blood-curdling—horrible—hellish—and as he reached the side of Shiela, who had fallen a crumpled heap on the floor, it disappeared.

"Help me," he cried to his sister. "God! I believe she is injured."

He picked up the fainting girl, carried her into his sister's boudoir, and laid her gently on the settee. Her eyes were closed, her lips blue and swollen, and there was the tiniest wound on her cheek from which blood oozed. It was like a toothmark, and he shuddered as he saw it.

"Turn the light on full," he cried. "Where's the brandy?"

But as the electric light blazed out, he turned to his sister in horror. For Shiela was covered from head to foot in a thin slime that smelt like death. It was in glistening streaks all over her face, in glistening streaks all over her dress. A slime that was horrible, filthy, and evil-smelling. And even as he brushed her cheeks clean of the malodorous matter he felt a burning sensation in his finger, and he saw a blister had risen, as though he had passed his hand through a flame!

"This is awful," he cried, never heeding the growing pain in his hands. "Hillary, get Mrs. Black—wash Shiela"—unconsciously he used her Christian name— "wash her in milk. I'll get a doctor. Burn all her clothes," and he gently held the icy cold hands. He had forced brandy between her tightly clenched teeth, but it had done her no good, and she still remained unconscious. Mrs. Black, the house-keeper, a Highland woman of the old school, came quickly in an-swer to the bell. Gently she and Hillary undressed the senseless girl, and bathed her in oil and milk.

"Put her in my bed," said Lady Morven. "I'll sit up with her tonight."

Mrs. Black asked no questions, but tended the newcomer, who was popular with everyone.

With gloves on her hands, Lady Morven picked up the girl's clothing and placed it on the open fire. And as she did so, there came that awful cry, as if a living creature was in pain. As the last remnant disappeared into ashes the dreadful cry was repeated, and, as it died away into an unearthly moan, a sobbing breath came from the girl on the bed—she shivered violently and opened her eyes.

"It's gone," she whispered. "But oh, it burnt so."

"My dear, my dear," said Lady Morven brokenly. "I shall not allow you to put yourself into such danger again. I have been a very wicked woman. I shall leave here." A knock sounded.

"The doctor," said Mrs. Black.

The canny doctor entered. He had been told a little of what had happened, but he put it all down to excessive imagination on the part of Shiela.

"H'm. Burnt rather badly. How did it happen?" He examined the wound at the side of her cheek. "What's this? It looks like a bite," and, even as he spoke, Shiela grew whiter than before.

"I'm bitten, you say? Oh, God help me," and she burst into tears.

When the doctor had gone she said to Lady Morven, "I mustn't stay. I am a danger to you all. Oh, let me go now."

"My dear, don't be foolish. Of course I shan't let you go. How do you mean you will be a danger?"

"I think I have discovered what has been haunting this place. It is an elemental. Now it has tasted my blood, and it will be even more fearless. Oh, send me away. I had armed myself with a crucifix when I threw myself at it, but in my excitement I dropped it. Thus it was able to feast upon me without interruption."

That night was a night of terror to them all. Even Stavordale Hartland, a man of iron nerves, felt his blood run cold at the incessant cries of horror that rang throughout the night. Shiela was almost too weak to move, but suddenly, when there had been a hush for a time, she cried out, "Beat it off, oh, don't let it come. Get a Bible. Keep it away from me."

The "Death Vapour" was materialising in the sick room. It drew nearer and nearer until it enveloped the figure on the sick bed.

"Stavordale, help me, help me," cried his sister.

Together they bent over the writhing vapour, and the man placed a Bible on Shiela's breast.

With a hoarse cry of rage the vapour disappeared, but the watchers saw another tiny wound on the girl's neck.

All that night they wrestled with the "Death Vapour." The house rang with cries of rage and hate. The very rafters echoed with hoarse laughter and choking screams.

When the morning came Shiela announced her intention of getting up.

"I can't rest here," she said pathetically. "I want to get out into the fresh air."

Later in the day she said, "Was there any other strange clause in your husband's will?"

"No, I don't think so—only the one relating to my staying here."

"Was that all?"

"Yes, except, of course, the crucifixes."

"What was that?" quickly.

"Oh, from time immemorial, a crucifix has hung in every room in this house. I think it dated from the time when the monastery was dismantled, and this house was built. My husband said in his will that he wanted every crucifix in the house to be buried with him."

"Ah, I think we may have your husband to thank for these unpleasant manifestations. It seems wicked to accuse the dead, but

I'm afraid he knew what he was doing when he made that dastardly will."

After a pause Shiela went on:

"Should you die, Lady Morven, who would benefit?"

A shadow passed over the face of Lady Morven.

"A very distant cousin, Miss Crerar, someone my late husband at one time wanted to marry."

"Oh," and Shiela looked sympathetically at the woman beside her. "I've been looking up the history of this place and it makes very strange reading. Part of this house existed at the time of the monastery, and part of the foundations belong to the time of the monastery itself. History is very vague about it, but the Priory was completely dismantled in 1587." Stavordale Hartland looked perplexed.

"What has this to do with the unpleasant happenings of last night, Miss Crerar?"

"A great deal. I have spent a considerable time in the library lately, Mr. Hartland, and I have discovered a lot about this place which I believe you are in ignorance of."

"Well?"

"In 1539 the Priory was at the height of its fame. The Prior, a holy man, was beloved of all, and you can judge his horror and dismay, when one day he found two of his most trusted monks offering up the 'Black Mass' in the vault below the chapel."

"This is getting exciting," said Lady Morven. "It sounds like a novel."

"The whole matter was thrashed out, and it was discovered that Brothers Ambrose and Aloysius were in the habit of visiting the neighbouring hamlets and villages ostensibly on errands of mercy. In reality they enticed children from their homes and inaugurated the 'Black Mass' sacrifices. They offered the children's warm, living blood to Sathanas, their chosen master, and drank it in communion."

"How shocking!"

"Justice was meted out to them by the Prior. They were locked up in the vault they had profaned, and left there to die a slow death of starvation."

"Still, I cannot see what all this has to do with the question in point," said Hartland. "After all it is only a legend."

"No, that is where you are wrong. It really happened, and I believe the bones of those two unfortunates will still be found in the vault under the chapel."

"But there isn't one," said Lady Morven. "At least I have never heard of one."

"Suppose we find there is," said Hartland. "Suppose the bones are there, even. What is your theory with regard to the vapour that appears now?"

"I believe the place is haunted by an elemental—"

"What is that?" asked Lady Morven.

"It is difficult to explain. It is a—something that possesses an existence; it belongs to neither death nor heaven. It draws its life from humanity, or from the astral spirits it may come into contact with. I believe that, in the last moments of those two monks, this elemental took possession of them. It took hold of their astral selves and lived with them even when their flesh rotted and their bones decayed. In the far-off ages the monks and inhabitants of this place took the precaution of having crucifixes about to prevent evil spirits visiting them. That is the true origin of them being kept about this house."

Stavordale Hartland looked with interest at the frail girl who spoke so convincingly about phenomena in which, in the twentieth century, it seemed almost impossible to believe.

"I believe that the elemental has inhabited this house ever since then, but by the precautions taken by the believers, its power has remained dormant, and it simply existed in a kind of trance condition in the vault below. Your husband, Lady Morven, left a will in which he ordered all the crucifixes to be taken away from this house, and you were to stay here for nine consecutive months in the year. Soon after his death the house became haunted—surely the deduction is obvious?"

"I think you are right, Miss Crerar. James hoped that the hauntings would occur, and either I should be frightened to death, or I should refuse to go on living here. In either case I should lose my income."

"You have worked out a very ingenious theory, Miss Crerar," said Mr. Hartland, "and knowing my late brother-in-law's particular refined cruelty, I really believe you are right."

"Then, if I put the crucifixes back . . ." began Lady Morven.

"I don't think that will have much effect now. You see the elemental has tasted my blood—it will become more venturesome. It has now a living vitality. It will—"

And even as she spoke, the column of "Vapour" rose on the air. But this time it was more solid, and in the moving, writhing mass they could see the form of a face. A malignant face, with eyes that gleamed and shone like sparks of living fire. It could only be called a semblance of a face, for although it possessed eyes, and nose, and mouth, it seemed but a shapeless mask. The most dominant feeling was the utter malignity of the creature, the almost devilish cruelty that seemed to exude from it.

Quickly Lady Morven and Hartland joined hands round Shiela, regardless of themselves. With "Holy Book" outspread, they gradually fought their way across the garden to where a deep shadow rested under a cypress tree. As they reached the darkness under the branches the "Vapour" lost its shape and was once more just a thin column of mist; but an awful screaming rent the air as it disappeared from sight.

"There's no time to be lost," said Shiela. "An elemental lives by light. I am safe as long as I am in the dark or in shadow. Mr. Hartland, will you motor at once to the monastery on the Oban road?"

"But—"

"Please don't ask questions. I want to get everything done today. Twice has the 'thing' feasted on my blood. Already it has become fearless. Ask there if they can send a priest with holy water to bless a house, and also to come prepared to say the Burial Service."

"The Burial Service?" said Lady Morven, aghast.

"Yes, yes. I'll explain all to him when he comes. Only be as quick as you can."

"Now, Lady Morven," she went on, as soon as they had seen the car disappear round the bend, "Is there any one here who would know if there is a vault that can be opened easily in the chapel?"

"Peter Dougal, our head gamekeeper, has been on the estate for over fifty years. He was here in my father-in-law's time, and—"

"Where is he?" shortly.

"At his cottage, I expect."

"Let's go at once to him."

Peter Dougal, a man of seventy-odd years, looked surprised when Shiela questioned him.

"Aye, 'deed, mem, of course, there's a vault. It was in '80 I think when it was last opened. The last master, mem, had it closed up."

"He knew of it?" breathed Lady Morven.

"Why, yes, mem. He always said it was an evil place, and—"

"Would it be easy to open it?" asked Shiela, breaking in.

"Oh, aye. It's under the big pew in the chancel. Angus Malloch and me could move the big stone easily."

"It's not sealed then?"

"No. Juist fixed in and wedged, that's a'."

"Well, open it at once," commanded Lady Morven, "and tell me as soon as it is done."

"Let us stay under the shadow of the trees," said Shiela. "We can watch for the car coming back."

"How do you know what to do?" asked Lady Morven, curiously. "Have you had experience with an elemental before?"

"No," said Shiela laughing. "And I don't want it again. But I have always been interested in the occult. My uncle and I were both psychic, and I remember many of the things he told me. He was always experimenting in psychical things, and, of course, I helped him."

The time passed all too slowly. Shiela was very excited. She knew she was in danger—now the elemental had regained its hold on life through her; she knew that unless it was exterminated her very existence was in danger.

At length they heard the sound of the car and hurried to meet it. The priest, a jovial-looking man of middle age, was plainly mystified.

"Father," commenced Shiela in her most winning way. "I have a strange thing to ask you to do. You may think it is almost unorthodox, but I want you to help me—lay a ghost."

The genial father looked distressed.

"Is it a joke?" he asked.

Quickly Shiela told him the story of the "Death Vapour," and the whole history as she had learnt it.

"Now, Father," she concluded. "All I want you to do is to say the last prayers over the bones of those unhappy monks if we find them in the crypt. If they are not there, then just say the Burial Service without a body. Afterwards I want you to bless every room in the house."

"Poor souls," said the father gravely. "Poor misguided men. May they rest in peace!"

"They will if you do as I ask."

"It's a strange thing you have told me, Miss Crerar; but, as far as I can see, I shall be doing no harm by acceding to your request, and I may be doing a great deal of good. Where is the vault?"

"We'll go there in a minute. Lady Morven—can you find me two very long steel knitting needles and a spirit stove? Mr. Hartland, will you get some lamps, as I expect the vault will be dark?"

When everything was ready they entered the tiny chapel.

"You are sure you all want to come?" asked Shiela. "Something very horrible may happen down there—are you willing to risk it?"

Without a word Hartland began to descend the steps that led to the crypt below. They found it was quite small and very musty. They hadn't far to look for that which they sought. In one corner, on the earthy floor, were some human remains. Two skeletons lay close together, their bony arms embracing, as if in their last moments of agony they had drawn near to each other for sympathy. Their bones were white, and every scrap of flesh had long since disappeared. Shiela examined the skeletons closely, and gave a cry. "It's as I thought. Look!" she said.

And there, in the bony frames, remained the hearts, slightly withered and parchment-like it is true, but retaining the shape and appearance of living flesh.

"I've never seen such an extraordinary thing," said Stavordale Hartland. "Those hearts look as if there is life in them still, and yet the bodies must have been dead for nearly four hundred years."

"That explains what I meant," said Shiela. "Those monks have never really died, in the full sense of the word. Their flesh rotted and their bones are now like powder, but in the moment of their last agony the elemental enveloped them and took its life from them. There"—pointing to the two hearts— "there is the very existence of the elemental. It is that I am hoping to destroy."

Stavordale bent forward with his hand outstretched to touch them.

"Don't, don't," cried Shiela. But she was too late.

The soft yielding flesh, still warm, filled with blood, burnt him; not with the pain of fire, but as if he had touched some foul, corrosive acid.

"Let us begin," said the priest. "I don't like this dabbling in the unknown. The whole thing savours too much of witchcraft."

He lifted a crucifix on high and got out his breviary. Slowly he droned the Latin prayers.

Shiela stood close to the skeletons with her needles, already made red-hot in the little stove. Her nerves were all on edge, she was waiting—waiting.

Suddenly the watchers became aware of a little shuddering sigh that seemed to rise from the very hearts themselves. It grew in volume until the whole place reverberated with the strange ghostly sound. Still the priest droned on. Lady Morven drew nearer to her brother, and he put a protecting arm about her.

Then the skeletons became enveloped in the thick, greyish vapour that had for so long terrified the inhabitants of Duroch Lodge. It was faint at first, but it grew stronger and stronger until it had once more assumed its malignant shape. A shape that had no definite outline, but yet seemed half human. The hideous face peered at Shiela—it was a grinning, cruel, demoniacal face. It grew plainer, the body had formed; there was the semblance of arms and legs.

"Quick, father!" breathed Shiela. The priest never looked up, but his words tumbled over each other in his eagerness to finish.

The bones were sprinkled with holy water, and at that moment Shiela plunged the red-hot needles into the soft yielding hearts. Hearts of men who had been dead for centuries, yet still retained the semblance of life.

There was the smell of burning flesh, and a dismal howl came from the elemental, as it enfolded Shiela in its deadly embrace. But she was fortified, and it had lost its power. The whole place echoed with wild laughter—with yells of rage—and, even as the skeletons fell to pieces, the "Death Vapour" grew fainter and vanished from sight. For a few seconds smothered screams rent the air, then they, too, died away, and the whole place was plunged in silence once more.

They all bent over the poor bones—the hearts had crumbled into a powdery dust—the bones were no longer whole. No longer was there anything evil about them, they seemed to breathe peace. Silently the little party made their way back to the chapel above, a silent group. The priest was the first to speak.

"Why, who are those?" he asked in amazement.

Hartland and Lady Morven saw nothing, but Shiela put her arm on his.

"The souls you have set free, father," she said, softly. For she also saw two figures with shaven heads and habits of brown, girdles of rope about their waists, kneeling with bowed heads before the altar.

"*Requiescant in pace*," murmured the priest, and, even as he spoke, a brilliant light surrounded them, they held out their arms in supplication, and disappeared.

THE ROOM OF FEAR

Menzies Castle was a house of mourning! Sir John Baverie—delightful guest and most companionable of friends—was dead. Mollie, Lady Menzies, the youthful chatelaine of the historic house was red-eyed with weeping, as she flung herself into her husband's arms.

"Archie, I shall go mad if we stay here another day. It's too awful!"

Lord Menzies smoothed his wife's hair and fondled her tenderly. He was a gaunt man of forty-odd years, and his young wife was the apple of his eye.

"Little one, don't worry," he said quietly. "It's just a coincidence. You heard what the doctors said. Sir John died of heart failure and—"

"Yes," she broke in, "but so did Tom Estcourt. Tom—who was never ill in his life. And then Rosa Mullindon. No one could deny that Rosa was healthy enough—yet she died. And now dear old Sir John. I'm sure the Tower Room is haunted!"

"My dear Mollie, you really must not give way to such fancies. We live in the twentieth century, and rooms and places aren't haunted now. The Tower Room is perfectly safe, and it is only an extraordinary coincidence that on the three occasions it has been used as a bedchamber, its occupants have died of heart failure."

But little Mollie Menzies shook her head. She still believed in the uncanny.

"Look here," he said at last. "I'll sleep there myself, one day soon. You see, I shall be quite all right."

"No, no," cried his wife. "You mustn't—I'm so afraid, Archie, I—"

A bell clanged through the great hall. A second later the butler announced "Miss Shiela Crerar."

Lord Menzies smiled.

"All right, little girl. See your Psychic Detective. She has evidently agreed to take your case up for you."

Shiela came forward quickly.

"I was so sorry to hear of your trouble, Lady Menzies, and I do hope I shall be able to help you."

"You don't know how thankful I was to hear you were still staying with Lady Morven, Miss Crerar. She told me how wonderful you were over that peculiar affair at Duroch Lodge, and so I telephoned through on chance."

"And as it was only a matter of fifteen miles I motored here at once," finished Shiela with a smile.

"My husband, Miss Crerar. Now you must go, Archie, I can't possibly talk in front of you. You don't know how horribly material he is, Miss Crerar."

As soon as the two women were alone Lady Menzies began.

"There isn't a great deal to tell," she said thoughtfully. "I will show you over the Castle later on. The Tower Room is the oldest part of it, and dates from the tenth century. There were originally four stories to it, now nothing is left but the Tower Room itself, which is built on a higher level than the rest of the Castle. Underneath it are cellars, which were originally used as kitchens, I believe. The room was closed up in my husband's grandfather's time—it was supposed to be damp. About two years ago, the Earl had the door re-opened, and the room furnished as a studio for me. The light is excellent there for painting. That is my great hobby, you know."

"Well?" said Shiela interestedly.

"Well, there is no more to tell. I used the room constantly with no ill effect. A year ago this very month we had the entire west wing redecorated. There was a small house party here at the time, and I was rather pushed for room. I—I had the Tower Room fitted up as a bedroom for a distant cousin of mine." Her voice broke slightly. "I had known Tom Estcourt all my life. He was a sailor—a jolly, lighthearted fellow that nothing could upset. He slept in that room for three nights. He never complained about anything, on the fourth he was found dead in bed. It was 'just heart failure' the doctor said. A few weeks later Rosa Mullindon came to stay with me. She had been engaged to Tom, and expressed a desire to occupy the same room in which he died. We tried to dissuade her, but she urged us to give in to her wishes; she was broken-hearted over his death. I went in to her at eleven—she was quite happy, reading a book of his that had never been removed. Next morning she was dead. Everyone thought it was just a coincidence, and when the ceiling fell down in Sir John's bedroom, he it was who suggested sleeping in the Tower Room. He knew of the deaths of Tom and Rosa, and always laughed at me when I said that some uncanny influence must be at work. I told him there was plenty of room, and there was not the slightest necessity to use that horrible room, but he insisted. That was last night. He was as merry as could be, and made arrangements to be called earlier this morning, as he had arranged to play nine holes of golf with the minister before breakfast. When his man went in to call him, he was dead, had been dead for some hours. Dr. Brown was sent for at once, and certified, as before, heart failure. He seemed dissatisfied with his own diagnosis, however, and phoned to Taynuilt for Dr. Andrew, and to Oban for Professor Weymiss. They arrived an hour ago, and corroborated his verdict. Just heart failure, with no complications. But I am not satisfied, Miss Crerar."

"But it seems a very straightforward story," said Shiela. "So far it is strange that three deaths should have taken place there, but you say you used the room constantly as a studio with no ill effects?"

Lady Menzies held out her hands pathetically.

"That's the story," she said. "Sir John's relatives are very anxious that his body should be taken to England to his home there. It will leave by the night express tomorrow, so you can commence your investigations the day after. Meanwhile, the house is too sad to offer much entertainment. Sir John was very popular, you know."

"Please don't bother about me," said Shiela. "If you will let me go to my room I shall be quite happy with a book."

"Most of my guests left considerately this morning," went on Mollie, "and by lunch tomorrow the last one will have gone, so there will be a quiet house in which you can work. I'll take you to your room. We dine at seven."

When Shiela was alone she sat at her open window and drank in the balmy air. Her life was altered by the merest chance. So far she had been successful. Would she continue so? On the following evening the minister held a brief service in the darkened death-chamber, and then the coffin was carried on stalwart shoulders to the ferry, where it was taken across the Loch to the nearest station—Taynuilt.

The castle was empty at last—Shiela its only guest. It was with mixed feelings she entered the Tower Room. In her heart she hoped that if some sinister influence was at work she would be able to discover it. But, on the whole, she felt rather sceptical, and thought Lady Menzies was distressing herself over nothing.

There was certainly nothing ghostly about the Tower Room. It was a long apartment, with a circular alcove at one end, lighted as well by large windows on either side. In the alcove was a glass door, which led down a short flight of steps to the garden and the cellars below. A huge stone hearth, with massive brass dogs, was built cornerwise across the room, which added considerably to its picturesque appearance.

There was neither cupboard nor recess, and nowhere where anyone could hide. Lady Menzies led the way down to the cellars. There was nothing even gloomy about these. They were lit by electricity, and the sandy floor was dry and clean. Both the Tower Room and the vaults seemed above reproach.

"I'll stay here all night," announced Shiela, when once they were in the Tower Room.

"No, no," gasped Lady Menzies. "I am sure it's not safe. I couldn't allow it—"

"Nonsense," smiled Shiela. "If I am to investigate, I must stay here. Now please don't worry. I promise you I shall be quite all right. Oh, there is a bell. Is it in working order?" and she pulled at an old-fashioned bell cord.

Immediately there clanged out a cracked and plaintive call, and a maid came scared into the room.

"It's all right, Sanders," said Lady Menzies. "Miss Crerar was trying the bell."

"Now," said Shiela, "if anything happens I'll peal the bell, and you can send someone in to me."

It was not without misgivings that Lady Menzies left her in the ill-fated room that night. But Shiela was very cheerful. The lights were full on and a fire burnt merrily, and as Lady Menzies shut the door after her, Shiela heard the muffled tones of the big grandfather clock outside strike eleven. She had really no preparations to make. She had no plan of campaign, for she didn't know what she was waiting for—what she expected even. However, she drew a chair close to the blazing fire and began to read.

The book was rather dull, and she dozed over it; the fire burned low, and suddenly she awoke with a start. The grandfather clock outside chimed the three-quarters. It must be a quarter to one! She had been asleep nearly an hour. She stretched her arms in delicious contentment, her mouth was wide open in a yawn, but even as the last silvery notes died away in the silence she became conscious of fear, fear of something intangible, and she realised she was shivering from head to foot. With an effort she relaxed her muscles, and her arms fell to her sides, but the effort left her weak and trembling. Her mouth was stiff with horror, and she closed it with a jerk.

She looked round the room—there was nothing to be seen—the lights shone steadily, and a faint glow came from the fast-dying embers. Suddenly her knees gave way under her, and she sank exhausted to the floor. The grandfather clock chimed again and in a mellow tone proclaimed the hour of one.

For fifteen minutes she had lain upon the floor in an uncontrollable fit of fear. She tried to reason with herself, but could scarcely command her thoughts. She was only conscious of one thing, one sensation—terror, a blind terror that was all the more hideous as its source was nameless.

There was no unreal quiet about the room—no ghostly calm. There was no strange light to be seen or unaccustomed cry to be heard. Everything was quite natural—there was absolutely nothing to account for her nervous state. She managed to raise herself on one elbow, and was shocked to find the sweat pouring off her forehead, while her heart pumped painfully. She dragged herself to her chair and fell back exhausted into it. As the minutes passed so her terror increased until she felt suffocated. The grandfather clock chimed with monotonous regularity, and presently struck two. An hour and a quarter had passed! Shiela felt powerless to move—the minutes were the most awful in her life. The fire burnt lower still until the embers of wood became white and lifeless. Again and again the silvery chimes rent the air, but the girl was as if under a spell, and remained motionless, her eyes glazed with terror, her face white and drawn, and her limbs quaking.

Three o'clock—four! Already the grey dawn was creeping in through the curtained windows and the birds had commenced their morning song.

As the last stroke of four died away the nauseating pall that had hung over Shiela like an unwholesome garment lifted. She became aware of a sense of relief. Her limbs ceased trembling. She was weak, it was true, but she was clothed once more in her right mind. Tired and worn out with her vigil of terror, she flung herself on the bed and drew the eiderdown about her cold shoulders.

At eight tea was brought her by a frightened maid, who feared what she might find in that room of tragedy. But Shiela was sleeping peacefully, and there was no hint of mystery or horror.

She awoke lazily, and drank her tea greedily. She was tired and very thirsty. She looked round the room, and gradually the night's events unfolded themselves to her sleepy brain. She remembered the unholy terror she had suffered. From a quarter to one until four she had been within its awful grasp. She had suffered the tortures of the damned, yet there was nothing to account for it. She dressed slowly, and thought deeply. Yes, there must be something wrong with the room! She knew now that the doctor's verdict of heart failure was correct. The inmates had died of heart failure brought on by fear. But fear of what?

She tapped the walls; they were all solid stone, and gave out no hollow sound. She looked up the chimney; it was a very old-fashioned one, and she could see the glimmer of light beyond the gloom. It was a very puzzled Shiela that appeared at breakfast. Lady Menzies looked at her anxiously.

"How did you sleep?" she asked.

"When I got to bed—very well indeed. But I sat up rather late. I feel tired this morning."

"You saw nothing—heard nothing?"

"Nothing."

Her hostess seemed relieved, and spent the day with Shiela in the open air. They had a round of golf, and in the afternoon explored the glens and woods.

The second night she sat up as before. Again the room had no perceptible change, but as the last sound of the clock chiming the quarter to one broke the stillness, the same terror came over her. This time the fear was more intense. She experienced her old childish fears of the dark, but they were intensified a thousandfold. She was horribly frightened, she crouched down in a corner of the room as if waiting for some terrible doom. Her heart beat painfully—her throat was parched—her lips cracked. She tried to remonstrate with herself for her stupidity, but the ever present feeling of terror overwhelmed her. Her head was bent as if waiting for a blow—she anticipated the hideousness of pain.

Her wonderful will power was hardly strong enough to help her in her fears, and as she involuntarily gave way to them, her sufferings were more acute than before.

She made one more effort to reach the door, but her limbs refused to work, and she sank down, muttering incoherent gibberings. Time passed—she had lost the sense of where she was. Dimly she heard four silvery notes. Four o'clock! And as if by magic, the fear left her.

This time she felt weaker than on the previous night, and when the maid called her in the morning she was flushed and feverish, and said she would have her breakfast in bed.

Lady Menzies came in to see her, and realised at once that something had happened. Shiela, however, refused to tell her anything, and only announced that she intended going on with her investigations.

Three more nights passed, but the strain was growing too much for the girl. She grew to dread the days, because they would lead to the nights. She dreaded the nights, and longed for day to dawn. Every night, as regularly as clockwork, as soon as the clock chimed the quarter to one, the feeling of terror claimed her, and for hours she was in its cold embrace.

She was very reticent about her discovery, but Lady Menzies felt alarmed as she saw the roses fading from her cheeks, and the deep shadows under her eyes growing darker day by day.

The mystery remained unsolved. Try as she might, she could discover no reason for the paroxysms that oppressed her.

One day she asked Lord Menzies to send for Robert Moffat, a well-known chemical analyst of Glasgow. Carefully he examined the room, but could find not the slightest sign of poison or noxious gas concealed in the wallpapers or furniture. After a long examination he announced that there was absolutely nothing the matter with the room at all!

Then they brought an architect in to see if he could discover any secret chamber leading from the Tower Room, but his examinations only proved that the walls were quite solid.

A fortnight passed, and Shiela had become very nervy and restless. The nightly torment she went through was beginning to undermine her constitution. Each night left her weaker than the previous one; she began to suffer from palpitations of the heart, and experienced great pain when she breathed.

"I won't give in," she said to herself, between tightly clenched teeth. "I will master this stupid terror."

Although the fear was still intangible, it had become more real. She suffered actual physical pain at times. It varied in intensity, but, always sensitive to the slightest scratch, her sufferings at times were almost unbearable. Then came the night when her whole body felt as if it was on the rack. Her joints cracked—her muscles swelled, and when she woke in the morning, her arms were inflamed and sore.

She felt the time had come to speak of the terror she was going through. Lord Menzies looked grave.

"If there is anything supernatural at work, don't you think it would be wiser if I had the door blocked up again? The room needn't be used, and I think it would be wiser for you to give up this search."

"No," said Shiela, defiantly; "I am determined to get to the bottom of this mystery. I wonder if you would have the room entirely re-decorated?"

"Why, certainly, if you think it will make any difference."

"And the chimney swept?"

"Certainly."

The orders were given, and for a week Shiela slept in peace, and to some extent recovered her nerve.

When the room was finished, Shiela again insisted on sleeping there, but the horror was worse, if anything, than it was before. She felt the cold sweat running down her body; her hands were clammy and cold, and as the clock outside struck three, she realised she could no longer stand the strain. She dragged herself across the floor to the bell-pull—unconsciously her lips moved. "Stavordale! Stavordale! help me," she cried. A harsh bell clanged through the oaken corridors with startling suddenness. Lady Menzies stirred uneasily, and then woke to life.

"Archie—It's Miss Crerar; she's in danger," she cried. "Quickly— quickly."

But the servants were before her, and when she reached the Tower Room, Shiela was being carried out. She was quite stiff; her eyes were closed, and her breath came in short convulsive gasps. Tenderly she was placed on a settee, and brandy was forced between her tightly clenched teeth. She moaned slightly, and opened her eyes, and then fell into a rather restless sleep.

Lady Menzies watched by her side through the rest of the night, and in the morning, although she was much better, a doctor was sent for.

"Heart trouble," he said, quickly, when he first glanced at her, but after examination— "Very strange. She shows every sign of having a badly strained heart. Yet it is working quite normally now. I should say she has had some great shock. Plenty of rest and quiet, a light diet, and she will be quite all right in a couple of days."

About ten, Stavordale Hartland came over in a great state of excitement.

"Shiela—Miss Crerar?" he asked. "Is she ill?"

"Why, how did you know?" asked Lady Menzies in some surprise. "She is certainly not very well. She fainted last night, but there is not the slightest cause for alarm."

Stavordale's face whitened.

"It's damnable," he cried. "I beg your pardon, Lady Menzies, but it really is. It's perfectly mad of a child like Shiela to meddle with the unknown. When may I see her?" eagerly.

"Tomorrow. She will be quite herself, I hope."

Next morning Stavordale arrived with an armful of flowers for Shiela. She smiled shyly as she took them.

"How did you know I was ill?" she asked.

"You told me yourself," he said, grimly.

"I did?" in some astonishment.

"Yes. I awoke and heard you calling me. 'Stavordale, Stavordale, help me,' you seemed to say. Oh, so distinctly that I thought for the moment you were still with us in the house. The horror in your voice nearly maddened me—I knew something was wrong. Little girl," he went on hoarsely, "if you called for me in distress, surely it proves you think of me sometimes? Won't you give all this up and be my wife?"

"Oh, I can't," she cried tremulously. "I—I can't. I have a mission to fulfil I can't explain. If you will only be patient—"

"Will you send for me if you ever want any help?" he pleaded. "I promise you I will be patient. I won't worry you any more—"

"If I ever need any help I will send for you," she said sweetly, and he had to be content with that.

"I am going to stay in the cellars under the Tower Room," announced Shiela a few days later. In vain they threatened—forbade—commanded.

"Won't you let someone watch with you?" pleaded Lady Menzies, but she refused all help.

At eleven she went down and turned the lights on full. It was rather chilly, and she buttoned up her coat and drew a rug round her shoulders. The hours passed slowly. One—two—three—four. At seven she went to her own room, and slept peacefully until late in the morning. The next night found her in the cellars again, but nothing disturbed her tranquility. The cellars were obviously immune from the phenomena that haunted the upper chamber.

In desperation she fulfilled her promise to Stavordale and sent for him.

"I can't fathom this at all," she said. "I wonder if you and Lord Menzies would sit up with me tonight in the Tower Room? I want to see if the same fear will affect you both."

That night there were three watchers. It was very still, and there was a pleasant smell of cigar smoke in the room. They talked on all subjects but one—psychology was taboo. Lord Menzies was in the midst of a funny story when the clock chimed the quarter to one. He stopped in the middle of a word, his face whitened, and he stared at Shiela out of glassy eyes. Stavordale moved restlessly. Shiela had lost consciousness, fear the omnipotent held her within its thrall.

Lord Menzies staggered to his feet, and gasped in unnatural tones, "I'm stifling. Let's get out of this accursed place."

It took the united efforts of the three to force themselves out of the room. They staggered, supported each other, staggered again, and eventually reached the door. The sweat was running down the two men's faces, and it was with a sigh of relief that they closed the door behind them. But as they reached the passage the terror left them.

"This is the end," said Lord Menzies dryly. "You don't sleep there again, young lady. Tomorrow I have the door bricked up. Why, it's worse than uncanny—it's unholy."

Next day Shiela went to the Tower Room. She was very disappointed. All the suffering she had gone through had been for nought. She had not discovered the sinister secret of the room. Already the furniture was gone, and the carpet had been taken away. The sunlight streamed in and its beams strayed into the passage beyond. Almost without thinking, she noticed the difference in the flooring. Out in the passage it was black and shining, slightly rough and uneven in places. In the Tower Room itself the floor was more even—newer, smoother.

"I wonder," she said to herself, and went in search of the earl.

"Before the door is bricked up," she said abruptly, "I wonder if you would try and prise up some of the flooring in the Tower Room?"

"Why?" he asked.

"I was looking at it just now, and the floor looks altogether newer than that outside. Surely if the Tower is the oldest part of the castle, and the original flooring is in the passage, the Tower Room ought to have still older boards?"

"Start at the door," she directed. "One of the boards looks quite loose there."

With great difficulty he succeeded in raising one of the narrow boards. Eagerly they peered underneath. A wooden step, black with age, worm-eaten, and uneven, met their astonished gaze. He prised open a second and a third board, and three more steps were laid bare before them.

"This room was on a lower level at one time," said Shiela in excitement. "Oh, have the floor all taken up, Lord Menzies."

With the help of some of the outdoor servants, the whole of the flooring was removed, and the original floor was open to view, some three and a half feet below; three stairs led down to it from the other portion of the house.

Shiela gazed at it uncomprehendingly. It was a very rough, uneven floor, great knots were in the wood, and in parts it was very frail. Here and there iron rings and rusty bolts were fixed to the ground. In one corner an iron slab was raised perhaps a foot from the ground. On the slab itself were fastened metal sockets in the shape of a boot. Shiela gazed at them curiously, and slipped her little feet into them.

"Whatever are they for?" she asked, and suddenly gave a cry of pain. "Oh, help me, Lord Menzies. I can't get out. Something is hurting me."

The earl bent over her. A rusty catch on one side still worked, and he opened the boot-shaped metal. Inside were sharp iron spikes that fell into position when the foot was slipped into the "boot"; but they were so cunningly fixed that they would not allow the feet to come out again, and the slightest movement gave the most excruciating pain.

Shiela was scared. "What is it?" she asked.

"Torture," he breathed.

He picked up an old and rusty pair of thumbscrews. "A torture chamber," he repeated, "and I should say one of the most horrible of its kind, yet I have never heard of it. Who used it—whether it was civil or religious—I don't know. It must have been complete in its terrors."

Blood stains on the floor had turned brown and rusty, but they were ominous reminders of the horrors of bygone days. In one corner lay a spiked iron club, rusted with blood. There was a rack fixed to the floor itself. Chains, clubs, iron masks with bloody spikes inside—the room was completely equipped for its dreadful purpose.

"It's horrible," said Shiela, shuddering. "I wonder I didn't think of the solution myself. This was a torture chamber, and probably always used at the dead of night."

"From about a quarter to one until four o'clock," put in Lord Menzies.

"Yes. It would be the most unlikely time for discovery. It was no doubt entirely secret. That is the reason you have no records of its existence. You see," she went on excitedly, "the hideous fear of the unhappy victims communicated itself to the very room. The walls, the wood, the bricks, were impregnated with wave upon wave of terror from the suffering ones. They retained it throughout the ages, and each night the terror that was once inflicted here, is let loose again at the hour it used to take place."

"But is such a thing possible?" asked the earl.

Shiela smiled. "It seems like it, doesn't it? What other explanation can you give? At any rate, may I suggest that you have the old floor taken away altogether?"

"Well?"

"Have the cavity between the old and new floors filled in, and destroy"—pointing with a shudder— "these."

"And you think that the room will be all right then?"

"I don't know. It seems possible."

"You will stay till it is all complete," urged Lady Menzies.

"With pleasure."

The work was set in motion at once, and in the course of excavations the workmen discovered a charred skeleton. The fingers were gone, and the way the bones were twisted proved only too plainly the pain that the unhappy creature must have suffered.

"May it rest in peace," said Lord Menzies, and he gave orders for its burial.

The hideous belts and torture instruments the earl caused to be thrown into the loch. He never found any records of the terrible place. He searched his own family histories, but never a sign or clue was given to point to its existence.

Shiela, Lord Menzies, and Stavordale Hartland stayed in the room the first night that the floor had been relaid. At a quarter to one they all became nervous, but the night passed with no ill effects. Clearly the Room of Fear no longer justified its name. The intangible horrors of the past had gone.

The sounds of agony, the horror and terror, the awe inspiring spectacles that had been absorbed into the very room itself, and that were nightly exuded from it, had gone never to return. The

Torture Chamber was no more. It was early September when Shiela once more boarded a train en route for Edinburgh.

Stavordale Hartland saw her off from Benderloch. She had stayed a couple of nights at Duroch Lodge after leaving Menzies Castle. As the guard waved his flag, Stavordale drew towards her, and instinctively their lips met. The whistle blew, and Shiela, blushing rosy red, slipped back into her corner seat, trembling with happiness.

Stavordale Hartland watched the train fade away in the distance. What mattered it that no smiling face leant out of the window and waved him a farewell? He pictured the rosy face in the corner, the tremulous lips, the downcast eyes. He was well content.

THE PHANTOM ISLE

Shiela Crerar had wandered delightedly over Roslyn Chapel. She had tenderly touched the 'Prentice Pillar, had feasted her eyes on the legendary carvings, had listened to the guide's tuneful voice as he told the story of the Chapel, and of the hate and violence that had been fostered there.

She went down the narrow roadway with the wonder of the past still in her heart. She was a very radiant Shiela. Her first cases had been so successful that she had many minor calls made upon her, which, though they had all proved uninteresting, had at least been remunerative. And now she was spending a few days at Roslyn, and revelling in the beauties of the famous chapel.

A telegram was waiting for her when she reached the hotel. She opened it tremulously—she hoped it was from Stavordale Hartland. She had not seen him since the memorable day he had kissed her farewell as the train was on the point of steaming out of Benderloch station. It had been re-directed from her Edinburgh rooms. It ran:

> Can you see me tomorrow. Urgent. Lady Menzies recommends. Murdoch, Caledonian Hotel, Princes Street.

The name was unfamiliar, and she felt disappointed. She had so hoped it was from Stavordale!

"Resting. Undertaking no cases," she wired, but early next day there was another telegram for her:

Motoring Roslyn immediately. Please see me and hear details. Most urgent. Murdoch.

Shiela was vexed. She had told her landlady to give no one her address, and now a stranger was coming to worry her. She wanted a rest badly, but her better nature prevailed, and she waited in for her visitor. About twelve a card was brought to her.

MRS. MURDOCH

ACH-NA-DINDOCH

SKYE

Mrs. Murdoch proved to be a prematurely aged woman. Her hair was white, and her face lined and wrinkled; but her eyes, bright and piercing, gave lie to the thought that proclaimed her old.

"Miss Crerar," she said brokenly. "I am in such trouble. Do forgive me for intruding upon you, but I feel that you are the only one that can help me."

Her distress was so real that Shiela was touched.

"Sit down by the fire and tell me what your trouble is, and I will promise to help you if I can."

Mrs. Murdoch remained silent a moment, and then: "It all seems so little, when I try and put it into words," she began, "but"— apologetically— "at the bottom of my heart I feel that there is something wrong. A year ago, Elspeth, my only daughter and child, returned from the Continent, where she had been at a finishing school. She came back a blithe, heartsome lassie, full of fun, loving, kind. Her first season was a brilliant success. She became engaged to the Duke of Cremont's eldest son, and the two were inseparable. It was a most desirable match in every way. They were both young, and had wealth and love to help them. Their marriage was to have taken place at the New Year."

"Then the engagement is broken?" asked Shiela.

"Yes, Miss Crerar. Two months ago Elspeth went out sailing. It was quite a usual thing for her to do, but she came back inexplicably changed. She seemed no longer a girl—but a discontented woman; old before her time, peevish, miserable. I thought she was sickening for some illness, but she became very irritable when I suggested she should go to bed."

"Well?"

"From that moment she has never been the same. Next day she was up at dawn, and spent the whole of it in her little sailing boat. The days passed—she would hardly speak to me, and she spent her whole time on the sea. Then I received a broken-hearted letter from the young Marquis of Mavoir—"

"Her *fiancé*?"

Mrs. Murdoch nodded. "Elspeth had written to him breaking off her engagement. It was done without my knowledge, so you will understand that the news came as a great shock. I wired Cedric to come to us at once. He had a very stormy interview with Elspeth. She gave him no reason for her change—simply refused to marry him, that was all. Cedric was broken-hearted, and left the same day for London. I've not heard from him since."

"If she no longer cared for him—" suggested Shiela.

"Don't think I am a mercenary, match-making mother, Miss Crerar," said Mrs. Murdoch. "I only want my daughter to marry for love, and it was because I felt she really cared for Cedric and he for her, that I was anxious for their union. Two days ago, my daughter told me quite casually that she was to be married on her twenty-first birthday."

"And that is?"

"Next Friday week."

"And you don't approve?"

"Miss Crerar, this is the real source of my trouble. She told me she is to marry Malcolm MacLaurie, Laird of Tath-Gart Isle. Well, there is *no* Laird of Tath-Gart now. This is where I want your aid. The last of the MacLauries was foully murdered in 1745 by the Chief of the Clan Murdoch—our clan. As far as I know, there is no living MacLaurie left—yet my daughter avows that she is going to marry the Chief. Now do you understand my fears?"

"I think so," said Shiela. "Where does your daughter meet this— this man?"

"On Tath-Gart Isle."

"Where is that?"

"About eight and a half miles from us—to the north."

"How did the last MacLaurie die?" asked Shiela.

"Old Malcolm MacLaurie was mortally wounded at Culloden," continued Mrs. Murdoch, "and his only son, young Malcolm, fled with the Prince to the hills. After a great deal of suffering and privation, they reached the coast in safety, and eventually gained Tath-Gart Isle. A traitor, however, was in their ranks. Wolf Murdoch, Chief of the Clan, left the island secretly, and—for a price—gave information to the English General. He and a boatload of redcoats made their way to the isle, but a faithful gillie gave the alarm, and the Prince and his retinue escaped to Skye. When the English soldiers landed, headed by the Wolf, they found the young chieftain at dinner with his sisters, alone.

"The castle was ransacked, but no trace of the fugitives was found. Young MacLaurie denied all knowledge of the Prince. There had long been enmity between the two houses, and in his baffled rage, Wolf Murdoch drew his sword and killed the elder girl in front of her brother and sister. Mad with grief and anger MacLaurie fell upon the Murdoch, but a score of soldiers overpowered him. Then the Wolf tore the living sister from the body of the dead one, and in cold blood murdered her before her brother's eyes."

"How horrible!"

"Not content with that, for now the pent-up hatred and petty jealousies of a rival clan were let loose, young Tath-Gart was forced to witness the burning of his home and his crops. He saw his servants and clansmen slaughtered, and when his home had been reduced to ruins, he was hanged upon his own castle walls. That is the history of the last MacLaurie, Miss Crerar. There have been none since."

"And yet your daughter is to marry a MacLaurie?"

"Yes. She told me he was Malcolm MacLaurie, Laird of Tath-Gart, and Earl of the Kelden Isles. It is the very title that lapsed in '45."

"And she says her wedding-day is fixed!"

"Yes, Friday week."

"Then we have a clear ten days before us. May I return with you to Ach-na-Dindoch?" said Shiela briskly.

"Thank you, oh, thank you," said the broken-hearted mother.

The journey was not eventful. They crossed from Mallaig on the mainland to Armadale in Skye. The mail-boat was rather cheerless and Shiela, tired and cold, was glad to wrap herself cosily up in the fur rugs in the Rolls Royce that was waiting for them at the pierhead.

When they arrived at the house, Mrs. Murdoch asked at once for Elspeth.

"She is in her room, madam," said the servant. "She has not been out all day."

A look of relief passed over the mother's face.

"Dinner will be served in half an hour, madam," went on the servant.

"Thank you. That will give us plenty of time, Miss Crerar. We won't dress tonight. I am sure we are both too tired."

The gong sounded, and Shiela made her way to the dining-room. Mrs. Murdoch was waiting for her excitedly.

"I've persuaded Elspeth to have dinner with us. I told her you were going to stay with us for a little. I never mentioned the real reason, of course, but she showed no curiosity—"

At that moment the door opened and Elspeth Murdoch entered. She was a very sweet-looking girl of the ethereal type. Pale, fair-haired, and petite, she gave one the impression that a sudden gust of wind would blow her away. Yet Shiela knew she was athletic, and could handle a yacht with the ease of a man.

"Elspeth, this is Miss Crerar."

"How do you do?"

"How do you do?"

The girl talked brightly throughout the meal, but Shiela noticed the nervous twitching of her hands, and the artificial gaiety of her manner. At times, too, she looked away into the distance and seemed hardly to be aware of her surroundings.

They made their way into the drawing room, but at the threshold she halted.

"I won't have any coffee, thank you. Good night, Miss Crerar. Good night, mother."

Shiela felt unable to pierce the veil of mystery that hung over Elspeth Murdoch's love story. That she was engaged to a man who had been hanged nearly two hundred years ago was absurd, yet, who was the mysterious stranger she had fallen in love with? Why had her whole nature changed? Was it someone impersonating the MacLaurie, or was it something far worse—the visitation of the dead to the living for the purposes of revenge?

Elspeth was absent in her yacht all the next day, but as the twilight deepened, the watchers caught the glint of a sail coming round the furthermost corner of the bay, and a few seconds later the pretty little craft drew close in, was beached neatly, and a moment later Elspeth vaulted out on to the dry silver sand.

"Elspeth," said her mother wistfully, "we came down to meet you."

The girl passed a hand across her brow wearily. "I'm sorry you troubled, mother," she said.

"You're very late," hazarded the unhappy woman.

"I'm sorry, mother, but Malcolm kept me later than usual. The castle is being made ready for the festival. The island is quite gay, and the servants are already making preparations for the wedding banquet."

"My dear, my dear," said her mother brokenly, "don't be so foolish. Why, you know there is no castle now. It was demolished long ago; as a child you played among the ruins."

A softer tone crept into the girl's voice. "You want me to be happy, mother, yet you deny me my love. You question the fidelity of my lover, almost his reality. Why, he has bidden three hundred guests to our wedding. All his clansmen will welcome me, a Murdoch, as his bride. The old feud is broken. No longer will Murdoch fight MacLaurie, or MacLaurie raid Murdoch. Love has healed the breach. Love has conquered all."

"Won't you bring the—the MacLaurie to see me, dearie?"

A shadow passed over the girl's face. "He won't come, mother. He bids you to the marriage feast. On that joyous day, he says all old scores will for ever be wiped out. By giving myself in marriage to him, I shall obliterate a thousand-fold the injuries that my ancestors did to his."

"May I come over to the island with you tomorrow, Miss Murdoch?" asked Shiela.

The girl trembled violently.

"No! No! No!" she cried. "I can take no one until my bridal day. It is his wish. Oh, how happy I am. I love him so. I love him so!"

Then suddenly her mood changed. Once more she was hard, callous. A woman had taken the place of a young girl. "I am sorry you bothered to meet me, mother, I am going straight to my room now. Flora will bring me my supper on a tray." And she walked quickly away.

"I am going to the island tomorrow," said Shiela determinedly. "Is it possible to hire a little motor boat anywhere?"

"Yes, old Sandy Black has one."

"Is it safe to go alone?"

"If it is a fairly calm day, yes. But what if Elspeth sees you?"

"I shall start at sunrise, before she is up."

"There is only one safe landing—in a little bay under the shadow of the castle ruins."

Next morning, Shiela started alone on her adventure. She saw Tath-Gart in the distance, hazy in the morning mist. As the sun rose red the island loomed out quite distinctly. The bay was easy to find, and she made the little boat safe, where it lay hidden behind a rugged rock. The island was even more barren than she had anticipated, and of the old castle practically nothing remained. One wall only stood sentinel at the cliff's edge, the remainder had been swallowed up by time.

There were high cliffs all round, but the top of the island was a barren plateau, with not a bush behind which to hide. She walked carefully round the little place, but could find not the slightest sign of life. Even the sea-birds seemed to have neglected it, and made their homes elsewhere. As she reached the bay she caught sight of *The Mermaid*, Elspeth's little white craft. It was quite close in, and instinctively she flung herself down flat upon the ground.

And then the scene changed. The whole island seemed to become full of life. Two stalwart men in kilts leapt knee deep in the water, and drew the little boat high on to the beach. A tall man with flowing locks and a long, straggling beard came towards the boat. Elspeth gave a cry of joy and held out her arms invitingly. He lifted her out of the boat, and held her close in an embrace. Elspeth gave herself up to the delight of his presence, and buried her head on his shoulder.

The man raised his head and looked at the serving men who were near, and Shiela shuddered at his malignant expression.

"Malcolm, Malcolm, you love me?" cried the girl, and for answer the man kissed her hair, her eyes, her lips. But Shiela shivered, for the embrace seemed to her to signify a fierce hatred, instead of love. Then the man drew roughly away, and the two walked up the steep incline towards the castle. Shiela gazed in amazement at the scene.

No longer was the ruined wall standing swaying at the cliff's edge, the piteous remnant of a glory that had gone. In its place a giant castle stood, a castle with smoke curling from its chimneys and one that bore sign of habitation.

The two passed close to Shiela, and she followed them. A drawbridge was lowered, and although a sentry was posted at the portcullis, he gave no challenge when Shiela walked in. By this time she scarcely realised the phenomena she was witnessing. Through corridors and passages she wandered; through gaunt rooms, with bare stone walls; now through tapestried apartments, and bedchambers hung with silk. But although servants were continually passing her, although in the distance she saw soldiers and guests disporting in the gloom, no sound was made. The everyday life was being carried on, yet there was not the slightest noise.

In the kitchen she saw a whole ox roasting before a blazing fire, yet when she put her hand near the blaze, no warmth came from it, and the contact seemed to chill her. Then the realisation came upon her suddenly, that the whole castle had been destroyed long ago. Where then was she?

A woman in a mob cap and kirtle of green hurried past her carrying a tray of crockery. Shiela called to her, but the woman made no answer—it was as though she had not heard her voice.

She ran from the kitchen to the wide stairs. Men in Highland dress with claymores bare, stood on either side of it but they seemed not to see her, as she sped past them. In a large apartment at the top of the stairs she caught a glimpse of Elspeth and her lover. Two girls were with them, girls with flowing hair and robed in white, but again the appalling hatred in their expressions terrified her.

Elspeth bent to kiss the elder girl, and as she did so Shiela cried out: "Oh, don't, don't." Then everything seemed to darken, and when she looked round again, she found she was standing in front of the old castle wall. The sun was sinking, and already Elspeth was halfway to the mainland in her yacht.

Shuddering slightly, Shiela went swiftly down to the little bay to the motor boat, and soon had left the uncanny island far behind her. What had she seen? Was it the ghostly past come to life again? Had the dying hatred of the MacLauries existed through death itself, and would their curse be visited on the last fair daughter of the Murdochs? The thought was horrible.

"Well?" asked Mrs. Murdoch eagerly, when she saw Shiela.

"You are right, Mrs. Murdoch. There *is* an evil influence at work, and I hardly know how we can combat it." She told the story of her visit, and Mrs. Murdoch was incredulous.

"Yes," went on Shiela. "Your daughter's lover is just a phantom lover, with a phantom home and phantom retinue. If you went to Tath-Gart you would probably see nothing. I am psychic, the wonders of the supernatural are often revealed to me. In this case, I saw eye to eye with Elspeth. I entered the castle in a negative state of mind. I was excited, inquisitive. I hardly realised what I was doing. My presence had no effect on the supernatural element there. They took no notice of me at all until they felt my hostility. When I saw Elspeth bend to kiss that horrible, malignant face, I tried to prevent her, and I succeeded. The whole scene vanished, it was not my actual words which caused it, but my will opposing the wills of the evil spirits. It's easy now to explain everything. Throughout the ages, he has no doubt haunted the isle that was once his pride and joy. He has concentrated all his power of thought on the last Murdoch. His will power has drawn her to the island, has made her see the castle as it was in 1745, has caused her to give her heart to him—a phantom. It is a fitting vengeance for the wrongs he suffered at the hands of a Murdoch. And now he in his turn is weaving a diabolical plot in which he will destroy the heiress to the Murdoch estates. He in turn will wipe out the last remaining Murdoch. In a hideous marriage ceremony in which the living is united to the dead, he will slay his bride."

"Don't, don't!" cried the distressed mother. "It can't be true."

"It is true," said Shiela grimly. "His object is to wipe out the Murdochs, and I intend preventing him."

"How? How?"

Shiela shook her head. "I don't know. I must think—think."

"Mother," said Elspeth later in the evening. "I am not going to Tath-Gart again until my wedding day. My wedding robe is only half completed, and my lover wishes me to be handsomely arrayed. I must work hard—hard."

"What are you using for your wedding dress?" asked her mother.

"Why, the old white satin dress belonging to Lady Elspeth, mother. It is too big for me, and it is difficult to make it fit."

Mrs. Murdoch gave a cry of horror. It was the wedding dress that had been worn by the bride of Wolf Murdoch—the slaughterer of the MacLaurie! It had been preserved through the ages—for this.

Every day during that last week, Shiela visited the island, and once Mrs. Murdoch herself went with her. They saw no psychic demonstrations, heard no sound of ghostly laughter, felt no uncanny presence.

The wedding morning arrived at last, and Shiela interviewed the servants and begged them to humour Miss Elspeth. She explained that she was "not well, and must not be thwarted."

Elspeth came slowly down the stairs. She had not altered the style of her dress, and she looked like an old painting that had come to life. She had left her hair unbound, and it hung in a rippling cascade down to her waist. She had caught her veil demurely round her face, and it looked like an old-fashioned mob cap. In her arms she carried a huge bunch of purple heather. Heather that had been gathered some months before, and was now dry and withered, its colour faded, its beauty gone.

She insisted on navigating the yacht herself, but was strangely silent. They reached the little bay in safety, and Shiela prayed that she might be guided in her actions. She was extremely nervous and highly strung, indeed, the only member of the little party that seemed to be at all composed was Elspeth herself.

Throughout the scenes that followed, Mrs. Murdoch saw nothing but the gaunt island with its ruins, and her two companions; heard nothing but the whining moan of the wind, the lashing of the waves, and the voices of her two companions; felt nothing but the bleakness of a raw November day! But all the same she nearly fainted with terror—terror of scenes that were not visible to her, yet which she knew were being enacted beneath her very eyes!

"Don't come too close," whispered Shiela to Mrs. Murdoch, "and don't interfere at all, no matter what happens."

Elspeth seemed to forget the two who had brought her to the isle, and boldly walked up the steep incline alone. Shiela followed closely, and again she saw the phantom castle, and again she crossed the phantom draw-bridge.

Two girls in white came towards the bride. Shiela gazed at them in horror. She recognised them to be the murdered sisters of the MacLaurie. Their faces were white and lifeless; their eyes lacked lustre, and their expressions of unholy loathing frightened her.

Elspeth seemed to be in a trance, and, noticing nothing, walked by their side. They led her into a large, tapestried hall, where the bridegroom awaited her. A bridegroom dressed in mourning, a bridegroom whose face was livid and discoloured; whose eyes bulged from their sockets; whose tongue, swollen and hideous, projected from his mouth. A bridegroom who bore in his face the signs of having met his death by strangulation. Yes—the MacLaurie had been hanged in 1745!

The hall was full of guests, but their clothing was rotten and worn, and their faces were those of dead men. Slowly a priest walked up the great hall. A priest with the face of a skull; a priest with fleshless fingers, and with vestments that covered a skeleton body. The ghastly ceremony had commenced. The living was being united to the dead.

For a moment only, Shiela hesitated. The sepulchral tones came distinctly on her ear:

"Wilt thou take this woman to be thy wedded wife?"

Her mind was made up. Swiftly she crossed the hall and flung her arm protectively round Elspeth.

The girl made a movement towards the bridegroom.

"Malcolm, my love," she murmured.

"In the name of God I command you—Go," cried Shiela.

She concentrated every ounce of will-power she possessed upon the phantoms. The brother and two sisters beat at her with long, bony fingers. The priest laughed hollowly. The guests grew blurred and vanished.

"Go, go," she cried vehemently, still with her arms tightly round the now senseless Elspeth.

The priest vanished—the castle walls were gone, but the hatred of the MacLauries remained. It was will against will—the will of the living against the will of the dead.

But Shiela was the strongest in that unholy contest.

First she saw one sister—then the other—fade away; but still the MacLaurie remained.

She was conscious now of only one thing—she must defeat him. Once that was done, he would vanish to return no more.

The maddened spirit loomed upon her—he seemed to envelop her. His breath was foetid and choked her. He uttered maniacal cries of thwarted rage and hatred, but her eyes met his fearlessly.

"In the name of Christ—Go!" she cried. Her breath was coming fast and the sweat was pouring off her, the result of the mental strain she was undergoing. The victory was nearly won. The form

of the dead MacLaurie was growing fainter, she felt his demoniacal hatred less intense, and even as he vanished, she laid Elspeth
on the ground, and fell exhausted by her side.

Elspeth was still sleeping when she was carried from the yacht
to the house. Gently she was undressed and put to bed.

"There are a lot of red marks on her frock," said Mrs. Murdoch.
"They look like blood. Do you know what it can be, Miss Crerar?"

But Shiela shook her head. "Some stain from the ground, I
expect," she said quietly. "That's all."

The details of the horrible scene would never pass her lips.

Elspeth slept the round of the clock, and when she awoke, all
memory of the past few months had left her. She had not the slightest recollection of the part she had played. She greeted Shiela shyly,
as if she had never seen her before—and Shiela was well content.

A few weeks later Shiela read the following in the *Scotsman*:

> The marriage which was arranged between the
> Marquis of Mavoir, the Duke of Cremont's son and
> heir, and Miss Elspeth Murdoch, only daughter of
> the late Murdoch of Murdoch, and Mrs. Murdoch of
> Ach-na-Dindoch, Skye, will take place on the 18th
> inst. at Armadale, Skye. Owing to the recent illness
> of the bride-elect, the ceremony will be an extremely
> quiet one, only the nearest relatives being present.

THE WEREWOLF OF RANNOCH

It was a chill night in late January. The snow lay thick upon the ground; the wind howled among the trees; and the full moon shone down on a desolate wilderness.

Half-a-mile from the little village of Dhuvhair—a village situated in the very heart and desolation of Rannoch—stood the little unpretentious house tenanted by Doctor Chisholm and his sister. It was a wild, dreary spot in which to live, and the mystery and horrors which had fallen upon the little community were in keeping with the weirdness of the place itself.

For some months Dhuvhair had suffered from an "evil visitation," to put it in the words of the "Wee Free Meenister." Cattle and sheep had been found dead in their pens, bloody and torn. Horses in their stalls had not escaped, pigs in their sties, dogs in their kennels, chickens in their runs had all suffered. And the manner of the kill was always the same, the throat of the victim was lacerated and bleeding, and the bowels torn from the body were left partly devoured.

"It's a Killer," said the Moorland folk. "It's a Killer. Keep your cattle under lock and key."

For a Killer is a dread thing among the shepherds and cottars of the North. By a Killer they mean a sheep-dog that has gone mad for blood; a dog that can no longer be trusted to look after the sheep, but one that will steal away as soon as darkness falls, and will slay the very creatures he is trained to guard.

But when children disappeared, and grown men and women, and their bodies were afterwards found torn and bleeding, lacerated with savage toothmarks, the people looked at each other timidly, and kept behind bolted doors at night, and prayed with the minister in the kirk on the Sabbath that "the visitation" might be lifted from them.

And it was the Reverend Evan Macintosh himself who wrote to Shiela Crerar and asked her to come and investigate the mystery that surrounded Dhuvhair; for he had known her since she was a little girl, and had heard of her marvellous successes. She had accepted, and Miss Chisholm had offered to put her up, as the manse was only a bachelor establishment.

So Shiela arrived at the little Highland clachan, situated in the heart of remote Rannoch Moor, and set to work on perhaps the most gruesome mystery she ever had to solve.

The days passed, and she was still unsuccessful. Each morning she chose a new theory upon which to work, and each night had to abandon it as being either impossible or absurd.

There was certainly the element of the unreal about the visitation. Crofters averred they saw "a shaggy shape with eyes like burning coal, slinking about the hillside at the full of the moon." And always, after the creature had been seen, there was a Kill. Children were kept indoors at night and came screaming from the "ben" room, saying they had seen the face of a wolf at the window. The whole countryside was in a ferment of terror, and Shiela felt powerless to cope with it. She followed up clue after clue that proved useless, and all her nerves were on edge.

Doctor Chisholm, her host, a cheery soul of sixty-odd years, gave her all the help in his power, but he was openly sceptical about her theory that the Killer was possessed of a supernatural element. "I am sure we shall find that it is simply some mad dog loose on the country, Miss Crerar. What else can it be?"

"Have you never heard of werewolves, Doctor?" she asked, quietly.

"Yes," he replied, "but I don't think I am quite sure in my own mind as to what they are supposed to be."

"They are men with dual personalities, Doctor, who have the power to change themselves into the form of a wolf or some other carnivorous animal."

"My dear Miss Crerar—" smiled the Doctor, genially, and ran his hand through his snowy hair.

"Oh, I believe in it, Doctor. It is another form of the 'Jekyll and Hyde' theory, that's all, only a much worse form. The astral spirit leaves the body in a sleeping condition, while it assumes an animal shape itself. Thus free, it roams round the world at will, and lengthens its existence by drinking fresh, warm blood drawn from a new kill."

"Surely that is quite a mediaeval superstition, Miss Crerar," protested the Doctor again. "We are in the prosaic twentieth century, and—"

But Shiela refused to answer. She had been in touch with the unreal too often to doubt. She knew the power of the spirits from the other world—the tangibility of the elemental—she had come across the very essence of witchcraft. Nothing was impossible.

And that night, as she stood at the garden gate after dinner and enjoyed the glory of a white earth under a full moon, she caught sight of a shadowy grey shape creeping among the trees. It was her first glimpse of the Killer. Without a thought of fear she bounded after it—hatless, coatless, breathless, she followed it. It turned its head—its eyes gleamed viciously, and it snarled angrily. Shiela pulled a branch of whitethorn—a protection against witchcraft—and held it high above her head. The wolf leapt at her, but as it touched the tree, it whined, slunk round a corner, and when Shiela moved a second later it had vanished from sight. There was no place in which it could hide, yet it had gone completely, and the only living thing in sight was a man who was walking quickly into the distance. She hurried after him, but the space between them never seemed to lessen. His walk, his figure, his manner seemed familiar to her, but there suddenly came a flash, and when she opened her eyes, he, too, was gone. She walked back slowly and ran into Doctor Chisholm.

"I've proved my theory," she said, with quiet concentration. "The visitant *is* a Werewolf. I have seen it tonight, and I must now set to work to discover who it is that is the menace to this little place. I believe some men have no knowledge that they possess this power, and while their astral spirit is absent, they are asleep and unconscious of their evil doings. This Werewolf is different. I am convinced he knows his own powers."

"Why, what makes you think that?"

"Because just now he appeared as a wolf—a second later the animal had gone, but a man had taken his place. I tried to reach the man. At first I didn't realise that the change had taken place, but when I drew near he used his magical powers, blinded me with a light for a moment, and when I could see, he too had vanished."

"Have you any idea who this—this man is?"

"Not the slightest at present. Although he seemed familiar to me, I find I am unable to place him. But I shall work hard to discover him, and then—" She left the sentence unfinished, and the kindly doctor tucked his arm though hers, and led the way back to his house.

But although Shiela saw the ominous grey shape many times, she was never able to track it to its lair.

"Will you watch with me tonight, Doctor?" she asked one day. "I want to try and discover the direction from which the Werewolf comes. Let us hide in the bushes by the churchyard. We shall be safe there on consecrated ground."

So they waited that night at the edge of the little graveyard—a spot eerie and forlorn.

"Get behind that tombstone," said the Doctor genially, "and I'll wait here."

"But I can't see you, Doctor."

"Never mind. I can see you."

So they waited. The moon was hidden beneath heavy clouds, the wind was piercing, and heavy flakes of snow cut Shiela's face and made it smart. Suddenly, as the clock in the church tower boomed twelve, there came the sound of ghostly laughter—laughter that seemed to come from the regions of the damned.

Shiela felt her blood run cold, and, as she watched, she heard the baying of hounds in the distance—and knew them to be the ghostly hounds of the wicked dead. Nearer they drew, and nearer. Shiela watched their approach, and counted them mechanically. Five—six—seven—eight. And they strained at a leash that was held taut by their invisible master. And even as they passed her Shiela heard the crack of a whip, and saw the quiver of the flesh that was flayed—yet of the whip itself there was nothing to be seen. As they passed, leaving a luminous trail behind them, she saw the "grey hulking shapes" speed swiftly by, there was the snapping of hungry jaws, a cry of pain, and the ghostly pack only numbered seven! They had passed, and all was still and quiet.

"Doctor, Doctor! Don't say now that you don't believe!" said Shiela.

"Doctor, Doctor!" she cried again.

"Doctor Chisholm, are you there?" and a frightened note crept into her voice.

But the genial doctor answered her, his voice grave and low. "Forgive me, Miss Crerar, I scarcely realised you were speaking. I was carried away by the scene."

Shiela left her hiding-place and crossed to him. He was rising from the shelter of a large whin bush, and the girl cried out in dismay.

"Oh, Doctor, thank God you are safe!"

"Why, what is the matter, Miss Crerar?"

"Do you realise you have not been on consecrated ground at all? You were on the path that separates the graveyard from the flower gardens that surround it."

He gave a little wry smile.

"Then it was your presence that no doubt saved me from harm, my dear."

Then one day Shiela saw the Werewolf lurking in the meadow near the Chisholms' byre. With the protecting whitethorn spray, she tracked it, but it disappeared behind the building itself, and as she turned the corner she came face to face with Doctor Chisholm's partner. They passed with a curt "Good night," and Shiela thought no more about the incident.

A week later it was, however, brought back to her mind. She was waiting again in the churchyard, but this time alone. Midnight boomed out, and the Killer passed. But even as he vanished from sight the Doctor's partner appeared from the copse at the side of the road. This time she passed him without speaking, for the moment her eyes lighted upon him a wild possibility suggested itself to her mind, and she felt at last that she had a clue—that at last she was on the right track.

When she had first met Doctor Chisholm's partner she had taken a dislike to him. He was a Dane—Olaf Sylmak by name—a dark, taciturn man of late middle life. She felt sorry he was an inmate of Cnoc-na-Ruaidh, as the Chisholm's house was called. She never spoke to him more than courtesy demanded of her.

She read craft in his expression, cruelty in his tight, thin lips, and shivered at the touch of his damp, flaccid hand. And now—well, she hoped the denouement was not far off. The Killer was always abroad when the moon was full, and tonight she would try and track the malefactor to its lair.

"Well," said Doctor Chisholm genially, as she said good night, "you have not discovered the identity of our unpleasant visitor yet?"

"Not yet. But I think I am at last on his track."

The old man's eyes twinkled, and he gave an exaggerated little shudder.

"Oh, you modern women! You dabble in science and medicine, you dabble in politics and law, and now you dabble in the occult. What else is there left for mere man?"

"Well, Doctor, you'll be glad if this mysterious horror is satisfactorily cleared up, won't you?"

"Of course I shall, my dear young lady—and so will Mary." He nodded affectionately at his sister. "Why, Mary scarcely ever sleeps a wink at nights now, do you?"

Miss Chisholm, a delicate spinster, many years her brother's junior, looked up flutteringly.

"Indeed, Miss Crerar, I have not. If it were not for Doctor Sylmak's kindness to me, his cheery presence, and the wonderful tonic he had made up for me for nerves, I am sure I should have had a breakdown long ago. The suspense is terrible, not to know from one minute to the next whether the—the Killer will make his visitation here."

Shiela looked grave. "You like Doctor Sylmak, don't you, Miss Chisholm?"

The little lady flushed.

"It is quite a secret. My brother, of course, knows; but if Doctor Sylmak is successful in a big experiment he is making, we are to be married."

Shiela was unable to look into the candid eyes of the little young-old lady.

"I—I hope he—he will be successful," she murmured, and then she not only surprised herself by bending over the spinster and kissing her on the forehead, saying, "But, above all, I hope you will be happy."

When she reached her room she muttered angrily to herself, "If I am right in my conjectures, I shall bring unhappiness on that poor little soul who trusts him. Yet better one heart broken than distress and desolation on many."

It was a bitterly cold night, and she wrapped herself up very warmly, put on snow-shoes, and pulled a woollen cap close about her ears. She loaded a little automatic revolver, and carefully opened a French window that led from her room to the outside stair, so prevalent in Scottish houses. Quickly she descended it, and crept into the shadow of a holly bush, and remained waiting— waiting.

It was an eerie night. The moon was brilliant, but the huge rings round it foretold stormy weather. The wind moaned and whistled, and Shiela drew her cloak close around her. She looked at her watch, and saw that it wanted but a few seconds to midnight, when she suddenly stiffened and her nostrils quivered. She had caught the scent of her prey!

There was a *crunch! crunch!* on the frozen snow, and a great grey beast slunk round the corner of the house. His nose was high in the air, and his red eyes gleamed banefully. The foam dropped from his slobbering jowl, and the steam rose from his heated body. She raised her revolver, and the beast seemed to scent danger, for with a whimper of fear it slunk into the shadows and vanished from sight. Quickly Shiela followed the direction it had taken. Among the trees she saw a grey shape flitting. It was the malevolent beast she knew to be responsible for the killings.

Night after night she had waited for it; tracked it among the peat hags and morasses of the moor; had followed it along the banks of lochs and peaty tarns; across heathery hummocks and granite boulders. But always the uncanny brute had evaded her. But now she had seen it come from the shadow of Cnoc-na-Ruaidh, and she felt that the Doctor's house was indeed the lair of the Werewolf—a thing loathsome, treacherous, vile. And even as she sped after it she shook with anger at the thought of the gentle spinster who had given her heart to Olaf Sylmak—the Wolf-man. Shiela had no doubts now—she had been suspicious of him from the first; but she had now to prove that he and the Killer were one.

As she crossed the dreary wasteland she heard a choking cry of pain—a cry that was hideous in the silence of the night. Still on she went, and at last came on the body of a stag. It was the beautiful creature that had cried out in its death agony. Its throat was completely gone, its body ripped open, and its entrails partly devoured. Drops of crimson stained the whiteness of the snow, and Shiela followed the bloody track. On it went across the uneven moorland, and at last came to a sudden stop, and Shiela saw the marks on the snow where the brute had wiped its jaws after its ghoulish meal.

The girl found she had journeyed to the edge of the moor. The spot was unfamiliar to her. A rugged mountain rose precipitously from the side of a melancholy loch. Her quest was done for the night. She could trail the beast no further, and she turned back to Cnoc-na-Ruaidh.

And even as she came in sight of the house she caught a glimpse of a hulking grey form crossing the front lawn. It seemed unconscious of the watchful eyes upon it, and stealthily crept beneath the shelter of a half-opened lobby window. For a second or two it remained quite quiet, then even as the girl watched it, it disappeared, and a moment later she saw the window shut and heard it latched from the inside.

Next day, as soon as breakfast was over, she retraced her steps of the previous night. The body of the stag was still in the same place, and the bloodstains, faint and blurred, still directed her. At the edge of the loch she hesitated and wondered which way to turn. A quarter way up the mountain side a huge lichen-covered boulder jutted out. At its base grew thick bushes of stunted holly, and Shiela's practiced eye told her that some massive body had crept hastily beneath the shelter of the low branches. She climbed swiftly up to it, and peered beneath. There was an opening at the foot of the rock, and, fearless as ever, she crept into the passage-way. The way proved to be very narrow, and ran perhaps thirty feet down into a large cavern. As Shiela entered it she gave a cry of excited pleasure. She had found the Wolf-man's lair!

The place was full of strange devices and mechanical appliances, the use of which she did not know. High up the rocky wall was a tiny ledge. Quickly she tried to reach it. It was an arduous task, but she was sure-footed, the rocky wall gave her foothold, and she reached it safely. It was in reality the mouth of a tiny cave, and she could stay there in safety, and watch all unseen anyone who might be down below. It commanded a perfect view of the whole cavern.

She hurried home and rested, preparing for her nocturnal adventure; but she was not destined to go out that night. A sudden storm came on, the rain came down in torrents, and she knew it would be a physical impossibility to walk the five miles alone. She went to bed early, however, and quivered with indignation as she saw Dr. Sylmak bend tenderly over the gentle spinster, who looked with such trust into his eyes.

He was a Werewolf! A man whose astral spirit took on the form of a wolf, and prowled at night in search of prey! A man who left his body in his chamber while his real self gorged on cannibalistic feasts. It was terrible—horrible—abhorrent!

Shiela was restless in her sleep, her dreams were uneasy, and she tossed from side to side in the large canopied bed. Suddenly she realised she was awake, and listened. There was a soft pad-padding outside her door, and she heard the snuffling of an animal, followed by a tiny whimper. Now, there were no animals at Cnoc-na-Ruaidh—neither cat nor dog nor bird. The house possessed no pets.

She lit her candle and looked round quickly, and gave a sigh of relief as she saw the branch of whitethorn by her side. She caught it up in her hand and opened her door. There was nothing outside. She felt a little mystified. She expected an encounter with the ghostly creature itself, and was a little disappointed. She shut her door and listened. Again she heard the whimper. This time she crept behind the door and waited. Slowly the door opened, yet neither handle turned nor lock clicked. It seemed to glide through rather than open, and through the crack in the hinges she saw the Wolf outside. There was no mistaking it! Its little red eyes gleamed with hatred, and its tongue lolled out of its mouth hungrily. It entered her bedchamber. Round and round it stalked, and she, ever watchful, held the whitethorn high above her head. It was a mighty duel of wits and strength.

The great grey shape crouched at her feet. Its breath was foetid and vile, and its coat gave forth a sulphurous vapour. Its murderous little eyes seemed to laugh as it saw the effort Shiela had to make to keep her arms above her head. How long they faced each other she never knew. She felt at any moment she must let her arms drop for very weariness. The stench of the creature was unbearable; the fumes from its body choked and nauseated her.

She saw her little revolver on her dressing-table, but was unable to reach it. Her eyes grew dim—her head ached. Then suddenly the Wolf was gone, and a pure white kitten clawed at her skirts and mewed piteously. Its foot was hurt, and in the prettiest way imaginable it lifted up its little paw. For a moment only Shiela hesitated, then with a swift movement she slashed viciously at the pretty little creature with her weapon of whitethorn, and the same instant reached her revolver. When she looked again there was no pretty white kitten, but a hideous grey creature, that whined savagely and licked the blood that oozed from a jagged wound across its body.

At that moment Shiela fired, and, with a cry, the Wolf leapt out of the door, and she realised she had missed it.

But had she, after all?

Dr. Sylmak appeared at her door, and there was blood upon his hand.

"What is the matter, Miss Crerar? I heard a noise, and came to see what it was. At that minute you must have fired, for see—the bullet just grazed my little finger."

Shiela gazed at him in horror. Then she had touched the grey shape after all. She thought she had missed; but was there not such a thing as repercussion?

If she wounded the Wolf, would not the man also suffer? If she killed the Wolf, would not the man die in a like manner? Although she had levelled the revolver at the Wolf, Olaf Sylmak had received the discharge. It was indeed curious!

But she did not mean to show her hand yet.

"Pray accept my apology," she said sweetly. "I thought I saw a burglar. I woke from a bad dream. I do hope I have not hurt you much?"

"Nothing to worry about, Miss Crerar. Go back to bed, and sleep better. Good night."

"Goodnight."

But Shiela did not intend delaying further, and directly after dinner the next night she slipped out of her room and started on her walk to the Wolf-man's cave. She had plenty of time; it was still before nine. She reached the place in safety, climbed the rocky wall, and waited.

It was very dreary in that place of fear, and she wished she had told Dr. Chisholm of her discovery, and invited him to accompany her. Time dragged. She must have fallen asleep, for suddenly she realised the place was lighted by huge torches that were fitted in brackets on the wall. In the centre of the cavern a brazier burned, its flames blue and red. A hooded man in a red gown, covered in strange hieroglyphics, stood over it, muttering in a monotone as he sprinkled a powder on the glowing coals that caused the flames to shoot up about the feet, assuming the colours of the rainbow.

A faint cry came from a darkened corner, and Shiela gazed in horror as she saw the magician stoop down and lift up in his arms a tiny naked child of perhaps two years. The plump little body squirmed and struggled with fear, but the man held it deftly while he anointed it with oils and sweet-smelling spices. Suddenly he held a knife aloft, and Shiela buried her face in her hands. There was an agonising cry—a cry that ended with a muffled, choking moan—and silence!

The girl felt too sick to watch; but the scene had its fascination as well as its horror, and tightly clasped in her hand was her loaded revolver. She would make no mistake tonight! But the wizard had not yet finished his revels. He dragged a stool in front of the brazier, and on it he placed two quaint figures. Subconsciously Shiela realised they were familiar. She peered cautiously down from her hiding-place, and realised that one was dressed like Miss Chisholm, while the other was wrapped round in a black hood, the exact counterpart of the one she was wearing at that moment.

The figure below raised the effigy of Miss Chisholm, and in a low voice called on Satan the Mighty, and Shiela knew she was looking at a *corp chréidh** ceremony. She did not know that the practice still existed: the cult of fashioning a body in clay, and by aid of ghastly spells and prayers to the devil, working harm through its medium upon the person it represented.

* Gaelic for clay body.

The sorcerer held the little clay figure in one hand, and with a long, pincer-shaped instrument twisted off the right hand from the wrist. And as he did so, a cry of pain came from the effigy, and a second later Shiela heard Miss Chisholm's voice cry out, "It hurts! It hurts!"

Then the image was flung contemptuously aside, and the man picked up the one dressed in the likeness of Shiela.

He lifted the *corp chréidh* in his hand, and with muffled words of hatred, bent over it for a moment before he plunged the entire left arm into the flames. And as the limb was shrivelled up by the furnace it uttered a wail of agony.

But Shiela had turned white and deadly faint, and she realised she was suffering the pain of burns. She hesitated no longer, and fired twice in quick succession at the monster below.

A piercing shriek broke the stillness of the night, and the man below had vanished; but Shiela saw a grey shape lift up its muzzle in the air and howl dismally, and even as it did so, it, too, disappeared from her ken.

Shiela, trembling and terror-stricken, crept home in the grey morning. Her arm was painful, but she had bound it up with strips torn from her petticoat. In the dim light she saw great blisters had risen from the inflamed flesh. She was worn out and tired, and hoped to creep into her room unseen. But she found the house full of excitement and trouble. Miss Chisholm was in the dining-room, weeping convulsively. Dr. Olaf Sylmak was bending over her, and soothing her.

"Why, whatever is the matter?" asked Shiela.

"My—my brother!" sobbed the woman. "He—he is dead!"

"What?" And as she spoke she noticed Miss Chisholm's right hand was bandaged.

"Shot twice through the heart, Miss Crerar. I heard the sound of a revolver fired twice in quick succession, and when I rushed into Dr. Chisholm's room—he was quite dead."

Shiela looked full into Olaf Sylmak's eyes, and read the truth there.

"May I see him?" she asked quietly.

It was Dr. Sylmak himself who led her into the darkened death-chamber. The face of Robert Chisholm had lost its benignity—its contour. The lips were drawn back, and revealed sharp fangs—fangs that scarcely seemed to belong to a human creature.

"There will be no more killings now, Miss Crerar," said Olaf Sylmak softly.

"You knew?" breathed Shiela.

The man nodded.

"I suspected it some time ago. I've been watching."

"Forgive me! Oh, forgive me!" cried the girl.

But Olaf Sylmak never knew what she meant.

THE WRAITH OF FERGUS MCGINTY

Five years had nearly passed since Shiela Crerar had first taken up her strange occupation. They had been years full of incident—life—success, and they had been years of love. Love mainly unspoken, it is true, but she knew that Stavordale Hartland's very life was hers, and she revelled in the thought. And now she had completed her task. Kencraig was once more her own. Every debt was paid, and although her banking account was small her heart was light.

She was staying with Doctor and Mrs. Chalmers at their Glasgow house for a short holiday, and Stavordale was coming on the morrow. She had written him a quaint, prim little note in which she told him her news, and now?—well, she was glad he was on such terms with the Chalmers that he could invite himself to their home.

She leant back in the depths of an armchair, and surrendered herself to the delight of a favourite author. She was glad she had no "case" on hand, for she was worn out with the strain of her psychic investigations, and she felt she needed a rest. Motherly Mrs. Chalmers was looking after and fussing over her, and the change was a joy to the sensitive girl.

The door opened and she looked up. A man entered—a man with white hair and a flowing white beard. His air was a little old-fashioned, his kilt of homespun was threadbare in places, but his manner was gentle and courteous.

He sat down opposite her and looked round him curiously. He touched a modern writing table and sighed heavily, and a tear coursed down his furrowed cheek. The girl watched him; he did not speak to her, yet his whole manner suggested that he had something on his mind.

The doctor's bell rang out, and she knew he was waiting for another patient. The old man rose, and with the same old-world dignity and courtesy bowed himself out of the room. Immediately afterwards she heard the doctor's door close, and she presumed the queer stranger had gone in to consult him.

She thought no more of the incident until dinner that night, when she suddenly said, "What a dear that old man was who came to see you this afternoon, doctor!"

"What old man, my dear?"

"The old man with the long white beard. He came into the drawing-room, but when he heard your bell, he went out. He looked exactly like a picture of an old patriarch."

The doctor looked puzzled. "No one answering to that description came to see me this afternoon," he said.

"But he went into your room," she persisted. "I heard the clock strike four as he left the room."

"He never came into me," said the doctor with a smile. "At four I saw Lady Mackleton to the door myself. She was anxious to get to Buchanan Street by a quarter-past as she was meeting a friend. I put her into her motor, and closed the door myself."

"I expect the old man got tired of waiting," said Shiela vaguely.

"A great number of people are that," said the doctor with a little chuckle, for he was the most popular practitioner in Glasgow.

The doctor's house was very old—new flats, ugly houses, shops, had grown up round it, but in spite of modern innovations it still retained a certain amount of old-world charm.

As Shiela went along the corridor to her room that night, she perceived a kilted figure in front of her. A gust of wind came from an open window, and she saw him shade his burning candle with his hand. He turned into a room known as "The Panelled Room," and Shiela caught sight of a flowing beard. It was her visitor of the afternoon! It was a very guilty Shiela that entered her bedroom. The old man was no patient, but an inmate of the doctor's house. Perhaps a relative who lived there quietly, unknown to the outside world—a recluse. And she had seemed to spy into the affairs of her friends!

She slept well—the noise of the thundering city failed to keep her awake, and as she rose, her heart sang—Stavordale! Stavordale! He would be with her at noon.

There was a double hall to the big house, and the inner formed a comfortable and picturesque smoking room, with its open grate and galleried stairway. Mrs. Chalmers was sitting there on a settee by the fire when she came down, ready to go to the station to meet Stavordale—and at the further end of the same settee sat the white-bearded old man.

Shiela felt embarrassed and would have passed with a smile, but Mrs. Chalmers called her.

"You have plenty of time, dear. The doctor has ordered the car to take you to the station. It isn't round yet. Sit down by me until it comes."

With a little apologetic smile the girl sat down between Mrs. Chalmers and the stranger. She felt horribly uncomfortable, for her hostess made no attempt to introduce her, and she was thankful when she heard the car at the door.

All the way to the station Shiela pondered over the matter. Could her friends be so heartless as to treat possibly a dependant relative in so churlish a manner? The thought disturbed her, but she was resolved to say nothing to Stavordale. The old man or his relations with her friends was not her business, and she—well, she was going to meet Stavordale!

His train was to time. They had no need of words, for as their lips met they realised they had found each other at last.

"I had your letter, little woman," he said. "I think I could read between the lines. You won't keep me waiting much longer, will you?"

"I am ready when you want me," was her shy confession.

For answer he touched his breast pocket. "I have a special licence here, my darling. Will you marry me soon—next week?"

Her face was suffused with rosy blushes as she gave him the answer he so longed to hear.

Dr. and Mrs. Chalmers greeted Stavordale warmly.

"My old room, I suppose?" he asked gaily.

"Yes, dear boy, the Panelled Room is reserved for you."

A curious shiver ran through Shiela—she scarcely knew why. It was the room that the old man had entered the night before! He was being turned out for Stavordale.

They spent the evening quietly and Shiela went upstairs with Mrs. Chalmers. Again she saw the white-bearded man, and again she watched him enter the Panelled Room!

She felt her heart beat rapidly, but her hostess seemed uncon-cerned. "Good night, sleep well, dear," she said, kissing her, and crossed the corridor and put her hand on the panelled door. "I hope Mary remembered to light the fire in here," she went on brightly. "The room was quite chilly when I went in earlier in the day."

Shiela watched her in open-mouthed amazement. Mrs. Chal-mers went straight into the room—the room the old man had en-tered only a few seconds before—and she heard her poking the fire. Her voice came through the door. "Shiela, my dear, have you a large lump of coal to spare in your room? They are all such small pieces here."

Mechanically Shiela lifted a piece out with the tongs and car-ried it on a shovel, but she hesitated at the door a second before she entered the room. It was large, with old-fashioned eighteenth century furniture, and the fire blazed merrily. She looked round it—there on a chair lay a pile of neatly folded clothes. A pair of brogues with the taws torn were underneath, while sitting up right in the very centre of the huge four-poster was the little old man. He wore a night-cap, and was eating from a bowl from which the steam rose. Shiela rubbed her eyes. Why was the stranger there? Why didn't Mrs. Chalmers notice him?

The old man nodded pleasantly, and quickly the girl crossed to the other woman, but before she could reach her, Mrs. Chalmers was standing by the bed and smoothing the sheets. Sheets that had never been rumpled with wear—and the bed was empty.

Shiela went to her bedroom in a thoughtful mood. She knew now that her power of "sight" was no unmixed blessing. She could foresee no rest from psychic labours now! In grey Glasgow—a city of work and toil—she hardly expected to meet with the unseen. The house stood in a little cul-de-sac off Bath Street. The roar of Sauchiehall Street was near at hand. The lights were bright out-side—all was modernity and rush. Yet—within sound of the city—"vision" had come to her, the meaning of which was as yet obscured.

"I had a strange dream," began Stavordale at breakfast next morning. "I seemed to see an old man with a long—" but Shiela heard no more. She rose and left the table and her heart felt sick within her. All that day she was nervous and irritable. She couldn't tell why, but the presence of the affable, white-bearded old man harassed her.

As she sat down at dinner that night she looked up suddenly. There, opposite her, sat the old man. He was unfolding his nap-kin, and when he had finished he helped himself liberally from a decanter at his elbow. A basin of soup stood in front of him, he seasoned it well, and began to eat.

Shiela gazed with horror at the figure, and Doctor Chalmers noticed her. He followed the direction of her eyes.

"Why, Madeline," he said to his wife, "are you expecting a visi-tor tonight?"

"No. Why?"

"See, an extra cover has been set."

"How careless," she replied, and then to the maid: "Did you set the table tonight, Hoskins?"

"Yes, Ma'am. It was quite an accident. I can't think how I came to make such a mistake. I'm very sorry."

But although she removed the knives and forks, and put the glasses on the sideboard, when Shiela looked again the old man was still in his place enjoying his dinner—but he was two courses ahead of the others!

That night the Wraith appeared in the drawing-room. He seemed to enjoy the music, and sat gently nodding his head in quiet appreciation. Then he rose and crossed to Shiela, and so she sat—her lover on one side, and an unknown wraith on the other!

The situation was incongruous. She felt a wild desire to laugh aloud. Stavordale bent to her.

"What is the matter, dear one?" he asked. "You look tired—anxious. Thank God I shall soon have the right to take care of you altogether."

"Stav," she whispered. "That dream you spoke of—the old man," but the figure on her left turned slightly and met her gaze, and she found she was unable to say what she intended, and passed it off with a smile.

The next afternoon she watched the old man descend the broad stairs in the hall. As he reached the open door the doctor appeared and stared at the unbidden guest for a moment. Shiela saw him hesitate for a second, and then stride after him, but the old man had reached the door and it had swung to behind him.

"You saw?" she asked.

"Yes, of all the confounded impertinence—excuse me, my dear—but did you see? He walked down my stairs as if they belonged to him, and let himself out of my front door, as if he owned the whole place. Who the deuce is he? Why, my dear, isn't he the same man that was in the drawing-room with you one day?"

"Yes."

"Who is he? Do you know?"

"Doctor"—hesitatingly— "I am glad you have seen him too, for the matter has been troubling me greatly. As a matter of fact he has sat with us at dinner for the last few nights!"

The doctor looked at her as if she had gone mad.

"My dear Shiela," he exploded. "Don't bring all your psychic stuff and nonsense here. The man's real enough."

"He's not, doctor. I don't know who he is, but he is certainly not human."

The doctor was clearly a disbeliever, but even his calm was shaken that afternoon, for his wife came into him with an alarmed expression.

"My dear," she said, "I am sorry to disturb you, but I really feel rather nervous. A white-bearded man has gone into the Panelled Room. I saw him go down the corridor, but although I called to him, he took no notice. I distinctly saw him go into the room, yet when I followed him a few seconds later, the room was empty."

The doctor with angry mutterings went upstairs, but although he searched everywhere, he could find not the slightest trace of the stranger.

Then Stavordale came in.

"Hullo!" he said. "I see you have a visitor. Who's the patriarchal old chap in the library? He seems to be making himself very much at home among the books there."

The doctor made no reply. The whole situation annoyed him. He was material himself, and he did not like to have his theory of an entirely material world shaken like this.

Then followed a period of unrest for the four in that house. Every day they caught a glimpse of the stranger in one part of the house or another. He sat with them at dinner; he listened to the music afterwards; Stavordale saw him in his bed. But whenever they tried to touch him, he melted into nothingness and vanished.

"I don't like it at all," cried Mrs. Chalmers. "My dear, you are to be married at the end of next week—won't you try and settle us here first? That old man is on my nerves. I know he seems quite quiet and peaceable, but I—well, the truth is, I'm not used to ghosts and I don't like it."

Shiela comforted the motherly woman.

"I am sure his presence is no menace to any of us," she said. "Try not to bother about it. I am sure sooner or later I shall find a solution to the mystery."

Several times Shiela tried to get into communication with the stranger, but he never uttered a word, and when she addressed him he just faded from sight. Faded is the only word to describe how he vanished. His appearance became lighter and lighter until he looked like a figure of vapour—transparent and ethereal.

Shiela seemed unable to get to the bottom of the mystery. The old man was certainly harmless—he had no sinister effect upon anyone in the house, yet his presence caused a vague feeling of disquiet. They could feel his presence even when they could not see him, and Mrs. Chalmers became quite hysterical. It was her first introduction to the unreal.

Shiela was walking up the broad stairway when she became aware that the old man was in front of her. She followed him down the corridor and he vanished into the Panelled Room. Hardly realising what she was doing, she followed him in. As she entered she was in time to see him disappear behind a piece of wainscotting that swung to after him. Delighted with her discovery she hurried downstairs, and told her story to the others.

"Let's go up at once," said Stavordale eagerly. "We must see if we can find a hidden door there."

They tapped on the wall—it certainly emitted a hollow sound, but the secret spring was very cleverly hidden. The carving represented a huge vine laden with fruit, and Shiela noticed that one grape seemed larger, fuller than the others.

"Push that one," she said excitedly. But although he pressed it, turned it to the right and turned it to the left, nothing happened.

"Can you pull it out?" she asked at last.

He obeyed her instructions. The carved wooden fruit moved ever so slightly, and then slowly the panels swung back and left revealed a small stairway.

"Get some candles quickly," cried Stavordale, and then slowly and cautiously the others followed him, Mrs. Chalmers nervously bringing up the rear, having first carefully propped the secret door open with a chair, "in case of accidents" as she explained.

The stairway was long and steep, and at the bottom a bolted door met their gaze, but even as Stavordale put forward a hand to unfasten it, the stranger mysteriously appeared, and lo! the door was open wide.

Courteously he bowed the little party through. They found they were in a very tiny room, so small that it might once have been used as a Priest's Hole. There was neither window nor grating to be seen, yet the air was pleasantly fresh. It was quite empty, except for a large chest that stood in one corner. Tears fell down the furrowed cheeks of the old man as he silently pointed to it.

Stavordale tried to open it, but it was heavily bolted, and its locks were of a mechanism that needed careful manipulation.

"We must carry it upstairs," he said, and with a smile, it seemed almost of relief, the old man faded away.

It was a difficult task to get the heavy chest up the narrow stairway, but they managed it, and at last, with patience and care, the lid was opened.

They clustered round the ancient chest—eager to see the contents. Tenderly Shiela lifted out a silken dress, a hooped dress of flowered silk that almost crumbled to pieces at a touch. Its style was of more than a century ago. Underneath it were more dresses—suits and a jewelled sword. A duelling sword with rusty stains on its blade—stains that told an ominous story.

But at the bottom of the chest a wonderful treasure was displayed. Plate of gold heavily chased came into sight, and on each piece was engraved a coat of arms, a broken key surmounted by a coronet. Piece by piece the plate was lifted out until forty pieces of solid gold were exposed to view.

"Where can it have come from?" said Mrs. Chalmers.

But Shiela found a clue. In faded writing on the lid of the box itself was scrawled:

> All this is the property of Strathbolla.
> I hide it while there is still time. F. McG.
> Anno Domini 1801.

"Look! Look!" she cried eagerly.

Mrs. Chalmers read it uncomprehendingly. Still she repeated, "Whatever does it mean?"

"It means we have stumbled on some property of the Strathbolla," said her husband, "and mighty queer it is to think we have lived here over thirty years, and yet had no suspicion of that hiding-place."

"How did it ever get here?" asked his wife.

"Ah! that is a mystery we shall never solve," he replied.

But Shiela thought differently.

"We shall have to communicate with the present Laird of Strathbolla," she said. "Do you know anything about him, Doctor?"

"Yes; his place is quite near Aberfeldy. He has only recently come into the estates."

All that day they were eagerly speculating upon the mystery, and wondered what part in the long-forgotten past the white-bearded old man had played.

The Stranger did not appear at dinner that night, and Shiela felt that he knew his mission was accomplished.

Early next day Strathbolla came in person to see the Doctor. In the presence of Doctor and Mrs. Chalmers and Stavordale, Shiela told her story.

She spoke of the haunting of the house by the old man, and of the subsequent finding of the chest.

The man's eyes glowed. He looked at the writing on the chest.

"F. McG.," he murmured. "Poor, faithful old Fergus McGinty!"

"Why, you know the initials?" asked the Doctor in surprise.

"Yes, and now I will tell you my story. Really I should have told it first, for, had you but known, yours is the sequel. This is the famous Strathbolla plate, Doctor, though perhaps you have never heard of it. The story was told me by my grandfather, for he knew and loved Fergus McGinty well, although he was still a lad when the old man died."

"When did he die?" asked Shiela.

"In 1801. My grandfather was then about six—you know, he died in 1888, and had lived nearly a century."

"Well?"

"Well, the story goes back a long way. It was about 1740 that Fergus McGinty first entered the service of the Strathbollas. He was—well, factor we should call him today; but he was far more than that, he was confidential friend as well. Niel Strathbolla, the young heir to the estates, was his dearest charge, and later when he grew up, and became restless and wanted to go to London, it was Fergus McGinty who accompanied him there. He valeted him—looked after him—lent him money when he needed it—in fact, was to him a second father. And, to the young man's credit be it said, he trusted him and loved him. Young Strathbolla got mixed up with a very fast set. He gambled, fought, and became entangled with a worthless woman, whom he married. In 1796, I think it was, he fought a duel, and killed his adversary, and for a time had to leave the country. He sent his wife and small son—my grandfather—to Scotland, and with Fergus McGinty went to Holland." The man stopped for a moment and looked at the jewelled sword that lay open on the table. "Probably that is the very sword that was used in the fatal quarrel," he went on dreamily. "At any rate, after that everything seemed to go wrong for him, and he returned to Scotland in 1799 a ruined man. His father was dead, and he had heavily mortgaged the estates—he hardly had enough money left to buy the barest necessities of life. Nothing was left but the famous gold plate—the very plate on the table yonder—that was given to the family by James V. It was Fergus McGinty who hid the plate from the hungry creditors who came to see what they could get. They burst into the house at Aberfeldy, and seized everything they could lay hands upon. The house was completely sacked, and afterwards burned, and Niel Strathbolla and his son escaped by the aid of loyal Fergus."

All the company in the room were listening to the story with rapt attention. They were being carried into the past ages, and they could picture the stirring deeds that were performed in the "good old days."

"Well, Niel died shortly afterwards—I regret to say it—of *delirium tremens*; his wife had predeceased him; and Fergus McGinty, now an old man, took charge of the little son, and it was that son—my grandfather—from whom I learnt the story. Fergus went back to the ruined house and dug up the gold plate, which he had buried, and took it to Glasgow. There he hid it in what he considered was a safer place, and he told my grandfather that it was kept safe for him, and that one day he would show him his wonderful possessions.

"Unfortunately, that day never came. He was overheard talking about it by a servant, and it was repeated to the creditors of the estate—that it was Fergus McGinty who had done them out of what they considered their just due. Six men came to the little cottage where Fergus and my grandfather were living, and demanded to know the hiding-place of the plate. He refused.

"'It is safe,' he cried boldly. 'It is in trust for my little master here. No one shall ever possess it but a Strathbolla.' Brutally he was knocked down, and a Campbell stood over him and menaced him. 'Tell us where it is,' he demanded; but to neither cajolery nor threats, menace or promise, would the old man yield. 'It belongs to Strathbolla,' he said, 'and Strathbolla's it shall remain.' But the men of those days paid little attention to law and order. In front of my grandfather—a wee, scared bairn—they cut Fergus McGinty's tongue from his mouth. With a wild oath the Campbell stabbed him through the heart. 'If we are not to benefit, then neither shall the Strathbolla!' and they left the bleeding body, over which a poor, little, terrified child wept.

"Many times my grandfather has described the hideous scene, for it remained vivid in his mind all his life. He told me he scarcely realised what had happened, but suddenly the dead Fergus raised himself up, and from his tongueless, bleeding mouth came the words, 'One day Strathbolla shall come into its own!' The child saw no more, for he was found later fainting on the dead body of his friend. There is little more to tell. He was taken care of by a distant relative, who left him his fortune. He paid off all his father's debts and rebuilt the old house—the very one I now possess. He made many attempts to discover the missing plate, but the secret was locked in the heart of his faithful Fergus—Fergus, who had lost his life and lost his tongue in the service of the Strathbolla."

"It's wonderful!" said Shiela, and Stavordale saw the tears in her eyes.

"My grandfather was convinced that one day the secret of the hidden treasure would be revealed; but neither my father nor I ever thought we should see the plate again."

"Then it was Fergus McGinty who told the secret!" said Shiela. "It was Fergus McGinty who invited us here! Poor dumb Fergus!"

"Did your grandfather ever describe him?" asked the Doctor.

"Often," replied Strathbolla. "He was a shortish man, well-built, but not stout. His eyes were blue—pale—but of a piercing brilliancy, and his hair was white, while his long white beard hung down well past his waist."

"The Stranger!" ejaculated Mrs. Chalmers, and, even as she spoke, the Wraith appeared at the side of Strathbolla. He raised one hand, as if in benediction, and with a smile of infinite tenderness faded away into nothingness.

Shiela and Stavordale were married on the following Saturday. In the large dining-room of the Chalmers' house the simple Scottish ceremony was performed. The house, they found upon enquiry, was once tenanted by a certain John McGinty. What relation he was to Fergus they never knew, but the secret had been well kept.

As the happy pair left the house for the car that was to take them to Kencraig, where their honeymoon was to be spent, the Wraith of Fergus McGinty followed them. Shiela saw him, and smiled; and as she did so a wonderful expression of peace came on the old face, and his features were lit up with happiness. Stavordale tucked his arm through hers as the car drove off.

"Happy, little one?" he asked.

"Oh, so happy."

And as he bent to kiss her: "Don't 'see' anything during our honeymoon, my dearest. Do have a perfect holiday."

"I'll try," she said quietly; but her expression was thoughtfully serious, and he realised that her "power of sight" was a gift—a gift that she could not shake on and off at will. But he loved her, and was content.

LUNA BARTENDALE & THE UNDYING MONSTER

Jessie Douglas Kerruish

BOOK I
SEARCH BY THE SUPERSENSITIVE

1

TO THUNDERBARROW SHAW

The end of the Fifty-two Months' War left the family of Hammand of Dannow reduced to two members. The two had always been good pals, Oliver Hammand and Swanhild his sister, and now they were left alone the bond between them was intensified.

Swanhild told herself that as she waited on that winter night. It was to allay her growing nervousness that she dwelt on it. She fidgeted too much over Oliver, so she impressed on herself as she looked at the clock for the fifth time between 11.35 and midnight. It was not true, but it served to reassure her for several seconds. She really had cause for uneasiness. Oliver was out late, and it was the kind of night against which the ancient family rhyme warned the Hammands of Dannow:

> "*Where grow pines and firs amain,*
> Under Stars, sans heat or rain,
> *Chief of Hammand, 'ware thy Bane!*"

Starlit, that is, and dry and cold. There was a breeze down in the Weald of Sussex, which meant that Dannow, up on the Downs, was in the track of half a gale. It was not a noisy wind, but the kind that suggests something very big and thin fresh from the horror of Infinite Space. Swanhild could not hear it distinctly, the Manor walls are a yard thick, only she felt it sweep round the building, and there is nothing more harrowing than a deadly hush with the feel of a great noise round it.

She waited in the Holbein Room, not the best place in the circumstances. Flanking the fireplace were the two dubious Holbeins;
portraits of Godfrey Hammand and his wife—both killed by the
Undying Monster of Dannow on a frosty night in 1556. Over the
mantelpiece the little, black, Streete portrait of Godfrey's father,
Sir Magnus the Warlock, who committed suicide after surviving
an encounter with the Monster on a frosty night of 1526. Swanhild
saw all three whenever she consulted the clock, as only one lamp
was lit, over the mantel, and they were enshrined in a little oasis
of warmth and light in the vast spread of wainscoted room.

The rest of the apartment was all shifting shadows, Swanhild
herself the only bright and vivid feature of it when the fire had
gone down to a sullen smoulder. She was a big woman of twenty,
slimly but largely built, with aquiline features, big grey eyes, calm
and wide-set, and a wonderful crown of glowing curls, every lock a
separate shade of gold, from coppery to that pale tint that suggests warmed silver. She was a typical Hammand of Dannow, evidently a descendant of the Warlock Sir Magnus, for the portrait,
the face outlined palely in a black wilderness of background and
Tudor cap, and the features traced like rivers on a map, might have
been a coarsened likeness of her.

Soon after midnight appeared Walton, the butler, with some
trifling enquiry as transparent excuse for a little talk. His manner
was one of nicely suppressed alarm.

"Mr. Oliver's very late, Miss Swanhild," he observed uneasily.

"We can trust him not to get into mischief, Walton."

"It's mischief getting at him I dread, Miss Swanhild. Those two
Ades are likely to be about their tricks on a night like this."

Swanhild laughed. "They're only poachers, Walton."

"You observed yourself, Miss Swanhild, that fellows who set
traps that mauled the poor beasts would be capable of anything.
The Ades were always a vengeful lot, a gipsy strain about them,
you know, Miss Swanhild. And Charlie Ade owes Mr. Oliver one
for that thrashing last month."

"Strictly he owes me one. It was I who sent Oliver round directly
I found the traps. Oliver would have been content with jailing him."

"He swore, and so did young Bob, to do for Mr. Oliver when he was out of Lewes, Miss Swanhild."

"Just so, hence my confidence, Walton. They wouldn't dare to do anything after saying it."

"Well, Miss Swanhild, there's no knowing." He hesitated. "As Mr. Oliver went to Lower Dannow it's to be hoped he won't take the short cut back by the Shaw—"

As he was voicing her own unconfessed fear Swanhild was curt. "Don't worry about the Monster," she advised. "Why, it hasn't been about for forty years."

"There's no timing it, Miss Swanhild. Once it was quiet a hundred and twenty years, and then it came up worse than ever—" He glanced involuntarily at the Warlock portrait.

The girl shuddered and abandoned her pretence of indifference. "If one only knew beforehand when it was going to manifest itself!" she sighed.

"If you knew when to expect it, Miss Swanhild, might I venture to ask what you would do?"

"Call in—Oh, Doyle, or Professor Lodge, or Miss Bartendale."

"Miss Bartendale, Miss Swanhild? I do not seem to recognise the name. May I ask if we have ever entertained the lady?"

"No, I only know her by reputation. She is the greatest hand at hunting down ghosts and anything supernatural that ever was known. She appears to combine the functions of a White Witch and detective."

Walton shook his head. "It was before your time, Miss Swanhild, but I remember Madame Blavatsky and Professor Crookes coming down after your grandfather's death and failing to find out anything. I doubt, with all respect to your opinion, if this lady, or anyone, could do anything with our Monster."

Swanhild laughed again. "I believe you would be half sorry if anyone could, Walton! It would lower the prestige of the family to lose its old-established Ghost, eh? A supernatural Bane and Luck combined that has gone on for a thousand years at least—"

She stopped suddenly. The door was ajar and from the hall came the noise of the telephone bell. Both the girl and the old man were unreasonably startled. Walton hurried out, and Swanhild followed him after a moment's pause. The hall was poorly lit, at the further end of it the maid who had been sitting up pending the master's return was at the telephone.

She turned, and across the dusk of the long apartment her face shewed with the uncanny luminosity of live flesh in a dim distance. Through the hush her voice came in almost a shriek.

"Oh, Mr. Walton—Miss Hammand. They've rung us up from the Lodge—the Monster's in the Shaw—Will heard it howl. And Mr. Hammand isn't home yet!"

As she ran the length of the hall Swanhild's heart seemed to miss one beat and then she was suddenly very calm. She must be calm, for Oliver's sake. "Hullo, hullo!" came the voice of the Lodge-keeper's son as she took the receiver from the frightened maid. "Why don't you call Miss Hammand?"

"It's Miss Hammand. Steady, Will. What's up?"

"The Monster's in the Shaw, miss. I heard on en. Killin' Mus' Hammand, most like. I heard on en a mile away. Horrible, it were, like a dog an' a devil to onct!"

"How do you know it's the Monster? It might be a trapped dog."

"Miss, I heard en! I were comin' home from Lower Dannow, after gettin' a bottle for Father from the Doctor, and on the bridge I heard en. Like a bark, an' a voice, an' a woman in 'sterics all to-gether! Wind bein' from the Shaw, miss, an' it carryin' all the way to the bridge! It warn't no dog."

"Very well, stand ready with a lantern to open the gates when you see a car coming."

Three violent applications to the house telephone brought the voice of the chauffeur, scared and sleepy. "'lo! Wha's 'time o' night?" it demanded.

"It's Miss Hammand. Run the Maxwell round, Stredwick. As quick as you can."

She ran upstairs and carne down within three minutes, buckling her brother's service revolver on round her motor coat. Walton and the maid, the only servants up at the time, still stood by the telephone, as though paralysed. "Miss Swan, surely you're not going to the Shaw?" the old man exclaimed.

The horror in his eyes brought home to Swanhild the incredible possibilities of the crisis. As a youth he had seen her own grandfather, Reginald Hammand, brought home from the Shaw after such an alarm as this: living, but with his hair turned partly white in a couple of hours. She could see the picture of it was growing in his mind's eye, and to break the spell of horror motioned him to open the hall door.

The inrush of wind almost took her off her feet. Sudden frost had crisped the ivy round the porch to brittleness, it made an odd undertone in the wind. Before, her was the courtyard, all black, the pines across the moat tossing their arms fantastically over the girding-wall, the sky overhead tenderly grey, with big, hard winter stars in it. Past the wall shewed copses and hangers like so many clumps of hearse-plumes; ground in the valley between all a soft mistiness of starlit frost-fog. Beyond the valley the last Northern wave of the Downs humping itself up to the crowning height of Thunderbarrow Beacon. The Monster Shaw, at the foot of the Beacon, plumily dusk above the mist. The summit over the Shaw only to be distinguished from the sky by token of its blocking out some stars and having the Monstrous Man of Dannow sprawled on it.

Dannow Monstrous Man is a giant figure outlined by stripping the turf from the chalk beneath, own brother to the Long Man near Eastbourne and the White Horses of many places in England. In that night of half-light and dull darkness it shone strangely distinct and menacing, looking, as shifting mist-shadows chased over it, like a Titan's ghost pegged down on the hillside and writhing in agony.

Swanhild, in the compulsory pause, up in the sounding emptiness of night, realised herself for a feeble atom bound to pit herself against what had baffled the wits and courage of thirty generations. She chafed over the car's delay, but knew it was unavoidable. And every moment was precious. What was happening to Oliver in that dark patch under the Monstrous Man that was the wood where so many Hammands had died hideously? If it was no false alarm, if he had truly fallen into the too tangible clutches of the Monster, then she was probably only going to share his fate—death in a horrible form, or madness that would end in self-destruction.

They had all committed suicide, all the Hammands who encountered the Monster and were not killed by it. Her grandfather and the Warlock Sir Magnus, and Godfrey whom Holbein painted, and many others. And not one had described what he had seen. They just killed themselves, rather than live with the horror of it in their brains. . . . That was the very worst of it—if only one had described what it was—any horror is preferable to that of utter uncertainty.

As she strained eyes and ears for the car's coming, a soft nose was thrust into her hand. "I had forgotten you Alex," she said, patting the Great Dane that had lounged after her from the hall fire. She would not go utterly alone, after all, though no man within ten miles would have ventured into Thunderbarrow Shaw on a frosty night.

"Miss Swanhild, I can't see a lady of the family run into danger without a man to back her. I'll come." Walton spoke with the explosiveness of desperation. His teeth chattered over the words, he clutched the doorpost as though staggered at his own temerity. He would be less use than hindrance. "No, thanks, Walton," she returned. "It may be a false alarm, and you must mind the house. Just get Mrs. Walton up quietly."

He opened his mouth to protest, but at that moment a dazzling light flowed round the house, to stop, purring, before the steps. Swanhild was down and in almost before it was stationary. The chauffeur jumped out; a ridiculous figure, his livery jacket huddled over the diverse garments he had snatched when awakened.

"It's the Shaw, Thunderbarrow Shaw, Mr. Stredwick!"

The maid called it down—she had an understanding with him. The man's face turned to a mask of panic. "Miss—I can't go!" he quavered to Swanhild. "The Monster's taken a Stredwick already, besides Hammands!"

Swanhild remembered the man's grandfather had been one of the victims whose death in the Shaw had been too horrible for her grandfather to explain or survive. "You'll open the wall gate," she ordered, settling in the driver's seat and calling Alex up beside her. He had it only half open when she guided the car through.

It bumped, thunderously, ever the moat-bridge, and shot into the avenue.

2
IN THUNDERBARROW SHAW

The wind lashed Swanhild's face icily as she put the car to half speed down the clear span of avenue. It glided over the smooth gravel steadily; the splash of white glare from the lamps slipping along the ground in front; tree trunks seeming to scurry past frantically as the light rippled against them in the pitch darkness that brooded under the roof of meeting beech branches. The Lodge was marked by a pink scintillation that was Will's lantern and a flicker of twisted ironwork as the open gates were passed.

Outside, the road curved to the right, beside the park railings, ran high and bleaky parallel to the valley, and dipped to the bridge. So far the wind came to them straight from the Beacon. The girl strained her ears for any unusual sound on it. She heard nothing, but felt the Great Dane start and stiffen beside her. The great creature suddenly drooped down on the cushions, whimpered once, and huddled against her, shuddering. Swanhild's brain crept—Alex, fearless, thoroughbred Alex, was abjectly frightened, with nothing to account for it save that the wind was from the Beacon and animals can sense what human beings cannot. Then the bridge was reached, a turn to the left made, and the car sped along a glimmering ribbon of highway with the wind no longer from the Beacon. Hedges ran to either hand, fluffily black, dipping to give a glimpse of the rivulet that ran down from the uplands like a flash of dull, meandering lightning. Then came cobbles, rough-cast garden walls to the right, cottages beyond them peaking, unlit, up amongst the stars. To the other hand the misty valley and the uplands beyond sloping to the spectral enormity of the Monstrous Man on the Beacon's dark bulk. The village well past, the flanks of the Beacon and another Down-hump swooped together and then opened to show the road rippling, ethereally pale, into the hazy immensity of the Weald.

Swanhild knew Oliver had gone to Mansby Place in Lower Dannow village, round the far curve of the Beacon's base. She had clung to one faint hope: that her brother had merely stayed gossiping with Goddard Covert unreasonably late. Her country-bred eyes could make out the Place, on its hillock, black but for one tiny glimmer towards the top. Oliver was not there. Goddard was up, pottering over his chemicals, but she thanked Heaven the Place was to windward of the Beacon that night. Oliver must have gone by the borstal; the sheep track that ran below the Shaw and through the valley almost to the Manor Lodge. All this went through her mind in the moment it took to turn the car and race back through the gap. A twist to the right sent it slashing and slicing through frozen grass and dead bracken, and so down to the turf-grown Roman cutting through the valley.

It seemed an eternity while she drove principally by instinct and memory into the dull, wet sea of mist in the valley-trough. The car rushed down into it, seemed to stand hummingly still in the smother of it, bumped, and began to climb in free starlight again, the Beacon rising in front, to be drawn up on a grass slope with the fringe of the Shaw not far above it.

Alex had recovered herself; she sniffed towards the wood, but shewed no uneasiness. The sounds of a wind-tortured plantation came down, full and loud: boughs beaten together creakily, the rustle of bushes and bracken, the swish of lashed grass. A very tornado of dismal noises met Swanhild when she unshipped a lamp and stepped towards the outer fringe of trees. She was hot and cold at the same time, and calm with sheer dread. The Shaw was mainly full of pines, firs and beech, that stretched up funereally, shutting out the dimly lit sky, save where a birch here and there let a few stars glimmer down between bare branches. The noisy, crowded spaciousness would have been terrifying to any solitary wanderer not country-bred, to Swanhild the terror was what might manifest itself at any moment; from the treetops, behind or in front, or from the very earth.

Alex loped in front, with swaying head. Swanhild called her brother's name at intervals, steeling herself against the dread that her voice might bring other hearers than Oliver. The whole Shaw was like a dark cave, a cave with endless turnings, where anything might lurk. Possibly Something that made sane men kill themselves after meeting it. Once an indistinct sound made her face round, and far away the other lamp was shining on the car.

A turn hid it, breaking the last link with the wholesome outer world, and landed her in a clearing whence several rides branched.

Someone had been there recently. The earth was too frost-bound to hold footmarks, but crushed grass and snapped fern told the tale. Alex suddenly ran up the nearest path to an oak that stood at one side of another small clearing. She nosed uneasily some-thing on the ground. It was a splash of blood, frozen and slightly opalescent. Swanhild flashed the light round, and on the side of the tree facing the open space was a dark mark, splashed head-high, and at the foot a ghastly huddle of torn flesh.

Swanhild's heart sucked, but this was not Oliver. It was the next worse thing, his dog. A gigantic mastiff, its body looked as large as a pony as it lay there. One hind leg had been torn off, the whole body had been twisted and squeezed to an almost shapeless mass before being flung against the tree. Some diabolic force must have been needed to perform such an atrocity. Alex, after snuffing mournfully at her dead kennel friend, led on again, across the clear-ing to a curve in the line of trees, where the lightning-struck ruin of a beech stood over-shadowed by a large pine. At the pine's foot the light lit on black curls prone on the shuffled brown needles and cones.

It was Oliver, sprawled over the roots with his head in a puddle of blood.

Setting the lamp down, Swanhild turned him over and propped him against the pine. His face was covered with blood, his hair matted with it; a thick silk muffler round his neck was black and soaked and frozen into folds. All the blood was congealed, it had ceased to flow some time before, though whether from cold or because Oliver had died Swanhild could not tell. The sleeves of his thick overcoat were torn to ribbons and his hands and forearms were black and scarlet and frozen almost stiff. Swanhild could not tell if his heart showed any sign of life, with the beating of her own and the noise around almost deafening her.

She stood up and squared her shoulders. A thicket of brambles and bracken backed the trees, it was torn and broken in a way that indicated a titanic struggle. Nothing could be done there; alive or dead she must get her brother home. Suddenly a little uncertain sound came from the hollow of the burnt beech. Her scalp crept, she stepped before Oliver, listening and staring from the beech to Alex.

The dog lifted and swayed her head uncertainly, sniffing towards the beech, then resumed her watch on Oliver. Swanhild could not see into the tree, a gap to the ground existed but it was round at the other side. There were scores of different sounds on the wind as it poured through boughs and over the hill edge; she could not decide if she had been mistaken. At last: "Come out of that hollow tree or I'll fire!" she ordered, in a scared voice she scarcely knew for her own.

There was no answer, and she fired into the trunk, waist high. Nothing ensued but a shower of rotten wood. The explosion of the revolver seemed to blow aside all other noises for a moment and leave her in a little clear space of silence. No sound came from the tree. She would have been satisfied but for the dog's action. Driven by impulse, almost without conscious volition, she snatched the lamp and ran to flash it in the hollow.

She had not cried out over her brother, but at what the light showed a half-scream of: "Kate Stringer!" seemed to ring in her ears without her knowing she had spoken. The sight was indescribable, the broken mastiff was nothing to it. And the worst was that the torn flesh she could scarcely distinguish from the torn clothing was still alive.

Nothing to be done there. With strength born of desperation she thrust Oliver up the pine-roots until he almost stood, sagging horridly as she propped him, butted a shoulder under one of his arms, and so slung him on her back. He was an enormous man, his feet trailed on the ground and both hands were needed to hold him by the limp arms she pulled round her neck. The butt of the revolver, thrust in the breast of her coat, touched her right hand as she held him. The lamp must be left behind; she turned it with one foot so that the light carried as far as possible along the way she had come. Summoning all her strength she started off, bent nearly double beneath her overwhelming burden.

Alex kept in front of her. The mastiff's body was within the lamp's ray, seeing it she realised afresh what a mark she made, weighed down and in the dark, for whatever had done the night's work. A turn took her beyond the light and a trailing bramble caught her round one ankle like a clutching hand; she jammed Oliver between herself and a tree while she reached up the foot and found what it was. Her eyes were now adjusted to the dark, she could distinguish Alex for a lighter patch in it as the animal led her over the first clearing, and so, presently, the light of the car hove into sight in a frame of black tree silhouettes. She summoned all her strength and in a last spurt reached the blessed open, between Shaw and car, tumbled her brother on the turf, and sank down beside him, sobbing for breath.

His head rolled over in a hideously limp way when she lifted his shoulders and held him in her arms while she recovered breath, her eyes on the Shaw all the time. So far, good. The Monster never attacked anyone save under pines or firs. Oliver was safe from it for the time. Only she ought to go back for the other victim. She tried to think it over, frantically, in the enforced pause to gather strength. She was almost sure Oliver was dead; but if he were taken to the Doctor at once there might be a chance for him. She knew poor Kate in the beech had been just alive—but she might be dead by now. Anyhow, a woman's first duty is to her own menfolk.

Kate was probably dead. She got up and dragged Oliver into the tonneau, tucked the rugs round him, and ran round the car to crank up. The girl who might be alive—her brother who might be

dead. The Monster had not molested her, but if she went in again—
She could come back after taking Oliver home.

Oh, yes, and Oliver might survive—at the expense of a girl's
possible chance of living. She dropped the handle and pelted off to
the Shaw again, after ordering Alex to stay with Oliver. There were
things a Hammand of Dannow could not do, even to save the only
brother the war had left her. She charged blindly through the darkness of the unholy wood now, no more conscious of the horror that
dark might hold in leash than of the ground under her speeding
feet, exalted past fear by plain duty to be done.

Only a thrill of horror had power to come when she reached
the beech and was stripping off her coat to wrap and hold together
the ghastly thing that was a girl like herself; a girl she had played
with years before, had talked and laughed with that past afternoon.
A pair of pale blue eyes opened in the mutilated thing that had
been the prettiest face in the village, and looked at her a moment
before closing again. In a few minutes she was back and had stowed
the close wrapped figure beside Oliver. To turn the car it had to be
run under the fringe of the Shaw, to a wider turf stretch, and so
round to the Roman way. Then it shot down the incline and along
the mist-filled trough of the valley, bumped, and climbed again.

To Swanhild it seemed a thousand years' stretch of wind that
lashed the face like sleet, stars racing backwards, smothering mist,
and sounding, empty space with a menacing horror ready to
materialise out of the murk, before the car swooped on to cobbles
in the safety of the village street.

It was best to head for the Manor. The doctor lived half an
hour's run away over the worst roads in Sussex. It was ten minutes' smooth scurry to the now brightly lit lodge. Will was on guard,
she called to him to call the doctor at once as the car flashed
through.

3

OLIVER HALF-REMEMBERS

In the courtyard Stredwick and Walton, both pale and wide-eyed, got Oliver out of the car and into the hall. Mrs. Walton waited there with the maid, large, composed, capable. She had been a trained nurse before her marriage and her nerves were dependable.

"Put him on that settle," she ordered. Swanhild followed, carrying the girl. Vaguely she reflected that the run must have been a record one, or the cloth between her hands and the tattered body would have been soaked through; then, with a shiver, she recollected that the Monster was a vampire, and a vampire's victims do not bleed much after meeting it. She laid her burden on the other settle.

"A bad knock on the head," pronounced Mrs. Walton, examining Oliver. "The wounds on his face and neck are shallow: his muffler saved him a lot, and the cold must have checked the bleeding. He's beginning to come round; Walton, get some brandy!"

Swanhild felt the room swaying for a moment. Oliver was not dead after all! Mrs. Walton turned to open out the coat that hid the other victim. Even her trained nerves broke at what was revealed. "Good Lord!" she gasped hushedly. "I've never seen the like—and twice I've helped clear the bodies from a wrecked train! Kate Stringer—I didn't know her at first—why, it's like the work of a tiger—a mad and starving tiger! We'll just make her comfortable, Miss Swan, my dear, against the Doctor's coming—"

Here Oliver opened his eyes. They were grey, and they looked diabolically grotesque, pale in the blood-blackened mask that was his face, as they turned about, dim and clouded, from Swanhild to the others. "What—" he began, huskily. Then his gaze found the figure on the other settle, the cloudiness passed away, a stare of utter horror came instead, and before anyone could stop him he sprang to his feet and bent a long look on the mangled girl. "Kate! My heavens, the beast got her after all!" he screamed, and collapsed into Swanhild's arms.

"A plain faint, from shock," Mrs. Walton diagnosed. "You and me, Miss Swan, can manage those wounds. Walton, you and Stredwick carry him to his bedroom."

The telephone bell rang. "From the Lodge, Dr. Newton will come at once," the maid announced.

Before the doctor came Oliver was conscious again. Swanhild was alone with him. He stirred, sighed, and looked round slowly. "Hullo, Swan!" he said, hoarsely. "How did I get here? I thought I was at the Place with old Goddard—" He lifted a bandaged hand and put it to his forehead. "Bandages? And how the deuce did I get into bed?" he said, confusedly.

He was very like his sister, an enormous, black-haired male copy of her, and his eyes were like hers, only now they were clouded. His face had been little injured, but on the left temple was a huge purple swelling.

"I found you in the Shaw and brought you home, dear," Swanhild said hastily.

"But how—I don't remember—after leaving Lower Dannow—" His voice trailed off to an indistinct stop. "How did I—I begin to remember—I fought the Monster   " Raising a bandaged hand to the bruise: "Oh, Swan!" he cried; "Kate—the brute got her!"

Swanhild perched on the side of the bed and laid a cool hand on his burning forehead. "Don't worry, dear old boy," she crooned.

"I'm all right, Swan," he retorted. "She—oh, I saw her!" He almost sobbed. "It must have taken her after I fought it off. It's our Bane—and it's taken a woman! The brute never comes except for one of the family—if I hadn't fought it off it might have taken me and spared her—"

"Oliver, dear," said Swanhild, abruptly, "what was the Monster like?

He blinked at her. "Oh, I see. You want to jerk a description out of me unawares. For fear—oh, for fear I'd keep it to myself and go mad brooding over it, like—like grandfather and the others. But I don't remember—" Suddenly a red light glimmered at the back of his eyes, as always happened when he was excited or profoundly shocked. "Reggie!" he gasped.

"Oh, Oliver!" cried Swanhild. "You don't mean—you're mad—I *hope* you are mad!"

"I'm not. I mean people will say it," he answered. "It's the first frost since he went west. They'll say in the villages he's returned as a—as a vam—. Good Lord, Swan, they'll call him *that!*"

"Hush!" she soothed. "You can put that right with a description of whatever you saw, dear."

"But I did not see anything. At least I can't remember. What's the matter with my head?"

"There's a lump on it, you must have hit the ground there—"

"Jove, that's it!" He pressed his least bandaged hand to his temple. "It feels all squashy. That must be why I can't quite remember—"

Dr. Newton hurried in; a big-built man, dapper in spite of the midnight call. "You were shouting, Mr. Hammand. That's a good sign at least," he announced. He believed in an optimistic bedside manner.

"I'm all right, Doctor, only sore. I suppose Mrs. Walton's been cauterising me. What of Kate?"

"Young people are tenacious of life. More I cannot say at present. She can't be moved; Mrs. Walton is preparing a room, Miss Hammand; she did not think it necessary to consult you." While he talked he felt Oliver's pulse and made a quick general examination. "We are doing very well," he nodded to Swanhild. "Nothing but a bit of tying-up left for me to do. Miss Hammand has cauterised you to a turn, it must have hurt her more than it did you! There," he slipped the last safety pin into position. "Let us hear about it."

"It's soon told." Oliver leant back against the pillows, a grotesque figure with his bandaged arms and neck and the bruise splashed over the larger part of his forehead now the swelling had gone down. "I'd been to Mansby Place and was taking the borstal short cut home. When I reached the Shaw I saw something glimmering in it and went in to investigate. Thought it might be some beast setting traps, you know, Swan. It was Kate—she lives with her grandfather in the little cottage at the far end of Lower Dannow, Doctor. She said the old man had been taken very ill, and she was going to the Lodge to ask them to ring you up."

"Very good: Mrs. Walton has rung up Dr. Albury and Nurse Black, when they come we'll send to old Stringer. You met Kate—?"

"I told her to nip back to the old chap, and I'd hurry to the Lodge. We'd walked back on her track nearly as far as the burnt beech as we talked, then all of a sudden I felt rotten." He put his hand to the bruise again, and hesitated. The Doctor, who had been mixing something in a glass while he talked, handed it to him. He drank the contents mechanically. Swanhild noted the scent of laudanum. "All at once," he resumed, "I felt rotten. Not ill, you know, but simply—oh, putrid! Kate screamed, it sounded awful in the dark; and I knew something was coming. Coming on me from all sides at once. My brain went round. All in the dark but for a bit of starlight, with my tyke rubbing against me. And, Swan, the worst of it was I didn't feel utterly strange. As sure as I knew it was the Monster coming I knew I'd been through it before."

"Yes, dear," she assented.

He flared up irritably. "You needn't talk as though I were a scared kid or a lunatic, Swanhild. Only it *was* queer, it didn't feel novel to me. Stars, and pines, and cold, and the Monster coming. I couldn't get away from it, it came from all round and closed on me like—oh, like the blast from furnace doors opening all round me. All round and above, and under me. And the air from them sweeping right through me. But it wasn't hot; only horrible. Horrible. Then Holder started to whimper, and my hair fairly rose. He didn't challenge at all, just began to whimper. A thoroughbred whimpering without warning could only mean something bestial. I seemed to know that what was coming would be the end of me, soul as well as body. If I didn't fight it it would annihilate me. Soul and body. I heard myself calling to God for help—out loud. That'll tell you how I felt. Then it closed on me, Kate screamed somewhere, and Holder screamed too. He absolutely screamed, I tell you, Doctor. A mastiff! Then I was fighting It. Fighting it anyhow, in a darkness that went red. All red dark until a splash of fire split it up and put it out. Put the red out and left proper black darkness. That must have been when I pitched on my head. Then I opened my eyes again in light, and saw the hall, and saw you, Swan, and oh, I saw Kate!"

He put his arm over his face and groaned. "Where's Holder?" he asked, noting Alex, who was standing with her forepaws on the bed eyeing him sympathetically.

"Dead." Swanhild thought brevity was best.

Oliver started up. "Holder dead?"

"He died helping you against the Monster, Oliver. It must have got Kate first, and you and he must have drawn it away. Why, it was a death a gallant dog might pray for!"

"If I hadn't fought it off it might have spared him and Kate too. I believe it went for me first." His voice was getting indistinct. On the verge of sleep he suddenly roused. "Why, Swanhild, you're the next! The only Hammand left, beside me! Whenever it appears the Monster will complete its sacrifice—if I die you'll be the Head!" He was in a frenzy of horror that overpowered the opiate temporarily. "Swan, promise me this: whether I live or die, go mad or stay sane, you'll have this investigated at once."

"I will, Oliver."

"You'll get Lodge, or the S.P.R., or that—that lady the Kynastons had."

On my word of honour, Oliver."

"Blavatsky and Crookes failed over grandfather, but people have found a lot more out since then." For a few minutes he was awake, a man thinking for the woman dependent on him. "I can't rest, alive or dead, unless you promise to have the investigation as soon as it is daylight. Whether I'm alive or dead, mad or sane."

"I promise, Oliver. As soon as it is day. On my honour."

"Ah," he sighed and fell back as though exhausted. "You're next Chief of Hammands—inherit the Curse—get Lodge, or the lady the Kynastons had—on your word of hon—"

His voice trailed into silence, and he slept.

4

A WITCH HUNT IN PROSPECT

The hours that followed were a reminiscent nightmare to Swanhild. A dreaming-over of the time when all efforts failed to save her elder brother some months before. The same reek of drugs and hushed bustle, the same horror of too much white linen overflowing everywhere. Everyone was needed, the Waltons, the other indoor servants, Swanhild herself and the second doctor and trained nurse when they arrived. The medicos had to be helped, one despatched to old Stringer, Oliver watched, a thousand things done for the other victim.

The smallest hours were well past before the full difficulty of the situation really dawned on Swanhild. The first exaltation of hurried action over, she waited in the Holbein room and the grotesque horror of it all became evident. Oliver was safe at home, his injuries were severe but superficial, but if he remembered fully what he had seen that night madness and suicide would be inevitable. She must do something. Something that thirty generations had failed to do. Find out what the Monster really was.

It was a desperate project, and it did not follow that finding out the secret would mean finding salvation for Oliver. What could this thousand-year-old horror be, anyhow? Why had it not attacked her? Had it left the Shaw before she reached it? Where had it gone, then? Where had it come from? No trace of it had been found after any of the previous tragedies. There was only one thing to be done, and she embarked on it by consulting the Post Office London Directory.

The door opened and Dr. Newton entered. She stared up at him dumbly. He nodded: "The verdict: joint verdict of Albury and myself, is that your brother has rallied splendidly, my dear Miss Hammand. His pulse is normal, and he is sleeping healthily under my opiate. The wounds should do well, also; thanks to your promptitude in bringing him in and cauterising them. Exposure might have finished him."

"What of the girl?"

"It is also thanks to your promptitude that she has a chance of life. Very microscopic, but still a chance. She can't be moved; I should like to call in a specialist."

"I give you *carte blanche*, of course, Doctor. What of Oliver's mind?"

"I cannot tell until he wakes. However, it seems unaffected except in the matter of his not remembering what happened immediately before that knock on the head."

"Does the blow account for his partial loss of memory?"

"Can't say off-hand. The bone is not disturbed, and after a good sleep his memory may be perfect again."

"He may wake with his memory restored?"

"Possibly, possibly not."

"In the latter case, may it return later?"

"That is also a possibility. I shall advise you if it becomes necessary to call in a mental specialist."

"A mental specialist will be no use if he remembers what he saw in the Shaw," returned Swanhild, bitterly.

"Now, now, my dear Miss Hammand!" the doctor chided. "Nothing I have seen this night is due to any but a material cause."

She reminded herself he had only bought the local practice when her grandfather's death was becoming a legend, and merely asked: "Well, what sort of creature made the wounds?"

"That is the one uncertain point. They are so ferociously torn and mauled that no mark is distinct enough to indicate what made them. It is fair season, however, a half-starved beast may have escaped from some show. I've warned the Dannow constable. Also, Walton has been telling me that those two Ades have been threatening your brother lately. They own three peculiarly large and vicious curs, if the masters attacked Hammand the dogs might have attended to anyone else who had the bad luck to be present. I hope, Miss Hammand, that our patient will wake in a fit state to laugh at his fancies of the night. By the way, what is the rhyme about the alleged Monster? I might as well know just what he fancies."

"It is I who fancy he may kill himself, if he remembers what he saw in the Shaw," returned Swanhild, defensively. "This is the correct version of our family rhyme:

> 'Dannow Monster, do ye wit.
>   With the race is firmly knit.
> While the Monster is alive
>   Hammand's race shall live and thrive.
> If it die; if die it may;
>   Hammond's race shall fade away.
> Who its monstrousness espieth
>   God grant grace that swift he dieth!
> Whoso, spying, dieth not,
>   Worse than death shall be his lot!'"

"H'm. What does the last line mean?" asked the doctor.

"That any Hammand who sees the Monster and is not killed by it will pine away through horror, or commit suicide. They did, both of them."

Swanhild indicated the Streete and Holbein defiantly. The doctor pursed his lips. "It is centuries since those ancestors of yours met their fate, my dear Miss Hammand, plenty of time for traditions to grow around them."

"My grandfather met a similar fate in 1890," she returned. "We have the Times of October 10 in that year, with an account of the inquest."

He frowned at her thoughtfully. "I seem to have read it some time or other. There was some mention of a legend accounting for it. That every now and then one of you Hammands must be sacrificed to the Devil, who claims his prey in a pine wood on frosty, starlit nights, in the shape of something called the Undying Monster."

Swanhild nodded. "That's one of the traditions. Only it has to be the Head of the family who is sacrificed. As long as the Monster lives to take his toll so long shall we hold Dannow."

"And that's the idea your brother has in his head? No wonder he was upset! My dear Miss Hammand you are upset yourself; and no wonder, after your exertions of the night. By daylight you will be yourself again, and the police will probably bring round the body of the escaped animal that did the very material damage to your brother and the girl. Now I must go back to my patients."

When he had gone Swanhild turned to the directory and made out a little list of names and addresses. She looked up again as the door was opened. "Goddard!" she exclaimed.

"Swanhild!" the newcomer responded, in a voice wherein reproach, relief and horror were blended. He was a tall and thin young man, a few years her senior, with a lean face, bright brown eyes, dark hair, and a humorous mouth. He was dressed in tweeds thrown on anyhow, a tweed cap squashed down on his head, and a motor lamp swinging in the gloved hand at the end of his left arm; hand and arm being expensive substitutes for the original limb.

From his face Swanhild's eyes travelled to the lamp. "Yes," said Goddard Covert, severely. "It's your Maxwell's starboard light."

"Oh, Goddard! You've been in the Shaw!"

"Oh, Swanhild, you never called me when you went in the Shaw!"

"Your wire is out of order, you know," she excused.

"You were glad it was," he retorted. "I was restless early, saw this burning in the Shaw, and went to investigate. And, oh, Swanhild! I saw the dog!"

He had set the lamp down and held her hands bunched together in his while they talked. "You in the Shaw—during frost—and after *that*—oh, Swanhild!" he went on, reproachfully. "Walton has told me all."

He became aware of the cap, and pulled it off. "I *was* upset," he observed, staring at it.

"You went into the Shaw!" she exclaimed again.

"It was safe—drizzling by that time. Swan, my dear, what are we to do?"

His acceptance of the Monster as a fact was bracing after the doctor's incredulity. Very briefly she gave him an account of her night's experience. "It didn't attack you," he said, at the end. "But, Oliver; since he's alive and sane what do you fear exactly?"

"That the sacrifice will be completed. Whenever the Monster has manifested itself the life of the Hammand attacked has paid the penalty, either at its hands or later on. If Oliver remembers what he saw in the Shaw he will be sure to—to do what grandfather did."

Goddard nodded gravely. "You have an idea, Swan."

"He may never remember; he may wake with his memory restored; or he may suddenly have it restored later. That's what I dread. If it comes directly he wakes I shall be with him, and Mrs. Walton, and we can do what we think is right. But we can't keep him under observation for the rest of his life, and if he remembered suddenly—"

She faltered. "I see," Goddard returned. "The shock of sudden remembrance might throw him off his balance. Well?"

"I'm going to try and find out what the Monster is. If we could do it before he remembers and explained it quietly to him the shock would be much lessened."

"Exactly. How do you purpose to find out?"

Swanhild indicated the directory. "I've been looking up the S.P.R. and Miss Bartendale. She's not in it, though."

"Miss Bartendale? I seem to remember the name."

"Lady Grace Kynaston told me about her. There was something wrong in the family last year. Nobody knows just what it was, but they say the family vault at Stoke Kynaston Church had to be hermetically sealed. Miss Bartendale succeeded when the S.P.R. failed. Unfortunately Lady Grace is abroad now, and she only mentioned that Miss Bartendale lives in London. Her name is not in the book, but she may live with her family, so I've made a list of all the Bartendales in town; eleven in all."

"What do you propose to do with that list?"

"Call on all, if Oliver can be left."

"It's rather a tribe to tackle." Goddard wrinkled his forehead up as though trying to remember something. "Bartendale, Bar-ten-dale," he repeated mumblingly. Swanhild crossed the room and opened the window facing north. The wind slashed in, with some rain on it, they looked over the dusky country to the Monstrous Man sprawling in the now overcast sky in what light came through cloud gaps, and the blur beneath him that was the Shaw.

"It's so grotesque!" the girl broke out. "Oliver is safe and sane so far, yet if we cannot find out this mystery that has been un-solved a thousand years he will go mad and—"

She could not complete it. Instead she cried: "I'm a coward, Goddard! A beastly coward—only Oliver's all I've got left! The doc-tors said he could not live when he was sent home with Reggie, and I made him live—and now it might have been better if I had let him die decently—"

"Hush, Swan, my dear!" Goddard's pleasant light tenor was commanding. "It's the dismal small hours, by daylight you'll be your plucky old self again, ready to fight for old Oliver once more—"

"How can we fight it? This incredible, unseen thing—"

"Steady, dear!" It was a crooning protest, like a woman's way with another woman. Briskly he went on: "It reminds me of a couple of years ago. Stuck in a trench dug in packed nastiness, with no way of reckoning when, how, or from where annihilation might descend on you. The only way to be any good was to keep quiet and alert—and not look too far ahead. At present we will look no further than the prospect of the impending Witch-Hunt. And, Swanhild, it wasn't true, wasn't absolutely nice, was it?—saying Oliver's all you've got left? I thought we understood one another ages ago."

He looked good-humoured reproach down into her eyes. It seemed to her, in that little pause after hours of frantic hurry, that the world stood still for a moment and there was nothing alive in the universe save the two of them, man and woman, in the hushed

room with windswept dark outside stretching to Infinity's mea-
sureless void.

"It just shows how you love old Oliver," Goddard said, tenderly.
He took her in his arms, kissed her very gently, and held her close
a minute. It was almost as Oliver had done on the night when the
elder brother died and he became the only kin left to her. With the
wakened memory of that the horror of the Monster closed down
on her again, but with someone to share it it was not so paralysing
as before, though she cried out:

"But you're not the only one! Oliver's still here!"

He held her at arm's length. "Exactly. Oliver's still on this nice
old globe, and it's up to us to keep him there, safe and sane, please
God! And I gather the sooner we get an investigator down the more
chance we have of doing it."

5

SUEZ-WEST-OF-SUEZ

It was the chilly, stillest hour of day when Swanhild came down again half an hour later. The deadly hush that had settled on the big house after the hours of scurry gave a shivering impression of a dead and hollow world. A nurse flitting across the hall the subdued reek of iodoform explained it too well.

In the Holbein room however, lights and a fire waited, Alex and divers other dogs shared the rug with several cats, and Goddard and Mrs. Walton were holding a not uncheerful consultation beside a table laid for two.

"I've taken the liberty of ordering the Mercedes round, Swanhild," said Goddard. "Mrs. Walton agrees with me that a couple of hours' spin will do you good."

"A run—now?" said Swanhild.

"Exactly," put in Mrs. Walton. "I can take charge of the house for that time."

"It's really a sporting effort to get Miss Bartendale, of Kynaston Vault celebrity, on the spot within two hours," Goddard explained. "Don't hope too much, but there's a microscopic chance you may see her and ascertain if she can and will help us within an hour."

"Oh, Goddard! What—"

"No questions, my dear, until you've had some brekker."

"I'm not hungry."

"Well, the witch hunt won't start until you have demolished this cup of coffee at least. The car isn't quite ready; directly she is we start for Suez-West-Of-Suez."

"Suez-What?"

"My designation for a place for which everyone has a pet name. Ranging from plain 'Brighton' to 'New Jerusalem-By-Sea.' It is said that everyone in the eastern half of our hemisphere blows through Suez some time or other, and you'll meet everyone worth calling anyone in the western fraction if you loaf about Brighton long enough. I have just remembered that somebody told me yesterday Miss Bartendale was seen taking the air, with other tepidly distinguished folk, on Brighton front the day before."

You know where she's staying?" gasped Swanhild.

"No, but it's easier to find a notable visitor to Brighton than a regular Londoner who isn't in the directory. I hear the car."

Swanhild jumped up, but hesitated. "If Oliver wakes while I'm away—" she began.

"Mrs. Walton's here," he replied. "If she had been in charge of your grandfather he wouldn't have needed a verdict tempered with charity."

Mrs. Walton nodded grimly. "He ought to sleep another six hours, Miss Swan, dear. When he wakes he'll get a nice breakfast or a dose of something that'll keep him quiet, according to his state of mind. The little trip will do you good, otherwise you'll fidget yourself to fiddlestrings and be unfit company for the boy when he wakes."

Then Swanhild hurried without further protest. Once in the driver's seat of the big car the growing uneasiness that had been coming to her began to abate. Open air, coming day, and the fact that she was doing something definite for Oliver made a different woman of her. "What are you going to do, Goddard?" she asked, when the bridge was negotiated.

"Question the gilded hirelings of the night watch in the hotels. If that draws blank, see if an early opening newsagent has a *Standard and Visitors' List* left from Saturday."

The rain had stopped, the stars, in a clear sky, were glittering their wintry brightest as the car shot through the village. The valley, mist-filled, slip past on their left, the Shaw twisted like a black scarf round the Beacon beyond it, the Monstrous Man livid above the Shaw. In the hazy spaciousness of the Weald they turned west,

Beeding was passed in the last of the starlight; the Shorehams, Old and New, threaded in the blackest minutes of the twenty-four hours. They spoke little, Swanhild only voiced her ruling thought when Southwick's twin Towers of Babel were in the rear, Portslade's twisty undulations safely negotiated, and the smutty blur under a pink palpitation that is Brighton against a winter's daybreak massed up ahead.

"What if she isn't there, Goddard?"

It was eerie on the nearly deserted road. Between the lamps they seemed to chase through a dreary chaos: sea and sky, near houses and distant downs alike one insubstantial, tattered mass of varied grey. The hush of that silentest of hours was intensified by the motor's throb and the sough of the wind that brought clammy dead gusts of sea-fret from the lapping waves. Swanhild's voice sounded hushed and shrill, hopeless and excited, at once. "If she isn't there she'll be elsewhere," replied Goddard briskly. "Now, Swan, don't get excited. Here's the Victoria Statue, first turn to the left and our enquiries begin."

She stayed in the car while he ran up and spoke to the night porters. Miss Bartendale was not in the first hotel, nor the second. In the end they worked nearly along the whole length of the front, alternately stopping for enquiries and making digressions up side streets to newsvendors' shops, until the sun rose, invisibly, somewhere in the newly-clouded heavens. Incidentally they learnt the degrees by which hotels wake up, from the first stirrings of step-cleaners to the aroma of frying and coffee which met them at the eighth hostelry. There a clerk presented Goddard with a spare *Visitors List*, and they consulted its smudgy columns under a lamp.

"Eureka!" chuckled Goddard. "See—'Hesse House, Hesse Square. Thursday. Lady Adams, Miss L. Bartendale.' We must hark westward again, but first up Ship Street."

"Why?" asked Swanhild, turning north obediently.

"P.O. telephone, dear. It's early for a call; we'll break ourselves gently to the victim."

Traffic was getting into its first stride, and it seemed ages to Swanhild while they crawled the length of Ship Street. Her gloves stuck to her hands and her face felt deadly cold, now that a few minutes would decide if this stranger would help or not. It was then, in the homely bustle around, that she realised the incredibility of it all. Oliver sane, but likely to go mad at any moment—the thousand-years-old Monster waiting in the misty world but a few miles away. In the Post Office she soon found the number of Hesse House, and the voice of a well-trained maidservant made reply. Miss Bartendale was there, she was up; preparing to take the early train to town. What name, please? Would Miss Hammand kindly hold the wire?

In a minute another voice came. "Hallo! I'm Luna Bartendale. I suppose the Monster has manifested itself again, Miss Hammand?"

Swanhild quite jumped. "Yes. Why?"

"My dear girl (you are a girl by your voice) when a Hammand of Dannow Old Manor rings up a total stranger who happens to be a Sensitive the inference is fairly evident!" The voice was a light soprano, the kind that does not make much noise but carries a long way. "The Monster's in all the Haunted Houses books and County Guides," it added. "When did it appear?"

"A few hours ago—" Swanhild put the night's doings in a few sentences. At the conclusion: "And what am I to do?" asked the soprano.

"You helped Lady Grace Kynaston last year—"

"The Stoke Kynaston affair was not a thousand years old. Don't hope too much, Miss Hammand, but I am at your service as far as my powers go. Where are you?"

"The Ship Street Post Office. I motored over with Godd—Mr. Covert, to try and find you, as I mentioned. I cannot thank you enough—"

"We'll take all that as said, dear girl. Is there any chance of my examining this Thunderbarrow Shaw before the police and sightseers trample it up?"

"Nobody, even our local constable, will venture in before full daylight. We can get you there in an hour."

"Very good. Come round here slowly, and I shall be ready for you. Au revoir."

"She's coming and she sounds nice," was all Swanhild could say to Goddard at first. He exchanged into the driver's seat and she told him all the conversation while they travelled slowly to the front and westward again.

Hesse Square is one of the cluster of aristocratically named streets, aggressively redolent of when they were not mainly devoted to the boarding business, in the southwest corner of Brighton. A haunt of hushed dullness on sunshiny days; deadly in the winter dawn as the car drew up between the funereal trees of the central enclosure and the light-spattered cliff that was Hesse House. "Jove, just the place for a witch!" said Goddard.

Swanhild had barely stepped to the pavement when the door opened and a little woman and big dog came down the steps. "Miss Hammand?" said the voice that had come over the telephone, and the owner stopped and held out a hand. The advantage of the steps brought her face level with Swanhild's. And it was a very charming face. The stray curls that glinted amidst the swathings of a motor veil were of that fine pale golden tint that so rarely survives childhood, and her features were so delicate that only eyebrows much darker than her hair and the pronounced cheekbones and high bridged nose saved the ensemble from dollishness. Her skin was creamy, touched with pink on either cheek and with a sharp-cut splash of red at the lips, her daintily rounded chin had a deep dimple in it, and she kept her lids habitually drooped so that her eyes flickered darkly behind a screen of golden lashes. She was slightly built, carried herself very upright, and was muffled in a voluminous coat of the heavy woollen stuff humane women wear in place of furs.

Swanhild took it all in in the moment it took her to stammer: "Miss Bartendale? The White Witch?"

"The Supersensitive," the other corrected. The hard red lips curved in a smile. "I'm older than I look," she supplemented, answering the girl's thought. "I am thankful I don't 'look my job' as Americans so poetically put it."

She canted her head to look at Swanhild fairly, and raised her lids. It was like an electric shock. Swanhild stared into blue-grey eyes of a lightness that seemed almost transparent, like ice in shade, diamond-bright, and so searching that she instinctively felt glad she had nothing on her conscience to conceal. The lids drooped again, and: "You'll take my word I'm It—myself?" Luna Bartendale said. Then, looking at Goddard: "Mr. Covert, to whom I owe the chance of inspecting the Shaw at once? We'll take the introductions as accomplished, and you'll drive, please, while Miss Hammand posts me in necessary details. I see my dog approves you both. That'll do, Smith, thanks. Pray don't forget the wire to my aunt."

She settled herself comfortably beside Swanhild with her feet on the dog; a creature of indeterminate breed with touches of Dalmatian and bloodhound; and took a little leather bag from the maid who had followed her. In a minute the car was on its way again.

6
THE VAMPIRE HAMMANDS

Miss Bartendale nestled in her corner and smiled at Swanhild. "You've got an *idée fixe* that I can help you, and now you've caught me you are bewildered with relief," she observed, casually.

Swanhild stammered: "I wasn't sure you'd come—and at this hour—"

"Bless you, I'm used to being rung up at unseemly times. I was quite relieved when you rang me up, I'd just finished breakfast, and breakfast alone by gaslight is about as ghastly as champagne in daylight. Now, please tell me your brother's account of what happened in the Shaw."

Swanhild repeated it, as they sped through the misty dullness. "Ve-ry curious," said the Supersensitive. Swanhild had learnt by then that she always spoke with a kind of little patronising drawl, and her voice grew fascinating with longer acquaintance and had a caressing suggestion of a northern burr in it. "Don't you notice something queer in it, Miss Hammand?"

"It was very confused—queer all through."

"Yes; still, one point is concretely odd. But he may have omitted to mention what— We'll hear what he has to say. Now for the Monster's history. Like everyone who has ever read a book about ghosts I am acquainted with the main details. Briefly, the family of Hammand of Dannow is said to be haunted by an apparition known as the Undying Monster. At different times members of the family have died mysteriously, and their deaths have been attributed to a meeting with the Monster. That, stripped of all details, is the matter in a nutshell, I believe. When did it last appear?"

"Nearly thirty years ago, in 1890. It killed my grandfather and two other people."

"I'll trouble you for full details."

"Well," Swanhild hesitated, then plunged in boldly. "Grandfather had no business to be meeting a lady from the Mansby Place house party in the Shaw. I don't suppose there was any real harm, but he was married and so was she. And it seems a gamekeeper, our chauffeur's grandfather, was spying on them. Anyhow the man and the lady were killed in a horrible way; as the Monster's victims always are killed: all torn, just as poor Kate was last night, and—and with pieces gone from them. Like Kate. Three dogs were there, grandfather's big spaniels and the keeper's lurcher, and they were torn to bits, but not—not eaten. When search was made the bodies were found near Thunder's Barrow, beyond the Shaw, and grandfather was wandering about, horribly mangled, but alive with his hair gone partly white. He refused to say what he had seen, and shot himself next day. Now you know what I fear for Oliver. If he recovers his memory of what he saw he will kill himself."

Luna Bartendale patted her hand gently. "My dear girl, I fail to see why he should do such a thing."

"Because everyone who escaped alive from the Monster invariably killed himself later."

"But, why?"

"Because they have learnt what the Monster is, and the knowledge is so horrible that they chose death rather than to live with it on their minds."

"But what is it like?"

"Nobody knows. I told you they refused, like grandfather, to describe it."

"We must hear some of the other cases. First, though, Dannow is one of the oldest inhabited houses in England, is it not?"

"The hall has some of the lath and plaster work of the original Saxon manor house incorporated in the walls behind the panelling."

"And how long has your family owned the place?"

"Since it was built."

"And the Monster has been haunting it all the time? How far do your written records go?"

"We have a deed sealed by Canute confirming Reginald, Hammand's Son in the manor."

"And what's the earliest record of the Monster's appearing?"

"There's a pedigree, drawn up in 1650 from older documents, with all its appearances to that date marked in red ink against the names of the victims, and another continuing the record to 1890."

"Can you give some details of a few of the appearances?"

"There's a Crusader effigy in our church, at Dannow, with a lump of a figure at the feet that's supposed to represent the Monster. By the 1650 pedigree this monument is to Sir Oliver Hammand, who met the Monster, lived, and drowned recollection of it by getting himself killed in the First Crusade. And there's a brass to Godfrey Hammand, dated 1387, with a queer beast under his feet. He met the Monster and spent the rest of his life in prayer and penance, turning Anchorite and living in a little cell built up against the church till his death. Those are the only two people who met the Monster and did not kill themselves afterwards. And you know, going crusading or turning Anchorite was a sort of suicide."

"Did they leave any account of what the Monster looks like? No? And yet they put portraits of it in a public place! What are those beasts like?"

"Impossible to tell. The effigy's nearly shapeless now, and the brass has been scratched and defaced badly."

"Did anyone, other than a Hammand, meet it and live to describe it?"

"None but Hammands have ever survived a meeting with it; other people were all killed or died of fright."

"This girl—Kate Stringer. She has survived."

"The doctors don't think she will last long."

"There's a rhyme about the Monster. Please let me hear it."

Swanhild repeated it. "Curious," commented Luna. "'While the Monster is alive, Hammand's race shall live and thrive.' It suggests that the thing is a Luck as well as a Bane. That brings us to the legends that account for it. You will know that a number of stories are in circulation that never find their way into print owing to our excellent law of libel. One is that a Hammand's life must be sacrificed every now and then to keep the Monster alive?"

Swanhild frowned and nodded curtly. Luna went on.

"It is said that Dannow contains a hidden room whose situation and contents are only revealed to the heir presumptive, under seal of secrecy, on his twenty-first birthday; and it is averred that the secret contained in it is so fearful that no one has ever betrayed it."

Swanhild seemed inclined to interrupt, the Supersensitive held up a checking hand. "I'm stating it baldly. One, popular tradition is that the first Hammand made a compact with the devil, selling his own soul on condition that his heirs should hold Dannow till the Day of Judgment, and that he should live that time to see the bargain carried out. He therefore still lives in the secret room, and at intervals issues forth to make the sacrifice of a human life in order to prolong his own. In short, the Undying Monster is your first ancestor, who perpetuates his unholy existence by swallowing the blood of at least one live human being. And one of the victims at least must be a Hammand."

"Yes, that's the most popular tale," Swanhild agreed. "It is also said that this thousand-year-old ancestor of mine has grown so incredibly revolting in appearance that the mere memory of it makes anyone he doesn't kill commit suicide later. But I can tell you one thing for certain, Miss Bartendale, there's no real secret room at all. I've often been in the room in question myself."

"There's another tale—that every now and then a creature half-human and half-animal is born in the line and kept hidden away somewhere in the Manor till it dies. A creature which occasionally gets loose with sinister results to whoever it meets—"

Swanhild interrupted hotly. "As a member of the family—"

"My dear girl, these tales were merely invented to titillate the love of nastiness ingrained in the common herd, before a too-free press arose to cater for it daily. Still, traditions exist. Isn't there another one?"

"The worst!" Swanhild exclaimed indignantly. "That we Hammands have a vampire strain in us, and if one of us is killed prematurely he—or she—will turn vampire and come back to Dannow, and—"

She stopped, shivering with indignation.

"Well?" Luna prompted.

"People will say it was Reggie!" Swanhild broke out wretchedly. "My elder brother—who—who died three months ago."

"Three months ago! The delay—"

"This is the first frost since he went west. And it is only in frost and starlight they can appear. You may not believe me, Miss Bartendale, but in our district people will say it. Why after grandfather's death it was said it was his young daughter who—who killed the keeper and lady. She had been killed out hunting the autumn before. They say it accounted for grandfather's refusal to state what he saw, and for his hair going white, and his suicide."

Miss Bartendale lifted her eyebrows gently. In the overcast morning light her eyes were suddenly all pupil, like a white cat's in twilight. "I have a fairly extensive knowledge of what people can believe," she replied sedately. "In my native Ribblesdale an animal is still drowned in the river every seventh year to placate a ghost named Peg O'Nell. Of course this nonsense will worry your brother."

"Oliver broods over things so," exclaimed Swanhild. "You see, our father died early in the war, mother didn't survive him long, and both the brothers were sent home last year, and the doctors said neither could live. Reggie went this summer, but I simply could not let Oliver go. He was quite well and strong by now—and I wish I had not saved him—for this!"

"Hush, my dear girl!" Luna's voice was gentle. "We're all in the same boat now. An aunt is the only blood relative the last few years have left me."

"Oh," said Swanhild, ashamed. Dropping her voice she whispered: "And there's Goddard, Mr. Covert, he's all alone. I don't know why I let myself go like this—to a stranger!" she wound up.

"Because I have come to try and help you, and you trust me, and I must know everything about you if I am to be of use," Luna made prompt reply. "Now, does the Monster invariably manifest itself in this Shaw?"

Swanhild was herself again, and replied quietly: "No; there's two heart-brasses in our church, to Oliver Hammand, the Anchorite's father, and his daughter. They were killed by it when on pilgrimage to Rocamadour. Godfrey was there when they met it, but survived and turned Anchorite, as I told you."

"It is very curious and unusual, the connection between the Monster and frosty weather."

"It's described in another rhyme," said Swanhild.

> "*Where grow pines and firs amain,*
> Under Stars, sans heat or rain,
> Chief of Hammand, 'ware thy Bane!

"Meaning that the Monster can only attack the head of the family on frosty nights near pines and firs."

"In short, the thing's a sort of curse attached to the ownership of the place? Does it only appear out of doors, then?"

"Once it manifested itself in the house, to Sir Magnus the Warlock, the Anchorite's grandson."

"Eh? I seem to remember the name. Isn't Magnus Hammand the Warlock the hero of a fairly presentable tradition?"

"He practiced black art in the hidden room, which has pines outside the window. The tale is that he raised the Monster to help him with his studies, and it got out of his control and killed his little son in the hidden room."

Luna seemed to wake and prick her ears. "A widespread tale," she commented. "It is also related, with differences, in connection with St. Dunstan and Friar Bacon. What became of the Warlock?"

"Oh, his wife saw the Monster kill and eat the child, and died of shock on the spot, and he committed suicide from horror."

"And to what extent did he practice black art?"

"Some say he sold his soul to Satan, and used to hold black masses in the hidden room, and sacrifice children. Oh, all sorts of utterly odious stuff! That he fed the Monster with live babies is the least disgusting. His tomb's in our church; some village people say it's his ghost that helps other dead Hammands to become vampires; others that the Monster lives on in the hidden room, as he died without laying it."

7

MORE DIMENSIONS THAN FOUR

The Supersensitive seemed to fall into reverie, fingering the dimple on her chin absently. "The main point is: however they vary all traditions agree in connecting the Monster equally with the place and the family. Now what's at the bottom of it all? There's no smoke without fire, and few legends without a substructure of truth. You have mentioned a secret room, Miss Hammand."

Swanhild almost laughed. "You shall see the hidden room. We only keep it to ourselves because we don't want people tramping all over it and disturbing the things."

"What things?"

"The books and crockery the Warlock left there. It was his laboratory, and when he died he said the secret of the Monster would be found in it."

At this Luna opened her eyes wide. "He said that four centuries ago, and the secret has not been found out yet? Am I to understand the room has been kept as he left it four hundred years?"

"Yes, except when Cromwell's men went over the house and stole or broke a lot of things. They may have removed or destroyed the clue; Madame Blavatsky and Sir William Crookes thought so. They were called in after grandfather's death."

"Yet you hope I may be more successful?"

"Knowledge has advanced since then?" Swanhild said it tentatively.

"It has," returned Luna with emphasis. "Blavatsky was a Sensitive, but I'm a Supersensitive."

"What does that mean?" asked Swanhild.

"That in the Shaw I may be able to trace the way the Monster came and went, by means of my cultivated Sixth Sense."

"What is that Sixth Sense?"

"One you've got yourself, dear girl."

"How do you know?"

"Because every normally decent person has it. You sometimes distrust people intensely, without concrete reason, don't you?—and afterwards find out they are undesirables?"

"That's only instinct."

"It's the sense of harmony in life. The normal rhythm of existence comprehends all that is true, kindly, and cleanly. Anything that errs against that rule, be it mental, moral or physical, jars on the rhythm, causes a break in the harmony which is perceived by the Sixth Sense. Bad thoughts, a sensual nature, a body to which death has come by violence; all these equally outrage the orderly harmony of existence. All people have this instinctive sense, so long as they keep themselves decent, but in some it amounts to a gift; like an eye for colour or ear for music; and it can be cultivated like other gifts. 'Sensitive' is the new name for such individuals. If anything out of the ordinary course of nature—anything belonging to the Fourth Dimension which is commonly called the Supernatural—went through the Shaw in the night I should be able to trace its tracks. If it *was* Fourth Dimensional," the Supersensitive added. "Your dog called your attention to nothing but your brother and the girl?"

"Yes; she was quite satisfied when both were brought out."

"And this is the point I noted in your brother's narrative as you have reported it. Mr. Hammand's dog did not warn him of the approach of his assailant."

"Jove?" Goddard, who had been driving silently so far, twisted his head round for a second. "I didn't notice that. Of course, though, Oliver wasn't his bright young self when he handed out the tale, and he may have omitted to mention no end of details."

"That's possible." Luna lapsed into thoughtful silence again. Swanhild hinted anxiously: "Have you come to some conclusion, Miss Bartendale?"

Luna smiled kindly up at her. "Only that I'll have a tough task searching the mists of ages for information that was evidently confined to a chosen few at any time. Also I sincerely trust your brother may be able to say the dog warned him. Even the Fourth Dimension cannot account for a dog's not noting the approach of an enemy to his master."

"Then what can explain it?"

Luna's eyes clouded. "There are more Dimensions than Four."

"What's the Fifth Dimension?"

"The Dimension that surrounds and pervades the Fourth—known as the Supernatural—as the Fourth surrounds and pervades the Third Dimension of our ordinary material life. The incredible Dimension that is now faintly glimpsed by the most advanced thinkers. The Dimension I have named and made my peculiar study. And isn't that your Monstrous Man, Miss Hammand?"

The northern escarpment of the Downs swept up like a titanic wave over them as the car leapt to the ascent, closed in when it slid into the gap, and swept apart to let it into the open with the village and uplands in view.

"The Shaw, Miss Bartendale," Goddard began, and suddenly put on the brake. Swanhild looked towards Thunderbarrow Beacon with incredulous eyes; Luna stood up to look over her head. It was clearer on the heights than in the Weald, and it was possible to see a fair way off, hilltops faintly greyer in the general greyness, rivulets like tarnished steel, the Shaw greenish-grey. The ground was beginning to be boggy, every individual leaf dripped slowly, and big drops dribbled off the cuffs and hat brims of the village folk who huddled in groups near the Roman track, gaping in a fascinated horror and ready for instant flight if need was. Over the valley, at the end of the track and under the Shaw, could be seen a tiny car and two men, one very big and with the glimmer of white bandages round his head and arms. Goddard turned the car and sent it down the track while Swanhild exclaimed, horror-struck:

"Oliver! He must be delirious—or mad! And I wasn't there when he woke!"

Goddard put the Mercedes to top speed, Swanhild was out and running up the slope before the big car had stopped behind the little one. Oliver hastened to meet her half-way. What could be seen of the left temple and the eye beneath was horribly discoloured, but for all that he looked wonderfully hale and sane.

"Cheer-o, Swan!" he called. "Don't worry, there's a good kid! I'm more sore from your beastly caustic than anything. And—to spare you suspense—I don't remember what I saw last night. I woke before schedule time, the doctor had to admit I was sound and sane, and I wasn't going to leave poor Holder out all day, you know. I say, Swan, is that the Witch?"

He stared past her, his eyes opening wide. She hugged his least hurt arm as hard as she dared while she piloted him to the car. In a less public situation she knew she might have cried with relief.

"My brother Oliver, Miss Bartendale," she began.

"So you have come again when you were needed!"

Thus Oliver, pleasantly and cheerily, as he enfolded Lana's hand in his left. "Directly I saw you I seemed to smell ivy flower," he added, nodding to himself complacently. He was looking full in Luna's eyes. Luna glanced sharply back, as a doctor does when a patient is losing hold of his nerves.

"I've not used that perfume for two years," she said.

"It was memory. You had it on your handkerchief—yes, fully two years ago. I'm not crazy," he supplemented, aside, to Swanhild. "Only I've met Miss Bartendale before. She saved my reason then."

Luna regarded him in a thoughtful manner. "I was attached to the Sloane Shell-Shock Hospital two years ago. I seem to half-remember your eyes. Did we meet at the Hospital?"

"No, it was a casual affair. You probably did as much for scores of other fellows. You couldn't remember them all, but they'd all remember you. I'll tell you later."

She was puzzled, but tranquil. "Very well, Mr. Hammand. At present my business is with the Shaw." It was at that point she noticed he was still holding her hand, and withdrew it. "How's the girl?" she asked.

The radiance left his face. "Delirious, and raving of something 'as big as a house' that attacked her. After all, even finding the Monster won't help her—" He broke off.

"It may save others in the future," she returned sharply. He started.

"Good Lord, I'd forgotten for the moment! It's what I want you for; Swanhild's next in the line."

She nodded gravely. "You don't recollect more than you did when you first came to, Mr. Hammand?"

"Not a scrap. I compared notes with the doctor, and found nothing to add or alter."

She stepped out briskly. "Now for the Shaw. I gather nobody has been in it since last night's happenings?"

"Warren, over there, has." He nodded to where a big, haggard young man in the velveteens of a keeper was speaking to Goddard aside. "He's poor Kate's sweetheart, and he's certain the Ades did it, and means to get them hung for it. Besides—he'll tell you. Warren!"

The man came forward. His face was horribly drawn, and mottled as though with repressed passions. He held a horse blanket over one arm, a gun sloped under the other.

"I wanted to be the first to enter the Shaw," said Luna.

He looked at her with the sullen, blankly—agonised eyes of a man stunned by calamity. "Asking your pardon, ma'am, I had to go through right along. 'Twas bare light when that born fool Will from the Lodge came to the village with a tale that made every grout-headed idiot there start saying the same thing: 'The fust frost sence Squire Reggie died—' they said—"

"Now, Warren!" Goddard glanced at Swanhild apprehensively.

"Asking your pardon, sir, I'm saying here, all being friends of the Hammand family, what others is whispering elsewhere. Squire Reggie!" he burst out, hoarse with loosened fury. "Him that 'listed along with you and me, Mr. Oliver! Him that gave me his water bottle half full at Cambrai saying he'd drunk the other half! And me mopping it up before I saw what a liar he was. And now, not content with what's happened to my girl, them that did it must shame his name in the grave!" He controlled himself, and was suddenly calm again. "So I went through the Shaw, and I asked some questions about the two Ades, and then went to the Manor, and Mr. Hammand would come with me to fetch the poor tyke home."

"What of the Ades?" asked Swanhild.

"Charlie's in bed, with a broken collar bone, and Joe has been knocked about considerably. Both bitten, too. It's true Miles, Squire Hudson's keeper, had a fight with two poachers he couldn't recognise in the dark, last night, but even if it was them there's only their word that Miles was responsible for all the damage."

"Exactly, one must bear in mind the possibility of a natural explanation of last night," said Luna, opening her little bag.

"I hope and pray it's natural, ma'am," the man responded grimly. "And I believe it. It's natural, and being natural I'll see Squire Reggie's name cleared and my girl avenged. Hey, dowsing? Water-finding?"

She had taken a forked twig from the bag and balanced it between her palms, the third limb dangling loosely. "The Divining Rod finds other things besides water," she replied. "Roska; to heel!"

The big dog took up her position obediently. With the twig dangling between her outstretched hands Luna stood, chin up and eyelids puckered, and turned on her heels in a semi-circle. Her golden curls and pale oval of face were the brightest spots in the dusky scene. Above her the Shaw was a louring patch of darkness against the grey sky, with dim scraps of the Monstrous Man glimpsed between the treetops; behind her the grey-green grass slope, the glistening motors blocked out by clusters of drab peasantry who had ventured near. Their vague blue eyes stared at her, half frightened, out of weatherbeaten faces. To Swanhild a curious feeling came: an impression that this was no new thing: the Downs with no house in sight, the Monstrous Man on his hill, and dimly scared people round a woman whose face glowed with inward light as she did silent incantations. It had happened before.

8

"ANOTHER DIMENSION—POSSIBLY A FIFTH"

Stopping abruptly in her circular movement, Luna stepped forward a few paces, paused, and looked down. The third limb of the Divining twig had risen and stood out horizontally. She was standing on a patch of sodden turf, the grass clotted in places with a sticky blackness that the late rain had not quite washed into the earth. It was where Swanhild had put Oliver down when she bore him from the Shaw.

Then Luna walked steadily, the twig rising and falling at intervals, straight into the ride down which Swanhild had come, to the clearing, and across it; always on Swanhild's track of the night before. Swanhild and the three men followed, Goddard carrying a lamp from the car, for it was dark in the plantation. As she entered the path leading to the second clearing the twig turned right over. Oliver, nearest to her, gave an exclamation. She looked down at Roska, who was nosing the first real splash of blood.

Now her course zigzagged in such a way that the twig came over every trace of blood. At each it rose. When she reached the body of the mastiff it rotated violently. Oliver made a little sound of grief and anger. She looked gently from the dead animal to him, and went on. Past the oak where he had lain, and into the burnt beech. Stepping out again, she hesitated and turned slowly round. The twig only moved over the track by which she had come. The bramble thicket that huddled against the dead tree was so close-grown that only a snake could have got through without breaking it. And unbroken it was.

"The assailant? He—she—it—came and went—which way?" she commented, as though to herself, as she returned down the track, trying every path that led from it. The twig only indicated the way back to the dog.

"You've missed my first track," Oliver volunteered. "Poor Kate and I both passed along that ride—"

He pointed. She turned to him, her wide-opened eyes all pupil; sombre, sparkling, blank and soft at once. "I can't follow the paths of normal people, Mr. Hammand. Spilt blood is out of the normal. The rod is only an indicator—like the hands of a watch—in myself resides the Sixth Sense which detects anything abnormal, or super-natural—as the Fourth Dimension is generally named. And blood is the only wrong thing I detect here." She looked down at the dog. "Will you have him put where I can examine him, Mr. Hammand?"

"What do you want to examine him for?" asked Swanhild.

"Teeth marks, and, possibly, a hair or other clue to the nature of what attacked him."

"You think something material did this, after Holder didn't warn me of its coming?" asked Oliver incredulously.

"A supernatural being would have to take to itself a material form with which to inflict these injuries. Even Fourth Dimensional be-ings—ghosts—have command of Third Dimensional Matter; at least that's how spiritualists explain their manifestations at *séances*."

Warren rose from rolling the dog in the blanket. "Begging your pardon, ma'am, ain't there room for explanation without calling in spooks?"

"Could you tear off a dog that size, Warren?" asked Oliver.

"No, sir. Nor pull it fairly in two, bones and skin included, as has been done to him here. But two men could between them."

Luna turned her shadowy eyes to him. "You *want* it to prove a mortal criminal; or criminals," she said.

"I do, ma'am. To hang what did for my girl."

"Exactly. Several men in league." Her voice became dreamy. "Else we must figure a creature strong as a horse, that tears with grasping paws—the poor dog's leg was torn off, not bitten at all—bites ferociously, and comes and goes Heaven knows how."

She glanced up casually. Warren started and looked up also. "A big monkey!" he exclaimed. "We'd best ask if one has escaped anywhere. Seems a likely notion, though I hope it ain't true. I want some one to swing for this."

She looked round at the other three, and under her look they said nothing. "The police ought to be informed, Mr. Hammand," she said.

"Very well," he agreed. "After you've helped Mr. Covert take him to the little car, Warren, run it to the Manor and tell Walton to have him put where Miss Bartendale can examine him. Then warn the police."

"When in doubt one can always fall back on the Murder in the Rue Morgue," commented Luna, when the two men were out of sight with their burden.

"You don't believe the ape theory?" said Oliver.

"No, but it will give the police something to play about with, and you had to warn them. There's one possibility left: that the creature took the same road, both coming and going, along which you and the girl were carried. In which case its trail will be blended with that of the blood; as far as that goes, and will continue beyond the spot where I started. We'll try."

But the rod only led straight back to the spot where Oliver had lain. She returned to the beech and tried about unavailingly. Warren and Goddard were delayed by a hitch in the little car's mechanism. She went through to the further side of the Shaw, without eliciting a single movement of the twig, and paused at the fringe, where a long hillock crowned with pines and firs intervened between the trees and the Beacon sloping up before them. "Artificial?" she enquired, indicating the mound.

"That's Thunder's Barrow, an Ancient British burial hill," Swanhild answered. Luna climbed to the top of it, and they followed her. The twig made no sign. "Any connection with the Monster?" she asked, standing on the top and looking at the Monstrous Man.

"I'm not sure," Swanhild returned, looking at Oliver.

He shook his head. "Nor I. Fact is, Miss Bartendale, we were not allowed to hear tales of the Monster when we were kids, and have had enough to think about these last years without it."

"Well, let us look at the Monster's portraits in the church."

Luna turned to descend. He checked her. "One moment, Miss Bartendale. You said you could trace nothing supernatural—Fourth Dimensional you called it—and there's no sign of a big animal having passed through the Shaw lately. A creature big enough to tear Holder like that must have left traces. If it isn't a mortal creature, and isn't an evil spirit, what can it be?"

"I must remind you of the first question I asked, Mr. Hammand. Did your dog warn you of its approach? A dog's senses are keen both for mortal and ghostly beings. There is a possibility your dog *did* warn you, but you have forgotten it, in consequence of the blow on the head. If it is not so, your Monster may prove to be a being of another Dimension—say a Fifth."

"What's the Fifth Dimension?" he asked.

Her eyes were very grave. "The Dimension beyond the Fourth; beyond the supernatural. The Dimension whose embodied powers can do physical destruction, though even a dog cannot detect their presence. The incredible Dimension in which science and Holy church are equally powerless, but which I, who unite science with so-called superstition, have made my peculiar study. I pray heaven your family bane may not prove to be one of its inhabitants."

She turned to descend again. Swanhild suddenly recalled how she had shirked discussion of the Fifth Dimension before, and laid a detaining hand on her arm. Her voice, to her own surprise, had an imploring note in it as she said: "Your power with the divining-rod may have a limit, Miss Bartendale. You followed the blood all right, but though there's dead people in the Barrow under your feet the rod gave no indication of it."

Luna glanced from the mound to the Man again. "Blood spilt about is one thing, Miss Hammand, people buried with the rites of whatever creed they believed are another. Whoever this tumulus holds is at rest. During daylight at least. Night is another matter." She broke off and shivered. "It's cold out here. Now, if you please, for the church."

9

"PARDON FOR . . . 26,000 YEARES AND 26 DAIES."

Swanhild drove the long length of the village at a circumspect pace; it was a winter of harlequin changes in weather, and now the wind had dropped to a languid breeze, not unwarm, that drifted thin billows of mist along the lower ground. Only heights and tree-tops were really distinct at any distance, between shifting grey ground and dull grey sky. From the road cottages showed indistinctly behind their winter-naked gardens, and beyond the far end of the village a peaked lych gate stepped out of the fog to meet them. They left the dogs in charge of the car and climbed the gravestone-flagged path to the porch. Dannow church stands on a wooded knoll in the middle of a hollow in a maze of sunk lanes, half a mile away from any habitations save a small farm and two cottages; a not uncommon circumstance in the county where:

> "Little, lost, Down churches praise
> The Lord Who made the hills."

There is a tinge of deceit about many small Sussex churches. With them a frontage of Churchwarden Gothic may enshrine an interior of Saxon stonework or Norman wall paintings, and Dannow's outer elevation of a flintwork barn hides an infinite richness of English art in the shape of the Hammand monuments. On that dark day the little place was in deep twilight; Swanhild flashed her torch round and Luna watched, gravely silent, while the memorials of the girl's forbears heaved into the light and sank back into shade. The nearly shapeless Crusader in his niche, brasses on floor and walls, the marble faces of the Warlock and his lady set in a glory of fretted stone and gilt blazonry. Also the little altar, and the copy of James Clarke's picture, and the column of names and fresh laurel wreath beside it.

She said nothing, but her eyes were again what they had been in the Shaw; blank, yet living globes of sombre tourmaline; as she paced round part of the building, only pausing to cross herself before the altar. "I thought these psychic people were all Agnostics or Jezreelites or something," Oliver whispered, surprised.

"Hush," returned Swanhild. "It's underbred to whisper—in church too. Besides, she'll hear you."

Lima took no notice of them as she examined with eyes and fingers the rubbed figure on which the Crusader's feet rested. Finally she spoke, her voice respectfully lowered: "It's sadly defaced," she said. "But it has animal paws—round paws."

"Well?" asked Swanhild.

"Doesn't it strike you as strange? It's ve-ry curious." She stopped and stared musingly from Sir Oliver Hammand the Crusader to the modest brass plate on the wall above him which stated that Reginald Hammand, Late of This Parish, died at Jerusalem, 1918. "We will see if the Anchorite brass sheds any light on these paws," she said at last.

It was in the floor of the nave. Goddard rolled up the matting and displayed a great sheet of metal incised with the figure of a man in monastic garb, a nondescript beast under his feet and a battered inscription below it. The beast's head was vaguely dog-like, with long nose and prick ears, the body slim in the waist, and the tail snaky and ending in what might have been either a tuft of hair or the conventional barb that ends a conventional devil's tail. Luna went on her knees to trace every line of it.

"It might be meant for anything on four feet," she commented, getting up and studying it with her head on one side. "Monumental natural history is of a go-as-you-please nature, and people have always bred the dog into *outre* shapes, but that's no canine tail. And those paws— It's inexplicable."

She crossed to the Warlock's tomb. There was that about the blank concentration of her eyes that made the others refrain from questions, though all three glanced at the brass animal's paws as they followed her. Commonplace, doglike paws, after a brass-engraver's stock pattern. Swanhild ran her light along the rigid figures of the Warlock and his wife, stiff garments, set faces, and hands pointed in prayer four centuries.

"No animal at their feet," observed Luna. Swanhild directed the light to the only other figure on the tomb. It was at the side, a small child, shrouded and resting on a skull.

"That, according to the village, is one of the kids he sacrificed to Satan or else fed to the Monster," Oliver remarked. "Of course it's really one of their own that died young. Really, you mustn't do that, Miss Bartendale!" he protested, horrified, as she went on her knees to examine the pavement where the base of the tomb rested. "Let me—"

She smiled up at him. "Thanks, I must do it myself. I'm looking for a possible crack leading to the vault beneath."

"My hat!" he exclaimed. "Do you believe that yarn about the old blighter's spook coming out at night?"

"I'm testing every tradition, searching every Dimension." She sat back on her heels and got out the rod. "There's one small chink under the skull—"

Balancing the rod, she laid her face against the skull.

"The cheekbone is very sensitive," she explained. Her eyes were blank, but the rod made no movement, and after a minute she rose and replaced it. "The old Necromancer apparently rests in peace; by daylight at least."

"Do you think his soul's at rest on account of this?" Swanhild indicated the inscription on the tomb. The names of the Warlock and his wife and the dates of their decease—8th and 10th February, 1526—in Latin; then, in English:

YE PARDON FOR SAYING OF V PATnost AND V AVE AND
A CRED IS XXVI MILT YEARES AND XXVI DAIES.

"I suppose you know it means that anyone who says so many prayers for the souls' repose of his wife and himself will be let off twenty six thousand years and twenty-six days of Purgatory," she added.

Luna nodded. "It's very significant."

"Do you believe this sort of thing helps to keep the old perisher quiet?" asked Oliver, staring.

"Sincere prayer can do much, but I certainly have no belief in the bought-and-paid-for-article. The point is this: 'Pardons' of this description were sold by the Old Church in the time of her lowest corruption, and this—" she touched the XXVI MILT YEARES— "is the longest ever granted. On a tomb and at such an early date it is unique. Now, what monstrous crime can the buyer have had on his conscience that he felt impelled to bribe posterity so monstrously to pray for his soul's rest?"

"His wife and kiddie, you know—" Swanhild reminded her.

Luna folded her lips and shook her head. Her eyes had gone back to their normal state, her fair curls and vivid little face were uncannily alive against the cold grey of the tomb as she leant an elbow on it and frowned thoughtfully at the effigy, the pleasant conversational tone of her lovely voice cut eerily clear through the hush of the church as she went on placidly: "The Monster had done such things before, it had haunted the family centuries before he was born. Why should he feel the need of pardon for a mere repetition of previous happenings? A man who had the nerve to follow studies forbidden by Holy Church when it *was* Holy Church was not likely to go insane over such a catastrophe—unless he blamed himself for it."

"Well—?" Swanhild prompted.

"I'm testing every tradition, you know," Luna proceeded. "This Pardon confirms most emphatically the one which alleges that the Warlock gave the Monster a fresh lease of life. If we can find what he did to rouse it we may find the opposite process—how to bind it."

"*If*," said Goddard, with meaning.

"Quite right. If. We must not raise too much hope, after the way Cromwell's men knocked about the hidden room. They may have stolen or destroyed the clue to the Warlock's reference to it. Still, we have something to work on. We know the Warlock dabbled in occultism: or necromancy as it was then called. Occultism pre-supposes the existence of Abnormal Dimensions whose inhabit-ants are divided from our wholesome Normal, or Third Dimen-sional, world by barriers they cannot pass. Only by the practice of Black Magic presumptuous mortals can outrage nature; break the barriers and admit abnormal beings into our world. And once they have entered keeping them in hand is another matter."

"Then you believe the tale that the Monster's a devil the War-lock raised, and that it got out of control and he left it loose when he died?" Oliver asked.

"I'm testing traditions. The inference from the Pardon is clear, while the brass—"

She checked herself, and glanced over to the nave. "What's wrong with the brass?" Swanhild demanded anxiously.

"I don't quite understand something about it. We'll shunt it into my subconscious mind *pro tem*, and concentrate on the War-lock. It is certain he blamed himself for the tragedy of February 8th, 1526. It is equally certain it had something to do with the monstrous sins into which occultism leads its votaries. And, un-less Cromwell's men spoilt it, it is certain he left the clue to the matter in the hidden room."

She stood up and looked at the effigy again. "What monstrous sin led to that pardon?" she repeated, half to herself. "It is not a bad face:

> '*So in the moonlit minster your fathers ye may see,*
> *By the side of the ancient mothers, await the Day to Be.*'

Not a bad face," she repeated. "Ascetic if anything. Evidently a portrait. Strong family likeness to you both, Miss Hammand. And he seems to be at rest. Yet—"

Swanhild, whose susceptible 'teens had been passed in an atmo-sphere of "A stout fighter can do little wrong," answered eagerly. "He fought at Bosworth, as one of Henry VII's standard keepers, and was knighted on the field. There's his helmet and sword hanging on the wall."

"If Miss Bartendale says he was a rotter he must have been a rotter, Swan," Oliver reproved.

"I don't say he was," Luna returned. "Still he dabbled in arts forbidden, between the gallant days of Bosworth and the final rest in the odour of bought sanctity. The early Tudor period was a time of great mental progress, good and bad, like our own early Windsor era. Some strong intellects unravelled the wholesome, useful secrets of nature. Others gorged like ghouls on the unholy remains of mental abominations an elder age had tested and tried to consign to the grave. Necromancy will seduce the noblest minds, as we have painful evidence in our own age. And the evil a man does may haunt those who come after him to the end of time, while he rests in peace himself. So that's his helmet?" She touched with a finger the dinted globe of rusty iron. "Our object is to get what's inside my skull connected with what was once protected by that metal."

"But there's four hundred years between you and the old blighter, and his brain's been dust long ago," Oliver protested.

"Four hundred years, or four thousand, can be bridged sometimes, when it's a question of connecting two human brains."

"You'll hold a *séance* and summon his spirit?" Swanhild put in.

"My dear girl!" Luna looked pained. "I thought I made some observations about occultism just now. I never resort to the antiquated and noisome fashion of sitting in a dark room looking for nervous self-deception. The Warlock's brain has been non-existent for centuries, but what fed it and dictated its thoughts still exists. I'll consult the Black Magical text-books of his era as last resort. Now to see if Cromwell's men really ruined the hidden room."

In the nave she reached the brass, glanced down, and turned to inspect it again, her back to the others. After a minute she went on her way with them. Oliver and Swanhild looked at each other over her head as she walked between them, but neither dared to ask a question. A new and overpowering sobriety had come to her.

"It's awfully cold," she remarked. They exchanged another look, for her voice had betrayed her. It was suddenly flat, as though she had received a shock.

Now what could she have seen in a minute's second inspection of the brass that had taken the sparkle from voice and eyes?

10

THE HAND OF GLORY

The mist had begun to shred away a little by the time Dannow's foursquare bulk loured into sight. Dark smears and rags of ivy draped it like a frayed shroud, twisted chimneys writhed snakelike up into the fog above it, and round its girding wall the weedy moat faded into the murk to either hand. Before the moat bridge Swanhild stopped the car and Oliver called Luna's attention to an uncertain mass glooming up beyond where the moat was lost to sight.

"That's a clump of pines on the edge of the moat, and the hidden room's opposite them," he told her. "If it wasn't so wet underfoot I'd take you round to see the grating that ventilates it."

"A grating? Then one can see into it from outside?"

"No, that's where the artfulness comes in. There's two iron grilles, one flush with the outer face of the wall, one with the inner. The wall's four feet thick, and the bottom of the outside grille is level with the top of the other. Even if the room is lit up anyone outside could only see a bit of the floor."

In the Holbein room Walton had a tray ready and a fire that made all four realise they were cold and stiff. They gathered round it while he went upstairs for certain keys, and Oliver inspected the tray and chuckled grimly. "Topping old souls, our house-keeper-cook and butler-valet, eh, Swan? There's everything I'm likely to fancy about this time of day here, and the inference is pretty obvious. Walton and Mrs. W. have laid their heads together and agreed to make my possible last hours as comfy as possible. They evidently expect I may run away and hang myself all of a sudden—"

"Oh, Oliver—" protested Swanhild.

"They do. Even you, Miss Bartendale, have looked at me closely once or twice."

She looked up from her occupation of warming her dainty, beringed little hands, and replied placidly, "So I have. Didn't you mention we have met before, though I can't remember the occasion? And here, I think, are the keys."

As he could not use his hands, Swanhild took charge of the keys, and led the way to the old part of the house. They all kept their coats on, Goddard carried a lamp, and the dogs followed at their owners' heels. At the end of a corridor Swanhild attended to the Yale, the old-fashioned spring lock, and the padlock that secured an iron-bound door. Damp, cold air slapped their faces like a gigantic hand when they stepped through. Half Dannow is like that; cold even in summer, a complex of twisting passages, damp walls, peeling plaster and rotted woodwork, with cobwebbed windows and dangerous stairs.

"Flowing water somewhere," said Luna when they had descended to a stone built passage. Swanhild turned the keys of two more locks and flung open another metal-bound door. The gurgle and swirl of water sounded like the chuckling of a drunken ogre where the threshold stone ended over a black gap. Goddard held the lamp in; the light flashed from a rippling black surface some feet down. "Cellar," said Oliver; "and the spring that feeds the moat. Go first, Goddard, you've been this way before."

The wall in which the door was set was not as thick as that of the water-filled cellar, consequently a foot wide ledge stretched away to left and right. Goddard stepped along that on the right to the corner. There another door was set in a niche some six feet square and deep, and from it he lit the way for the others. "A movable stone used to be here, this is a comparatively recent addition," Oliver explained, while Swanhild unlocked the door. Again Goddard led the way, passing down a stair made of mere chunks of oak pegged together. At the foot of it he stood with the light; Luna suddenly drew back with a start. Her eyes turned sideways to the light shining up the stair; they were wide and black again and her face had gone very white.

"Eh—what?" gasped Oliver. Swanhild turned her torch on; in the white glare Luna's forehead glistened and her eyes were uncanny with their sombre calm ringed by golden lashes. "There's something very wrong down there," she said, in a detached tone, glancing down at the dogs. Her own animal looked up at her sympathetically, otherwise both exhibited no emotion.

"Then you must not—" Oliver began, but she was already on the stairs. He plunged after her, his most usable arm ready to lunge at any danger, and in a few moments all stood within the hidden room.

"Something very wrong here," she repeated, standing by the oak table in the middle, "but nothing that threatens active harm. Some-out of the Normal, but not Abnormal with a capital A."

"Fourth Dimensional?" Swanhild prompted.

"Oh, no, my dear girl. More like Three and a Half Dimensional. It can't be full Fourth, or the dogs would notice it."

The animals had settled themselves placidly under the table. "My dog didn't notice anything coming in the Shaw before I did," Oliver put in nervously. "You'd better go back—"

She started to pace round the room, taking the torch, for the lamp Goddard had put on the table lit the walls but dimly. "I am safe from danger in any dimension, through my knowledge," she said, but he followed her, obviously ready to put himself between her and any danger. The room was solid stonework, walls and floor of large blocks, ceiling of narrow ones laid on oaken rafters. Two large oil-heaters, incongruously new and shiny, explained why, for all its nearness to the moat, the place was fairly free from damp: only the wall opposite the stairs was smeared with fine moss round the iron-bound oak shutters. These Goddard opened, letting in a gush of cold fresh air through a grating of twisted ironwork. They looked through this up an oblique shaft; smoke blackened, to another grating and a glimpse of pines and grey sky seen dully in mist. The ceiling and upper part of the walls were also darkened with smoke, evidently the product of a brick furnace that was erected against the wall between stairs and grating.

On the table lay four great leather bound books, a little mildewed. About a dozen jars and bowls of red earthenware; some fire-blackened, stood beside the furnace, on the floor, together with a scattered pile of smashed glass and potsherds drifted with dust and cobwebs. At the other side of the furnace were laid out several chunks of stone, the fragments of a single broken block, all drifted up with dust also. After looking closely at everything Luna opened her bag and took out the rod again.

"There's something wrong here," she repeated. "Is there any hiding place—in the thickness of the walls, for instance?

"It's been proved over and over that not an inch of the walls or floor or ceiling sounds hollow," returned Swanhild.

Luna stared round under level brows. "The Roundheads must have destroyed the clue—yet I feel something. What's that broken stone?"

"It's inscribed with the rhyme I told you about the pines and bane. Somebody must have smashed it while getting it out of the wall—you can see the hole there—under the impression that the secret might be hidden behind it."

Now Luna balanced the rod between her palms, and at once the third limb rose to the horizontal. With her eyes at their widest and blackest she began a tour of the room, the rod rising and falling again as she approached and passed the furnace. When she rested a wrist on the brickwork the twig turned over languidly. "Puzzling, very puzzling," she commented to herself. "Indications, but faint and insufficient."

Moving on to the jars she placed a foot on each in turn. At the fifth the rod rotated briskly. It was a big jar with a cover, like a bread crock. Swanhild ran and removed the cover, revealing a layer of dust under the brim. Goddard elbowed her aside gently and paddled in it with his fingers. "A hard, level surface," he reported. "Excuse my shoving, Swan, but where I was raised men are supposed to attend to unclean jobs."

He scooped the dust aside, and felt the surface beneath with his nails. "A solid mass, like hardened sand and salt, Miss Bartendale."

"Smash it," said Oliver, dribbling a lump of stone from the broken inscription across the floor with his feet. "Oh, I say!" he added suddenly, "I hope it isn't any old Isabella-and-the-pot-of-basil stunt! If it is, salt's just the thing—"

"There's no room for a head in it," Swanhild returned. Goddard took the stone and soon the crock and its contents lay in a scattered heap of shards and powder and lumps of unclean crystals. "There's nothing but filthy sand and salt," he reported, after flattening it all out with the stone.

Luna put the toe of one shoe on the mass, and again the rod moved. "There's something amiss with it, but not powerful enough to account for my feeling. We'll leave it for the time."

She walked past the stairs to the third wall. At once the rod began to turn over rapidly. She drew in a quick breath and ran one finger lightly up and down the wall. The pace of the rod increased as her hands went upwards, slackened when they were as far up as she could reach, and when she brought them down level with her shoulders it whirled at a tremendous pace and leapt out of her hold. The little tap of it on the floor made the others realise the tense silence in which they had been watching.

She turned to them, passed a hand over her forehead, and looked at them with her eyes normal again and full of horror. "This is the centre of the influence," she exclaimed, touching a stone level with her shoulder, "and it's horrible—horrible!"

"But the wall's solid!" Goddard pounded it with the stone.

"It is; yet it's the centre of influence." She blinked at them, her face drawn and white and her mouth squared as though with intense strain, and crossed to the open shutters. Her features lost their tenseness in the mist-streaked draught that stirred the little curls about her ears and forehead. "The rod rather takes it out of one," she remarked, apologetically. "Moreover, that stone, though it's not a foot square, has something incredibly revolting about it.

In thirteen years' practice the rod has only jumped out of my hands twice before."

"The plaster's crumbling, in fact it isn't real plaster, only clay smeared in." Goddard looked round from picking at the stone. "I do believe the block's movable."

"A sucker is what we want," said Swanhild quietly. She had already wrenched the tongue off one of her shoes. She took a knife and hank of twine out of her pockets, trimmed the leather to a circle and knotted the stout string through the middle. "There's a smugglers' hiding hole in a cottage here, and you pull up a brick in this way," she said, talking as she worked. "I'll soak it in the spring."

While she was gone Goddard picked the clay out, Luna turned over the books on the table. "The *Desir Desire*, the *Book of Abraham*, the *Duodecim Portarum*, and Albertus Magnus," she observed. "Fine MSS., Mr. Hammand, and comparatively harmless. Merely alchemy and vulgarity. But, of course, Cromwell's men may have stolen worse works."

Swanhild returned and the wet sucker was flattened on the stone. A good pull brought out a block about two feet long and apparently solid, which slid out like a tight fitting drawer. Goddard got his shoulder under it and with Swanhild's help deposited it on the table. "By Jove, I see!" he cried. "The back half lifts like a lid. Will you—Miss Bartendale—?"

She moved nearer the open shutter. "Hang this lint! You open it, Goddard," said Oliver.

Goddard lifted it and with it came a gush of scent, like a faint rush of compressed stale air. Dry, and vapid, and sickly without being absolutely offensive. Swanhild shivered and involuntarily drew back from the table. The hollowed place at the rear of the block only held two bundles, long narrow bundles wrapped in musty linen. Goddard took the uppermost, shook it, and rolled into the lamplight a dry, wrinkled object less than a foot long.

"A bundle of cigars gone wrong?" Oliver hazarded, staring at this secret of four hundred years.

"A piece of cut leather?" Swanhild faltered, feeling oddly uncomfortable about the spine and scalp.

Goddard turned it over gingerly, and then wiped his fingers on his coat. "Ugh!" he grunted. "It's a hand! A filthy, disgusting old mummied hand!"

They all looked at Luna. From her distance she regarded it with unsurprised disgust.

"*It is a Hand of Glory*," she said.

11

RUNIC WRITING

The mist-laden draught brought enough of daylight through the grilles to impart a garish suggestion of the unnatural to the lamplight, the faces grotesquely shadowed around it, and the dried brown horror in the glare of it. Only Luna, full in what natural light there was, seemed wholesome and real. There was a little silence while the three round the table groped mentally after vague recollections of old horror-tales. Then, with a start of mild surprise, Swanhild was aware of her own voice repeating the Ingoldsby jingle:

> "*Now open, lock, to the Dead Man's knock!*
>   Fly, bolt, and bar and band!
> Nor move, nor swerve, Joint, muscle, or nerve,
>   At the Spell of the Dead Man's Hand!
> Sleep, all who sleep! Wake, all who wake:
> *But be as the dead for the Dead Man's sake!*"

"What's the beast, anyhow, Miss Bartendale?" asked Oliver, in a hushed voice.

"The hand of a hanged murderer, pickled with saltpetre and long pepper"—she glanced at the broken crock— "and dried by a fire of male fern and vervain."

Oliver's gaze followed hers to the furnace. "And what are the disgusting blobs of grease on the finger-tips?"

"Candles. Made from the same source that supplied the hand. The directions are in the *Dictionaire Infernal*, also, I think, in Albertus Magnus, by your elbow there."

Goddard shivered. "I once read a yarn in a magazine about a chap who got a hand out of an old burial mound, and used to send it to murder people he disliked—"

Luna smiled drily. "O. W. Holmes declared the world was a thin solution of books in his days. Now it is a turgid one of journalistic misinformation. The function of the Hand of Glory is to reveal hidden treasure; also, while the candles on it burn, anyone who is on guard is supposed to be paralysed."

"Then can it have any connection with the Monster?" asked Swanhild.

"Heaven knows. Perhaps the other parcel may shed light on the matter. Pray open it, Mr. Covert."

Goddard took up the second bundle. "Bigger and heavier. If it's even beastlier don't say I didn't warn you, ladies," he said, and jerked out the contents beside the hand. They were all keyed up in expectation of a further horror; it was almost a shock when a green and golden thing of beauty clattered out. The upper part of a sword, a golden hilt, a hand's length of bronze, green with verdigris, below it, and two flat ribbons of verdigrised bronze curling from the pommel, like a crossguard in the wrong place. For the first time that day Luna's expression was one of surprise. She came over and picked up the object to examine it closely.

"What's it?" asked Oliver, flatly. "Another obscenity?"

She gently shook her head. "Without doubt your Warlock ancestor made the hand for his own unlawful uses. But this is past my comprehension. How, when, where and why he secured it and hid it with the hand is a puzzle. Particularly as there is nothing objectionable about it. That is centred in the hand. Perhaps the runes may have something to do with his treasuring it."

She handed it to Swanhild and indicated the golden part. This consisted of two plates riveted on the bronze foundation; they were much worn, but rude figures could be discerned in low relief on both. "Runic writing," she said.

"What does it say?" demanded Swanhild.

"Nobody alive can read runes offhand, and I cannot read them at all. They may contain some hallowed spell; ancient northern tradition abounds with tales of broadswords with runic charms on them."

"Then this is ancient? Older than the Warlock's time?"

"If genuine it was about two thousand years old before your Tudor ancestor lived. These 'Antennæ hilted' swords belong to the Later Bronze Age, which ended about 700 B.C. The gold plates may be a later addition, but this blade was most likely made when Rome was one row of mud huts and the Ten Tribes were still unlost."

Oliver stared at her with eyes that could open no wider. "Do you mean that the Monster, the thing that mauled me and tore the flesh right off poor Kate last night, is something that came from the north in the Bronze Age?"

"We don't know if these discoveries have anything to do with the Monster at all. Only it is significant that this is Northern because Northern demonology and necromancy have been strangely neglected in these days of occultism, occultism everywhere. Some dreadful thing begotten of Northern gloom and frost, and—" She checked herself. "I confess I am at sea for the time."

"You have already found out more than anyone else has in four hundred years," he consoled heartily.

"I've only lit on disconnected data that make the matter more confusing than it was at the start. However, I don't despair. In one case I handled the trouble happened to a colonial soldier during the war, I traced its origin to the fourteenth century, and found the remedy in America. Fact, I assure you. Your Monster has been in evidence a thousand years at least, such incredibly powerful and persistent manifestations may well have thousands of years of growth behind them. Now, let us turn to the Warlock's statement that the secret of the Monster was to be found in this room. Why did he content himself with this vague declaration? If the hand and hilt were what he meant, why did he not specify their location? If they are not connected with it, why did he say anything at all?"

"Something else may be hidden here," Swanhild suggested.

"Impossible," Luna declared. "The hand, and the jar and furnace used in preparing it, are the only abnormalities in the place."

"You called them Three and a Half Dimensional," the girl persisted. "What if the Warlock's secret is Fourth Dimensional?"

"Fourth? What's commonly known as a spirit? I should at once detect its presence, and so would the dogs."

"What if it's Fifth Dimensional?" demanded Swanhild, looking her straight in the eyes.

A little frown drew down Luna's brows ever so slightly, but she returned smoothly: "At present I do not care to advance a positive opinion on the possible connection of a Fifth Dimensional influence with this room."

Under her direction they probed and pried, sounded every stone, and raked out the broken glass and pottery. Finally they took a book each and went over every page in search of marginal notes, pin pricks, or dotted letters that might point to a cipher message. The search was without result, Luna finished her volume first and went roaming about while the other three still pored over their task. When Swanhild finally closed the *Desir Desire* she was engaged in scraping the dirt out of the sunk letters on the broken stone.

"I can let you have a good photo, taken when the lettering was cleaned up for the purpose," said Swanhild. "Its only the rhyme I repeated about the Monster and frost and pines."

"It's ve-ry curious," rejoined Luna. "It must be older than the Warlock's time, as the hole it came from is as black as the wall around it. I understand the furnace has not been lit since he left it in 1526? Then he left the broken block lying about all the years he was at work there?"

"Oh, no. The pieces were used to build part of the furnace. Look, there are the clean holes they were taken from afterwards."

"I meant to ask about those holes. Then he didn't understand the meaning of the rhyme. He simply found a broken stone hanging about and used it. He saw nothing interesting in the words."

"They are very simple. Only a plain warning."

"My dear girl, there's nothing that rouses my suspicions like an apparently simple article over which anybody has made a mystery. That the Warlock saw nothing more about these lines than Peter Bell did about a primrose by the river's brim is evident; the puzzle is this: Why were these simple lines ever carved here?"

Swanhild eyed the broken block gravely. "I never thought of that. Have you got a theory, Miss Bartendale?"

"No. At present I'm suffering from an overplus of data. Yet every detail, from the Bronze Age sword to the Warlock's easy utilising of this block, may have some bearing on the matter. We have heard of such things as jigsaw puzzles. I see the men are shutting their tomes simultaneously. What luck, gentlemen?"

"The old perisher didn't add marking valuable books to his other crimes," Oliver answered.

"Apparently. This was only a cursory inspection; if necessary I shall go through all four later. Just now we have done all we can here, and it's getting a bit chilly. I understand nothing has to be moved from the room, Mr. Hammand?"

"You may do as you like, of course. Only you surely don't want to take that away?" Oliver indicated the hand.

"The fates forbid! I shouldn't like to touch it with a hop pole. I merely wish to submit the inscription to an authority on runic lore I know."

"Would it be safe for you to take it?"

"I've told you the evil influence is centred in the hand and where it was prepared. Look"—she took up the sword— "I could not handle this bonny bit of metal work if it were not wholesome."

"Then we'll pack it for you. What of the hand?"

"Put it back in its place and I'll make it safe."

When Goddard had replaced the sliding stone she plastered the join between it and the wall all round with some malleable white stuff and dried herb which she produced from the bag and kneaded together. "Evil powers are not supposed to get past garlic and purified beeswax," she explained.

Then smiling at their blank looks, she supplemented: "I don't say I believe in this kind of hocus pocus, but there's no harm in taking precautions."

Then they went up again. After the hidden room it was refreshing to have the bubble of the spring at their feet and to see the light glint on moss-slimed walls and crawling black water. Oliver drew a deep breath and shivered. "Even a water-logged cellar feels sweet to stickiness after the abode of our friend the hand!" said Goddard.

Oliver was very grave. "I didn't notice it at the time, either because it came on gradually, or with the excitement of finding the things, but I now realise how beastly it was in the room. Yet it wasn't stuffy. What do you think, Swan?"

"The hand was ghastly, Oliver. Otherwise I didn't notice anything queer."

"I didn't mind the hand." He frowned thoughtfully. "Still, there was a putrid feeling—as though the air was full of something I half recognised. Full of—of—"

"Black butterflies ridden by blue devils?" suggested Goddard, gaily. "We've had our fill of nastiness this morning, Oliver. Don't get silly ideas into that cracked headpiece of yours."

Luna gave the speaker an approving glance, but Oliver turned on him indignantly. "This is a serious matter, Goddard, even if you don't think so. There was a feeling about, especially after the hand was on the table. If I stayed there long enough—with the hand—by myself—I think I might remember—"

His voice tailed off and he put his hand hesitatingly up to his hurt temple. Swanhild, quivering with apprehension but afraid to interfere, cast an agonised look at Luna. In response: "You'll remember when I order you to do so," Luna snapped, in a thin, imperative voice that acted like a bugle call on Oliver.

He straightened galvanically, and the confused look left his face. "When you order me to remember?" he said.

"That is what I said. Until then, if you have any regard for your sister's peace of mind, and do not wish to risk possible danger to more than mind and body, you will not trouble your head at all with efforts to remember."

"You have a theory—" he accused.

Almost sternly the answer came. "I found the hand and hilt—more than anyone else has done in four centuries!" Her tone changed: "Come, Mr. Hammand, we have had enough work and horrors for the time! Don't forget I am a specialist, and specialists never advance a premature opinion—unless some wretched journalist catches them off their guard! When the runes are read by my professor it will be time enough for theorising."

She laughed, but there was something in tone and laugh that stopped further questioning.

12
"? ? ? ? ? ? : HAMMAND—"

To step from the deserted part of the house into the lived-in portion was like getting away from the oppression of a bad dream. They did not realise how long they had been in the hidden room until Swanhild opened the final door and they found Walton hovering nervously in the corridor on the other side. The old man's evident relief at their appearance told plainly that he had been hanging about for a long time in the throes of anxiety; he explained that the Inspector from Steyning was waiting to hear an account of the last night's doings. As Miss Bartendale would not be needed for that purpose Swanhild established her in the Holbein room with certain genealogical MSS. and the photograph of the inscription.

When the three returned she was curled in a chair before the fire, frowningly regarding a huge sheet of parchment that was spread on the rug. "What's that?" asked Oliver, lowering himself into another chair.

"What? Don't you recognise your family tree to 1650?"

"Never saw it unrolled before, and I don't suppose Swan has."

"Ah, I see. You've simply taken it for granted that some people came between you and Adam. Then I presume you don't even know you are of Danish descent?"

"Danish?

"I suspected it, from the very unusual name Swanhild, that seems as much a fixture in the line as the distinctly Scandinavian cast of features which I noted both in you two and the Warlock's effigy and the portraits here." She glanced at the Streete, then indicated the parchment's branching tree of angular pen lines with clumps of elaborate writing and tiny coloured shields dotted all over it. "Look, that recumbent individual in the idea of Danish mail entertained in 1650, from whose person the tree springs, is your first notable ancestor. The entry about him is in Latin, but I'll translate:

> *'Magnus Hamandr's son, who was kin of the*
> *Royal House of Denmark, married her.'*

"The 'her' in question is Edith, the Saxon heiress of the place at the time."

"By Jove! And that Bronze Age sword—you said it is northern!"

"Getting warm, aren't we? Some dashing Dane married the heiress of the old Saxon line. Probably he was a pirate and slaughtered the rest of the family prior to the nuptials, but that doesn't concern us. The main fact is that his father, Hamandr, must have been a distinguished individual, since his name was given to the line when surnames came in. And look here, under his name is the first red entry. He was the first of the Monster's victims—in England at least."

She emphasized the last words, and paused. Swanhild took up the discourse. "A Magnus came into the line from Denmark, and with him the Monster first appeared."

"Exactly. And one of his descendants, also a Magnus, seven centuries later, practiced Black Art and treasured a Bronze Age sword of Scandinavian origin. He even kept it with his most private necromantic tool. It all points to Denmark, the Danish ancestor, the sword, even the northern trees—pine and fir—that are to be avoided. We have learnt something this morning."

She leant back in her chair and added in a different tone: "As a Bachelor of Medicine I ought to know better than to read by firelight! It's two o'clock, don't I hear a gong somewhere? While my conscious mind is attending to lunch its sub-conscious mate will sift the facts we have gathered and compare them with others stored in my memory, and later I may be able to shed some light on the initiatory ritual of the hidden room."

"The—what?" asked Oliver, but she got up, slipped her arm in Swanhild's, and answered lightly.

"Here ends the morning's work. Talking shop at mealtimes is the unforgivable sin. At least that's one of the maxims on which I have been brought up."

"Hear, hear!" assented Goddard. "A misdemeanour has to be pretty poisonous to outrage Nature and good manners concurrently." To Swanhild he whispered: "Whatever that little woman may be in the occult line she understands managing men who want it. You've noted, haven't you, how admirably she pulls up old Oliver when ever he starts to try and recollect?"

Never were the two sides of a normal personality kept more strictly separate than in Luna Bartendale. The slight aloofness that had seemed to enfold her like a veil when she worked vanished at will and left her nothing but her unprofessional self: the prettiest and most debonair little woman that ever made other women like her as easily as men did. Throughout lunch she confined the talk to the Russian Ballet and Home Rule, *Raymond*, the *Young Visiters*, and other light topics. In a short time the Hammands felt as though they had known her for years, and Swanhild was so absorbed in noting that Oliver was brighter than he had been since 1914 that it never dawned on her the visitor pumped them both exhaustively concerning their history, characters, and habits. The girl was divided between relief over her brother's temporary recovery and dread of what revelation might be waiting for when she could get a private talk with the occultist, and had no attention to bestow on anything else. Only when the coffee and cigarette stage was prolonging itself unduly, Luna looked at her watch, and switched back to business.

"We will have another look at the documents," she announced, in the voice that went with the divining rod.

"Don't be in an indecent hurry," Oliver urged. "After a couple of hours' rest—"

"In a couple of hours I must be on the way to Hassocks," she returned, and led the way back to the Holbein room. There she spread the MSS. and photograph out on the table. "Now we will have my sub-conscious mind's reconstruction of the family history. The Monster came into the line with Magnus the Dane, and its nature was known to the family until the year 1456—"

"The year 1456?" Swanhild repeated.

"These are my conclusions, you shall hear the reasons later. The secret, as I said, was lost in the year 1456, when the initiatory ritual of the hidden room was discontinued. Many years later the secret was rediscovered by Magnus the Warlock, apparently as a result of his necromantic studies, with terrible consequences. Since then the Monster has manifested itself at irregular intervals, but no one has ever been able to explain what it is. Now for the ritual."

She took up the photograph. "Look at this. It explains the story: repeated in books and magazine articles to this day, of the heir of the manor being initiated into some secret in the hidden room. You have assured me it is not done, but evidently it *was* done—up to 1456. This inscription was hacked by someone unused to such a task. Not scratched casually, but the labour of many hours. Now why was not a proper workman employed?"

"Because there was something in the room, at that time, that could not be concealed from anyone who entered it?" suggested Oliver.

"Precisely. But the rhyme is a simple thing. Why was it not carved by a professional and the block then inserted in the wall?"

"The block was in the wall already?"

"No. It is Sussex marble, easier to carve than the harder stone of which the room is built. It was specially inserted by those who were allowed to know the room's secret. This implies that the rhyme—though it is public property now—was considered unfit for general circulation—*when the clue to its exact meaning was known.*"

"The meaning seems so plain," said Oliver.

"Seems, *seems!*" she returned. "Language is so wonderful! So far we make out that each successive heir was taken into the room when he was of age, and made to learn the lines: after their occult meaning had been explained to him."

"How did the knowledge disappear, then, in the year you specified?" asked Swanhild.

"Because, as I gather, the family was practically wiped out, as regards the male members, at the battle of Blore Heath in 1456. The owner of Dannow was killed there, and the only male Hammand left was Magnus; the Warlock-to-be; who was only born in the previous year. Don't you see? All the holders of the secret died at once."

"Oh!" Oliver nodded emphatically. "The Yorkists sacked the place, too, they must have destroyed all clues to the secret. It was always said they broke up the inscription."

"Exactly. The secret lapsed utterly, until Magnus, many years after, rediscovered it. That is, he found out part of it. He 'raised' the Monster after it had been at rest or bound over a century, but did not know how to control it; a matter that was probably taught by the ritual."

"All that sounds logical," said Goddard, glancing down the parchment and then at the second one which continued the genealogy to "Oliver, born 1893." "Only; look at this, Miss Bartendale. From the first Magnus, about 830, to the Anchorite, 1392, is 562 years, and in that time the Monster appeared eighteen times. From the Warlock, 1526, to this year is nearly three hundred years, but it has only appeared seven times. Three cases and more to a century while the ritual was known, barely two to the same time when it was forgotten. Yet you hold the ritual was of a protective nature. What do you make of that?

She met the glance of his searching brown eyes without a change in her own. "That possibly the ritual, instead of being a guard, ensured the supplying of the Monster with frequent victims, of course."

Oliver gave an exclamation of disgusted horror. "Miss Bartendale! That's too beastly! The tale of the human sacrifices—"

"I don't credit that wholly: though you must remember sacrifice is never beastly *if it is voluntary.*"

"But those people who were killed didn't die voluntarily—"

"I am merely pointing out data; not advancing any theory at this early stage." She lapsed into a fit of musing, turning the photograph about with one hand while the other toyed with the dimple on her chin. Oliver, sitting opposite her, mused also. He could not decide which was most to be envied; the lucky fingers that might caress the dimple, or the happy dimple that might be caressed by the fingers. At last she had to look up, compelled by his steady gaze.

"The first two lines are complete: '*Where grow pines and firs amain, Under stars sans heat or rain*'— The third begins with a gap in the stone. Your version of the missing link, Miss Hammand, was—?"

"'*Chief of.*'"

"'*Chief of Hammand, 'ware thy Bane.*' Really, you know, it doesn't sound absolutely it, with the dot and cross! '*Chief of Hammands*' might be better, though still feeble."

"The exigencies of metrical composition may have compelled the author to jolly with the sense," suggested Goddard.

"Not very likely. In medieval rhymes when it was a question of sacrificing sense or scansion, scansion went. One word is lost, that is certain, and the accepted restoration does not make too much sense."

"The first letter is a C," he pointed out. "Half of it is left."

"The upper half of a rounded letter. It might be O or Q, G or S, as well as C."

"Does it matter?"

"It might and it might not. Also the remains of the last letter cannot be connected with F at all. This is a home-made travesty of Lombardic lettering, and a horizontal line at the bottom of a letter can only belong to Z or L." She began to measure the lines with a pencil. "Moreover, the letters are evenly spaced, in spite of their uncouth formation, and each word is divided from the other by two dots, which occupy the same space as a letter. '*Chief of*' contains seven letters—seven spaces—the necessary division marks for two words bring it up to nine spaces. But from the initial of

'Hammand' to the beginning of the line there's only room for seven spaces, including the double dot that remains *in situ*. It appears that instead of '*Chief of Hammand*' we have—"

She jotted on a piece of paper:

"? ? ? ? ? ? : Hammand:"

13

"O, C, G, Q, OR S, AND L, OR Z"

"This is like a weekly paper puzzle," said Goddard. "You have proved that '*Chief of*' can't be the opening of the third line, Miss Bartendale; does that mean that the missing word, or words, may alter the sense of the whole rhyme?"

"Nothing is impossible; though what you suggest does not seem unduly probable, with only six spaces for letters. We have O, C, G, Q, or S, for possible initial, and the last character can only be L or Z."

She noted down the possible combinations on the paper.

OxxxxL		OxxxxZ
CxxxxL		CxxxxZ
GxxxxL	or	GxxxxZ
QxxxxL		QxxxxZ
SxxxxL		SxxxxZ

"And, after all, it may be nothing of any moment," she concluded, pushing the paper away. But Goddard considered it gravely. "C-r-u-e-l, that's a letter short," he said. "But they might have spelt it with ll: 'C-r-u-e-ll' Hammand."

"Obvious, but no sense," commented Luna.

"C-o-r-b-e-l," he spelt. "Much worse, let's try G. G-o-s-p-e-l-; worse than ever! How about O? O-r-i-e-l, or two words: O-d-u-double l— 'O, dull Hammand' isn't bad, but still without sense.

The English language is copious enough when an Old Army Sergeant is dressing you down, but wonderfully restricted when it's a missing word. The Z endings I dare not tackle."

"It may not be anything," Luna repeated. She bent over the photograph again, her elbows on the table and her head on her hands. "The rest is plain: '*Where grow pines and firs amain, under stars sans—*'" She paused abruptly, and stayed as she was, her face almost hidden by her palms, her finger-tips tapping her temples. "Oh, there's no disguising it—I'm fagged out now, and this trifle is getting on my mind!" she exclaimed, raising her head and giving herself a little shake.

"You are tired to death—on our account," Oliver began, concerned.

"Fairly," she conceded. "I've done enough for the time, perhaps, but I must examine the poor dog's body."

The others all rose. She waved a forbidding hand. "No, thanks. The butler is to show me where it is. You all knew the poor fellow in life, and there's no need to harrow your feelings. I prefer to do my inspecting by myself."

It was a command, and they obeyed. She returned within half an hour. "Jove, but you look rotten, Miss Bartendale!" exclaimed Oliver.

She smiled wryly. "It was not a pleasant task for an animal-lover. By the way, the police have not yet examined him, I gather?"

"No, they have wired for a Scotland Yard man."

"Well, he will not find any clues in that direction. There are no tooth-marks whatever, and I don't think he ever had his own teeth into anything. And now I have finished my day's work."

"But—" gasped Swanhild.

"It is a bit inconclusive," Luna completed for her as she came to a stammering stop. "Ve-ry inconclusive, but all I can do until I get a translation of the runes. On them I depend as the thread that will string together all the scattered facts we have gathered to-day. And I really am tired."

"But—" poor Swanhild began again, and again disappointment and dread choked her.

"Miss Bartendale's used up—on our account," said Oliver, in a big soft voice that was a command. "If you don't care to tell us your conclusions at present, Miss Bartendale, we accept your decision without question."

It was the tone of a master in his own house, a tone he had not used, in Swanhild's memory, since he became owner of Dannow. Still, out of the depths of her sudden despair and helpless fear for him she persisted. "Then you mean to leave us helpless, Miss Bartendale?" she protested.

"By no means," answered Luna briskly. "I shall leave you fully protected against this Abnormal danger. It can be put in a sentence: you, Mr. Hammand, are alone in any danger from it, and you must not go into the hidden room or any place where pines and firs grow, by night, until you see me again."

"When will that be?" he asked eagerly.

"To-morrow. When you come to see me, all of you, and learn one of my reasons for not enlightening you further to-day."

"To-morrow? Run up and see you?" he repeated, brightening.

"You are quite well enough to go about freely. Will you promise me—for your own good and your sister's peace of mind—not to do what I have forbidden you to do until I release you from the promise?"

"It's a bet. What of your address?"

"15, Bispham Gardens, Chelsea. I live with my nearest relative, Madame Yorke, the pianist. We had better pack the hilt now."

"I've a cigar box that'll fit it like a dinner."

He went in search of it. "Whew!" whistled Goddard, softly. "Old Oliver's uncommonly bright and biddable all of a sudden, Swanhild!"

"I've given him something to look forward to," said Luna.

"Is that why you have put off telling us anything?" Swanhild asked.

Luna turned to her quickly. "No, it is not," she answered. "It's merely a convenient by-product of my plan, that may keep him from brooding. I cannot tell you any more to-day—not even to still the anxiety of a sister who is shivering with it on her only brother's account!"

As she spoke she laid her hands on Swanhild's shoulders and looked full into the girl's eyes. Her own were, now, neither brooding nor scintillating, but very soft and kind, and though her hands were small the touch of them sent something through Swanhild that stiffened her backbone. She did not know she had been trembling until she now felt it stop. "Trust me a little while; I beg," Luna went on. "Believe me, I know what I am about. I have dealt with similar manifestations before; though none so ancient and powerful. I am speaking to you, too, Mr. Covert," she supplemented, over her shoulder.

Goddard laughed guiltily, without losing the sobriety of his look. "I certainly think you make too much mystery about it, Miss Bartendale," he admitted. "Moreover, I find it hard to believe you are on the right track. You are certain the secret was known before the Wars of the Roses, yet during that period the deaths were more frequent."

"They were. I don't mind telling you two what I make of this detail; then, perhaps, you will trust me better. In this world, then, every happening resolves itself into three parts—cause, agency, and effect. Effect, the visible result, agency by which that result is worked; and cause behind agency. Since Blore Heath the effects of the Monster's manifestations are all that have been known. Before that period the agency—the form the Monster had power to take for the working of the effects—was known. But the cause—the exact nature of the Monster, and why it was able to have such power in connection with the Hammand family—was not known. I suspect I have rediscovered the agency, and may possibly discover the cause."

"So you believe," he conceded grudgingly. "Only that does not explain why the disasters were most frequent when the agency was known."

"On the contrary, it does. With the best possible intention the worst possible means may have been adopted to control the agency. To use a familiar simile: the remedy was worse than the disease."

"If you find the cause can you stop the effect?" Swanhild asked eagerly.

"I don't say I can find the cause. I don't profess to be wiser than all the sages of the past, but I can try to find it in the light of new knowledge that has been added to what had been gathered when the agency was known before. Cause is sometimes incomprehensible: as the primal cause of the universe is still, though mankind has always known of its effects in nature, and exact science has latterly found out some of its agencies."

"Can you guess at the cause of it all: from your previous experiences? The generic nature of the cause, I mean?" Goddard asked.

" I can:

> 'To me dim shapes of ancient crime
> Wail down the windy ways of Time,'

and this Monster is the result of some sin that is haunting down the sinners' line from age to age. No later than tomorrow afternoon you shall have a glimpse of my methods that ought to satisfy you."

14

THE FIRST OF THE FOURTH ESTATE

The wind had shredded the mist away by the time Luna had to start for Hassocks, but the sky still loured. The sun, glinting through a slit in the cloud-canopy of the Downs, suggested the narrowed, flaming eye of a malicious devil, peering over the sodden grey world in search of mischief to be done in the coming night. Luna, glancing back as the motor made for the gap leading to the Weald, saw a last view of Dannow against the forbidding sky. The crack of metallic red brightness behind resembled a red-hot blade plunged through its lumpish bulk; it looked a fit casket for the abominable hand and ominous inscription hidden in its keeping.

"In common fairness you must come and see our Sussex in more cheery circumstances," said Oliver Hammand. He had insisted on joining her escort to Hassocks, only agreeing, ostensibly as a concession to his sister's natural fussiness, to go in the tonneau with the guest and the dogs. Luna turned from the dreary scene to find his grey eyes looking full at her. Bright, pleasant eyes, frankly making no effort to shift their gaze on meeting hers. "What were you thinking about Dannow?" he asked, further.

"That if I owned it I would have every stone of it carted away, the Shaw rooted up and ploughed deep, and the name of the place altered. Also I'd change my own name and go to some Colony and start life afresh; away from all associations with this horrible patrimony!"

Luna was shocked at her outburst almost before she had finished speaking. Oliver looked kindly at her. "You are tired," he said.

His big round voice was itself again, and in spite of the dis-
colouration of one temple and the bandages round his throat he
radiated calm and strength. "We won't talk of Dannow any more
at present," he went on, "but of how you mastered something worse
than the Monster when we first met."

"What could be worse than the Monster?" she demanded, turning in her corner to face him.

"A grown, sane man, on the verge of hysteria. Bless you, Miss
Bartendale, I believe you tried to forget it, for vicarious shame!
There!" he nodded sharply; "you are beginning to recollect—"

"Was it a station?" She was groping, mentally, to fix a hovering
impression.

"Let me tell it. I want to. Yes, a London station. A Red Cross
train unloading. Myself in a corner, all alone and feeling worse
than I ever did before or since in my life—except when I saw poor
Kate, of course."

His voice dropped from the eager note it had taken on. "Never
mind that. Go on," she prompted.

"You see, there'd been a mistake in the wire, and nobody was
there to meet me. Oh, it was poisonous! I'd taken it for a dead cert.
Swan would have been there, spotting my compartment at a hundred yards and sprinting beside it—"

He lowered his voice and almost whispered. "Miss Bartendale,
if men tasted Hell in the years just behind us some of us also learnt
what Heaven will be like. Simply like getting out of the hospital
train straight into the charge of some strong, kind, dependable
woman of one's very own."

Luna's eyes dropped. "And there was no one for you?" she
prompted, in a low tone.

"Nobody," he resumed, quietly again. "I'd kept myself up so
far, but all the life fairly sucked out of the world then. The official
helpers were busy with the really sick chaps, I just stood a bit aside
and the tears ran down my face. In two more breaths I should have
begun screaming. Oh, yes, there was nothing from '14 to '18 to
match not being met when you expected to be. Then somebody
turned and came right out of the middle of the crowd, straight as a

bee to a hollyhock, drove me into a quiet corner, mopped my eyes
with her own handkerchief—that's how I know about the ivy-flower
scent—hid me from public view with her own person—you may have
noticed she's about half as big as I am—put a cigarette in my mouth
and lit it. Holding me stiff all the time with a pair of pale eyes
through which life seemed to run back into the world again and
make it firm and sane. I believe you don't enjoy listening to all
this."

"Go on," she returned hushedly.

"Then she got it all out of me, guessed about the wire mistake,
pointed out it would be a lark to take my people by surprise, made
a raid on another walking case who hadn't anyone to meet him,
compelled us to prop one another, and shoved us into a V.A.D.'s
charge right away. Through the long illness that followed, Miss
Bartendale, the memory of that incident kept me from giving up. I
had something to live for; to trace and thank a small lady with pale
eyes and ivy-flower scent about her."

"Any trifle amuses an invalid," she agreed.

"I did hunt, too, when I got about, but the station people were
all different by that time. Only I always had a feeling we should
meet again."

Then she looked up at him and in that moment she really saw
him, really realised him, for the first time. That's how it happens
in life. He had been in attendance on her since early morning, but
since that early morning she had been absorbed, isolated by her
work, and he had been nothing to her save a person in dire need of
her peculiar services. Now, suddenly, he was no longer an abstraction—a mere unfortunate client—but a living personality. An enormous man outwardly, quiet of manner, sober but genial; with
strong, refined features very like his sister's, and wide-set eyes
nearly as large and beautiful as hers. Behind the outward man a
nature highly strung, proud, affectionate, and emotional with that
appalling form of emotionalism that eats its possessor inwardly,
from his repression of all outer show of it, until it culminates in
some terrible outburst. She understood him suddenly, and through
him his ancestors; those men, decent to the core, who had pined

to death or killed themselves when the Monster was revealed to them.

And there was something more borne on her in that moment of meeting eyes. Something so new to her and so incredible that she thrust the bare idea out of her conscious, formulated thoughts. Only women think in thoughts—not words—in such matters, and her inner mind tossed to her outer a sentence written in one of the root-stories of the world when the bronze sword she had in her bag was new. "Her heart knew him with the knowledge of youth," it said.

"Isn't that Hassocks?" she said hastily. It was bathos, but bathos is in the best taste when an experience of the soul has reached its climax and any attempt to prolong it would vulgarise it.

"Yes, that's Hassocks," Oliver replied. He, too, realised that the commonplace was now the right and becoming note. He also knew that in that moment, in that modern car speeding over an ancient road with mist and the primaeval Downs around, the greatest and commonest of miracles had worked itself without word or touch. To him it was an inevitable, glorious fact, predestined since the world began, to be accepted in a spirit of ecstasy too great for expression. To Luna, with her knowledge, it was a thing most horrible, to be thrust aside in an attempt at rebellious unbelief, the very climax of Dannow's monstrous horror.

Hassocks really hove into view on the cloudy horizon, and Swanhild turned to apprise her of the fact. The *vade mecum* of overtried souls, the commonplace, decreed that they had cut the time close, and the blessed bustle of securing an empty compartment, and footwarmers, and smuggling Roska in, tided Luna over the worst moments of her life.

"You think he's safe for to-night?" Swanhild whispered wistfully.

"I know he is, outside of the hidden room and the vicinity of firs and pines. Send me a wire first thing in the morning, Miss Hammand, and any other time if you think there's anything to report. And don't forget—my address at eleven to-morrow."

Swanhild received the final warning running along the platform. Just as Oliver had expected her to be running by his carriage two years before. Over her head Luna caught his eyes, and knew he was remembering the fact too, and expected her to remember it. She subsided amidst her borrowed rugs and addressed her thoughts severely to the matter in hand.

The hush of the carriage, the hum of speed without and the last of the daylight skimming past the windows, was conductive to thought. With Roska's big head on her knees and the animal's eyes reflecting the perturbation in her loved owner's mind, the whole matter arranged itself in its hideous Fifth Dimensional entirety. Only after a long time the name of a station gliding by apprised her of London's nearness and woke her from abstraction. Noting the dog's sympathetic eye she shook herself impatiently. "Cheer up, old lass! It's only business!" she assured the animal, while she opened the window and scattered the contents of a bulky envelope into the foggy abyss that was London's fringe of outer slums. "Only business," she repeated to her reflection in the mirror as she straightened her hat and touched up her perturbed features in preparation for public exhibition at Victoria.

Once past the barrier she instinctively picked out the bills of the *Evening Post's* afternoon editions:

IS IT A GHOST?
MYSTERIOUS
SUSSEX
OUTRAGE

And

DANNOW OLD MANOR
MYSTERY
INCREASES
LATEST
DETAILS

A lanky young man had got out of another compartment of her train, and was waiting by the bookstall when she reached it. There he tendered a neatly folded copy of the *Post*, surmounted by a tiny bunch of primroses nicely arranged round a little sprig of fir. "Collected at Dannow, in the intervals of gathering ghastly details, dear Witch," he said, grinning.

Luna took the offering dubiously. "You are the prince of impudent dogs; which is euphuistic for pressmen, Tommy," she returned. "We'll go shares in a taxi, and I'll promise to shed a tear when you are publicly executed."

Mr. Thomas Curtis, of the *United Press, Ltd.*, chuckled. "Some journalists deserve hanging all the time, and all journalists deserve hanging some of the time," he agreed; "but all journalists don't deserve hanging all the time, and you've always declared I'm one of the most undeserving. That's why you wired me to cover it for the *Post* directly you learnt Dannow was on the tapis—eh, dear Witch?

"Perhaps; who knows?" agreed Luna, stepping into the cab.

He followed. "Luna," he remarked softly, "may Tommy, the friend of your pigtail days, dissociated from Curtis the special correspondent, ask if you have mastered the Dannow mystery?"

15

"AN ENTIRELY NEW CRIME—"

"Tommy, the friend of my pigtail days, dissociated from Curtis the special correspondent, may ask anything he likes," returned Luna mincingly. "Just let me hear what you've made of the case so far."

He chuckled again. "That sounded like the only Luna of pigtail days. Well, I've made half a column of village interviews. Half col. about Dannow. Quarter col. local bobby's war record. Half col. with clock-time, chronicling your arrival. Half col. interview with you. I phoned it up from Hassocks while you lunched at the moated grange. It's for our Daily to-morrow; front page. Shorter version in our Evening here." He tapped the paper. "Witch, darling, what'll you take to contribute an article, on ghost-chasing in general, to our Weekly on Sunday? Not untold gold, I assume?"

"Not untold Lucile frocks, Pressman, dearest. What's the interview with me like?"

"Simply the customary non-committal tepidities, couched in the customary painfully interviewese English. I did one of the Geddes family—I forget which—on the transport situation in the same style day before yesterday. In the afternoon I collected photos for our Pictorial. Tried to get a snap of the injured girl in bed and bandages (bed and bandages have been a long suit with pictorial journalism since the war) but was rudely repulsed by the Hammand butler. It's been a putrid day for outdoor snaps, but I caught something of you and the afflicted family coming out of the church. I think you want this case kept quiet, dear Witch."

"I want all my cases kept as quiet as is humanly possible, dear Pressman."

"That's why you whistled me up to cover it, as usual. I've got the scoop so pluperfectly to myself that the other rags will be forced to deprecate the whole matter. Thus saving you and the victims no end of Press persecution. As you intended." He grinned at her sideways. "Witch, you can do what kings and premiers sometimes cannot—manipulate the Fourth Estate, but you can't prevent the Fourth Estate knowing it's being manipulated!"

Luna laughed back. "Now, belovedst Witch," he went on, "can you tell me just this: if you have solved the mystery?"

"Belovedst Pressman, if I had I shouldn't tell."

"What if I ferret it out for myself?"

"In the interests of your firm?"

"In the interests of my firm, and our Daily, Evening, Pictorial and Weekly. Not to mention because the Dannow hidden room has intrigued me from my youth up."

"In many of my cases there's something that would make Tommy the ex-ornament of Maudlin sorry if Curtis the Pressman had to report it."

"You *have* learnt something!" he accused triumphantly. The cab had stopped now before a modest little tree-embowered house. Tommy followed her to the door with the rugs and bags. She paused before inserting her latchkey. "Tommy," she said seriously, "I've often been curious to learn the ethics of news-gathering. You are not an unmitigated bounder, what would happen if you got hold of something your birth and upbringing would incite you to hide? What, in that case, of loyalty to your firm?"

He became grave. "I'd stop short if it was an independent search, Luna, but if the firm ordered me to find out anything and it led to unexpected results, birth and breeding would go hang."

The strains of "See the Conquering Hero" floating downstairs intimated that Madame Terentia Yorke was back from a concert. "It was uncommonly good hunting, Luna," she announced, switching round from the piano as her relative entered the drawing-room. She was a big, radiant sort of woman, looking, with her white hair, peachy complexion and black eyebrows, like a girl pretending to be middle-aged. "Item Three missed a train and I stepped into the breach. It ought to take the coals off our minds this quarter. Upon my word, child, you look used up! I've seen the papers, don't tell me you have mastered the Dannow secret!"

"I wish I hadn't!" groaned Luna, shortly. "Of all the horrors—" She dropped limply into a chair. A cat and kitten came from the fireside to climb on her knees, Roska thrust a comforting muzzle into her hand, but she disregarded them all. Madame Yorke, much concerned, came across to her. "Now, Luna, this isn't like you," she protested.

"Home's a place where you do not need to keep up appearances all the time," returned Luna, "and I've had to keep up appearances with both hands since—since I supplied certain missing letters about three this afternoon!"

"Now, honey, you've been overdoing," Madame Yorke cooed, dropping into the northern burr that will out in moments of stress and caresses and soothes an overwrought brain from the ears in-wards. "If you want to tell me about it, do. It generally does you good to talk things over with someone who won't tell, though she can't help. Brooding over anything is the very old Hornie and all his angels—"

"I don't need to be told that, after this afternoon!" Luna snapped with sudden energy. "Oh, what a little rude worm I am—" she added, aghast at herself. "But you got me on the raw, uninten-tionally, there. I want to tell you about it."

"Very well, then." The elder woman's mien changed to one that had cowed American agents in its time. "We'll adjourn the matter till later. It's near dinner time, and as dinner comes but once a day, it's a pity to spoil it. I won't listen to a word, in spite of my devouring curiosity, until I've got you changed and fed and in your right mind. Why, my dear, from the time on the wire you sent me you must have worn your present attire since eight this morning, enough in itself to give anyone nervous prostration!"

Accordingly, it was much later and Luna was her impassive self again when, over the coffee and cigarettes, she set forth the

Hammand secret in its stark hideousness. Familiarity with her housemate's experiences had almost killed the faculty of amazement in Madame Yorke, but over this her eyes opened wide. "How utterly horrible, Luna!" she gasped at the conclusion. "How will you explain to those poor youngsters? Why it amounts to a thousand years of crime—such crime, too! An entirely new one—"

"Not new. Several people have been accused of it in the past. I remember two Sussex cases: one not much later than the Warlock's time, and one in the seventeenth century. There was a trial for it in London thirty years ago, too."

"I was going to say: an entirely new crime for the papers to bill if they learn of it. It's easy to understand why the Warlock killed himself—and your clients' grandfather, too."

Luna shrugged her shoulders. "Those were special cases. Now to ring up Professor Bergstrom about the sword."

It was her economical plan to make other people do her spade-work for her. She burdened her excellent memory with the first rudiments of most sciences, just sufficient to enable her to set her various friends in different walks of learning on the track when she needed information.

"He's tumbling into a taxi to come round," she announced presently. "Would you mind seeing him? I don't feel up to anything more to-night. I think I'll go to bed now. It's barely ten, but this has been a strenuous day, and that hidden room has taken it out of me. I must be growing old."

The other woman looked at her anxiously. "Don't you think, Luna, it's time you gave up your work?"

"I must exercise my talent. You know how many people I've helped where everything else from the Church down was of no use."

"You must exercise your talent. But what if your talent died—? I tell you, Luna, I wish it would. I used to dread the idea, because it would mean my losing your companionship, but now I cannot be so selfish."

"It never will die," Luna answered shortly. "By the way, the professor is to know the sword was found in an old house, nothing more."

For the first time she was sorry her relative knew that a sensitive's power can only be lost through two causes—degrading sin, or that grand passion that sweeps up all powers of soul and brain into itself.

BOOK II
THE MOUND OF THE GOLDEN PIGTAILS

1

TO SUMMON THE WARLOCK

Next morning Luna did not come downstairs until Swanhild's telegram arrived. "They will be round at eleven," she informed Madame Yorke over the breakfast table. "The girl died last night. Inquest to-morrow."

"Oh!" said the elder woman, as though it were past anything but that flexible monosyllable.

Luna shrugged her shoulders. "It had to be, but it was a dispensation of Providence she survived a few hours. Otherwise—well, I've made all safe; unless those poachers get involved. Have you seen the papers?"

"I have, and I'd like to hear you converse in the way interviewers allege you converse with them, Luna. The *Daily Speculum* has a page of photos. One of you accompanied by the afflicted family and the local church, taken in dense fog. Mr. Hammand larger than the sacred edifice; his sister and her fiancé mainly boots and blurs; you a mere smudge marked with a cross; like the fatal spot on the site of a crime. Portraits of the Monster, from effigy and brass. View of local policeman. Both rhymes in heavy type."

"Nice for my clients, eh? It won't be Tommy Curtis's fault if by this hour those rhymes are not being bandied about in city trains and offices, discussed at late breakfast tables all over England, and argued about in coffee houses and bars from Berwick to Southampton. I can only pray that the *Daily Post* may not be moved to offer a prize for the best suggestion as to their exact meaning. Now I'm going out about the Hammands' business until they are due."

There was no inordinately spicy murder or divorce current that week, so, although Curtis had skimmed the cream of it, the late morning and early afternoon editions of all the papers were billing the *Dannow Mystery*, alias the *Sussex Horror*, blatantly. The news of Kate Stringer's death was in the Stop Press columns. When Luna's taxi drew up behind the Hammand car, the maid was engaged in turning away three reporters from the front door. She had to stop and snub them all round while paying the driver, and by the time she entered the drawing room her three visitors had had time to get on intimate terms with her relative.

Oliver was the first to jump up and greet her. He looked uncommonly big in the little room, and uncommonly hale and normal but for the ugly liver-coloured splotch on his temple. His grave, wide-set eyes beamed down on her as he enfolded her hand between his own. "You don't appear the worse for your exertions on our behalf yesterday," he said cheerily. Then the light died in his eyes.

"You've got Swan's wire?" he added.

"I have. It was no more than I expected."

"If I hadn't fought off the thing from myself—" His eyes became absent. They stared into Luna's, unseen by those behind him, with a blank, awakening horror in them, as the morbid thought brooding at the back of his brain came to conscious expression. "You know, Miss Bartendale, the sacrifice must be completed—"

Swanhild's eyes sought Luna's over her brother's shoulder, anxious appeal behind their outer calm.

"That's quite enough, Mr. Hammand," said Luna sharply. "What is done cannot be undone. You are not responsible for the past, but you are for the future. Your duty, therefore, is to help me make sure that no more mischief may be done in time to come, not to waste your strength in useless repinings."

Her words and tone acted like magic on him. He stiffened visibly. Swanhild's eyes brightened, Madame Yorke looked at him, and at her niece at the same time, with the amiably blank expression that indicates acute observation.

"There!" quoth Goddard. "That's what I've been trying to din into your stupid head, Oliver! Perhaps you'll believe me now the omniscient Miss Bartendale has set her seal on it."

"I believed you all right," replied Oliver; "only sometimes one can't live, or think, up to one's beliefs."

"When working to fulfil them one can," declared Luna.

"What of the runes, Mist Bartendale?" Swanhild asked eagerly.

"Patience," Luna smiled at her. "They are still unread, though my Professor sat up all night over them. We consulted the British Museum Keeper of Scandinavian Antiquities this morning. They are a new form, but my authorities agree they approximate to the Flemlose Stone inscription. Which is Danish, of about 700 A.D."

Swanhild looked plainly disappointed. "I thought you said the sword dated back somewhere B.C., Miss Bartendale?" said Goddard.

"The bronze part does. The gold plates are a later addition. Yet I feel in my bones that in that inscription the clue lies. We are to send photos of it to divers savants and—we shall see."

"What about what you are to tell us to-day?" asked Swanhild.

"You shall help with the preliminaries, dear girl, if you'll come with me while my aunt amuses the men for a little while."

"I help you—"

"Exactly." She slipped an arm through the girl's, and turned to the door. "As one of the two remaining descendants of Magnus the Warlock you may be a priceless help. Come, the sooner we begin the sooner your legitimate curiosity will be slaked."

Oliver watched their exit complacently, but Goddard's face was somewhat stern, as it had been all through the interview. He felt he could not utterly trust Luna until her many small mysteries were explained.

In about half an hour the maid summoned all three to Luna's consulting room, for it was understood that the Sensitive had no professional secrets from her relative. The room was a small one, furnished severely with a divan and big desk, bookcases, and chairs that were evidently intended to keep the sitters awake and attentive to business. It was darkly papered, and the London day was a dull one. Swanhild looked uneasy and as nervously expectant as she ever permitted herself to look, Luna was her business self, cool, and quietly aloof. "You have something to tell us?" said Oliver.

"No. I want to learn what you can tell me, after I have put you in a hypnotic sleep."

He stared. "Why, what can I tell you?"

"What the Warlock knew about the Monster, perhaps."

"But I know nothing of what the old chap knew."

"Consciously you don't. Still, you are one of his descendants, your brain is descended from his, and in some nook of it may be hidden the information that will explain much to us."

He blinked, then understanding came to his eyes. "Oh, you'll summon his spirit—"

"I thought I mentioned I haven't the impudence to pry into the next world without invitation. It's what the Warlock's spirit did with the brain that I want to find out. People in hypnosis can sometimes remember what they cannot in a normal waking state."

"Oh, by Jove! I don't quite see your game, Miss Bartendale, but of course I'm in your hands. But must you mesmerise me? It's so—so undignified, you know."

"You are thinking of mountebank public exhibitions. You will only sit in that chair and answer the questions I put to you; as Miss Hammand did just now."

"What?" It was Goddard who almost shouted the questioning exclamation. "Swanhild! You never allowed yourself to be hypnotised?"

"Why not? I simply went to sleep and remembered nothing till I woke."

"Mesmerism is a risky and unreliable process."

He stopped, conscious that—since Swanhild had been hypnotised—it was too late to protest. "My dear chap, Miss Bartendale knows her business," said Oliver reprovingly. "I say, Miss Bartendale, why did you try Swan first?"

"To see if she would serve. She was unable to answer a single question, so I must try you, if you agree."

"I've told you I'm in your hands, under your guidance wherever it may lead."

His voice was round and steady, a scintillating gleam of red shone at the back of his eyes. Luna's shone back, lambently blue.

They stood quietly facing one another, but both felt as though they had jumped up and joined hands, as people might do with a dark and unknown road to be gallantly dared before them. "It will lead back through the ages till we meet the Warlock," she answered.

They were alone for a moment. The glorious isolation passed as she spoke. She waved him to a chair facing the window. "Oblige me by looking at this until further orders, Mr. Hammand," she said. "Now to summon the Warlock through the back of my watch!"

A tense, waiting silence ensued.

2

LEWES MARTYRS AND GOLDEN PIGTAILS

Luna had placed her watch, burnished back up, in Oliver's hand as it rested on his knee. "You shall now see the processes and hear the questions I used with you, Miss Hammand," she observed aside to Swanhild.

Oliver looked at the metal steadily. At the end of four minutes Luna spoke. "How do you feel mow?" she asked.

"A little fagged, Miss Bartendale."

"It's your eyes that are tired," she returned in a casual tone. "How they blink! You have difficulty in keeping them open, I see."

He began to blink violently. "You can close them, but not open them," she went on conversationally.

They closed. "You cannot open them, but try to do so," she purred on.

From the twitching of the surrounding muscles he evidently tried to obey. "I can't do it," he observed, "Yet I'm trying for all I'm worth. It's ridiculous."

"Then we'll end it." She gently fanned his eyelids with one hand, and they opened.

"You made me keep my eyes shut, but you didn't do or ask anything," he said, blinking. "I heard all you said."

"It was only a preliminary test. Now please look me in the eyes and count a hundred."

He complied. "How do you feel now?" she asked. "A bit fagged."

"Of course you do. You can scarcely keep your eyes open. How the lids are twitching!"

(Here his lids began to twitch.) "It's hard for you to keep awake," she proceeded, crooningly. "I see your eyes are closing—they are closed—"

(His eyes closed, and he collapsed limply in the chair.)

"—everything is running away from you—you cannot collect your thoughts—you cannot open your eyes—you are asleep."

And asleep Oliver now appeared to be. She took the wrist of his least injured arm and extended the limb. "You cannot put your arm down," she said, and left it stretched. "You can open your eyes, and can hear, but you must pay no attention to anyone but me."

His eyes opened; their expression was something between that of a sleepwalker and the sightless. They followed her as she stepped to the desk and took up a notebook. "He is an excellent subject," she observed.

"I thought nervy and hysterical people were the best ones," said Swanhild.

"An error. Speak to him, Miss Hammand."

"Are you comfortable, Oliver dear?" she asked. He took no notice.

"I have him in perfect control." Luna smiled at her look of dismay. "He is now in what is known as profound hypnosis. This is exactly the process I followed with you; let us see if he will answer more satisfactorily than you did." She seated herself opposite him. "In a normal state his arm would be tired and shake by now. Put down your arm," she ordered, and he complied. "I want to know what you remember of English History, Mr. Hammand."

She proceeded to ask him many questions, working back from the reign of George V, through the Guelph and Stuart dynasties. Some of the queries were simple, as Swanhild and Goddard could tell, some were beyond their knowledge. The simple ones he answered without hesitation, in a flat voice, the others after more or less consideration. When Charles I was mentioned a flicker of interest came into his eyes. "The Martyr," he said, promptly.

"Very good," Luna assented. "We will go further back. Do you remember Mary Tudor, the Queen?"

"Mary—Mary Tudor? Ah, yes, Bloody Mary. I—I seem to remember—"

He paused uncertainly. "Think about her and her times for three minutes," Luna ordered.

He remained staring blankly before him, his forehead gradually developing wrinkles. At the end of three minutes by the clock he spoke. "I have thought of her."

"And have you thought of Derek Carver?"

She rapped the question out suddenly. He started and sat up rigid. "Derek Carver!" he exclaimed. "Bloody Mary the Queen—and Derek Carver! I know the name. Derek Carver—and something else. Something horrible. A scent—a clean, horrible scent—and heat—and something else horrible. Derek Carver—good Lord, what's the horror about Derek Carver?"

The blankness had given place to unutterable terror in his eyes. Sweat broke out on his forehead; the fingers of his unbandaged hand twitched convulsively; his whole big body shook. He had all the appearance of a man struggling with nightmare or an agonising thought. Swanhild started from her chair to go to him, but Madame Yorke's hand laid on her wrist made her drop back again, trembling a little in sympathy with her brother. Luna's face was set like a mask, her lips folded to a hard line.

"Mary the Queen, Derek Carver," she said.

"I know!" he cried. "A scent—the same scent there was at Streatham when we came up to-day. They were tarmac-ing a by-road. Oh, yes, it was boiling tar—no—burning tar! Burning tar, and burning wood—and people burning. Tar burning, and people burning—Heavens, it is horrible!"

"Forget it and wake!" she ordered, waving her hand lightly past his forehead.

He shut his eyes, shivered, opened them, and stared round, blinking like a man newly roused from sleep. "Really, I feel—" he began, putting his hand to his forehead. "Have I been asleep? I remember now. I looked into your eyes, Miss Bartendale, until they seemed to grow, and fill the world, and swallow me up like a great pale wave. And then I don't remember any more. Only waking."

She opened a big book, where a sheet of foolscap, covered with typing, served as marker; read the sheet down and glanced at a page of the book. "Capital!" she exclaimed, and turned with alacrity. "Look in my eyes again, Mr. Hammand."

He obeyed, and in a few moments sank back asleep as before. "Open your eyes," she commanded. "We go on where we left off."

"Mary Tudor—and Carver—and the tar burning—" He looked at her with growing horror in his expression.

"Mary's gone—forget her!" Luna's voice rang out commandingly. "We have passed to Henry Tudor; Harry of Richmond. Think of Harry of Richmond and a double-handed sword. Of what does that combination remind you?"

"Of Magnus the Warlock keeping the standard at Bosworth."

"Very good; think of Magnus the Warlock. Of what else does his name remind you, beside the big sword?"

"Of lots of things." Oliver was not excited now, he spoke in a quietly considering way. "His tomb, and the hidden room, and the painting—"

"Think carefully, and repeat everything in order as it occurs to you. The tomb makes you think of the hidden room?"

"No, of the portrait. The portrait recalls the room it is in, that room recalls the other room in the same house—the hidden one. And the hidden room recalls what we found there yesterday. The hand and the hilt."

"And of what does the hand remind you?"

He considered a moment. "Of nothing."

"Did it belong to the Warlock?"

"You said you thought so."

"Never mind anything I may have said. Think of the time of Harry Tudor, the Seventh Henry, and Magnus the Warlock who lived in Dannow at the time. Think hard."

Her face was very white now, and the inner corners of her eyebrows were raised and compressed together, as though with mental strain. "What does the hand suggest?" she repeated.

"Nothing," he replied, deprecatingly. "Oh, the bronze sword!"

"Then the bronze sword—of what does it remind you?"

Evidently he was racking his memory. "Of something, but I can't quite grasp what."

She opened a drawer of the desk, took the bronze hilt out of a nest of cotton wool, and placed it in his hand. "Look at it," she ordered. "Feel it, smell it, and tell me of what it reminds you."

Obediently he turned it over, stared at it, and held it to his nose. "I know," he announced. "It reminds me of a scent, of a scent that is in this room."

Even Luna seemed a little astonished. He sat for a moment with his face raised, breathing lightly—as sensible people do when trying to locate a scent—then he rose and marched straight to the desk. There he pointed to a little glass that held Tommy Curtis's stolen offering. "That," he pronounced, with satisfaction. "Pine. That's it, only very big, over my head and all round. A grove of pines. And the sword. Pines and the sword. And something else. Three things altogether. Pines one, the sword, two, and the third—oh, two things really, but exactly alike. Long and thin and shining. Shining."

He stared round in perplexity. "Oh!" he cried, and stepped up to Swanhild. She watched him breathlessly, with dread in her eyes. He pointed to her head. "Hair," he said, triumphantly. "Bright golden hair. Plaited. Two plaits, thick as my arm. Each with a long curl at the end. And near them something else. The sword, the pines, the golden pigtails, and—oh, I remember."

In the air he drew a sign. "A swastika!" exclaimed Luna.

"We called it a different thing," he replied vaguely.

"Fylfot?"

"Yes, fyl-fot."

"And can you read the writing on the sword-hilt?"

"No."

"Do you know what it is?"

"Runes. You told me." He inspected the broken weapon critically. "There's more writing, on what's left of the blade. Under the verdegris."

Luna stared at him and put her hand up to her forehead. A mild look of distress came to his face. "*Sufficit*, Luna," said Madame Yorke, quietly.

Luna pulled herself together. "Sit down again," she commanded, and when he had obeyed she flicked her fingers over his eyelids, and: "Wake! Forget all and wake!" she said.

He woke very quietly, blinking and then looking round with placid interest in his eyes. "You look awfully tired, Miss Bartendale!" he observed with concern.

"I stopped the sitting, as it had gone on long enough," Madame Yorke took on herself to reply. "This sort of thing is wearing to both operator and subject; though they may not realise it at the time; and a woman who owns a clever niece ought to take care of it."

"Quite so!" he agreed, with emphasis. "Let me see, I don't seem to remember anything since your eyes swallowed me up as before, Miss Bartendale."

Now Swanhild found her voice. "Miss Bartendale," she exclaimed, "who told you we both have a mild antipathy to the smell of hot tar?

"Nobody," replied Luna. "I didn't know it. What caused it?"

"It's hereditary, our father and grandfather had it, too."

"Indeed. You knew of it, but didn't know the cause. I found the cause without knowing of it. That antipathy, Miss Hammand, began with the son of the Warlock and the Marian persecution of 1555. While I put my notes in order please give Mr. Hammand an account of what he said in answer to my questions, and then I shall give you a lecture on the science of Ancestral Autobiography as applied to our investigation."

3

ANCESTRAL AUTOBIOGRAPHY

Swanhild's account was full and exact. At the conclusion: "Golden pigtails!" Oliver repeated, and he seemed a little shocked over it.

"Now, in your normal waking state, do you remember anything of them?" asked Luna.

"Only—let me see. Oh, yes, Swan as a flapper. But she only had one."

"The pair were in connection with the sword."

"Then I don't know anything about them."

"The Warlock did. And in a hypnotic sleep you recollected it."

His eyes lit with sudden intelligence. "You mean I'm the reincarnation of the Warlock?"

"Reincarnation, as an explanation of mental phenomena, is as easy and unprovable as Spiritualism," she replied, with a laugh. "I don't deal in easy and unprovable theories. Come, let's get round the fire comfortably, and I'll explain how I tapped your *hereditary memory*.

"The brain is a vehicle for the registering of thoughts, emotions, accidents, encountered by the body or brought into being by the owner's spirit," she began, when they were settled. "Every experience and emotion makes a record of itself in the substance of the brain; records deeply or lightly impressed, according to their importance to the owner of the brain. They cause an alteration in the convolutions of its substance. Some of these alterations are soon obliterated, some last through the owner's lifetime, some will last for centuries—may last to the end of time. Do you follow me?"

"Ye-es," Oliver hesitated. "But, you know, a brain does not last for centuries."

"Its descendants do. Generation after generation. Some experiences—superhuman sorrows or joys, ecstatic religiosity, acute fear—can make a difference in part of the brain so powerful that it is reproduced in the brains of the owner's children, and their children after them, indefinitely."

"I begin to see what you're driving at."

"But hereditary memories, as a rule, lie dormant unless they happen to be awakened by some outer circumstance similar to that in which the original impression was received."

"Jove! I see!" he exclaimed. "That antipathy to the smell of hot tar, now?"

"It is an unconscious memory of when your ancestor, the Warlock's son, was profoundly shocked in heart, soul and brain, when he saw the burning of the Lewes Martyrs in 1555. Scents are the most subtle agents for awaking memory. The scent of hot tar, in your case, awakes a vague, faint sense of mental discomfort, too dim to be even defined as fear or horror, though the cause has been long forgotten. Only in a state of hypnotic sleep, Mr. Hammand, your memory is strengthened so that you can put that cause into definite words. You recognised the flame of one of the men who were burnt at Lewes and at once connected it with burning tar, and exhibited all the symptoms of extreme horror."

"Has that anything to do with finding out about the Monster?" Swanhild put in.

"Everything and nothing to do with it. It was a test, and it has proved I am on the right track. I'll explain, and you will then understand why I have made a minor mystery of this day's work. I laid my plans yesterday, as soon as I learnt you had neither of you ever looked at the pedigree of 1650. On that pedigree are notes respecting the Monster's appearances, and also about notable members of the family. The note about the Warlock's son, Godfrey, states that he turned Protestant in the reign of Mary, being converted by witnessing the terrible death and unshaken constancy of his friend, Master Derek Carver. During luncheon I ascertained that neither of you had even read the names of the Lewes martyrs on their memorial, though you had often seen it in Lewes. I considered that the shock which could make a man of family change his religion in Mary's days might have been profound enough to transmit some echo to his descendants. Accordingly, this morning I phoned the British Museum and ordered a professional 'reader' to find out all about Carver. His *précis* was ready when I called for it; I put it away in that copy of Foxe's *Book of Martyrs*, and read it over *after I had ascertained what you remembered of the matter.* After putting you in trance I so roused your memory of Mary's reign that the mere mention of Carver's name waked a vivid recollection of the martyrdom of your ancestor's friend. I then read the *précis*, and found your recollection remarkably accurate."

"Why didn't you read it before?"

"Because unconscious thought-transference is one of the dangers of this sort of investigation. If I had known all about it I might have unintentionally made you say what I knew myself."

"What had the smell of tar to do with it?" asked Oliver.

"Let us look at the *précis*." She read aloud:

"'Derek Carver, a Flemish Protestant refugee. Settled in Brighton, where he owned and worked the Black Lion Brewery in Black Lion Street. He was condemned for heresy in 1555. Particulars will be found in Foxe's *Acts and Monuments of the Martyrs*. He was executed at Lewes, before the "Star" Inn. Was burnt at the stake, *in a barrel of tar*, his Bible—'"

Both Oliver and Swanhild uttered a simultaneous exclamation of horror. Luna put the paper down. "That's all we need to know," she said gravely. "Yes, it's apparently a far cry from a prosperous Brighton tradesman dying for his faith in the sixteenth century and you youngsters feeling vaguely uncomfortable at the scent of tarmac on a road in the twentieth century, but the connection is direct. I found the connection—and perhaps you begin to understand my methods now?"

Swanhild leant forward, an unusual light in her eyes. "You found that Oliver recollected the incident; when you waked his memory in the right way. It follows you may be able to rouse his memory of what our ancestors knew of the Monster. That's it, isn't it?"

"Exactly," replied Luna. "There are layers of memory, so to put it, and I have worked back to the Warlock."

Oliver leant forward, too, his face acutely eager. "I see all now. What do you say, Goddard? Miss Bartendale knows her business, eh?"

Goddard inclined his head gravely. "I never doubted she did. It was the secrecy I—er—commented on."

"My dear Mr. Covert, don't you understand that yet?" Luna turned to him. "My object is to find what's in Mr. Hammand's memory, not to put ideas into his head beforehand. The Carver test had to be administered without warning. If I had told him of it beforehand, with the best will in the world he would have thought of it until the time came, and would have unconsciously invented particulars to oblige me with. Taking him without preparation I got the plain truth."

"I understand, if Goddard doesn't," declared Oliver sturdily. "Then you worked back and found out I remember something that happened to the Warlock in connection with the sword and a pair of golden pigtails. Now, what on earth could those things mean?"

"I have a faint suspicion, founded on previous researches of my own," answered Luna. "After finding out what we can of the Warlock's contributions to your dormant memory we shall go further back, in search of—never mind what."

"It's marvellous!" he exclaimed. "More wonderful than any tales of magic! Going through a fellow's mind as though one were turning the pages of a book backward. I say, Miss Bartendale, the Warlock met the Monster. That must have impressed him as much as Carver's death did his son."

Luna shook her head. "The task is not going to be so enviably easy. He died a few days after the meeting, and all his children were born some years before that. An idea cannot be passed on unless it is in the parent's mind before the child is born."

"Oh, I see. You must work back until you reach someone who learnt about it before his kids were born."

"It looks like it. The task will take some time, for an hour a day is as long as I care to keep anyone in hypnosis. Therefore I hope you will afford me one hour a day for a few days to follow."

"You have to command. Every day we'll run up until further orders."

"I am of no use?" said Swanhild.

"Apparently not, and I am sorry."

"It seems curious," said Oliver. "You'd think a woman's more sensitive mind would hold impressions best."

"A normal woman's mind isn't more sensitive than a normal man's. It only seems so because a woman is physically more highly strung. In the present case the explanation is simple. Hereditary memory, like other hereditary traits, sometimes plays tricks, often lying dormant for a long time, and often only showing full development in one person in every generation. Like the extra finger or singular teeth in some families. However, Miss Hammand, you have something to do to help the work. In old houses like yours one never knows what may turn up after diligent search. I want you to dragoon every lumber room, chest, and drawer in your home, in search of old papers. I learnt from the MSS. you showed me yesterday that the great *savant* and astrologer Nicholas Culpeper investigated the Monster in 1651; he may have written a report, and some scraps of it may be extant."

Swanhild brightened. "There's any amount of lumber rooms," she said.

"Very good. Now we have a threefold search going on: you ransacking the manor, several savants combing out Scandinavian archæology, I turning Mr. Hammand's mind inside out. To-morrow I shall be down at Dannow."

Oliver brightened. "I want to hear what's said at the inquest," she explained. "And I hereby declare the session closed, it is near the witching hour of two, just time for a cigarette and a change of subject before lunch. Whatever we do we must avoid mental staleness or over-brooding in this work."

4

"AARON'S GOLDEN CALF—IN SUSSEX"

The next day saw the public interest in Dannow in spate. Although Curtis had made such a scoop of it, it was too rich and varied for other pressmen to neglect. Freelance journalists resuscitated old articles on ghostly matters from the "rejected" drawers of their desks, and sold them at once. Junior reporters put in a spare hour in the nearest reference library, and amassed enough information during it to publish authoritative articles on Black Masses, Magic, Elementals, Family Banes, and the like, and sign them:

"By a Well Known Occultist," or "By a Distinguished Psychic Expert." And the current specimen of the *Daily Post's* celebrated brand of serials introduced a chapter obviously founded on the Thunderbarrow Shaw happenings into that day's instalment.

Dannow district was overrun with pressmen, morbid curiosity-mongers, souvenir hunters—who hacked all the bark off the beech and the oak on which the dog's body had struck—amateur detectives, and misguided individuals who mistook a degenerate taste in the gruesome for occult gifts. The Hammands were pestered in their own grounds by would-be interviewers and Oliver received fourteen requests for contributions on the subject of his family traditions from various periodicals and a cable from New York offering an incredible sum for a photograph of the hidden room.

These matters Swanhild imparted, indignantly, to Luna when they met her at Hassocks. Directly after, while Oliver spoke to the stationmaster, she added a rapturous whisper. Oliver turned and smiled at her indulgently. "I didn't need to hear what you said, Swan," he observed. "You were telling Miss Bartendale I'm very well and cheerful considering. Did you mention that you spent the night on my doormat?"

"Where is the inquest to be, Mr. Hammand?" asked Luna.

"The Hammand Arms, at Lower Dannow." His face clouded. "I'd actually forgotten why you've come, for a minute."

"Come, come, no useless brooding!" she chided. "You can help it."

"I can. Only I feel so indecently happy when I let myself go. And when I think of Kate—and poor Warren—" he ended indecisively.

Dannow suggested an *al fresco* motor and cycle exhibition. The late war, and press exploitation thereof, has much increased that class of humanity that takes its pleasure in gloating over the details of other people's sordid crimes or revolting accidents, and it was well represented; together with reporters, spiritualists, and other concomitants of an incomplete world. Oliver smuggled his party in by devious back lanes to the disappointment of a double line of cameras and three cinema operators. The proceedings were little more than formal, as the police wished to follow up the customary clue. A rumour that Miss Bartendale, the renowned psychic expert, would give evidence, proved erroneous. Luna followed the proceedings behind the shelter of a veil that did not allow anyone to judge if they really interested her. She sat next to Warren, who was as inscrutable until the Ades appeared.

The jury looked more or less unwell after viewing the body. No overt reference was made as to the possibility of a supernatural explanation of the tragedy, beyond a short speech at the start, in which the coroner bade the jury dismiss from their minds certain absurd rumours that were current. The circumstances with which they were concerned were very material, he pointed out, and to these circumstances attention must be confined.

The doctors concerned ascribed death to the injuries. Deceased was never in a fit state to give an account of what happened. In delirium she constantly raved of "something as big as a house" that she imagined was attacking her. The injuries were the result of an attack by some large animal. The wounds were too badly mauled to afford any data with respect to the assailant's formation of jaw. They might possibly have been inflicted by a very large dog. Dr. Newton disposed of the idea that Mr. Hammand's dog might have been responsible for them. He had examined the animal's body, and it had not swallowed anything but a dog biscuit for some time before death, whereas the injuries—

These injuries, coldly detailed, afforded a big sop to the public love of sensation. Swanhild described the finding of the girl. Oliver gave a brief account of his experience, merely stating that he felt something approach in the dark, fought blindly, and fell. Cross-examined by a sporting farmer on the jury he said the mastiff barked in a friendly way when near the girl, his memory of what ensued was confused—it *might* have warned him of the assailant's coming.

Will Cladpole described the unnatural noise he had heard from the Shaw, and how he had summoned Swanhild. He was succeeded by the Ades.

They were the most interesting witnesses to those who held to a material explanation of the affair. Warren paid the closest, un-friendly attention to every word and look of the two. In two days he had gone down to skin and bones; his face reminded Goddard of youthful ideas of Eugene Aram, and he watched the brothers with a fixed gaze under which they very soon came to dire confu-sion. They were a pair of ordinary, hulking country louts, incapable of lying with conviction, and had made the mistake of concocting an edited account of the night's doings in order to discount the seriousness of their poaching arrangements. In consequence they were soon involved in a web of counter-statements, and the coro-ner found it necessary to caution both. They were dismissed after making a very bad impression, and the inquiry was adjourned for ten days.

The manor party waited in the landlady's private sanctum while the first press dispersed. Luna stared silently through the window overlooking the road, until the Ades passed and loiterers peered and pointed after them. "A factor in the problem, those two," she said, meeting Oliver's inquiring look.

"You surely don't think they—" He stopped, astounded.

"I don't, but the police and population seem to entertain different ideas. Well, that I can't help, for the time, though I know those fellows were not the agents of the Undying Monster."

"Then why don't you clear them?" asked Swanhild.

"Because to reveal anything about the Monster's Fifth Dimensional nature at present will benefit nobody and ruin all my plans. Unless they are officially accused I decree silence."

"They're my tenants—" began Oliver.

"Exactly, but they're not mine, thank goodness! I cannot produce my evidence at present, but when I can—" She shut her mouth firmly, and the others knew better than to ask any more questions. From the window could be seen the Beacon; a number of people, daring in daylight and company, were swarming up it. "What was that tale about Thunder's Barrow you referred to, Mr. Hammand?" she asked suddenly.

Oliver looked at Goddard. "Oh, I know," said Goddard. "It's nothing to do with the Monster though, Miss Bartendale. Merely a vague yarn about Aaron's Golden Calf being buried in it."

"Aaron's Golden Calf?" repeated Luna. "In Sussex?"

Oliver nodded. "Why not? You never know what you'll find if you scratch the surface of our extensive and peculiar county of Sussex. They found a sky-blue skeleton in Beeding Level, a canoe left over from the Flood at Northiam and a solid amber teacup of the time of Adam at Hove; not to mention the pre-Adamite person—half a jawbone and a Christian name, according to the papers—at Piltdown."

"Some people say the Golden Calf is in the Trundle over Goodwood racecourse," Goddard supplemented. "I'm sure our Barrow's a more respectable situation."

"I didn't know you knew so much before, Goddard," said Swanhild.

"I had seven years' start of you. You came too late for the local fun. In cottages now the main talk is about Sunday paper scandals and football competitions; in my kidhood I've spent priceless hours listening to old folk chat about ghosts and buried treasure, smuggling, and hanging in chains."

Luna seemed to wake out of a reverie, and asked: "If a golden figure is there, why has nobody secured it?"

Goddard chuckled. "Because the Poor Man shifts it out of reach if anyone digs. 'Poor Man,' Miss Bartendale, is polite Sussex-ese for the Enemy of Mankind. It's nothing to help you, I'm afraid."

"Perhaps not," she assented. "Only I'm by way of being an expert in traditions, and this is a curious one. Aaron's Calf—in Sussex. It's a queer combination, and the more *outré* a tradition is the more the expert wonders what originated it. To-morrow we will have the second sitting."

5

"TO OPEN THUNDER'S BARROW"

For many ensuing days the Dannow mystery continued to reign paramount in public interest. After the inquest the Monster's victim was buried, next day photographs of the ceremony were in all the papers. By the end of the week publicity reached high-tide mark, and for the first time in living memory Dannow Church had to be locked in daylight; the Warlock's tomb having been disgracefully chipped by relic hunters and the whole building littered with the cigarette ends, matches, odd papers and other trade marks of the travelling masses. Every day Swanhild had two anxious times. The first every morning, between waking and her first sight of Oliver. Oliver's matutinal greeting became a formula:

"When I remember what's under the bump on my brow I'll tell you, old thing, but I don't at present."

The other was during each sitting, while she waited with silent dread what Luna's questions would elicit. Oliver was in excellent spirits, except when he happened to remember the other victim, and when they went up to London it was usually late before they returned, owing to his frank unwillingness to tear himself away from the Yorke–Bartendale abode. What was left of the day was invariably spent in ransacking every nook of Dannow, though at first they found nothing relating to the business in hand.

On Thursday, Luna, after putting Oliver in hypnosis, concentrated his attention on the bronze sword, of which she still had charge. She endeavoured to learn if he remembered anything of the inscription he had declared was on the blade. He said he could not remember it, but was sure it existed. She showed him photographs of various runic scripts, but he could recognise none.

On Friday Luna came to Dannow, with the hilt, and held the sitting in the hidden room. She led him very carefully back to the Warlock's time, and gave him both hand and hilt to examine. He remembered quite suddenly that the blade belonging to the hilt lay near the pigtails and fylfot, measured the length of it along his arm, and said it was leaf-shaped and green with verdegris. She made no comment.

It all seemed foolish and futile. Only Swanhild knew that behind the apparent futility Luna was working towards some end that was perfectly visible to the keen brain behind the diamond eyes and golden curls. Swanhild's trust was implicit, but essentially personal. In Luna's presence an atmosphere of normal life, of steady work towards some seen goal, braced her, but away from the other woman's influence the subconscious sense of abnormal horror brooding over Dannow and keeping its shadow over her brother and herself—the last Hammands—settled down immovably. Oliver did not reason about anything he simply surrendered himself to what he regarded as marking time until Luna should be ready to reveal her purpose. He was content to wait, nobody mentioned the dead girl in his hearing if possible, and he had the supreme happening of any lifetime to occupy his head and heart.

Goddard's feelings were tinged with a distrust that induced the persistent feeling of a pause before some tremendous happening; like the hush before a storm.

On Saturday Swanhild and Oliver came to Chelsea very early. Oliver with the stain of the bruise—which had been liver colour the day before—suddenly faded from his temple; Swanhild in a state of suppressed excitement.

"Well?" asked Luna. "Something's up?"

"A reference to the Monster and Nicholas Culpeper's signature!" answered Swanhild, producing an envelope and tenderly extracting two fragments of thick paper, frayed and yellow with age. With some difficulty Luna read the faded words on them.

"'. . . *that the Hammands are of a breed vampyrish, and if one be slaine prematurely he shall goe to neither Heaven nor Hell, but live unnatural in ye grave . . .*'—that's important, Miss Hammand! And, let me see '. . . *your most afft, frd, Nick. Culpep. . . .*' This is priceless. Where were they?"

"In the seat of an old chair. There was a tear and a bit of the stuffing poking out."

"Some handy and economical ancestor of ours must have done the job himself, for there's three chairs and a sofa all stuffed with written papers," Oliver supplemented.

Luna restored the scraps to their shelter. "The misery for which economy has always been responsible!" she sighed. "Are there any more pieces of this sheet, Miss Hammand?"

"We don't know yet. There's five clothes baskets full already of what we got out of one chair and the sofa. It's all in scraps and, as the furniture was stored where the roof leaks, a lot of it is in lumps almost like *papier mâché*. Goddard has stopped behind to try and separate some of it; he spotted the signature first, and we found the other bit when we split a lump. We're going back early to examine the rest of the disused furniture."

"Kindly speak for yourself, Swanhild," interposed Oliver. "You promised Goddard to go hunting, but I'm otherwise engaged."

"Otherwise engaged?" repeated Swanhild.

"My dear girl, you don't seem to understand that these sittings are a great strain for the principals. You looked utterly used up yesterday, Miss Bartendale. I'm sure you need a half-holiday as badly as I do myself, so I've booked stalls for *Chu Chin Chow* this afternoon. You mentioned you are one of its votaries. I knew it was no use asking you, Madame Yorke, you told me yesterday you have a concert on to-day."

Luna consulted an engagement book. Her aunt answered drily, "I distinctly remember you asking me yesterday if I had any engagement for to-day, Mr. Hammand."

Oliver looked her in the eyes and grinned winningly. Her own mouth twitched, but she straightened it and turned her gaze on

Luna, who was studying the book intently. "You booked stalls, Oliver?" said Swanhild.

"There's such a thing as a telephone. Now, Swan, you know you can't keep your eye on me for every minute of the rest of our lives! You mean well, but it's getting on my nerves a bit. You don't suppose we stopped at Clarkson's to get my eye toned down just to go and grub in an attic, do you? Miss Bartendale will take care of me, and pack me off to Victoria for the 6.30—that is, if you can spare the time to help me with my holiday, Miss Bartendale."

Luna announced that she could spare the time. Madame Yorke obviously dissembled surprise and disapproval. Swanhild remained silent after her half-hinted protest: she was used to the men of her family having their own way for good or ill. Luna checked Oliver's simple rejoicing over her acceptance by switching on her professional manner and ordering a move to the consulting-room. The sitting that day was short, and the net result was a repetition of Oliver's previous description of the missing blade, and his recollecting that the runic inscription on it was sunk in a meandering band.

A letter postmarked Dublin awaited Luna on her return that afternoon. "Luna, why did you go with Mr. Hammand?" demanded her aunt, over the dinner table.

"Auntie, am I the woman to decline a proffered bite of a child's sugar-stick?"

"You aren't, normally, the woman to trifle with anyone's feelings."

"If I had refused to accept this little attention from Mr. Hammand, when I tell the truth he would think I avoided him—"

"You should. That poor lad is the kind to take things hard, for all his stolid exterior."

"That's it. He's taking that girl's death hard; subconsciously, all the time." Luna flushed, then paled, as she saw in her mind's eye a picture of some hours before. The interior of a taxi speeding from His Majesty's, murky London outside, Oliver's eyes sparkling as he told her he was almost grateful to the Monster, then clouding with pity and horror and self-reproach as he added— "if it wasn't for Kate!"

"You have to tell him some time," the elder woman pursued. "After the sittings. My dear, do you fancy I haven't noticed how he gets you into a corner and plants his sister and Mr. Covert on me? And do you imagine Miss Hammand does not notice it either? She's only too thankful for anything that diverts his mind. She told me as much."

"This is a new departure for you, Auntie. As you are the sort of woman to whom all males are 'boys' from the newly-born tom kitten to the human grandfather, you don't suffer girls gladly as a rule—"

"I don't suffer the new sort of girl—who apparently takes Tony Lumpkin as her model—but Miss Hammands an old-fashioned young thing. You have her feelings to consider, as well as her brother's."

Luna smiled mockingly. "Love, hunger, and regard for other people's feelings are the most powerful motives in human nature, eh, Auntie?"

"Don't quibble, Luna. To put off telling them much longer would be the bitterest refinement of cruelty."

"Business is sometimes cruel to be kind. However, as there was the first spasm of a loathsome murder in the papers to-day, and to-morrow is Sunday, our investigation moves on a stage towards explanation."

"Luna!"

"The two facts mean that the Hammands' private affairs will interest the public less the day after to-morrow, and on it Dannow should be fairly free from sightseers. Accordingly I shall wire my clients not to come up to-morrow, and write to warn them to have a gang of labourers ready on Monday morning. Then I purpose to open Thunder's Barrow in search of what I hope to find there. Will you come with me? I must oversee the opening from the first sod, and it may take more than one day. I know our young friends have been urging you to urge me to take you down for a country visit. No, that is not a sudden freak. My Irish savant has read the gold runes, and in the Barrow something I want may be waiting."

6

CHURCHYARD MOULD

The early train had just disembarked Madame Yorke, Luna, Roska, and a pile of luggage on Monday morning when Oliver and Swanhild arrived at Hassocks. "Luna warned you in her letter that we fear we shall have to inflict ourselves on you for the night, Miss Hammand," the elder lady said. "She thinks the digging may last all day."

"With ca' cannyism pervading life it may take several days at least," replied Oliver, with conviction. "Goddard is drumming up labour, in accordance with your instructions, Miss Bartendale. Isn't it all rather sudden?"

"It's a job to be done and done with before the workers have time to talk about it. I'll explain in the car."

It had snowed a little, hailed a little, and rained a great deal the previous day, but this morning had turned out mild and muddy. A delicate vapour eddied about near distances in the low-lying Weald, made subtle mystery of the road fore and aft, and clung in shredding lumps in the bare hedges on either hand. Swanhild was at the wheel, Oliver in the tonneau with the elder visitor, leaning forward to join in the conversation. Luna, nestled back in her corner beside Swanhild, could see both faces, and beyond Oliver her relative. Madame Yorke was beautifully null and politely interested in whatever was under discussion.

"Any more Culpeper fragments turned up?" asked Luna.

"Goddard thinks he has spotted some in one of the sodden balls," replied Swanhild. "He's taken it home to steam it; he's awfully good at things like that."

"Capital. How are you off for visitors?"

Oliver almost groaned. "It was putrid yesterday. Some perishers of charabanc owners ran special trips from Brighton, and we were overrun with sightseers of a peculiarly noisome sort. By a dispensation of providence the weather was a caution, and so far we have not been worried to-day."

"Cap-i-tal. We don't require an audience; though there's no real mystery about the present move. We are simply going to look for something the Warlock may have left in Thunder's Barrow when he ransacked it."

She placidly surveyed their wide-eyed amazement. "For this matter hidden in the past we have to rely on that tricky jade Circumstantial Evidence," she proceeded. "Let us reconstruct a little local history. Your ancestor—Magnus Hammand's Son—was buried in the barrow, and with him his most cherished personal belongings were also interred, in the Danish way. Seven centuries later his descendant, heir of his name and possessions, Magnus the Warlock, decided to get those personal treasures as well. He made the Hand of Glory, dug into his rude forefather's tomb, and took what valuables he found. Only I hope and think he left behind the most precious article, the bronze blade with the inscription. Four hundred years later you, the descendant of Magnus Hammand's Son by way of Magnus the Warlock, are going to open the tomb again in search of the blade. That's all."

"But how do you make it out?" asked Oliver blankly.

"When Mr. Covert told us of the Golden Calf and the way it is supposed to be guarded I began to have suspicions of the Barrow and also of the Hand of Glory. Hand and tradition illustrated one another, for most traditions have a substratum of truth. Look at Washington, a hamlet you may know as it's not a dozen miles west of your home. From time immemorial it had a tradition of a long bearded ghost haunting a particular field, and awhile ago a hoard of Saxon pennies was unearthed in that field, buried a thousand years before by some long-bearded Saxon. The Warlock was an alchemist, by token of the books in the hidden room, and alchemists are a gentry who require much solid gold to aid in preparing a little of the phantom variety. He made the Hand of Glory, no doubt to stupefy the diabolical guardian of the Barrow's treasure. In the sword hilt we have one specimen of the gold he found there."

"By Jove, that's plausible!" declared Oliver.

"Only I've always understood the Barrow was ancient British, and connected with the Druids and their god the Monstrous Man," demurred Swanhild.

"When in doubt early archaeology always blamed everything to the Druids," replied Luna. "The name of the place gives its secret away in these days of more advanced knowledge. It is not the only Thunder's Barrow in the world. Thunder is an obvious corruption of Thor. Your ancestor was a pagan, a worshipper of Thor, and the Monstrous Man is an image of that god. He had it hewed in gratitude when his god cast his lot in the fair ground of Sussex, or else to guard his barrow when he was buried in it. Now, when I waked your memory connected with the Warlock and the broken sword, Mr. Hammand, you described the sword as being in company with golden plaits and a *fylfot*. Just what the Warlock may very well have found in the grave of a Danish chieftain."

"Those pigtails!" exclaimed Oliver.

"Precisely. No doubt they made you think of a woman, but Viking chieftains wore long hair and plaited it. And the *fylfot* is the symbol of Thor."

"My hat!" said Oliver simply.

"Stilt, I don't see the connection with our ancestor," Swanhild objected.

"Miss Bartendale does," reproved the loyal Oliver.

"And Miss Bartendale's going to explain the clinching connection she received last night," said Luna. "A Dublin savant has read the runes on the hilt. They run: '*I am named Helm Biter, my master is Magnus Fairlocks, Son*—' The rest is too rubbed to be legible. The runes on the blade may be better preserved."

"Jove!" said Oliver, in admiration that verged on awe. "Are you certain the inscription is so important?" asked Swanhild.

"It must be, since the memory of it has survived in Mr. Hammand's mind."

The car had turned north now, mounted, and slid through Thunder Barrow Gap. There was more wind in the heights, and the air was clearer, but the valley was full of mist and the rivulet invisible. Chalk has tricky ways, and by some atmospheric cantrip the Monstrous Man glowed like a pink ghost while nearer features were murky in mist like shredded black gauze. Goddard now met them, as he walked from the village, he greeted them with a wry grin, climbed in and advised a move for the Shaw.

"For we'll jolly well need every minute we can snatch, Oliver," he said. "I've only been able to collect a very scratch gang, and it's going to start for home half an hour before sunset. Hornblower is bringing Old Moore and the German watch his son looted to time the exodus. It's no use expecting local men to hang round the Shaw after official dusk."

"I didn't think of that," said Luna. "I'm not omniscient. How many men are there?"

"Four. Hornblower, who's the village atheist and professes no belief in anything but Bob Blatchford. He's coming because he has to prove he doesn't believe in the local spook. Our new gardener, an ex-boy scout. A labourer just come home from bettering himself in London and ready to do anything. These are coming on a cash basis, Warren, the chap you met in the Shaw, is coming for recklessness."

"Only four?" said Oliver. "Did you say I wanted them?"

"I did, Lord of the Manor, and the village practically downed feuded allegiance about it. Luckily my four are a hefty lot, also my bought and paid for arm is one of the best, and Swanhild is a garden maniac. You can reckon six spades. Am I to understand the object of it all, Miss Bartendale?"

Luna rehearsed her explanation while Swanhild drove carefully along the valley. "There's points I don't seem to understand," he commented. "If the Warlock went for gold alone, why did he keep the hilt hidden away, instead of using it with the rest of his loot? And simply meddling with the Barrow doesn't seem to explain his dying reference to the room, and the pardon. From what I've heard of them necromancers can't have reckoned grave-robbing much of a crime."

"These are points *I* don't understand," replied Luna. "I only know I'm going grave-robbing with an object myself. Oh, I know what you are thinking, Mr. Covert—it isn't nice to disturb the grave of Mr. Hammand's ancestor without even the chaperonage of an exhumation order."

He reddened guiltily. "It doesn't matter what anyone thinks as long as I am satisfied," Oliver interposed in the slow, masterful way he rarely indulged in. "It's my ancestor, my land, and my Bane."

They reached the end of the road here, descended, and walked through the Shaw to the Barrow. Though lower lying ground was sodden that day the close grown Downland turf of the mound was firm to the foot. The view from the top was all very grey, Luna's curls and Swanhild's, the brightest spots in sight, and after them the glowing Monstrous Man on his grey-green slope. The Shaw was darkly menacing, the edge of the hill, where it steeped down abruptly beyond the Barrow, suggested a coastal cliff with the mist that filled the Weald below lapping, sealike, a little beneath its overhanging turf rim. Only the sea of mist bore a muffled silence, unlike the sounding silence of the real sea. The eye, ranging dazed and flinching over its immensity could not tell where it merged in the uncoloured sky; only now and then some trick of wind in the higher atmosphere allowed a glimpse of Chanctonbury's crest, away to westward, and Wolstanbury's to east. The hoot of a motor came from some road hundreds of feet down in the mist, like the syren of a far-off ship.

The Barrow was unnaturally even in contour, only a slight depression ran down one of the long sides, near the end, facing the Man, with three small firs and a stunted yew in it. Luna hitched one end of a ball of white twine to one of the firs and walked round, paying it out on the ground, until she had marked a circle about fifteen feet across, including the four trees and the middle of the mound. By that time the workers put in an appearance. Hornblower deposited his watch and almanac on a stone, and all set to work to dig within the circle. The remainder of the forenoon was spent mainly in grubbing up the four trees.

At the men's dinner hour Swanhild and Goddard took a turn with the spades, while Luna, who could drive a car when she chose to exert herself, Madame Yorke and Oliver went to the manor for lunch and brought them a basket back. It was getting on for three when the men struck chalk.

Not natural chalk, but chips and knobs of it packed and tamped down as flat as a floor. Hornblower, working where the small trees had been, straightened himself to look round and then spaded up some soil from in front of him. "Summut tejus queer here, sir," he said to Oliver. Where the depression had been the regularity of the made chalk floor was broken by a patch of mould, and the spadeful of it the man held up was very black and fat, unlike the light-coloured virgin earth they had cleared off the chalk. Warren inspected it and said it was like the pocket of rich, much worked soil where the village stood. "And it never grew her by Natur'," he added. "Someone must ha' started a garden and then buried it."

Oliver stood on the edge of the cutting and frowned down at the hole. "A pocket of black mould put where the chalk's been broken through," he said, as though to himself. Then he put his hand to his temple, where the bruise, shorn of Clarkson's aid, was still a liver coloured splotch. "I seem to know—where have I seen it? Oh, to be sure, at a funeral! Of course—it's churchyard earth! Consecrated soil, put there to— Now what the deuce was it put there for?"

7

GOLDEN CALF AND DRAGON SHIP

"Oliver! Don't be beastly!" exclaimed Swanhild.

He started and blinked. "Eh? Good Lord, what was I saying? It just jumped out," he declared contritely.

All the men hesitated, save Warren. He elbowed Hornblower aside and began to spade up the black soil. There was but a little pocket of it, soon he was shovelling up chalk chips once more. The others set to work again.

"Superintending is chilly work," said Luna. "You might take us to see the Man and the rest of the place, Mr. Hammand."

Oliver, looking extremely dazed, accompanied the guests up the slope and the stripped chalk path, edged with brick, that was the Monstrous Man's left leg. "Whatever made me say that?" he demanded ruefully. "It seemed to slip out. Churchyard mould—my hat! I must have been rotting!"

"You were not. It's probably churchyard mould, and sudden memory of the fact woke in your mind at sight of it. I have been rousing your inherited memory so much of late that it must now be in a state of extreme activity."

"But what could churchyard earth be doing there?"

"Consecrated soil is supposed to possess some occult virtues, and there is something sinister about that Barrow. It may have been more than gold that the Warlock went after."

They did not talk very much while he conducted them over the Beacon's sights; the earthworks with the Roman mounds over them and the full dewpond and its sparse fringe of trees. Finally they returned to the bared flint platform, near fifty feet across, that was the Monstrous Man's head.

It was indescribably spacious. The Weald a far flung map; trees and roofs dizzily tiny down below the rim of the Beacon, beyond, long blue distances and shadows moving over it all from the vast grey and silver clouds that drove over the clear blue of the sky. The Downs past Dannow were black with the shadow of one, and cut the horizon as a billowy line of greenish-black, with the church and cottages crude against their bulk, like coloured paper figures glued on a backing of dusty black velvet.

Then the main body of clouds forged onward, and the shadow on the Downs slid to the middle distance, and left the top ripple of the uplands above it a wavering band of impossibly bright greens and unbelievable yellows and fawns, where turf and ploughland alternated, with an amazingly white scratch of road pouring down a gap and losing itself as a dim suggestion of a grey line in the shade below; like a silver ribbon hanging down in a turgid pool. Luna, leaning back against the wind that poured over the Beacon top, looked silently with level brows and wide eyes and found the airy splendour of it beautiful to the point of pain. Oliver glanced from the distant earth and enclosing sky and down the Monstrous Man's long perspective to the Shaw. In its semi-circle of trees the Barrow was plain to be seen, the chalk of the digging dull white, Swanhild's wool jumper a brighter white, the five men little black figures. Then he looked round at Luna, and her gaze turned from the calm contemplation of spaces past space to find his eyes intro-spective and distended with flinching contemplation of something without any bounds of space.

"It's all happened before!" he exclaimed breathlessly. "Sky and Downs, and the Barrow with little people working on it, and a golden-haired woman somewhere about! Only the people were building, not digging. And I was there, just as the sky and Downs and big clouds were."

"Another memory-wave," she replied. "The Barrow was piled by your ancestor, who sailed from Denmark twelve centuries ago,

and wasted the country and married Edith the Saxon. Hereditary
memory again."

"Oh, it doesn't matter what you call it. I know I was here long
ago, with a golden haired woman. And I'm here again. And you are
seeing our Sussex in more favourable circumstances, as I said you
ought to!"

He said the last sentence with a sheepish suddenness, as though
ashamed of his vehemence. The shame was but momentary, for he
looked to the Downs again and went on: "Oh, it's a country worth
fighting for! A country one can be happy in—and it's all mine, from
the Barrow to the Manor woods. My people have owned it and lived
on it for over a thousand years. They fought at need, and died at
need, for it. Even the Warlock did his share to stop the War of the
Roses and earned the right to it afresh. My father and brother died
for it, I've fought for it myself, and surely I've the right to be happy
in it. Yes, even with that bestial Monster shadowing life!"

He spoke with a curious defiance, so subtly mixed with joyous-
ness that it could not be told where one quality merged into the
other, and even in the daylight the red sparks flamed at the back
of his eyes. For the first time Madame Yorke broke the pleasant
silence she had kept since they stopped. "We all have the right to
be happy in this fine world," she said gently. "So far as our heri-
tage from the past, our own wrongdoings, circumstance, and the
woes of our fellow-mortals, will allow."

"Our fellow-mortals? You mean Kate—" he began, his voice
leaping to a note of protest that was almost shrill.

"Don't harp on that, for heaven's sake!" she protested. "Hasn't
Luna told you you are in no way to blame for that?"

"The sacrifice—if I hadn't fought it off—" He stopped, defiant
again. "But you said it was ancestral sin, a thing of the dead past."

"There's nothing so actively alive as the dead," Luna replied, a
blank sombreness in her eyes. "When I conjure up a mental picture of humankind it takes the form of a great round plain; the
present world, covered with its fifteen hundred millions of solid,
living folk. And behind them—mistier and dimmer the further one

strives to look—are the figures of the billions of people of the past. These are impalpable, yet extend hands that reach and grasp the living people grown from them, and guide them with power almost resistless both for good or evil. Clouds of people of the past; clouds beyond clouds I see them—the dead whose very essence, the fruit of their deeds and thoughts and words, lives in us, the living."

She shivered, as though with sudden cold. "Do you believe we are only reflections of our ancestors?" asked Oliver.

Luna roused herself. "Oh, no, and you must never let yourself think that, Mr. Hammand! We human beings are threefold. One part is hereditary, the result of what our ancestors did and thought; one the result of the circumstances in which our lives are spent; and the third the spark of Himself God puts in us all—the personality. The personality through which, by God's grace and our own effort, we can either rule hereditary and circumstance, or else rise superior to them. If I did not believe this, Mr. Hammand, I should not be here, desecrating the Barrow in which your ancestor is buried to find the secret that empowered your hereditary Bane to have power over his guiltless descendants."

"That's so." He agreed absently, for his attention had wandered, while she talked, to the Barrow. "Miss Bartendale, you said some time ago that old Magnus the Dane probably killed all Edith's people. I'm sure you were wrong there."

"Really? I cannot picture a Viking chief getting permission to marry a Saxon lady unless he killed her protectors first."

"Oh, I know. He loved her so—so largely that he made them take him as a friend because she did."

"I can still less picture a Dane suspending his pirate operations long enough to conduct a courtship."

"It didn't take long. They only needed a little while to understand each other. Only a few days—Monday to Monday, inclusive. I know it."

A little pink overspread the delicate pallor of Luna's cheeks. He looked quickly away from it.

"I'm talking like a fool," he said. "I don't know what you'll think of me, for I scarcely know what I'm thinking, myself, at times! I've been so happy the last few days, and it doesn't seem quite right. It seems too beautiful to last, and too callous with poor Kate—I'm sorry! Only I think I've just realised life's worth living, and my ancestors have been making this bit of land for me to live in and be happy in—happy as Magnus the Dane was when he came here and realised that life was worth living at last. I know he did that; it's come all over me just now, up here standing beside the god he carved in gratitude for the gift of a bit of Sussex to be happy in and his destined woman to be happy with him. Do you think I'm crazy?"

Luna hesitated, then replied in her driest manner:

"You are just better from a long illness, Mr. Hammand, and in an impressionable state, and I have roused your inherited memory to sudden consciousness of what has been implanted in you by ancestors who ruled here for a thousand years. There's a poet who may rank with Homer in the days when he also is of the past, living this same country of yours, and he has put the truth in words for ever:

> 'So to the land our hearts we give,
> 　　Till the sure Magic strike,
> And Memory, Use, and Love make live,
> 　　Us and our fields alike.
> That, deeper than our speech and thought,
> 　　Beyond our reason's sway,
> Clay of the pit whence we were wrought,
> 　　Yearns to its fellow clay.'"

"And there's a very nice clay figure running from the pit whence it was wrought!" said Madame Yorke. "Your sister scampering down from her ancestor's barrow, to be plain."

They hurried down the slope. Swanhild's voice came up. "Come at once!" she called. "We've found the golden calf!"

"Golden calf?" repeated Luna, joining her. "There should be no gold in that Barrow!"

The hole was very big now. The men stood in a knot at the edge, Goddard was down at the bottom, scraping soil off a bulky object over which he stood astride. This object was long as a man, but much thicker, it lay prone and was almost shapeless, mainly black, with some gleams of yellow where he was scraping. Warren held out something that he had rubbed on his corduroys to get the caked earth off. It was the size of a hatbox lid, and as thick, earth-smeared yellow, with green spikes thrust through the edges.

"It's pinewood, covered with gold plates fixed by copper nails," said Goddard, straightening himself. "As like a calf as anything."

The hired workers stiffened with one accord, and glanced at the west, now reddening as the rest of the sky paled. Hornblower went to consult old Moore and the watch. "A heathen idol made o' pine!" said Warren.

Oliver leaped into the excavation. "It's not a calf and not an idol!" he corrected. "It's—" He stopped, and looked round, over the edge of the cutting. At the pines' tops, the bulk of the Beacon, black against the incarnadined west, and the Man pale on it. "Not a calf, and not an idol," he repeated. "Now, what is it? There's two important things one makes of wood. Idols and— What's the other? It's made of wood, painted and gilded. Something that stands upright. This is lying flat." He suddenly slapped his thigh with his usable hand. "A figurehead! The figurehead of a ship—this is a ship's figurehead!"

Almost he shouted, in a culminating burst of delight. "A ship's figurehead in Magnus the Dane's barrow—why, it's a dragon, to be sure! The dragon figurehead of a dragon ship! We're standing on the deck, with some soil between, of our ancestor's dragon ship, Swan, old girl! Don't you remember? I do. He came up the Adur on board it, and when he died they dragged it over country and buried him in it. The bulwarks, with shields on them, are there, and there—" He stabbed a finger towards the earth a couple of yards on either side of the fallen figure. "And Magnus himself is under our feet, under his own deck, with the long green blade like a leaf at his feet."

"Boat-burial, and a figurehead!" exclaimed Luna as he stopped. "Why did I not think of it?"

"'Tes less than 'alf a' 'our o' sunset, Mus' Hammand!"

The voice of Hornblower made the announcement from a distance discreetly clear of the Shaw. While Oliver discoursed the three hirelings had taken but a few moments to get coated and on to the beech hangar south of the pines. Stolid Sussex was in every line of their figures, the unhired workers knew better than to remonstrate. Oliver ran his fingers through his curls. "Whatever have I been up to now?" he asked Luna.

"Another memory wave," she replied. "The question is: how are we to finish the work? If we leave it till morning the tale of gold those fellows spread will compel us to work under the eyes of half the reporters in London."

Oliver's eyes became introspective, while he stared at the ground on which he stood. "A yard of chalk, badly pressed, then the deck, then Old Magnus." He tossed his head and was himself again. "There's over an hour to dusk, three could do it in that time."

"Then you go home and we'll finish it." Swanhild took up her spade again.

"I'll stay. There's no danger till dark, even for me. Miss Bartendale said so."

"There's no danger even for you in dark when I'm present," Luna confirmed. "I know how to avert it."

"Then why don't you teach us the knowledge?" asked Goddard.

"Because mere knowledge is of no use without the training that enables the possessor to utilise it with safety. As you'll understand when I tell of the ritual and its disastrous consequences."

"A little grave-desecrating goes a long way with a person of my simple tastes," Madame Yorke put in. "I'd rather go back to the manor for a rest while you young things enjoy the finale. Also you'll need spuds and trowels for the later fine digging."

This settled it, and it was arranged that Oliver and Luna should take her home and return with the tools, while the others hastened the work on. Oliver promised they would keep to the track along which the hirelings had now vanished, clear of the pines.

8

"THE HIDDEN ROOM—TO-NIGHT—"

When the car stopped under the Shaw again darkness was still a thing of the future. The Downs were dull and dim; yet marvelously distinct and solid under a sky mainly devoid of positive colour, but waning to transparent pale orange beyond Thunderbarrow Beacon. Over the Beacon, one puce-coloured cloud jagged along its under-edge with red-hot copper seemed astonishingly distinct and harsh in the airy softness of the rest of the firmament. The moon; a shy, eroded crescent; sailed over the village where in cottage windows little reflections of the coppery cloud glowed luridly.

Frost had set in, it would have been a time of breathless silence, but the eternal wind of the Down heights was pouring, chill and steady, through Shaw and hanger, stirring the trees to a breathy droning like that of an angry sea. Luna and Oliver were halfway along the lower path when a cry came down wind: a shrill little squeal that made both start. "A rabbit, some brute's been setting traps again!" cried Oliver. His eyes gleamed red with the profound anger of a man who rarely gives way to passion. Luna's hands went up to her ears at the sound, and down again as it came once more, pitiful as the wail of a little lost soul crying out at worse than physical pain. "It's in the Shaw, not far!" she exclaimed. "To heel, Roska!"

Oliver caught her wrist. "There's no danger where I am," she said, then jerked free with: "Oh!" in pitying horror, as a third cry came.

"You must not go!" he called, but she darted up amongst the beeches, the dog at her heels. She was out of sight in the few moments it took him to realise she had gone and to start after her over the packed leaf-carpet between the wide-set trees. The beeches were passed before he caught sight of her again, speeding into the dark boscage of the Shaw, guided by another squeal. He called, and the wind brought his voice back to him as he darted into the black windings in turn.

There was a faint scent of smashed pine and fir needles under his feet, a little colourless sky showed translucently betwixt the close-shouldering trunks, and overhead in broken threads and rags between the masses of the boughs. In Oliver's head something seemed to turn over, heave itself, run down, catch at his heart, and send a warm wave along every nerve of his big body. He was joyfully, ecstatically conscious of every bone and muscle, working and rippling in harmony; of the wind that sang through his bristling curls; of his feet slapping crisply on the needle-carpet; and could trace every vein by the burring, singing thrill that ran along it. And back of it all was a consciousness that it was all familiar, had all happened before. It was no new thing; pinewood, and duskiness, and himself coursing like a young god after a woman who fled before him. He had forgotten the Monster; forgotten the cause of the chase; fear and pity alike had no power over him. He could not have recalled his own name without a pause to think. He was simply a fiercely live personality in a world that held nothing but dark woods and a golden-haired woman.

It had all happened before, that moment which held the joy of all the ages in it: the joy that was the more perfect because it was graciously just imperfect, with one step of culminating splendour yet to be reached.

Something scuttled past him, in two more steps he was towering over Luna at the end of a piny tunnel. She was rising from her knees, her curls and eyes glowing in what light came in cracks from all round. The dog stood beside her like a dusky phantom. She held the trap in her hands. "I let it go; its leg was only a little hurt and life is worth living here even if one's lame," she said.

Her eyes met his, and she stood still. He made no movement and did not speak, for through the warm ecstacy that enwrapped him he knew the culmination was not yet to be.

They stood at gaze a moment and she paled, then by an effort she turned from the mastery of his scarlet-glowing eyes and flung the trap away. The spell was broken, involuntarily his eyes followed the flight of the rusty metal through alternate flashes of shade and pale light, and its fall into the nearest bushes.

"Pines and firs, cold and stars!" he exclaimed suddenly. They were in a sort of inverted funnel of foliage, round them were the little cracks of pale, lingering daylight, but the funnel overhead was coal-black and in its patch of opening there glimmered two stars. "Come!" he cried, then: "It's coming—the Monster!"

It was coming. The sudden sense of dread and repulsion, the consciousness of something intangible closing round him, of an indescribable presence and pressure, acutely evident, though imperceptible to bodily senses. He gave a shout, a shout with whose utterance he had no conscious connection, and it rang in his ears as though some one else had roared the snarling, defiant drone of it.

"*Heysa-aa!*" it was. He caught up Luna on his usable arm, swirled round on his heels, and plunged back through the ride for the beeches. The dog followed without making any sound. At the same time Luna pulled from her pocket an electric torch she had brought for use in the excavation, and switched its white ray round on trees and ground and the scraps of daylight that shamed it, a turn of her wrist sending the light full in his eyes so that he was blinded for the while. "There's nothing here—now!" she said.

He knew she spoke truth, for with her words the sense of the abominable presence fled and there was nothing but wholesome dusky woods, the woman clutched on his arm, and the dog loping beside them. For all that he did not slacken his pace until he had dashed out on the turf beyond the Shaw, and halted with open country round and no stars to be seen in the still daylit sky.

"It's gone," he said, in a quiet tone that was a chant of triumph too tremendous for boasting.

"I can control it," she answered, hushedly.

"I mastered it," he contradicted. "God would not permit me to save myself from it—or other people. But to save you He gave me the power."

"No," she cried anxiously. "It was I who controlled it."

He laughed a low, triumphant laugh. "We will say we conquered it between us—together."

"You might put me down," she said, suddenly. Both had forgotten he was holding her still. While he talked to her with half his brain the other had been considering how natural it seemed to be holding her, with her face above his against the sky. She belonged to the place—so said the ecstatic half of his brain while the other gave words to his lips—it had all happened before. He holding her, and her face against a pale sky above his own. Only was she a part of the place, or the place a part of her? The stars just becoming visible round her; pale lights in the pallid sky, as her eyes were lights in the pallor of her face; pale stars, the ghosts of stars that shone in such a sky a thousand years before: a sky under which he held a woman on his arm and was glad to the point of pain. And either the yew berries on a vanguard tree just within his are of vision were harsh mimics of her scarlet lips, or her lips were ghosts of yew berries that glowed a thousand years before, when he held a woman and felt the pain of too much gladness. At her words the dreaming half-brain recollected itself and knew what it had been dreaming over: echoed echoes of when its owner's forbears carried off their destined women.

He set her down beside the car. He said no word of apology, and again something turned in his head and, without strain or any sense of bathos, the half-brain's visions ceased. "Do you know what you said in the wood?" demanded Luna.

"No, I don't. Only it sounded like—oh, *heysa-a.* That's it! It seemed to come into my mouth of itself. Was it a spell to keep the Monster away that I suddenly remembered?"

"No, but I recognised it. I know it, and if the runes are on the blade— Come."

They made for the lower track again. The man smiled to himself. They had resumed the relations of client and specialist. It was

as it should be: he was not the man to give his love where it was
not fated to be given, and he was not the man whose love would go
to a woman who did not expect the decorous, slow niceties of woo-
ing. She had read all that was in his eyes as he looked up at her, he
knew he had been beguiled by the gloaming and the shock of the
Monster's coming into prematurity—though only with his eyes. She
had glossed over it prettily, they had taken up ordinary intercourse
just where it had been interrupted.

He glanced up at the darkling Shaw and laughed outright at it.
He had met and escaped the Monster, and he had no more dread
of it. Such utter lack of dread that he did not mind his chosen
woman risking another meeting with it if pity called. That was it—
it could never harm her or him when they faced it together.

When he laughed Luna knew his thoughts, and for a moment
there tugged at her heart a desire to tell him all—to destroy his
fool's paradise, to take from her own heart the burden of seeing
him in it and anticipation of the inevitable agony when he must be
dragged from it.

Tell him—for her own comfort—and so destroy the web of protection her wits and learning were weaving round him and his for
ever! She spoke up sharply: "It has no power with me, but remember your promise not to risk a meeting with it."

"Exactly, I dare not risk a meeting without your protection,"
he assented. "Miss Bartendale, I believe I'm living a double life, in
the same place and same skin and at the same time! Simultaneously
I'm thinking of myself and how glad I am to be alive here, and
living over how glad my forbears were to be alive here. I suppose
it's your doing, stirring up my ancestral memory. It must be
affecting my sanity a bit—and it's very joyful madness!"

"You will be painfully sane when I tell you the full truth," she
answered, curt with the struggle in her own heart. Round the end
of the path Swanhild raced to them. "We've reached the deck!" she
called. "It's oak, and there's black mould on it, too!"

They ran back to the excavation. Warren was resting a moment,
seated on a slope of mingled chalk chips and virgin soil that ran
from the Barrow's centre down to the uneven surface of decaying
dark wood where Goddard was scraping with the edge of a spade.

"It's badly smashed about," Goddard reported. "The chalk has poured down through it there. I suppose we break through now?"

Luna shuddered. Because the end was in sight, and because it is one thing to lay plans with the impersonal aid of learning, and another to break in on the ancient dead with one's actual hands and eyes. Warren jumped up, but Oliver checked him. He knew what was in Luna's mind.

"No need to disturb the old Lord of the Manor," he said, in his roundest voice of command. He leapt down the hole and stared at the wasted oak, with inturned eyes. "Let me see—His helmet's where you stand, Goddard. His plaits stretch to my own feet. The blade was at *his* feet. Ah, yes!—It's under the chalk now. Dig there, and dig carefully."

So they dug as he directed, and within the half hour—before the moon was really a light—they found a rotten leather shoe with a golden clasp on it, and above it a little yellow dust that must have been bone of the living Hammands' bones. Those they buried back again in the thickness of black mould that was over them, and amid the chalk they found three sadly battered shards of coppery bronze that put together into the blade on which Luna's hopes centred.

In the dry chalk they had got little verdigris, but the chalk in its descent on them had wrought harm no mere tarnishing could have done. On the largest fragment rubbing with a leather glove was enough to clear the surface, and on it at least the damage seemed irreparable. The runes had been scratched on it, not properly graven as on the gold hilt-plates, and the sliding chalk had practically planed them away. While Goddard and Warren shovelled back part of the soil to close the digging until morning, Luna and the Hammands examined the shards under the light of the torch.

"Well—?" said Swanhild at last. She shivered as she put the decisive question.

"It is totally spoilt—" Luna hesitated. "You can do no more?" suggested Oliver.

"It is checkmate, and I must try another line of enquiry!" she snapped. "A line I don't like to pursue. I don't understand it!" she broke out, with more emotion than she had displayed so far. "I am so evidently right to a certain point. Someone has dug before us, and it must have been the Warlock. So I said, but why he left the gold on the dragon, and why he put the black soil there I do not know. It is utterly bewildering, yet every detail must have some bearing on the problem."

She turned impatiently, and led the way round to the car.

The twilight was changing to misty blue dusk; earth was gaunt, the Shaw darkling and evil; the Monstrous Man seemed to exult with a vast, callous, ghastly joy, to Swanhild. She tucked the rugs round Luna while the men made some final arrangements for filling in the excavation early next morning, and took the chance to whisper:

"Miss Bartendale, what is the other line of enquiry?"

"My *dernier ressort*. I shall compel the Monster to manifest itself in the hidden room to-night, and reveal its origin."

"You can compel it to appear?" Swanhild glanced at the Shaw, as though fearful that the declaration might bring the Monster forth.

"I can—in the hidden room. You shall be convinced, for you shall see it."

"I see it—I see the Monster?"

"Yes, you must be there. It will not harm you, for I can control it; nor will you die of the sight, nor kill yourself after; since I compel it to come; but life will never be the same to you afterwards. Yet for your brother's sake you must see it. Are you afraid?"

"I am, but I'll come. Surely, after the war—"

"Nothing the war brought could prepare one for this. Now, do not say anything to the men; it is between us—a matter women are better fit to bear than men."

Swanhild nodded. Somehow, it was not such a shock that she was to see the Monster, but that a time and place was fixed. "The hidden room—to-night!" she repeated.

Luna gave her a little, silencing frown. Goddard had come up behind her.

9

"IN THE NAMES OF THE ASA GODS—"

Goddard declined a dinner invitation, and went straight home. The Mound of the Golden Pigtails had proved a ghastly frost; so he expressed it to himself. He had seen that even Luna was somewhat discouraged, and had caught the horrified tone, though not many of the words, in which Swanhild addressed her before he came up.

Luna was at a loss, Swanhild patently aghast about it, and he fancied that in his desk might be waiting something of use in the crisis. The others had been too absorbed in the Barrow to ask how his work was getting on, and for fear of exciting undue hope in Swanhild's mind he had not mentioned that he had deciphered the word "Warlock" on three fragments overnight. Accordingly, he went back to his scraps and lumps of *papier mâché* with a brain freshened by the day's work out of doors, and woke out of an absorption of toil some hours later, with swimming head, aching eyes, and a hope that he had found out what might be of more use than all Luna's wandering data.

There could be no mistake: here was an account, fragmentary but clear, of Magnus the Warlock's motives, methods, and misadventures in opening the Mound of the Golden Pigtails. The account of an eye-witness, repeated at one remove, a hundred and thirty years after the actual happening.

The hour was not so very late, even for primitive Dannow, so, leaving word that he had gone to the Manor, he went out, anxious to hearten Swanhild with the least delay. It was very cold and very

clear, winter stars flickering overhead and the best part of a gale
helping him along.

He took a short cut through an ineffective patch of the park
railings and skirted the moat by the west side of the house. Dannow,
like all properly regulated Sussex houses, faces north, it towered
over him blackly, the world beyond it indistinct, trees and sky
blending together all round, only the eternal Monstrous Man strad-
dling along his hillside, creepily distinct, up in the heavens. At point
of turning the corner for the bridge he stopped and stood dum-
founded.

There was a light where no light should be. A dull glow from
the grille of the hidden room.

It might be nothing. So he told himself after the first involuntary jump of his startled brain. Only the tone of Swanhild's voice
speaking with Luna after the Barrow fiasco obtruded itself suddenly on his recollection, and the words he had scarcely noted at
the time came clear and sharp. "The hidden room—to-night!" Tone
and words repeated themselves over and over in his brain as he
stepped to the brim of the moat and hooked an arm round a fir's
trunk to save himself from being blown over into the lapping black
water. The grille's lower edge was above the level of his eyes, fifteen feet away over the moat; he could only see the twisted ironwork of it, in broken black lines against the glow on the wall behind. Such a curious glow, bluish-white, a secretive sort of light,
even when allowance was made for the sloping tunnel and two iron
nets. Besides, if anyone was there with a light why were not the
shutters closed? The wind was pouring straight into the room, it
would be inconvenient to say the least. His instinctive lover's fear
caught fire from, the words singing themselves in that terrified tone
of the beloved's voice through his head— "The hidden room—to-
night!" What business could anyone have within the hidden room
at night? On a Monster night, too, cold and windswept!

Afterwards, he could not recollect if he told himself spying was
justified in the circumstances, or if he, simply did not think of ethics at all, any more than he remembered the arrangement of the

grilles. If it was anything unholy he was the person to investigate; for he was not of the fated Hammands. He simply ran to the bridge, hung his overcoat on the parapet, and climbed over into the ivy. It was easy going, the old branches, thick as a liner's hawser, crawled in and out of the leaves, humping themselves against and away from the wall; like pythons cased in cocoa-matting and spikes. Very good foothold; Goddard simply ran sideways along the wall, like a spider, in spite of the wind that got between him and the stone-work; rounded the corner; scrambled to the grille; and came to anchor with his feet on the sill, the fingers of his real hand knitted in the ironwork, his artificial arm hooked round an ivy branch.

The tunnel was full of the glow, and the roar and sizzing of the wind down it. He could only see the inner grille, all black lines against light. As to hearing—he was beginning to realise what a consummate ass his fears had made of him when a voice came up the tunnel.

Luna's voice. He had noted before its curious carrying power, now it came quite distinctly against the wind, cutting, thin and low and vibrant, right through the clamour. At the same moment the light went out.

"Pines are around and above you; stars, clear and cold, above the pines. Wind, clear and cold, around all and soughing through all," the voice came, in a sort of hushed, monotonous chant, un-canny in the circumstances. "Starlight, cold wind, and fragrant pines, round you a pentacle erected beyond whose line you may not pass, and a victim for you without the pentacle's line. You are alone with one human victim; I empower you to manifest yourself visibly, Hamandr the Undying! In pines and wind and starlight—I empower you to manifest yourself—Skinturner! In names of the Asa Gods—of Odin Allfather, and Vingi Thor, and Asa Lok, Ham-andr! In pines, and wind, in starlight—*and the pentacle*—I com-mand and empower you to appear! Skinturner—Skinturner—In names of the Asa Gods, Hamandr Skinturner, turn your skin and come!"

She ceased. The wind held full sway in Goddard's ears for one hushed moment of expectation. Then, cutting through the blast by

main force, came an infernal sound that lifted the hair on his forehead with horror.

A demoniac cacophony. Shrill and droning at once; deep yet
crackling; bestial yet touching the human, human enough to make
the bestiality of it obscene; triumphant and despairing, glad and
bitter; all hate, all lust, all the abysmal passions of a lost soul kept
from annihilation by its own quenchless wickedness, put in a single
cry. So it swelled out into the dark, and Goddard knew he had heard
the Undying Monster.

He had heard it alone; it was the sight of it that made men kill
themselves rather than live with the memory in their brains. Three
times it snarled out, then stopped as a third voice rose; deep but
sharp.

"Oh, Luna—!" Swanhild cried, almost whimpering.

Again came the inexpressive drone of the Monster. "Oh, Luna!
Luna! I can't bear any more!" Swanhild repeated, frantic horror
and dread in her tone.

The light flashed on again, then, simultaneously, light and all
sound were cut off together.

Goddard was hanging to the ivy, windy darkness in front of him
as the blast that rushed round him and down the tunnel beat back
again. The shutters had been closed, and behind them Luna
Bartendale must be meddling as the Warlock had meddled to his
cost in the same room. With Swanhild there, already terrified to
the point of panic. Swanhild who had neither cried nor broken
down through all the shocks of the war years!

Her danger turned him suddenly cool and alert. The grille was
firm as the wall itself, yet he must get into the room quickly, if
only to share whatever catastrophe Luna's folly had involved
Swanhild in. To go round to the front, explain to whoever answered
the door—impossibly long. Hopeless, too; for Swanhild always
locked the corridor door automatically. But she did not usually lock
the room's actual entrance. He summed everything up in the moment it took him to take a fresh purchase on the ivy and set scram-
bling off to the right.

A glance down at the ripples crawling out from the house beneath him told when he was over the spring-cellar. He had not

played with Oliver and Reggie Hammand in bygone years without learning all the ins and outs of Dannow, and that the outlet to the moat was a plain arch under the water-level. An arch large enough for a slim boy to scramble through. Now he went hand over hand down by the ivy trails until his feet were in the water, his knees, his armpits. The lowest hold was reached: he took a deep breath and let himself slip down.

The wet blackness slid up over his head, he was caught in a slow wave from in front, turned on his back, and swept in a bunch against something immovable. His head bobbed into free air; he trod water, gasping, pinned firmly against the outer marge of the moat; marked carefully where the bubbles and ripples indicated the submerged arch, filled his lungs again; kicked off from the bank, and fought through the current to its centre.

It was a crazy effort. Three boys in daylight had just succeeded in "boosting" one of their number through against the compressed tide, but it was the short cut and only way to where Swanhild was, and strength came to him from the thought. Twice he was swirled back, but at the third effort a superhuman dive brought his fingers in reach of an inequality between stones. His head felt as though it would be pressed into his shoulders by the passionless smooth force of the flowing water, his lungs seemed ready to burst, but somehow he forged through the little tunnel until quite suddenly the pressure slackened and he shot up and could breathe again.

For a little while he had to remain, just making efforts enough to counteract the suction to the arch, pressed by the upper slack of the water against the wall of the cellar. When his eyes ceased to be filled with scarlet waves and black flashes everything was silent but for the bubble of the spring, and black but for a little indefinite patch of light high above him and far in front. From his position he knew the hidden room door was open, and this was the light from within on the cellar ceiling above the ledge.

The silence hit him like a physical blow as soon as breath and memory were back. The Monster's howl would have been preferable. Was all over? He asked it of himself as he felt his way with the strength of desperation, round to a corner in the darkness and then along the side wall to the ledge. Once a hand grasped that all was settled, he swung on to it and reached the niche in a couple of bounds.

There he hung on a foot while his heart missed a beat. The deathly stillness hit him afresh, but his hesitation scarcely delayed him one step's time. He leapt to the threshold and stared with the boldness of utter dread down into the room.

10

"... THE EXPLANATION—IN A SINGLE WORD"

Swanhild was the only person in the room, and in the first dazed glance Goddard thought she was dead. With the odd double consciousness that comes in times of shock or emotion he was mildly surprised with half his mind that he could take in everything so calmly.

The Warlock's table had been pulled into the corner before the stair foot, the lamp on it showing all the room distinctly, and in particular Swanhild's huddled figure; kneeling with arms sprawled on the table and her face hidden on them. The crocks and inscribed stone were pushed against the walls, and in the cleared space of most of the floor was chalked a large figure; the five-pointed star known as the pentacle. In the middle of it lay an overturned chair, and without its lines the Hand of Glory, the gold and bronze sword, and the plates from the dragon figurehead.

He noted every detail in the fraction of a second it took his advanced foot to descend on the top stair. The stair shook at the touch, Swanhild lifted her head and sprang to her feet. He came down quite placidly and they faced one another over the lamp.

"Goddard!" Swanhild exclaimed. "You have come—of course you would come when—" It had been a cry of relief; her tone changed as she stopped in the middle of her sentence. "Oh, why did you not come earlier?" she gasped. "Ten minutes ago—" She came to an inconclusive stop and put her hands over her eyes, as though the distraction of his coming had passed and horror come back again.

Goddard reached over the table and caught hold of a wrist. "Come away at once!" he repeated. "I heard the Monster and Miss Bartendale!"

"There was no danger. No danger with Luna there." She lowered her hands and stared at him over the lamp, her eyes calm to the point of expressionlessness in the pits of shadow the upcast light made round them. "It has gone, Goddard. Why, you are drenched! How did you come here?"

"Through the moat. After I'd heard the Monster—and you crying out. Swanhild, what is it all?"

"I've seen the Monster." Her calm was awful in its way. Control, learnt and inherent, had pulled her together. "There was no danger. I was simply startled. There was no danger," she reiterated dully. "No physical danger," she amended.

"Not as long as it stayed in the pentacle, eh?"

Goddard was more himself. He felt nothing sentient but their two selves was there now. The secret hiding-place gaped empty, the stone drawer was on the table, and the hand's musty, musky wrappings. Old reading reminded him the pentacle is a holy symbol; if you stand in one evil spirits cannot cross its chalked lines to you; if you drive an evil spirit into one it cannot get over the lines.

"What do you know?" Swanhild rapped out anxiously.

"What I heard through the grille before the shutter closed and made me come to you any way."

"Oh, Goddard!" Her eyes kindled, then clouded. "Ten minutes sooner—what did you hear altogether?"

"I heard Miss Bartendale summon it, it howled, you cried out and the shutter closed. Swanhild, you have learnt something."

"I must not tell you. I've met the Monster—seen it!" Her control broke and she hid her face again in her hands as she almost wailed: "I have met it, and lived—as the Anchorite and Crusader did! Only there's no war now to get killed in, and no real Church for final refuge—oh, why did God let us keep Oliver alive for this? If only he had died cleanly in the war—"

"Hush, dear," Goddard said patiently. "You've had some sort of shock, and don't know what you are say—"

"I know too well. I know why the Warlock and Grandfather killed themselves when they—"

"Swanhild! You are not thinking of—" He could not put it into words, but slipped round the table and clasped an arm round her, with some vague idea of stopping her from violence to herself.

"No, no, Goddard!" she cried hastily, dropping her arms and letting him see the blank horror in her eyes. "It's different with me. Luna prepared me; and raised it to convince me. I would not—could not—believe it without evidence. It could not have harmed anyone while she had it under control. Only I know all, and there's nothing left for me in life now—"

"Except to help whoever must learn the truth also."

It was Luna's voice. Actually Goddard had never thought of her absence from the room, in his consternation and concern for his own woman. She came down the stairs now, queerly suggestive of the priestess of some ancient cult in the thick grey coat that hung in severe folds round her.

"To think I brought you here!" Courtesy and ordinary decency went by the board as that crowning fact occurred to Goddard. Luna smiled coolly.

"Some day you will understand the inestimable good you did when you brought me in a hurry, Mr. Covert."

"You have exposed Swanhild to some unspeakable danger—"

"I have broken to her—with what gentleness the subject permitted—something she was bound to learn."

"Then let me know it, too."

"I have a perfectly valid reason for not doing so at present. Why, man, do you think I'm enjoying all this?"

The level voice broke to a note of bitter, appealing irony. Swanhild slipped away from Goddard's arm and passed one of her own round the smaller woman's shoulders. "You must not worry Luna, Goddard!" she protested. "She is suffering worse than I am."

"Hush! You must not say that, Swanhild!" Luna disengaged herself from Swanhild's arm, crossed to the pentacle, and, with her back to the others, bent to pick up the Hand of Glory. She turned again and addressed Goddard in her usual placid tone. "How do you happen to be here—and wet, Mr. Covert?"

"He only heard me shout, and came through the moat," Swanhild explained hurriedly. "He heard—heard the Monster, that's all. If he had only been ten minutes earlier, Luna—!"

"It is certainly a great pity, if you had to come at all, that you did not come ten minutes earlier, Mr. Covert," said Luna. While she was speaking she had wrapped the Hand in its mouldy coverings and replaced it in the stone box. Goddard suddenly woke to the oddity of it. "Miss Bartendale," he said; "on a previous occasion the mere proximity of that hand gave you acute physical distress. You have handled it casually now. It's a bit odd."

She flushed from neck to temples. "Perhaps it's another of my mysteries," she replied, defiantly. "Perhaps I simulated that distress for my own purposes. At least, that's what you think, it is evident."

Swanhild turned indignantly. "If you suspect Luna of anything mean I shall hate you, Goddard!" she exclaimed. Then Luna spoke again, mistress of herself and the situation once more.

"Mr. Covert, later you shall learn the meaning of our operations here, and at the same time you will understand why we cannot explain them now. What do you say about that, Swanhild?"

"I say you are right, Luna. I said it before. Nobody but we two must know anything until you succeed or fail utterly. Goddard, dear; will you take our assurance, on our honour, that we have run into no danger, and will run into none, however suspicious circumstances may appear?

Goddard hesitated. "I must consult Oliver," he began.

"On no account!" exclaimed Luna, emphatically. "He knows nothing of this, and is to know nothing until we choose to tell!" Swanhild chimed in almost fiercely:

"If you mention this to Oliver you will regret it all your life, Goddard! In a few days at most we shall tell him ourselves; and tell you; and then you will understand it all."

"I understand you keep much from him for fear of muddling his inherited memory," Goddard replied. "Only why can't you tell me? You know I shall be crazy with fear for you, Swanhild, if I don't know."

"There's no need," put in Luna. "We will not enter this room, nor attempt to make the Monster manifest itself again, unless it is with you and Mr. Hammand as willing witnesses. We have done what had to be done, and are none the worse for it, as you see. It had to be done, it is done, and will you accept our promise and keep your own counsel?"

"Everything you say makes it more mysterious," he protested.

"It does. Yet the explanation can be given in a sentence, perhaps in a single word." Luna was not herself, behind her outer calm, and as she spoke her eyes strayed involuntarily to the broken inscription. Goddard noted it. "In an Old English word?" he asked sharply.

Luna's eyes turned to his again. They did not flinch, but she half-smiled; the smile of a clever person caught napping. "Perhaps, perhaps not," she answered.

"Then possibly I may find out that word for myself."

Swanhild gave a little exclamation. Luna continued to regard him consideringly. "We can no more stop you from trying to find it out than we can tell you at present, Mr. Covert," she answered slowly.

"But you don't think I can find it out?" he accused.

"Honestly, I doubt it. Still, you have all the data that have come to light." She nodded with a great affectation of frankness to the objects on the floor and the hand in its drawer. "This is all I intend to say on the subject. Will you take our assurance that we will try no more experiments, and refrain from mentioning the subject at all to Mr. Hammand? There is method in all my secrecy."

He considered, not doubting their assurance, but deciding if the reference to the "one word" was mere mockery on her part. It could not be, for her glance at the inscription had been unpremeditated, a bad slip for anyone so self-controlled as she was usually. Swanhild broke in on his reflections.

"Goddard, we were forgetting; you are wet through—"

"It's happened before." Goddard was in a reaction of irritability, wondering how she could be so petty after what had passed. "Don't worry, Swanhild."

"You wouldn't be vexed if you knew what a relief it is to think of anything so wholesome as wet clothes and death of cold at present," said Luna. "I must point out, though, that a severe chill will incapacitate you from pursuing your researches more or less, Mr. Covert; so please make up your mind if you will accept our word of honour."

"Goddard, dear, we never were in danger," Swanhild said earnestly. "Nobody is in any danger indeed, but Oliver—poor, good old Oliver. It is on him the Monster has—has set a claim, and if Luna fails—" Her face had gone back to the stark, unutterable horror it had worn when she raised it from the table. In the distraction of arguing with him whatever she had seen had been pushed into the background of her conscious thought, now it had returned. She broke off and cried: "If only you had been ten minutes earlier!"

"Will you accept our assurance?" repeated Luna, coldly.

"Of course I shall," he answered. Two considerations decided him: First, that whatever risk they had run in the Monster's appearing was past. Secondly: he had more data than they thought.

"Then you shall see us safely out of the room," said Luna, obviously relieved.

In the corridor, with both doors locked behind them, Swanhild halted. "You'll come to Oliver, he's in the Holbein room with Madame Yorke, and get a change?" she said.

"I don't feel like meeting anyone at present. I can let myself out by the side door and run home. I won't take any harm." Standing in the corridor, in the lived-in house, a sense of unreality, of incredulity, came over him like a wave, but simultaneously an echo of the Monster's obscene cry stabbed through his brain. "I've got your promise, Swanhild," he said gently. "I won't add to your trouble by risking illness."

"Just one question," said Swanhild; "what brought you here at this time?"

"I was taking a short cut on business," he answered shortly; "and heard it howl. Dear, you do look rotten!"

"She'll break down as soon as you go, Mr. Covert," put in Luna, "and the longer you stay the worse the break will be. Go, for Heaven's sake!"

It was evident Luna also was near breaking point. Without further words Goddard went. Dannow had been a second home to him from boyhood, it was no feat to let himself out by a certain side door. Only as he stepped into the starlight Swanhild came running after him. "Do believe in us, dear!" she whispered brokenly. "We are in no danger; nobody but Oliver is—you'll understand when Luna tells you. I can't let you go without—without—"

"Hearing me say I do believe in you!" he completed. "Of course I do, dear."

"And you'll hurry home?"

"At once. It's all right, I've stood many a night wet through in the trenches."

She ran back, and he went on his way round the court and through the unlocked bridge gate. The open air felt unreal and his head spun with nothing definite in it save that Swanhild had safely passed some danger and the clue to all lay in the missing word of the stone.

11

"LET DOWN—BY THE GOLDEN PIGTAILS"

In a time of stress and surprise people act without realising the subconscious reasoning that dictates their procedure. Only when he was back home, dry, and settled in the lamplit familiarity of his own library did astonishment and incredulity come to Goddard. A sense of unreality tried to possess him, only held at bay by memory of the demoniac howling and the look in Swanhild's eyes. What most puzzled him was his own conduct: looked at in retrospect it seemed at first incredibly supine. He should have consulted Oliver at once. He should have forced Luna and Swanhild to take him into their confidence. He should have done a dozen things he had not done. Calmer consideration put another complexion on it, and ratified the unanswerable good sense of his subconscious promptings. The two women had acknowledged a great risk safely run. They had promised it should not be repeated. A man lets a lady run risks, but he does not disbelieve her word. He could not have done otherwise than he had done.

Only it was so utterly confusing. What mortal creature could have made the noise he had heard? All the old stories thronged his mind; the ever-living Hammand; the half-beast born at intervals and hidden away; dead Hammands coming back in vampire shape. They were lies, gangrenescent lies, of course; yet Miss Bartendale herself had spoken of unexpected truth woven in with the embroidery of tradition.

A ghost? He had a healthy derision for materialistic spiritualism, but Miss Bartendale had referred to Fifth Dimensional beings—beings beyond the alleged Fourth Dimension of ghostdom.

Only, he recollected it then, she had said Fifth Dimensional beings had to assume a material form in which to manifest themselves to the physical senses. Both she and the Monster had disappeared from the hidden room in the few minutes it had taken him to get in by the moat. The word "Ectoplasm" flashed into his mind. Mediums could let spirits take this substance from their own bodies in which to manifest themselves. He had seen about it in some magazine that very month. Had Miss Bartendale done something of the sort? Now he thought of it; she had never spoken in her own voice while the howls went on. As to her evanishment from the room: oh, mediums had all sorts of arrangements.

What, though, of Swanhild's exclamation: "If only you had been here ten minutes before!"—and Miss Bartendale's confirmation of it?

Everything was contradictory. The main question was: did he feel satisfied they were safe in the Manor? They had assured him no one was in danger but Oliver; he did not doubt their assurance, but he did fear that miscalculation or accident might attend Miss Bartendale's experiments. On an impulse he went to the telephone and rang up Oliver.

Oliver's voice, complacent and somewhat sleepy, answered. Goddard asked some small question about next day's arrangements as excuse for the call, and gently extracted the information he wanted. All the ladies had retired by then, replied Oliver; they were tired with the day out-of-doors. Poor old Swan had developed a touch of neuralgia as well. Got it showing Miss Bartendale the lumber rooms and things, while he entertained the elder guest. Swan wasn't the neuralgic kind as a rule, so took it hard when she did have it: she looked half-stupefied, poor girl!

Thus Oliver. Goddard put his own interpretation on the last item. Swanhild was suffering from shock.

When he entered the room she was overwhelmed with horror. Not fear, as he realised when he cast his mind's eye along the perspective of subconscious observation, but sheer horror. His arrival had served as a healthy counterstroke, had helped her to pull herself together for the time. She said she had seen the Monster; that she understood why the Warlock and her grandfather had laid violent hands on themselves after meeting it; that she would not

injure herself, because Luna Bartendale had prepared her beforehand. The inference from this was that tradition was right; it was
the sheer appearance of the creature, seen without warning, that
overturned the beholder's reason.

But, in that case, why did both wish he had come earlier—come
in time to see it without preparation? They would tell him all in a
few days. But anything might happen in a few days. Miss Bartendale
was human, she had tripped for once. She had not been able to
gloss over her involuntary glance towards the broken stone as she
said a single word would explain all.

Obviously the lost word at the beginning of the third line. "? ?
? ? ? ?: Hammand" it was. He would read down C, G, O, Q, and S in
a dictionary, in search of six letter words ending in L or Z.

He thought there would be no sleep for him that night when he
got out the largest dictionary in the house and started work on it.
He was young and healthy, however, his mind was at rest over
Swanhild's safety for the time, and reading solidly down a dictionary in the small hours is somnolent labour. Gradually his head
drooped on the page, and only when one of his dogs came scratch-
ing at the library door did he wake to the late winter dawn.

His first act was to ring up Dannow, and his heart acted oddly
until Oliver's placid voice brought relief. All was all right at the
manor, only poor old Swan looked like a nerve-ridden imitation of
herself; after a night of neuralgia. They were all four going to have
a paper-chase in the lumber rooms. Would Goddard come and
help? And—they'd forgotten to ask him overnight—what about the
papers he had already?

Goddard couldn't come over; thanks. As to the papers, he
wouldn't raise hopes, but he wished to devote the morning to them.
He would let them know when he was sure of anything.

Swanhild was safe for the day. That was a load off his mind,
and braced by it and bath and breakfast and his sleep a comforting
idea presented itself. Miss Bartendale had handled the glorious
hand quite casually, while before it had caused her acute discomfort when it was shut up in the wall. And that discomfort had been
genuine. It was her discretion he distrusted, not her honesty. It

looked as though, in some way, she had found means to weaken or control whatever abnormal influences were centered in the hidden room.

So far, so much comfort, but he could not tamely await her revelation. Afterwards, looking back to the steps that led to the final catastrophe of the Shaw, he saw direct inspiration in his obstinate decision to find out for himself.

In the afternoon, baffled temporarily, he tramped past the lodge and overtook Swanhild in the avenue. It had rained all day, more or less, this was one of the driest interludes: a thinning in the showers, full of the kind of lazy sprinkle with sunshine glinting through that makes a blank wall beautiful, and a spacious fairydom of huddled trees; particularly when a man's beloved is there in the dropping lines of light, austerely shapely in glistening oilskins.

Swanhild started as he ranged up beside her. "Hullo, Goddard!" she said uneasily.

Even in the four syllables the change in her voice was striking. Something had gone out of it, it was forced, old, tired behind its affection of heartiness. He replied: "Cheerio, Swan; this is topping! I'm sure we'll both feel nicer for a little talk before we face society together."

"I—you guessed—" Swanhild looked sideways at him as they walked on. "I meant to avoid you. For a bit."

"Bless you, of course you did! You've had a shock and have promised not to confide in me. In a reversal of the circumstances, I'd have funked your society myself. Only it wouldn't be sense."

"You always understand, Goddard!" She suddenly crooked her arm in his and squeezed it, looking in his eyes with an admiring trust such as he fancied Dian might have bestowed on Endymion. She made a very haggard Dian, though. She had aged ten years since their parting near the Barrow. She was composed as usual, but blue rings were under her eyes, and behind the calm of them they put him in mind of Dante's Frozen Circle.

"Dear," he said; "I understand you because I'm your lover; only a lover's a bundle of instincts, and I have a feeling that Miss Bartendale's secrecy is unsafe—"

She interrupted eagerly. "Nothing can happen, as long as we have Oliver's promise to avoid the Shaw and room. He alone is in any danger."

"But, you know, this promise can't go on for ever."

"It is only for a few days, Goddard. And for that time Oliver must not know anything—"

"Um'm. Hence that neuralgia stunt."

"Of course. Goddard, you promised not to tell him—"

"My dear, I did. You needn't think I'd peach, though I'd sooner have anyone, good old Oliver included, in the big bonfire than you worried for a minute."

She looked at him uneasily. "Goddard, dear, there's something I want to say about our engagement. If the truth has to be made public; as it must be if anyone is in danger of being charged with what happened in the Shaw—"

She ended falteringly, inexpressive horror in her eyes again. "You mean some men would be glad to creep out of the engagement?" He stared at her blankly. "Swanhild, will it be so bad as all that—telling the truth?"

"It will become a matter of history," she replied, her eyes seeming to cling to his despairingly. "The newspapers—you know. And it will be put in books, loathsome books about notorious scandals; all in a section by itself. And it will be raked up in articles and magazines for ever—"

"My dear," he interrupted; "that's quite enough. If public exposure becomes necessary I shall be compelled to procure a special licence at once. I don't approve of a hurried marriage for you, but even your dignity must go by the board when it's a question of my getting the official right within two days to be involved in whatever public odium you and Oliver have to stand. And I'm badly mistaken if Luna Bartendale will desert Oliver—"

"Goddard, you mustn't!" Swanhild cried it as though she had been struck. "You mustn't talk of them like that."

Goddard stared. "Oliver and Miss Bartendale? Why, haven't we been bucking ourselves for a week because the old boy's absorption in her has kept him from brooding?"

"The hidden room changed a lot last night. Changed everything in the world—"

"Except you and me, dear," he whispered.

They had wandered out of the avenue, under the shade of some beeches. Swanhild sat down abruptly on a fallen trunk and hid her face in her hands. Goddard put down the roll of papers he carried and sat beside her. After a while she was sitting up again, braced by the little breakdown with him to see her through it. "If only I could tell you!" she said.

"Just so. Now you are all right again, and we will converse on everyday topics. Such as why the deuce I'm here."

"Why? I forgot—the Culpeper manuscript?" She started eagerly. He shook his head.

"No use raising false hopes. It's another frost. It sheds no light on the Monster's nature, though it contains an account of the Warlock's opening of the Barrow, and how he let it loose after it had been laid there by the Anchorite."

Swanhild jumped to her feet. "So Luna was right as far as she got! You may not see anything in it, but she may."

"Right-o, dearest. She's an expert in such things, and can probably detect hidden meanings in my compilation. Just as a naturalist can reconstruct the entire beast from one chip of tooth. We'll barge along and consult her; but it's my belief we have been let down and landed in the cart by the Golden Pigtails."

12

THE CLUE OF CLUES, 1520–1651

Oliver and the guests were in the Holbein room, Goddard, entering, found himself trying to look narrowly at Luna and the Warlock's portrait simultaneously. Luna was quite herself, bland and insouciante, as he had expected. He knew she had no need to be upset as Swanhild was: Fifth Dimensional horrors were all in her work. Only he noticed a deep line right across her forehead, and was not sure if it had been there when he first met her, or even the day before.

"No success in the lumber rooms," announced Oliver. "Swan told you, I suppose?"

"Oh, yes, and I had to make a similar report about my efforts. A long narrative with nothing in it."

Luna shrugged her shoulders as though not surprised. "Still, we want to hear it, if you please," she said.

"Of course I meant I couldn't see anything in it," he returned, catching and keeping her eyes as he spoke. "You may detect hidden meanings. It happens to be an eye-witness's relation of the opening of the Barrow by the individual over there."

"Oh!" said Madame Yorke and Oliver. Luna's eyes opened. "We must hear it," she repeated. "Is that the manuscript?"

"I've sorted and fixed all the original scraps on transparent paper, but it is very gappy, so I drew out a shorthand *prècis* of it to read at once, thinking you could examine the other at your leisure."

Oliver, highly excited, started to pull chairs into position round the hearth.

"The document is in a deplorable state," Goddard explained, when they were settled, "there's so many holes and missing words that to make the main story intelligible my copy is a modernised paraphrase, with all the old flowery turns of speech omitted. First, Culpeper repeats the details of the case he came to investigate. It seems that the Lord of Dannow, Sir Gilbert Hammand, and his youngest son were returning home one night from Lower Dannow. One of the horses turned up at Dannow, riderless and with its throat horribly torn, and a search party found young Hammand, a boy of thirteen, dead and partly eaten, in the Shaw. The bodies of Sir Gilbert and his horse were lying in the road, at the spot where the Beacon almost overhangs it. It was evident they had either fallen over while struggling with the Monster; for the horse's flanks were somewhat torn, or else jumped it in a panic. Culpeper, therefore, came to make enquiries, for his friend, Reginald, Sir Gilbert's elder son, who was in hiding as a Royalist at the time. To begin:

> Fragments (modernised) of a letter from Nicholas Culpeper. Esq., written from next door to Ye Sign of Ye Red Lion, Spitalfields, London, to Reginald Hammand, Esq., address lost, December, 1651.
> . . . the tale that the Hammands be of a breed vampyrish, and if one be slain prematurely he shall hie him neither to Heaven nor Hell, but live unnatural in the grave his allotted span of life, so long as he may drink at certain times the blood of some creature that is quick. Which tale the vulgar do repeat, coupling it with the name of your brother Oliver, slain in Worcester fight and brought home for his burying this two months past. . . .
> *So I went down to Sowsex, and made my inquest: the time being the waxing of the moon, a period propitious for launching any work. And first I was intent to ascertain exact dates and hours of this Monster's coming, that, the same being applied to the rules of our Divine Science of Astrology, and the*

rules of the Science Divine applied to them, the two
interacting might formulate some warning where-
by you, my good Reginald, and future lords of
Dannow may be set at guard ad aeternum *against*
whatever heavenly configurations do enable the
comings of this ghost, apparition, wraith, succubus,
daemon, or whatever it be—

Goddard broke off, somewhat breathless after the sentence. "There's an enormous gap here," he said. "And I don't quite understand this preamble, anyway."

"I do," replied Luna. "Our astrologer was ahead of his time. He tried to find the origin of the Monster by means of astrology, as I am using archaeology and hypnotism. The same principle, utilising different branches of science. Go on, please."

"It's from here I've translated into more modern wording," said Goddard, and resumed his reading:

From family papers I gat me the time of your
great-grandfather's meeting the Monster: the
which was the tenth of November, Ao. Di. 1556, and
from your great-great-grandfather's tomb the date
of his affliction through it in the secret room, which
was Feb. 8th, 1526: but of the hours no record is
left. Then made I great inquiry, ranging from the
sluts of your lady mother's kitchen to your good
neighbours of Wiston and Danny and Newtimber,
and so finally learnt that in Steyning lives one Jos.
Blount, who boasts that in his youth he was inti-
mate with John Slinfold, that was skyrer *in his non-*
age to Sir Magnus Hammand the Warlock. . . .

"What's a *skyrer*?" Oliver interrupted.

"Nothing so awful as it sounds; only a sort of medium—preferably a boy who'd never been in love who looked into the necromancer's magic mirror for him," answered Luna.

. . . What he had heard from Jno. Slinfold Jos. Blount would not reveal to any being a chirurgeon by occupation, and used to keeping a shut mouth. To Steyning went I, therefore, and was directed to a decent dwelling where a grave citizen receives me coureously, being Master William Blount, chirurgeon also, and a man of somewhat more than my own age. "Ah, 'tis great-grandfather you would see, Mr. Culpeper," he says.

To whom I: "Your grandfather, surely, Master Blount!"

To whom he: "Nay, sir, grandfather died peacefully of natural decay at the age of seven-and-eighty last Martinmas."

And so conducts me to a room where, in the sunshine, sitteth one grey and all shrunken, but younger in the eyes than his great-grandson of forty. The great grandson, then, makes my name and errand known, and leaves us. Then we speak together after this fashion:

The ancient man: "Yes, Mr. Culpeper, I was 'prentice to John Slinfold until he died in my nonage, ninety years ago. For an hundred and nine shall I be next Candlemas, Mr. Culpeper, and my son died of old age last year."

I: "Then in sooth, Mr. Blount, I fear I trouble you fruitlessly; the matter being of such a time past."

He: "Indeed you do not, Mr. Culpeper. Life's like a good stage play (if one may name such in these days) whereof one retains good memory of Prologue and End, though scenes between be forgot. Truly I remember the savour of the lollipops and marchpane I had in childhood, five reigns ago, though I forget on what I supped last night. And I can tell you what Master Slinfold told me in the year 1559, though I forget at whiles there's no King in London now.

Master Slinfold once found me reading of a book that was Odomare his De Practice Magistri and with choler bid me stop reading of such. 'For, from the Philosopher's Stone,' says he, ''tis but one step, and that inevitable, to Black Necromancy. Whereby I am minded to tell thee, Joe, the woful ensample of my quondam master, Sir Magnus Hammand. The whom began as gallant and virtuous a gentleman as every England bred; yea as ever Sowsex bred; and is now a name to fright babes withal."

"And I said: 'Sir, I will listen and strive to profit.'

"'Sir Magnus (said Master Slinfold) was one that had no ardour for wine beyond the third cup; who scarce noted any woman's looks save his beloved lady's; and thought no twice of gold nor rank. Also he was one of the gigantic squires that kept the Red Rose standard at Bosworth, and his dinted helm and seven foot sword are in Dannow Church to this day: at the which I would folk would stare as often as they do at his shameful boughten pardon. King Harry of Richmond would fain have had him to Court and to great honour, but he chose to bide at home and give himself to study.

"'The which I tell you, my son (said Master Slinfold) to prove my contention—shewn in the past and afresh in the present—that the best of mankind, for whom the flesh and gold hold no temptation, will fall deep as greed or lust could drag them through the presumptuous sin of prying into what God hath hidden from men. Concerning Sir Magnus I can tell you one shameful thing he did that led to his end, I serving as his skyrer many years, being an orphan whom he took into his house and kindly nurtured.

"'During my first years with him his occupations were harmless enow, search after the stone that transmutes all metals to gold for King Harry his master, and for himself seeking the Elixir of Life. Which he did innocently, through drugs and distillations, capons fed on vipers and vinegar, and the like. But after I had left him, said rumour, he sought it with obscene ceremonies and black rites, even such as brought the Merechal De Retz to the stake in France. Of which I can give no evidence, for obscenity is ever added to obscenity as any evil tale passes from vulgar tongue to vulgar tongue. Only I know what he did over the opening of the Druid's Grave; the which he would never have done when first I worked for him.

"'Always a tale had been that the Mound of Thunderbarrow hid a great treasure, some holding it was Aaron his calf of gold; others it was the sacramental vessels of the Druids, the which they hid when Saint Wilfrid brought Our Redeemer to Sowsex. When Sir Magnus spoke with me of opening it I put him in mind that a many had searched but ever the treasure was shifted from their reach by the Devil that sits a-guarding it. Whereat he laughs and says: "You may keep all the gold we find, Jack, for your fee. I am after no metal, boy, but seek the Sign and Spell that empower whoso knoweth them to control all spirits, so that they go when he saith Go, and come when he saith Come!"

"'Then said he further: with, his eyes all a glowing flame: "I'll get me them, Jack, and when I've gotten them I'll use them more wisely than did Doctor Faustus—poor fool! Through the spirits I command I'll get me the Philosopher's Stone for making of gold from earth, and I'll get me the Water of Life, and through it I'll live for ever, and whomsoever I choose shall live together with me for ever! Yea, and never an army shall stand against the ghostly legions of devils and sprites I shall

*command by my Spell. And never Emperour or King
but will barter his kingdom or empiry for a little
life more and a little more life; and time will be
Magnus Hammand shall be Emperour of Earth, and
whom he will shall be his viceroys! Who knoweth?
in a few centuries hence—in 1800 or 1900—the am-
bassadors of subject nations may be abiding hum-
bly in the meaner rooms of Dannow, to do their
devoirs to Magnus Hammand, Goldmaker, Spirit
Controller, Owner of the Water of Life, and therefore Emperour of Earth? Emperour of Life and
Time, and therefore of Earth! Yea, verily, so shall
it be; and who knoweth but they may sue for
favours through Jack Slinfold, the ever-living Chief
Minister of Magnus Hammand, the ever-living
Emperour of Earth and Life and Time?"'"*

Goddard stopped and all looked up involuntarily at the
Warlock's little, dark portrait. "To live for ever—Emperor of Earth!"
said Oliver, a red flicker of admiration in his eyes. "To control the
world and the world of spirits! He was moved by a tremendous
ambition, nothing mean, when he went to search out the Barrow,
that ancestor of ours, eh, Swan?"

"And he ended by bribing Posterity to pray for his soul," said
Luna, drily. "Pray go on, Mr. Covert."

"'"But, sir," said I, with all meekness; "how know
you this wondrous Spell lieth in Thunder's Barrow?"

"'And he, answering: "Because there's a family
tradition the Anchorite, my forbear, laid the Monster in the said Barrow, having earned the power to
do so by his life of mortification. Yea, and 'tis true
the Monster hath never vext the family since his day.
Now I ask thee, Jack, my pupil, how could a spirit of
such age and power be laid save by the Spell of
Spells, which is Solomon's? By Solomon's Seal and

Spell, wherewith he controlled all spirits, good and evil alike. It is for written words and mystic signs we search Thunder's Barrow."

"'Then I: "But, sir, if we remove these signs will not the Monster be freed?"

"'And he: "Nay, Jack, we shall not touch the Signs, but make a fair draught to study at ease in our workroom."

"'Then I; bringing out my final objection: "Sir, many have dug in the Barrow, but never an one hath gotten aught save waste of labour for his fee; the Devil ever moving whatever is in it out of reach."

"'And he, laughing: "We shall go prepared as never diggers were prepared before. To wit with a Hand of Glory."

"'And I, shivering: "Master, this is Black Necromancy."

"'And he, concluding the matter: "Jack, the Master am I, and on my head be the guilt!"

"'For the hand Sir Magnus went after dark to the gallows above the Monstrous Man, where hung Will Stredwick, gibbeted three days before for killing of—

(Here is a break in the document, the next part begins in the middle of a sentence).

. . . and at the tips of the fingers and thumb we placed candles of fat, procured from Will also. Then all was ready, and on the first of the darks of February we went, with Hand, and spade and pick, to Thunderbarrow Shaw. These I carried, my Master, as the stronger, bearing a lanthorn and on his back a great bag of consecrated earth from the churchyard. Moreover, we had St. John's Wort—that keepeth evil spirits at bay—hung round our necks, and a sprig of garlic in our girdles, and my Master's

great boarhound to company us. Come to the Barrow we spread the earth on the ground by the
mound's side, Sir Magnus instructing me at any
alarm we were to spring into the midst of it and drew
a pentacle around us with the cold iron of his ra-
pier; the which he laid, ready drawn, on the mould.
Then we lit the Glorious Hand, and by light of it and
the tanthorn began to dig at the mid point of the
Barrow.

"'Under the turf was light soil with certain trees
that we had to remove, and beneath that a made soil
of chalkstones. Under the turf first we found a slab
of stone, of about the bigness of a coffin, laid flat.
My Master noted there was on it no figure of
Solomon his Seal, so we left it and dug on a wider
compass. You shall understand we got no further
than the chalk that night, for the candles of the Hand
burnt out; so home we went, wearied, as dawn was
coming, to rest and make more candles.

"'*To be short, 'twas the third night ere we came
to anything save chalk. That night was windy and
cold and whitely starlit. We had to hew a niche in
the side of our burrow to shelter the Hand from the
blast, but a man works lustily in cold, and ere midnight we ended the chalk, and part of our burrow's
side falling, there fell with it a great figure that I
took for Aaron his Calf of gold, it being of wood
thickly gold-encased—*'"

Oliver clapped his hands in rapture. "Miss Bartendale! You were
right all through! You couldn't help the accident that smeared the
inscription off the blade, but you did lead us after the Warlock."

"The old brute!" said Madame Yorke. "Still, he's interesting,
and some brutes aren't. Please go on, Mr. Covert."

13

THE CLUE OF CLUES, 1651–19—

(Goddard resumed:)

"'If was affrighted at first, but Sir Magnus laughed—saying no harm was done as there was no graving on the figure. Moreover, the dog sat unmoved. "And," says my Master; "she will warn us if ghostly visitant cometh anear." So we propped up the figure again and presently dug to a wooden flooring. "Unsealed and uninscribed," saith Sir Magnus; "we may safely break it up."

"'Wherewith he searched out where two wide planks ended, put his pick-tip under and heaves one up. 'Twas a great feat, but my Master had the strength of four men. To make space for his working he sent me to the top of the digged pit, and awesome it was there, with him down in the hole, the Glorious Hand burning steady in the calm that was there, whiles the wind hooned fiercely around me, with the roar of racked trees and the coughing of strained undergrowth in its breathy cry. Finally Sir Magnus heaved aside the second plank, and out rushes as it were foul air, that made my head to swim. And out went the candles of the Hand.

"'Mayhap my senses failed me awhile, there betwixt the dark of the pit and the dark trees and sprin-

kling of stars. Then was I roused and the hair of mine
head stood up by reason of a cry from Sir Magnus
down in the pit. "It is coming—it is coming!
Sathanas, avaunt!—In Nom—' and he gabbles the
exorcism of Father, Son, and Holy Ghost; his great
manly voice rising to a woman's scream. Then: "Look
to thyself to the holy soil, Jack!"

"'At that the hound begins to whimper, and from
the blackness of the pit there comes a cry that is
neither laugh nor wail, man's voice, nor beast's, nor
daemon's, but compound of all. I turned me round
about and fled down the Barrow's side and at a
bound to the middle of the consecrated earth, seiz-
ing the lanthorn as I went, and so stood there, with
lanthorn and garlick in mine hands. Out of the pit
comes the daemonic howling again and again, mixed
with screaming from the hound, then over the pit's
brim upleaps Sir Magnus, a last long bark snapping
short behind him, into the light's extremest rays.
One moment he stands there, then flings himself
down on the holy soil beside me, and so sits gasping
while I put down the lantern and with the naked iron
draw the pentacle around us both. So sat we with
the lanthorn between us and its upcast rays making
our faces strange and dreadful, most especially my
Master's, that was all blooded and with bites and
tears on it, his hands and forearms being in like case.

""It hath escaped!" he groans. "What I know not,
and how I know not. Only I felt something coming
as the hand went out, and I fought, all hoodman-
blind; yea, even to use of teeth and nails, and the
blackness went red—and so came the light of the
lanthorn in my face."

"'Whereat I cry: "The dog, sir?"

"'And he: "She fought likewise—" and he flashed
the light round, and behold the poor bitch lying at the

Barrow's foot, beyond our earth, dead and most shock-ingly handled with tooth and claw and her head near dragged from the shoulders. At which sight Sir Magnus cried out that she had died for him, and makes a long arm and pulls the body beside us, say-ing it shall not be further mauled dead that suffered in life for him. Then he redraws the pentacle round us, that was broken by his reaching over its line."

"Bravo," said Oliver, "the old fellow wasn't such a hopeless case after all! We ought to overlook a lot for that dog's body. Eh, Miss Bartendale?"

Luna looked at him freezingly. Swanhild frowned, and Goddard went on.

""And what now, sir?" I ask, looking round at the dark wherein might snook some foe of soul and life alike.

""To await daylight in this our harbour, Jack," he replies, taking the light and turning it round as far as its beams may reach; which showed under-growth, and the tumbled tree-trunks and turned forth orts of our digging, whereabouts anything might lurk and hide.

"'No doubt 'twas but a short while we waited, for the lanthorn candle was not burnt out when slats of grey skewed between the trees, but a life of alarm was lived in our pentacle. At last came first dawn and we could see in a way. Sir Magnus took the light and stepped to the Barrow. "Now is the time when evil sprites have no power," he says, with no word about God Who had preserved us. "We will explore our pit, Jack. What we have let loose is of power re-sistless at night, sith it blew out our hand, but the mischief is done and we will conclude our business in daylight."

"'So I lay on my belly over the pit's edge while he went down. And it was a grave he had opened, for under the raised planks lay a skeleton in armour, disposed seemly head to West. Nay, rather, there was a cuirass of mouldy leather with horn and iron rings on it, all fallen flat, and at its hem thigh bones—one broken by stamping of Sir Magnus on it as he fought hoodman-blind—and leather greaves, and a pair of shoes fallen this way and that. And over the cuirass was a helmet, horned and winged with bronze and gold, and beneath the helmet two monstrous golden plaits lying to the beginning of the thighbones. And on the left plait a round target with a sign on it like the Cross Potent of heraldry, and by the right a great broadsword, all massed rust, and across the thighs a doubled bladed axe, and below the shoes the hilt of a sword golden and engraven, and a leaf-shapen blade broke in three several pieces and green with vergris. For some breaths' space my Master remained astride of the hole, staring down. Then gave a great laugh and cried: "I fancied we had thrust unmannerly into a gentlewoman's final withdrawing-room, Jack!"

"'*And so stoops down and plucks from between the plaits two tufts of golden hair. "Moustachio'd like a Don Spaniard," he says, then, musing: "I do remember—on a time—squires wore their hair in plaits. Welladay! the Monster loosed, the mischief done, Jack, we may as well pouch this comely golden sword, for its inscription's sake." I remonstrated, but: "We'll pouch it," he returned, "moreover, something seems to tell me we can do it without danger. Also the writing on it is not utterly strange to me—Now, how do I remember all this, Jack? Can it be the sprite of the golden-plaited Squire is discoursing with me? This is a ship I stand*

>on—I know it. That image is the figure-head—I
>know it—Why, body o' God, Jack, how know I all
>this?'"'"

Oliver interrupted eagerly. "I knew it all, too, when I spied the figurehead."

"History repeats itself, Mr. Hammand," answered Luna. "The Warlock, like you, had an uprush of inherited memory. Pray go on, Mr. Covert."

"As a matter of fact, this is the end of the connected portion," Goddard answered sadly. "Of the rest I can give the baldest summary, collected from infinitesimal fragments of MSS. It appears Sir Magnus and Slinfold sprinkled churchyard mould on the armed skeleton, replaced the planks; with more mould on; and then filled in the hole. For the rest the Warlock told Slinfold that he never saw anything of what he fought in the excavation, and attributed his keeping his reason and escaping alive to that circumstance.

"Soon after the occurrence Slinfold lost his power as a *skyrer*, and was apprenticed, by his own request, to a surgeon. He could only speak from hearsay of the tragedy of the hidden room and the Warlock's reason for buying the Pardon. He ridiculed the idea that Sir Magnus had been engaged in offering his beloved youngest son to the Devil when Lady Hammand came in and died of the sight. He thought the Warlock was merely using the boy as *skyrer* when the Monster unexpectedly manifested itself, and that it was through his remorse for meddling with necromancy, in the shape of the hand, and so loosening the Monster from the Barrow, that the Warlock could not bear to live.

"That ended the Slinfold-Blount narrative. From it Culpeper learnt that the Monster was loosed from the Barrow about midnight on the third night of the New Moon, February, 1520. At this point the document peters out into a few scraps past deciphering, so we don't know to what conclusion the Astrologer arrived."

Goddard folded his papers. "An irritating discovery," he ended. "We should have found out what the Astrologer had to say about his deductions, not simply how he found his data."

"Quite the contrary." Luna's eyes scintillated. "I know enough of Astrology to be sure that the times he fixed were too vague to be of practical use. However, honest work is never lost, though the worker may not see the results. Providence allowed Blount to live over a century so that he might hand to Culpeper information that was of no use at that date, but which may prove my clue of clues three centuries later. It's dusk now, and all the sightseers who have been about to-day in consequence of our work yesterday will be clear of the place. Who will go to the Barrow for the Runestone?"

"The Runestone?" repeated Goddard.

"The stone the Warlock left where he found it. Do you remember what he said of it, according to Slinfold, Mr. Covert?"

She held his eyes mockingly. "That Solomon's Seal was not on it," he began, and suddenly saw the significance. "Why, from the way he put it—he did not say it was plain—"

"Precisely," Luna rose. "The particular symbol he looked for was not on it, but he didn't note it was plain. Ergo, it was inscribed. We shouldn't be long getting it, it is apparently under the turf a little out of the radius of our work yesterday. You and Swanhild ought to be able to get it out, and Mr. Hammand will help carry it."

They straightway loaded a couple of spades on the Mercedes, and within an hour the stone was out on the grass of the Barrow top. It was half as wide as an ordinary tomb-stone, as long, and twice as thick. Luna had come provided with a clothes' brush and a copy of the hilt-runes, and straightway she was on her knees, cleaning the caked mould from the signs deep cut in the stone on back and front. It had to be turned over before she found what she wanted and, looking up, gave a nod and a glance of almost frightened triumph to Swanhild, while she pointed from the photograph to a group of signs on the stone. A replica of the sword-runes came half-way down the longer one.

"It's what you wanted?" suggested Oliver, politely pleased. Luna became null and non-committal at once. "I cannot tell, Mr. Hammand, but it makes a new line of enquiry."

"We'll photograph it, I dare not trust it to the railway," she said, not long after, when it lay on the rug under the Warlock's portrait.

"And we'll take the photos up to Professor Meikelsen by the first train to-morrow."

"Oh, really, you said you'd stay till to-morrow evening," protested Oliver.

"No use trying to stop Luna when she's decided to hustle, Mr. Hammand," said the elder guest. "She never does anything she can shift on to anyone else, but when she starts to do anything she's as energetic as a monkey possessed of what you'd call the Poor Man."

Luna smiled at the tribute. "You think I hustled too much over the Barrow, Mr. Covert," she said, and Goddard reddened, for that was what he was thinking. "No labour is lost, however, as I observed about your deciphering of what the late Mr. Culpeper noted. I gained priceless data from yesterday's work. Only we must not cherish too much hope," she added, hurriedly looking at Swanhild's eager eyes. "We still have a thousand years of mystery against us."

That night Goddard read down C, G, O, Q, and S, in the dictionary again, lest he might have missed a pregnant word. It was in vain, and the Slinfold narrative added to the maze.

14

"...?????: HAMMAND: ...." AGAIN.

The guests departed betimes next morning. Goddard helped to escort them to Hassocks, and spent the rest of the day in supporting Oliver and Swanhild under a renewed Press infliction, reports of the Barrow operations having sent fresh swarms of reporters and sightseers to infest Dannow from the Shaw to the manor front door.

He reaped the reward for his efforts to brighten others that night, for at first sight of a photograph of the hidden room inscription which he had procured from Oliver an illuminating recollection was roused. A retrospective picture of Luna when she first studied it. She had read to "... *under stars, sans*..." then glanced down at the gap. The French sans was commonly used in medieval England, together with other Gallicisms: could the missing word be French?

He consulted the French dictionary left over from his schoolroom days, without result, and decided to run to London next day and purchase the fullest one, containing archaic words, he could find.

Next day, Thursday, found the newspaper-got flood still high. At noon came a telegram for Swanhild. The runes had been read overnight and Luna wanted all three to come up to Chelsea that afternoon, for a sitting.

Not having seen her for a couple of days, Goddard was struck by the change in Luna since her first coming. She *had* developed a line over the forehead, and her hands were not very steady. It was easy to diagnose her appearance as that of a very strong-willed person keeping down over-strung nerves with difficulty. Madame Yorke even seemed distinctly harassed, behind the mien of genial disapproval she had worn since the beginning of the sittings.

This one differed from all that had gone before. Luna would not let them know the translation of the runes. She produced two typed sheets of foolscap. "Duplicates," she announced. "When you are in trance, Mr. Hammand, Mr. Covert is to read one over to you, and note if you recognise any words or sentences. No," she added, holding them behind her; "you are not to read them first. We have to avoid putting ideas into your head, you know. After waking you we shall read the second copy, mark what you recollect in a waking state, and compare the two."

"It sounds interesting. Why don't you do the reading yourself?"

"Because I know what I think you ought to recognise, and so do Auntie and Swanhild in some degree, and any of us might give you a hint, unconsciously, by a chance of voice. We must leave you alone with Mr. Covert, also, to obviate any chance of unconscious thought-transference. Please sit there."

Oliver had reached the point at which a command and gesture from her sent him at once into a trance. Left alone with him Goddard found it rather loathsome. Oliver, having received instructions from Luna, could hear what he said, but apparently could not see him, staring with unspeculative eyes, and answering in a flat lifeless voice the queries that were read aloud. Like the animated corpse of old Oliver, Goddard thought. He worked carefully through the sheet and then called the women back.

Luna's hands shook and her eyes seemed to shoot sparks through their golden veil as she scanned the marked paper. Finally she gave a look of meaning to Swanhild, who was peering over her shoulder. "As far as it counts, not bad," she whispered. Then her habitual composure returned and she waked Oliver.

"Let's be comfortable while you read the other sheet, Mr. Hammand," she said. They seated themselves round the fire and Oliver read aloud:

JESSIE DOUGLAS KERRUISH

"'Do you know anything of the following?

SALVATOR ROSA.

RATTOTSKAR.

HVARENO.

VISHNU SIRANGUAN—'

"What a queer muddle!" he broke off.

"I concealed what I hoped you'd recognise in a jumble of any chance words that occurred to me."

"Oh, I see. To see if I'd pick out what you expected? Well, Salvator Rosa's a poet or sculptor, or something. Vishnu's a Hindu god of some sort. I don't know the others. Hullo, there's an old friend in the next line—ODIN,"

"What does the word suggest?"

"Myself sitting on the foot of Swan's bed and reading a book we had about Norse heroes to her when we were convalescing after measles."

Out of the list that followed he recognised a few classical names, and the following words and sentences:

"'THOR,' another Norse god, I remember.

"'BALDUR,' another of them.

"'TESTE DAVID CUM SYBILLA,' I don't know the words but they go to a tune like this"; he tapped on his knee the *Dies Irae*.

"'AESIR LOK.' It sounds like Loki; more Norse. I think he was the villain of the measles book.

"'SIGMUND,'—he's in Wagner.

"'MIOLNER,'—I half-know that, but am not sure."

He stopped, having reached the end. "In a waking state you have identified five of the words I hoped you would," said Lana. "In hypnosis you picked them out, and five others as well: RATTOTSKAR, YGDRASIL, JORMUNDGANDR, EINHEIRAR, and FIMBULVETER."

"I don't know those," he protested.

"In hypnosis your awakened memory did. They are all from ancient northern religious tradition. You Hammands have been English Christians for ten centuries at least, but for scores of centuries before your ancestors were pagans; and echoed echoes of their religious ideas are ingrained in your brain, and can be wakened to active knowledge when you are hypnotised."

He nodded slowly. She consulted Goddard's notes on the first paper. "You recollected vaguely the name of Sigmund, a merely mortal hero, but described Odin as the ALLFATHER, Thor as owner of the hammer Miolner, Baldur as the spring god, Lok as the devil, Ygdrasil you said was the Holy Ash Tree, the Einheirar you called deified heroes, Jormundgandr something long and round, and Fimbulveter the Final War."

"Well?" he asked. "Waking, I don't know them; as I said."

"You have a wonderful sub-conscious recollection of what your ancestors believed in when the bronze blade was new."

Then she began to discourse about it: what people believed when the blade was new. Jormundgandr, the serpent that held the sea in place round mid-earth, the Holy Ash, under whose branches the souls of the Einheirar—heroes slain in battle—feast until the Fimbulveter-Tide: when they should ride over the Rainbow–Bifrost Bridge—to help Odin and the other gods in the Final War with the devil-gods of Helheim. And the death of the gods, and the dying of the world, and the resurrection of them all, and the riding of them over the reviving earth.

Goddard could not deny it was tremendous in its way. Luna's fine, impassioned voice had something to do with the charm; and the sheer, clanging syllables of the ancient names themselves; and the barbaric splendour of the myths. When she stopped he woke up with a little gasp, and saw Swanhild's eyes wide and shining like stars, and Oliver blinking and staring. Only Madame Yorke was wide awake and calm; who had posted herself out of the radius of her niece's magic eyes. "As you talked," said Oliver, slowly; "it made me think of Wagner, and something beyond Wagner. The Ring music and something beyond it."

Goddard could not help an emphatic nod. Old Oliver had voiced his own feeling exactly. "Yes, Wagner," Luna assented. "He embodied in the Ring his remarkable hereditary memory of old Scandinavian intellectual atmosphere. Aristotle said of the Elusinian Mysteries that he considered the initiated did not learn anything in definite words, but received certain impressions that produced certain conditions of the soul. That is what is done by my reminding you of the beliefs of your ancestors—"

She broke off and looked full at Goddard. "It seems rather a deviation from the business in hand, eh, Mr. Covert? Only very soon I shall tell you all why it is not so long a way from the Danish Undying Monster to the Old Danish Day of Doom."

Goddard did not forget a huge French dictionary, and at night he settled down to read the necessary sections. C, G, O, Q, and S, in search of six letter words ending in L or Z. It was about midnight when the word and its meaning leapt at him from the page, and nearly until dawn came he was still sitting trying to grasp its ramified meanings.

It was past his understanding in some directions, only the horrible core of it was plain. Six letters—and he understood the ritual, and why Reginald Hammand and Magnus the Warlock killed themselves. Why the others who saw it pined away. Why the Warlock's wife died of what she saw. Why Swanhild and Luna could not tell him about it.

Thousands of years of it, from Oliver and Swanhild back past the Viking whose dust they had disturbed two days before; perhaps past the Bronze Age warrior whose blade was its first fixed point in Time. Sumless generations, and the Monster ever at their elbows, undying while son followed father. From before the Bronze Age to the twentieth century of salvation.

Undying.

Undying to Swanhild and Oliver—no, thank God, not to Swanhild. Only to Oliver—to Oliver, and an inquest in a little inn, with the worst result of civilisation ready to bruit it to the ends of the world if a couple of louts were in danger and the shame incredible of a hundred generations must be told to save them.

All explained in six letters.

1

THE SPIRIT OF THE AGE TAKES A HAND

Goddard did not wake until very late that Friday. After two days of rain and enervating mildness the morning was dry and breezy, with some frost on the Down heights and a little sunshine over it. A day to assist thought, the dreadful truth became more incredibly logical and more revolting as he tramped in the direction of the Manor.

By an impulse he turned into the church and inspected the brass. Coming out of the lych gate he almost ran into Oliver. He caught himself starting violently and drawing a sharp breath. The word in cold print was bad enough, the reality embodied in one of its living victims was shocking.

"Cheer-o, old man!" said Oliver "You jumped a bit! Church doesn't appear to agree with you in the morning."

"I was looking at the brass," Goddard blurted. He had to say something, and nothing else came to his mind. Self-consciousness foreign to his nature possessed him, and he dreaded lest it should betray itself in his manner, in an unintentional stare or too hurried withdrawal of his eyes from Oliver's frank regard. He felt a sudden consciousness of what a good sort Oliver was. How the kids used to hang round him in the refugee camps in Flanders—and oh, why hadn't a bullet found him in that same Flanders! It all flickered through Goddard's brain while he made his stupid reply,

"Did you spot anything about it?" asked Oliver.

"Nothing," replied Goddard truthfully.

"Miss Bartendale knows all, and we'll know before long," said Oliver. "We got a letter this morning asking Swan to run up early. She's got some information sooner than she hoped, and is coming down with Swan this evening; and Mrs. Yorke too, of course; to hold a final sitting in the hidden room. They want you, to assist, so will you come round and dine?"

"Of course I'll come." Goddard felt a great calm at the prospect of unburdening himself.

"Then shall I pick you up as I return from Steyning? I've got some business there, and ought to be on the way home about four."

"Right-o." Here a *char-a-bancs* swept past, involving the two men in its wake of powdered chalk, petrol fumes, and strident remarks.

"That's the place—them trees up there—it didn't 'arf eat the poor gal; didjer see the *Daily Post* ercount, and wot the doctors said? Fair made me sick, it did. Wot I say is: it's a thin tale erbout 'er reasons for bein' there at midnight—that young gent—"

"Damn!" said Oliver. Goddard said: "Amen!"

Real frost developed during the afternoon, dusk and dark culminated in clear starlight, checkered by the clouds that drove in flocks over the sky, driven by a bitter wind. At six o'clock the earth was faintly starlit, the valley full of soft frost-fog, the Shaw louring purple-black under the spectral greyness of the Monstrous Man.

All horribly like the night of the Monster's coming, so Goddard reflected as he stepped into Oliver's car. The drive was a silent one until they had left the village behind and were near the Manor turning.

"We're late," commented Oliver suddenly. "They'll be there before us. Gone to sleep, old son?"

Goddard started. He had unconsciously fallen into a reverie, reflecting that the old conception of the Monster—a ghastly, ghostly horror ready to materialise out of night without warning—was preferable to what the six letters had told him. Before he could reply:

"Hullo, what's that?" exclaimed Oliver.

It was Will Cladpole, racing for home, humped over the handlebars of his cycle. The car overshot him; he shouted, pedalled fiercely, and clutched the hood to keep beside it. His face was white and frightened. Oliver applied the brake.

"Oh, Mus' Hammand, sir!" the boy bleated. "There's murder a-gain' on if summun don't stop it! Down in t'Shaw, sir! I heard of her shriekin' out—"

"What on earth are you talking about?" demanded Oliver.

"The lady as went into t' Shaw, sir! With the gem'man as takes pictures for the noospaper; the *Post*, sir! There was a lot on 'em, in a big car, sir, a'goin' to t'Shaw. What nobody does arter dusk, you know, sir. An' I follered, an' they went in an' in a minute she shrieked out awful. That awful, sir, that I just didn't go in, but nipped right back to t' road."

It was all delivered like one sentence, and he stopped breathless. "Pull yourself together," Oliver ordered, in a voice Goddard remembered from Flanders days. A low, round voice that suggested command and the capacity to deal with any situation that might be impending. "Are you telling us some woman's being murdered in Thunderbarrow Shaw?"

"I'm tellin' you, Mus' Hammand, sir. She screamed awful. They left the car outside an' went in, you can see its lights."

The hedge blocked all view of the Shaw at that point. With one accord Oliver and Goddard jumped out and ran to a gap. Over the valley, at the end of the Roman byroad, above the mist level and at the rim of the Shaw, was a little red light. "Nobody has any business to be in that Shaw after dark," said Oliver, running back to the car, and jumping in. Goddard seized his sleeve. "You mustn't go, old man," he cried. "Remember what you promised—"

"A woman in danger—Miss Bartendale would understand—" Oliver replied curtly.

"Oliver—I'll go, you stay—" Goddard stepped up beside him.

"Old man, it's my Shaw, and my Bane. I'm going."

"Oliver, you don't understand! It's only you there's danger for— only—" Goddard broke off, conscious of the boy staring and listening from the road. "You mustn't go—" he cried, and sprang at Oliver and caught him round the body, pinioning his arms and trying for a ju-jitsu hold. Any sort of hold—it would pay to break one of Oliver's arms—anything to keep him out of the Shaw. "For Heaven's sake, old man, just wait while I tell you by ourselves—"

"While a woman's in danger, old son!" the other man replied. "If you won't come—"

"I'll go, but you must not!"

They grappled then. Oliver was half as heavy again as Goddard, and many times as strong: strong enough to do a rough act harmlessly. He plucked Goddard from himself as though he were a child, swung him at arms length, and sent him reeling backwards across the road.

Goddard pitched over in the embrace of the hedge, dragged himself out in a clutching tangle of bramble trails, and saw the rear light of the little car vanish back towards the village. Without a word he snatched the cycle from Will, mounted, and raced off in its track.

He drove the pedals frantically, almost standing on them, but the car light grew smaller and smaller. It disappeared from sight, turned into the Roman cutting, while the cycle was skimming bumpily over the village cobbles. He went the length of the street like a flash, looking neither to right or left. At the proper point he turned rather by instinct than sight and the cycle shot headlong but smoothly to the trough of the valley, into delicate fog that made everything invisible beyond the lamp's glare, ran along the level, and began to climb. To Goddard fog and sky alike seemed to be crossed by letters of fire writing before him the completed line of the rhyme:

"GAROUL : HAMMAND : WARE : THY : BANE :"

Up the slope loomed soughing blackness that was the Shaw, below it two red lights scintillated. He jumped off behind the little car where it stood untenanted behind an empty five-seater, and took a hurried glance forward. In the depths of the Shaw was a little glow, and on the wind there came to him through the stirred trees the echo of a woman's voice. Acting on a half-formulated thought, he snatched a rug from the car and slung it over his shoulder as he raced into the wood towards the light.

It was in the clearing before the burnt beech, down wind from it voices came to him as he ran; and once a squeal as of bodily pain or incipient hysteria. Speeding blindly, he stopped just short of colliding with a figure that bulked between him and the light.

"Oliver! Thank God!" he exclaimed.

Oliver, at the leeward rim of the clearing, was hidden from it by a thicket. He turned his head. "You, Goddard!" he exclaimed.

"Come away at once, dear old chap!" Goddard begged. "You should not be here, you know—"

"They shouldn't be here." Oliver indicated the clearing. "It's that blighter with an Oxford accent and Filbert hair—Miss Bartendale's Press jackal—"

His voice was hoarse with suppressed indignation. "You promised Miss Bartendale not to come in," Goddard urged. "Come away. Let me settle them, whatever they are—"

"It's *my* Shaw, old man! As to what they are—look! A séance, if you please!"

While the men talked singing had come spatteringly down breeze to them. Goddard glanced in. A motor lamp stood on a fallen log, its light turned to them, and in that Curtis of the *Post* leant against a tree, pencil and notebook in his hands, and looked across at the burnt beech. Owing to the efforts of souvenir-hunters, the interior of the beech was open to view; a woman stood there, Goddard could see her face dimly in the starlight; holding hands in a ring with three others. They were singing "Lead, kindly Light." Goddard said: "Never mind them, Oliver!" and plucked at the bigger man's sleeve.

Oliver pulled his arm away. "I must clear them out. Just listen to that!"

The singing stopped, the woman in the tree spoke in a low, impressive voice. "Is the spirit of Katherine Stringer here?" she demanded, staring before her with unfocussed eyes.

A pause succeeded. Another woman gave a strangled, half-hysterical yelp. The medium then answered herself. Her voice, middle-aged and deep when she spoke in her own person, was screwed up to a falsetto travesty of a girl's. "Katherine Stringer is here!" it wailed.

"Answer me, Katherine," the medium said, in her natural voice. "To what was your death due? To man, beast, or spirit?"

"To the Hammand Bane," she answered herself in the falsetto.

"And what is the Undying Monster, Katherine?" another woman demanded. "It is a Vampire? Or an Elemental? Or one of the Hierarchy of the Outer Planes?"

"I must not tell you," the falsetto answered. "I can but say it is able to manifest itself in one moment of your earthly reckoning of time; it is not perceptible to the keen senses of even a dog; it tears, and sucks, and devours."

All this came subconsciously to Goddard's ears while he spoke with Oliver. "It's an obvious rehash of what was said at the inquest," he whispered. "Why won't you come away, Oliver?"

"I can't leave them there, you know."

"Then order them off, and come away."

"I've heard you interrupt a séance the women may have hysterics."

"Let them!" exclaimed Goddard. He was in a fuming agony, owing to the limitations of his partial knowledge. It was evident that so far something was holding off what he dreaded, but he did not know what to do without the risk of blindly precipitating a catastrophe.

While they spoke the questioning went on. "But what does it look like, Katherine?" the questioner asked.

The falsetto replied: "I am barely as yet across the borders of the world of spirits, and have not the words to describe what I have learnt."

"But is it a vampire: a dead Hammand who can't rest in the grave?" persisted the querist.

To which the falsetto responded prudently: "I may not tell you of what has brought strong men to madness and suicide. I am but in the ante-chamber of this world."

"What is the world of spirits like?"

This was a deviation from the subject immediately in hand; but the querist was evidently not a person to miss opportunities.

The falsetto began this answer without hesitation; launching into a muddle of materialistic eschatology, blended with some elementary psychologic and biologic information, not unsuggestive of Lewis Carroll's "Phantasmagoria." "Hang it, I can't stand any more!" gasped Oliver. "That drivel—and on the spot where poor Kate met her death—women or no women—this abrogates courtesy!"

He stepped round the thicket. Goddard mechanically grasped the rug in both hands and followed him. His half-knowledge did not afford any information in the pressing question; whether to interfere bodily; or to wait supinely, hoping that the unknown restraining factor would continue to hold the Monster off. So the two stepped into the light and faced Curtis.

2

THE MONSTER AT LARGE

The Mercedes must have arrived at the Manor about the time Will reached the high road. Mr. Hammand was not yet back, so Walton replied to Swanhild's enquiry. Swanhild involuntarily glanced behind her. The stars were very vivid in a moonless sky, the wind cold and dry. A Monster night.

"We have his promise," Luna whispered, answering her thought.

Madame Yorke went to her room, Luna stopped to look at a trophy in the hall, and Swanhild stopped to explain its beauties. Both were in the state in which people ache to chatter incessantly about things indifferent. After many minutes the telephone issued its call. Telephones are apt to clamour at any time, but at the sound both startled, and Swanhild hurried to answer it.

She seemed to be switched back a fortnight, for it was Will's voice and the words of the midnight call two weeks before. "Hello, the manor—send Miss Hammand—quick!"

"It's Miss Hammand, Will. What's wrong?"

"It's the Monster, miss! At least Mr. Hammand's in the Shaw and somebody's murderin' somebody there. I heard her shriek—"

Swanhild was surprised at her own coolness. "Are you telling me my brother is in the Shaw?"

"Goin' there, miss. I heard of a lady shriekin' in it. I saw her go in, and heard her shriek, and came away and told him. And he pitched Mr. Covert out and set off for the Shaw."

"You mean my brother's going to the Shaw?"

"He must be there now, miss."

"And Mr. Covert, what of him?"

"He took my bike and started after the car. He didn't want Mr. Hammand to go, and Mr. Hammand chucked him into the hedge."

"Very well. Stand ready to open the gate for me." She rang up the garage. "Stredwick! Have you berthed the Mercedes?"

"Not yet, miss. I thought I might have my tea first, miss—"

"Good! She's plenty of petrol in. Run her round at once. At once, mind!"

She turned to find Luna behind her. "The only thing that would make Oliver break his word, Luna. Some woman in trouble in the Shaw. He's there—now, and Goddard is following him."

Walton stood beside Luna. Swanhild noted, quite calmly, the other woman's face was white but perfectly reposeful, only the close-drawn lips and the eyes smouldering under levelled brows indicating the dynamic force in leash. "You ordered the car round," said Luna. "Can we overtake Mr. Covert at least?"

"No. It is just a few minutes too late—" Swanhild paused and considered. "Not by the road," she amended, suddenly. "I remember—by the borstal we might intercept Goddard."

"There'll be three—" began Luna. "No, I forgot, the woman's there already. We may be in time to save Mr. Covert. What of the borstal?"

She buttoned up her coat as she spoke, Swanhild mechanically followed suit. "Reggie once drove the Maxwell down the turf beside the borstal. It was touch and go, by daylight, but I'll do it, or break my neck," she replied. "The roadway is hopeless. By this I can get to the Shaw in five minutes—or be killed."

"Oh, Miss Swanhild, the borstal bridge will be under water, with these rains!" protested Walton.

She ran and opened the front door. From the left the Mercedes purred up and Stredwick jumped down. Without wasting any time the two sprang into their places. The car seemed to take the moat bridge at a stride and shot down the avenue with the throttle open.

Luna was scarcely settled in her place before the frightened eyes
of Will, his lantern, and the ironwork of the gate flickered past
like a limelit picture. Swanhild turned the car to the left.

It ran for a short way on a smooth road, turned to the right,
slashed through long grass, and so leapt to the grassy slope beside
the white line of the chalk path.

They were facing the Beacon, and the breeze from it, their
lashed eyes could only make out the surrounding country as a dimly
illumined stretch of duskiness and deeper duskiness, with blurs of
frost-fog in the hollows, arched over with cold stars and driving
clouds. Luna, compulsorily inactive, shivered like a leashed grey-
hound, Swanhild was tense and cool, her eyes intent on the flaring
ribbon of path beside them. She saw before her a fan of light running over the short Down turf with the white line of borstal twink-
ling along the right-hand extremity of it. The white line was her
guide, to the left of it the Maxwell had been driven. The angle of
the slope steepened suddenly, the tilt at which the car rushed down
it almost flung the occupants on the screen. Swanhild leant back
and watched the rim of the light flow downwards, the white line of
safety ever near its right extremity. "Look for the bridge, Luna,"
she ordered, in a hissing shout that carried through the noise of
engine and wind.

Luna stood up, leaning back against the seat to keep her balance. Far in front she could see the dark bulk of the Beacon, topped
by the glimmer of the Monstrous Man. At the bottom of the valley
between, crossing the barely discernible line of sheep-track, was a
rippling line, dirty steel-colour in the fog. On the wind there came
to her a sharp, crackling echo. There was no mistaking the hideous, half-human note, far though it had carried.

"The bridge?" Swanhild repeated. "Is it over-water?"

Luna stared under level brows at the murk. "I see a kind of swirl
and break in the stream; no timbers."

"Sit down," ordered Swanhild grimly. "We'll jump it, and at
worst it's only drowning."

The angle became slightly less acute. She put the car almost on
the borstal, and gave it a swift turn to the right when the edge of

the lamplight flashed on water. It bumped violently, sank a wheel in the deep track, carried on out of it by sheer momentum, and splashed, thundering, and crashing, on the invisible bridge.

The bonnet drove through the stream like a ship's cut-water, and sent churned foam splashing over the panels. The car paused and seemed to sink backwards; recovered itself like a horse on its haunches; and landed on the opposite bank with a jar. Behind it sounded a rending of timber as the bridge collapsed.

There was now only a moderate slope up to the Shaw; as they breasted it a fusillade of the barking, unnatural howls burst forth. "There's a light creeping along the Roman road to the village—" exclaimed Luna. "I don't understand—" She broke off, bewildered, as the Mercedes stopped behind Oliver's little car.

She jumped out and unshipped a lamp. Swanhild seized the other. From the Shaw's depths the diabolic uproar of baying and barking came intermittently. Luna paused, with titled chin and narrowed eyes, locating the centre of disturbance, then sped into the labyrinth with Swanhild behind her. She ran like a sleepwalker, picking her way through the tangle of trees and massed under-growth without looking. As they ran the noises grew more distinct, they reached where the men had watched the séance, the monstrous screaming snarl droned out, a note of triumph in it, and Goddard's voice cried out shrilly. Luna swung the lamp in front of her and dashed into the clearing. Dead silence ensued.

3

IN THE FIFTH DIMENSION

Oliver stepped into the light before Curtis about the time Will neared home. "Do you know what you are doing here?" he asked, with menacing blandness.

"Reporting the séance," Curtis answered, too astonished for more than a bald reply, staring at the apparition that towered the best part of a foot above him.

"Also you are trespassing," said Oliver. His hand descended behind Curtis's head, bunched up the back of his collar and coat and the scruff of his neck in a grip made ferocious by the outraged sense of decency behind it, and administered a shake that jarred him from teeth to toes.

At Oliver's appearance the Medium stopped with her mouth open in the middle of a word, and silence held the four women for a moment. Then: "It's her!" one of them squealed: the grammatical reference being to their ghostly informant. "It's the Monster!" two others chorused, when Oliver advanced across the clearing, the lamp in one hand the other dragging Curtis. The Medium said nothing; she was hardened to violent interruptions of her performances. The circle came to pieces, and the three other pieces huddled round her, too startled for hysteria. They were young women, of differing types but alike in possessing the wild eyes of that faith that neither doubts nor reasons. The medium was middle-aged, and inscrutable now she had got over her first alarm.

"No, ladies; it's merely the proprietor of this wood, in which you are trespassing." Oliver's voice boomed forth tranquilly.

Goddard, following him in a state of quivering uncertainty, remembered that in Flanders Le Sergent Hammand had been notable for his management of frenzied refugees. Oliver was in his best form now; his large calm personality lifted the women's overwrought nerves clear from collapse to reassurance. "You will doubtless have the goodness to leave this place at once, ladies." He released Curtis, in order to pick up a scarf dropped by one of them, and handed it to her with a bow. "That pine-lined ride is the shortest way back to your car," he concluded pleasantly.

Curtis gathered together what was left of his dignity. "I am exceedingly sorry if we have annoyed you, Mr. Hammand," he began. "I fail to see, however, in what way we have given you any cause for the unpleasant assault you have just made on me. We were simply endeavouring to solve the mystery of this place, and Mrs. Robinson, whose celebrity as a medium is doubtless known to you—"

"It's only the presence of your friends that saves you from a worse assault," interrupted Oliver, in a low voice. "Go away before I lose control of myself—"

"Yes, get out, man, for your own sake!" supplemented Goddard. "You don't know what you are monkeying with, and you'll be to blame if anything happens—"

"Excuse me," Curtis interposed. "I am in no way responsible for these proceedings, and would never have proposed them myself. I was merely ordered to report—"

"Don't disgrace yourself utterly by excuses," snapped Oliver. "Go before I lose my temper."

He thrust the lamp into the Pressman's hand. Curtis took it without any more words, for the Medium was pulling at his sleeve meaningly, and hurried away with the women. Goddard linked his arm in Oliver's and took a step forward. Oliver stood firm. "Half a sec.," he said. "Let them get away first."

Goddard felt his face wet and warm, for all the dry cold. To follow or not? Which would be the least evil? He sweated and trembled in the misery of his half-knowledge. To let things proceed without attempting to guide them; in blind trust that the unknown factor that was keeping the Monster manifestation away might continue to act to the end; might be fatal. "Oliver, old man, don't you think you really ought to boot that beast all the way out of the place?" he suggested.

"It's not my habit to brawl before ladies." Oliver smiled at him in the last reflection of the departing lamp. "Also he must be left in a condition to see them safe off, you know. Why, old thing, you're fairly shivering yourself to pieces!"

The light vanished and left them in a dusk that was darkness to them after its going. "For God's sake, Oliver, let's get out of this!" exclaimed Goddard, after a few moments' pause. "They must be off by now. I—I'm in a blue funk, can't you see it? Miss Bartendale warned you—"

"Bless you, old son, it's all right! Hullo, what have you got that rug for?"

"I—I just happened to bring it. Oliver, I tell you I'm afraid—"

"Artful old Goddard! Swanhild told you to keep an eye on me! I know it's all right. I alone am in danger, and you know it, but I also know all about it—"

"You know what the Monster is?" Goddard almost shouted.

"No, but I know the spell that keeps it at bay. I dug it out of my inherited memory. *Heysaa*—That's it. *Heysa-aa!* Why—what—? Goddard, it's coming!"

His voice rose to a roar. "Run, Goddard! Run, run, man! It's coming—I tell you—! *Heysa-aa-a-a—*"

The word began as a human shout, broke halfway, turned to the unspeakable droning snarl of the hidden room, and swelled into a crackling, roaring, screaming, demoniac howl. It was like the hoarded lust and hunger and hate of all the ages, expressed in a voice that passed the bestial in its perversion of the human. Goddard sprang back a step. His eyes were now sufficiently adjusted to the faint starlight to distinguish movement; he saw Oliver's immense body drop to all fours and crouch back in momentary defensiveness while his eyes lit up and glowed red against the dark bulk of it.

A moment they remained so. Goddard, paralysed by the glare of them, stayed motionless. Then they soared up, phosphorescently opalescent, with a predominance of red, like two sinful dead planets escaping from Hell.

Kate's delirious words flashed through Goddard's brain: "Something big as a house—" As the eyes rose he waked and acted instinctively. He leapt sideways and flung the rug over the rising stars, keeping hold of two corners. It was bearskin, stoutly lined, but it was torn in three at once, while the demoniac voice swelled into a burst of baying and the immense body whirled round on him. Again Goddard stepped aside, and as he stepped he whisked part of the torn rug round his artificial arm. He was prepared as none of the other victims had been, though he knew any preparation would but stave off the end a while. The red eyes were over him again; he curved his real arm over his throat and presented the other before it as he went down under an irresistible weight.

He fell on his back, and so fought madly, again and again thrusting the insensate arm at the panting red-hot slavering jaws that strove to get at his throat, and the burning teeth that fixed once in his live arm and tore it hideously as he wrenched it away. Thus defending head and throat he staved off frantically, with feet and knees, the body that crouched over him. The rug did yeoman service with its loose, hindering fragments, but at last tearing fingers wore through the folds and raked the clothes from his shoulders, the red eyes were over his, nails tore at his chest, and a last triumphal snarl seemed to fill the world and vibrate the earth on which his head was pressed. In a final effort he thrust the skin-wrapped arm upwards, the howl was cut short, in the sudden silence he heard the cracking of the artificial limb as the jaws gripped it, and a white light swept over them like a wave. With the shock of it Goddard's thumping heart sucked and paused; he shut his eyes in the glare and fell back limply.

He only closed his eyes a moment, and opened them to this: He was flat on his back, his real arm crooked over his neck and a warm rain from it dribbling on his chin. His artificial arm was smashed and should have fallen limp, but was held up at full length, with ridiculous tatters of bearskin drooping from it over his chest. Over it was the upper line of Oliver's teeth, and over them a demoniac travesty of Oliver's face. Oliver was on his knees astride of him, his palms just off the ground, the blood-bedabbled fingers convulsively crooked as Luna's hand on his forehead forced him backwards. She was bending over Goddard's head, the lamp trained full on Oliver's face, and Goddard knew he would carry the picture of it to the grave.

It was the face of Oliver Hammand, devil-obsessed or else turned by some Circean spell to an animal with power of hatred and cold cruelty beyond the human or bestial. His hair stood on end; under it his ears laid themselves backwards; his upper lip had almost vanished from sight in a diabolic snarl; the whole mouth, blood-smeared and slavering, was distended and sucked in at the sides. The jaws protruded abnormally, and the big teeth appeared to project still further forward, while the upper part of the face seemed to be contracted and sloped back into insignificance, a mere setting for the red eyes. And the peculiar marvel was that the ensemble did not suggest the animal that is nearest man, but one quite diverse, for the face was fantastically wolfish; suggesting a man's capacity for hate blended with a wolf's ferocity and set in a body blended of both man and wolf and animated by a devil.

It was photographed on Goddard's brain while the arm dropped from the relaxed jaws. Oliver's face changed; his eyes lost their red and were stonily horror-struck; his jaws apparently retreated; his forehead came forward; his ears straightened and his hair subsided in damp curls. It all took but the few seconds that brought Swanhild to them, half a dozen paces after Luna. In those few seconds Oliver flickered back to his normal self, all but the blood on his mouth and fingers and the stony horror of his expression. Swanhild fell on her knees beside Goddard.

Slowly Oliver rose to his feet, without changing the pose of his head and arms, and stood astride of Goddard, arms taut, fingers crooked, and eyes staring glassily at Luna, who stood beyond

Goddard's head with the lamp. Finally he said, in a thin, blank sort of voice, like the hollow shell of his normal bass: "I—I have gone mad. I'm not dreaming. I've gone mad—gone mad and killed Goddard."

"Not killed, old man!" Goddard cried reassuringly. "I was only exhausted for a minute."

Swanhild jumped to her feet and flung her arms round her brother, forcibly bringing the rigid hands to his sides. "You are not mad, dear, dear old Oliver!" she almost cried. "You are sane, and you always will be—"

"I'm dreaming—" he said, tonelessly.

"No, dear, no! It's all right; perfectly all right, dear old boy!" Swanhild crooned, holding him tighter and tiptoeing to press her face against his. There was blood on her cheek when she canted her head to look in his eyes; he stared at her dully.

"There's blood on your face, Swan," he said. He slipped one arm up out of her bold, looked at the crimsoned fingers and clean back, drew it over his mouth, and eyed the resultant pink smear on it. "I am mad—or dreaming," he said, as though trying to find mental foothold. "I felt the Monster coming; coming round me; entering into me. And I wanted to kill you, Goddard—kill you and get at your throat with my teeth. Oh, say I am mad, for Heaven's sake!"

Goddard jumped up and caught his hand, squeezing it hard. "It's all right, dear old chap!" he declared. "Not your fault, and it won't happen again—"

"Won't happen again?" repeated Oliver. "How do you know? What do you know? Has it happened before?"

"Dozens and dozens of times, and no blame to anybody," Goddard assured him. "I know all about it. Do buck up and don't take it too seriously—"

Oliver pulled his hand away and put it to his head. His eyes travelled to Luna. "I shall go mad soon," he said quietly.

She stepped to him and looked him full in the eyes. "Mr. Hammand," she said slowly, "since this has happened it is best to tell you all simply and fully. You are not mad, though you attacked Mr. Covert just as a hungry wolf would have done. *Just as you attacked Kate Stringer here a fortnight ago—*"

"Oh, Luna!" It was Swanhild who interrupted.

"It is wisest and kindest to tell all at once," Luna went on unmoved. "The Monster did not enter into you, Mr. Hammand, simply because the Monster has never had any existence. It is purely a creature of the Fifth Dimension, and the Fifth Dimension is—the human mind."

She paused. The others stood in a bunch, Swanhild with her arms round her brother, Goddard grasping his hand firmly. The situation was past any words at the young people's command; both could only try blindly to impress on Oliver that their relations with him were unaltered. Luna's voice proceeded, cold as fate: "I have told you that a powerful impression on a human brain is passed along through the ages. A virtuous impulse, a vicious one, an unnatural one; all will repeat themselves throughout the centuries. You are in that way a victim, Mr. Hammand, of lycanthropy."

"Lycanthropy?" he repeated. "I seem to remember—"

"Lycanthropy is a form of erratic mania that causes the victim to imagine he is a wolf, and to act in accordance with that belief. It is a mental disease that has reached the form of an epidemic very often, and in the men of the line of Hammand it has become hereditary. It only appears when the victim is in a pinewood, in starlight, and with one human companion—"

"There!" exclaimed Goddard. "That's what I didn't know—*one* other person!"

Oliver's gaze never shifted from Luna. "Wolf madness?" he said. "I remember now—they called such people *wehr-wolves*, didn't they?"

"In German," Luna replied. "In Old English, 'turn-skins'; in French '*loups-garoux*'; in old French the term was '*garoul*,' as in the hidden room inscription."

She ceased. "I begin to understand," he said, without emotion. "I'll realise by and by. How long have you known this, all of you?"

"Since Monday," Swanhild answered, and: "Since last night," Goddard chimed in. He continued to look at Luna. "Since I first saw the brass," she said.

"Since your first day here?" He spoke dispassionately, and it was the more dreadful for the grotesque disorder of his face, blood smeared and scratched and beginning to discolour where Goddard had beaten it off. "You've known all the time I'm no better than a mad cannibal? That my ancestors were man-eating brutes in human shape? That if I had children they'd be the same? That I mauled and half ate a woman here—"

"I know that it was not you—yourself—it was an impulse of memory caused by the sin of an ancestor three thousand years ago."

"It's good of you to make excuses. I quite understand now. It explains everything. Pines and cold and starlight—and wolf-mania. Oh, I see it all—grandfather killed the woman he'd coaxed into the wood—and the Warlock started to eat his own child— Oh, I quite understand. Quite. Understand, you know." He smiled round at them. "By and by I'll realise it, I suppose. Cold, isn't it? We ought to go to the doctor and have your arm tied up, Goddard."

He strode into the pine ride. Swanhild ran and hooked her arm in his. He looked at her. "You've known it a week," he said. "You realise it, I suppose? Well, I shall later."

She only clung to him, and so they passed along the path. Luna and Goddard followed with the lanterns.

4

ONE LOOSE LINK

When they reached the cars, Goddard halted. "Half a sec. all of you," he exclaimed. "We must explain how we got knocked about, you know, Oliver! Swanhild, you're able bodied about the hands, will you kindly take that bike and hurl it violently on its front wheel on the road? You all perceive my game? I had a small accident, and bumped into Oliver in the course of it, hence my state, and his face. Topping, Swanhild!"

She had fallen in with his suggestion and flung the cycle slanting along the path so that the front wheel buckled. "You'll steer the Maxwell, Miss Bartendale?" Goddard concluded. "I suppose you'll go with Swanhild, Oliver?"

While the two cars crossed the valley Goddard explained his discoveries to Luna. Oliver, in the other car, sat with head up and eyes drooping, silently regarding the blood-tipped hands folded on his knees. When driving permitted Swanhild placed her disengaged hand over them. He turned his head and looked at her with vacant eyes. "I'll realise by and by," he said. "At least you're the same, Swan, dear."

"Everyone's the same, dear old thing," she whispered back. He smiled in a spiritless way. "They can't be, Swan. It's best to understand that at once."

People were flocking into the village street in knots from the south; in a way suggestive of a crowd returning from a sight; but the occupants of the cars were too intent on their own affairs to notice anything unusual. In the manor courtyard and hall there was a general hubbub; most of the house staff huddling about while Madame Yorke tried to persuade the terrified Stredwick to get some conveyance ready to take her on her niece's track. A hush fell as the cars appeared.

"It's all right, Madame Yorke." Oliver roused himself to address the guest in a voice meant for the audience in general. "Some spiritualists were holding a screaming séance in the Shaw, and Goddard and I had an accident after packing them off. That's all; I'm not hurt to mention, I'll just go and tidy myself a bit while Goddard is tinkered up. If I'm wanted to go for the doctor or anything I'll be in the Holbein room in ten minutes or so."

Luna gave her aunt a meaning glance, and swept it round to Goddard and Swanhild. "He's best by himself for a while," she whispered.

Within the ten minutes she entered the Holbein room. Oliver had turned on only one light, above the fireplace, and stood leaning on the mantelpiece. His face seemed flat and grey, curiously like the painted face of the Warlock above his head. There was a dull composure about his features. Luna had an irresistible impression that Sir Magnus had looked like that after his wife fell dead in the hidden room.

"Well?" said Oliver, his voice pleasantly unemotional.

"Mr. Covert's injuries are trifling. I came to tell you that while Swanhild and Auntie finish the bandaging. No need for the doctor."

"You came to reassure me. Oh, Luna, what's the use of pretending? You know what a dream I've had—and then to learn this!"

He almost cried it, with a break in his voice, and stretched out his hands appealingly. She would have taken them in hers, but he stared at them and drew them back. "There's blood on them!" he groaned.

"But there's none on your conscience!" she cried back, trying to snatch at them. He placed them behind him; she came close and put hers on his shoulders. Her bright curls barely reached his chin; irrelevantly there came to his mind a sunny line from one of the sunniest works in England's radiant literature. "'As high as my heart,'" he quoted aloud, and: "Oh, Luna, Luna!"

"Oh, Oliver, dear Oliver! You know it is hurting me as much as you—" She almost whimpered. Her face was drawn, her eyes wide black pools of anguish. For the moment her composure had dissolved and her underlip worked like that of a child on the point of breaking down. The temptation to stop its quivering in the easiest way presented itself, in that moment of revelation, as a mere obvious necessity, but in the fraction of a second it took Oliver to bring his hands round and bend his head something woke in him—the ingrained self-restraint that was too strong for temptation. He raised his head and, instead of closing round her, his hands lifted to remove hers from his shoulders. "I know it, Luna," he said gently. "I know it because I have dreamed dreams lately, and I know you would have let yourself dream them, too, but for your knowledge. Now I also have the knowledge, and perhaps it would be better if you did not touch me."

She drew back a step, composed again, and settled quietly in a chair by the fire. He seated himself opposite her, as quietly, and began to speak in a level tone. "It seems curious I don't feel excited," he began. "No, it isn't curious after all. One learnt that in war time: after a real disaster one was a bit numbed and quite cool. And this is a real cataclysm—waking from a dream to reality is the biggest cataclysm, isn't it? And it was such a heavenly dream: dreamed between the reality of war and the reality of hereditary madness—"

"Not madness," she interrupted. "Hallucination."

"What does it matter what one calls it?"

"Hallucinations may exist in a perfectly sane mind."

"But hallucination that is hereditary is another matter, dear." He spoke as one who argues gently with the self-deceiving. "An hallucination that has led to murder and madness along the ages has got to stop. And it rests with me to stop it."

She was silent. "I'm the last male Hammand, the last link in the chain—oh, it all fines down to me—no getting away from that! My ancestors thought it was an external evil spirit; we know it's in the brain, handed down from Hammand brain to Hammand brain, and that mine is now the sole repository of it, and must be the last. It's quite simple. And you knew it, Luna, while I dreamed dreams."

"I had your promise, and relied on it to avert accidents until it was time to tell you the truth."

"Quite wisely. No decent person could calculate what Spookery and the Press would do. I am not apologising for my broken promise."

"I should have been surprised if you had kept it, in the circumstances."

"Exactly. We understand one another. That's where the bitterness is—" His voice broke, but he controlled it. "Only you knew I was dreaming and did not wake me—"

"I had my reason—"

"I can imagine it. You who are so learned and gifted; who can find out the secret thoughts of the long-dead and go through the minds of the living like so many books; you are human yourself and dreaded to end my dream—"

She looked up as though ready to speak, but checked herself. He went on: "It was your dream, too; no use trying to deceive one another. The dream came to both of us when we met. Only you knew it could never become reality. When was that?"

"I suspected from the first. The brass was decisive."

"You knew from the first day? You've suffered all this time? And you are the worst sufferer; I've only had to bear the shattering of the dream, while you have had to shatter it yourself. Oh, Luna dear, you are the greatest sufferer. Only—the dream—I didn't realise how lovely it was until now it's broken. The dream every decent man dreams—"

He glanced up at the portrait, and his voice hardened.

"It isn't fair! He lived his dream before it was broken, and you have said he was to blame—his wife and kiddie, though! Good Lord, he may have suffered more!—but then he didn't lose *you*, Luna! He lived his dream—his ancestral house; his wife to make it home; his own little children to be loved and worried over—the dream every normal man has at the back of his mind, though he doesn't talk about it. Only I'm not a normal man—strictly, I shouldn't have been born at all—"

She hid her face in her hands. He checked himself. "Oh, yes, it was right I should. If it was only for the two hours during the retreat from C—," he went on in the tone of one who considers a question.

"I was half as big again and five times as strong as any man who was left alive. All thanks to generations of well-bred, well-living ancestors. That's why I was able to lift the Maxim into the gap and work it with the one hand I had fit to use; and that meant the grey-coats didn't get through before the Lancashires came up. They said it saved the line—my decent ancestors having bred me big and sound. It wasn't the line I considered, of course, but the crocked chaps behind me. We collected five lorry loads of them: a couple of hundred men with a fresh chance of life and fulfilled dreams; a couple of hundred who weren't stamped into the mud after all. The women of a couple of hundred men not needing to take up life without them—all depending, you know, on one of the sound strong arms I inherited—inherited straight from the Warlock's arms that swung that big sword at Bosworth. Oh, it was worth being born for, even if my own life had to be ruined—if only I had never met you, Luna! Are you crying, dear?" he ended gently.

"No!" came through the fingers interlocked before her face. "And if I were it would be for gladness that God hasn't made me love a man who would rail at Him in trouble."

"Oh, my dear, He didn't make you capable of loving a cur! My fate's just that of most people, after all. He allowed my forbears to hand to me mingled good and ill, a sound body to be of some ser-vice to my kind, a kink of the mind to wreck my own life because of the *noblesse oblige* that has also been handed down to me together with the blessing and curse. Oh, it was worth being born for; work-ing the Maxim; I would not have minded dying over it—but it's another matter to go on living after meeting you and learning I cannot have you—living in the same world with you!"

She made a little movement, yet did not speak, for she knew it was good for him to talk freely after the shock. "But, of course, I've got to do it," he went on "Live, and bolster up the family repu-tation until the line dies with me." He stopped, and the dreary com-posure of his eyes gave way to a red light of horror. "Good Lord! Those poaching brutes! If they are arrested—"

She lowered her hands and her eyes looked, into his, "A thou-sand years of disgrace—everything to be explained for the swine of the papers to exploit. I begin to realise it now—cannibalism, no less—past imagination—unique—" he stammered on.

She interrupted. "Not unique, there was a trial for it—on the high seas—in London thirty years ago. And men have been accused of it even in Sussex; Colonel Lunsford, and—"

"It's the last straw—that I may have to come forward and brand myself and my ancestors publicly. No, it is not—losing you is the worst!" Oliver sank his face in his hands, "With you I could have faced everything—"

Luna suddenly flung herself on her knees beside him. "Oliver, it's too hard. You shall have me; I'll stand by you, and nothing shall separate us. I was made for you, and God has brought us together, and He cannot mean us to be the victims of past folly and sin—"

"The *future* is our business, dear," he said.

"Why should we be slaves of the unborn future? Let the future look to itself, so long as I can make you happy. Your ancestors handed on the curse—"

The man was suddenly very calm and collected. "They did it in ignorance, dear. We should do it deliberately."

"What does it matter? We only live once in this fine world—"

"There's a life after, and we are responsible to those who come into possession of the fine world after us. Just look forward, dear, forward to the Lord knows how many Oliver Hammands with their lives ruined—perhaps just when they'd met the women of their hearts—and who knows how many Kates hideously done to death! No, dear—"

"I can see it all; I have seen it all for weeks; and I do not care—"

"Of course you don't, dear; for the time. You'd give your soul and wrong all the rest of humanity to make me happy temporarily. Only it would never answer. You'd come to your senses, and you'd hate yourself for stooping, and I'd hate myself for allowing you to stoop. You are learned and wise, and I'm commonplace, but in this matter the man must be master and save the woman from herself. And you know, dear, it might be better if you didn't touch me. I'm no Galahad, only a man who loves too well to sacrifice the woman he loves to her own love for him. Oh, my dear, you know how it hurts me—enough to give me some idea of how it must hurt you, Luna "

She threw her head back. "It takes away part of the sting to learn I love a man so much better than myself, Oliver."

"Dear, I'm not, yet it is grand that you should think it! And perhaps I should not have said I love you—though you knew it."

"I knew it," she replied triumphantly. "Only I had to have it in words before I could make you promise to marry me if the one loose link in my chain of investigation proves dependable."

His eyes stared incredulously into the calm starriness of hers. "Your chain?" he said.

"I did not forbear to tell you from cowardice, but because I hoped that when I told you of the Monster's nature I might perhaps give some feeble hope of its exorcism. Oh, do not hope, Oliver! One link is weak, but if it holds the Monster curse may be removed forever."

He put his hand to his head. "I've heard surgeons can do wonders—make blighters decent or idiots clever by operating on their brains—"

She laughed, an overwrought laugh. "Rubbish! Rubbish! Newspaper rubbish! A mental curse must have a mental cure—if one can find the First Cause. And I think I've found the cause—back in the Bronze Age; only one step is pure conjecture; one link uncertain. In a word, Oliver; if that link does not hold you must be the last Hammand, but if it holds you can marry me, for my fee, and let me stand shoulder to shoulder with you through life. Oh, don't hope, Oliver—" she burst out. "When I have told you all you will realise how doubtful the link is; but if it holds—"

In the middle of his amazement he heard a step. Quickly he sprang up and lifted her to her feet. The door opened; Swanhild came in and behind her Goddard, one sleeve empty and his hand bandaged, and Madame Yorke.

"Oh, Oliver!" cried Swanhild. "News has come from the lodge. The Ades were arrested half an hour ago. They resisted, that's what all the village was watching while we were in the Shaw. And Will learnt it was for—for poor Kate's death!"

Oliver turned to Luna with a bitter smile. "Thus passes, publicly, the good name of the Hammands!" he said.

5

BRONZE AGE TO JUDGMENT DAY

They all remained at gaze a full minute. Then Oliver said: "I must 'phone the police at once. Those fellows must not remain in suspense."

"No!" cried Luna sharply. "Before we make a move we must clearly understand the business. A few hours' arrest won't hurt them."

"Their women—" said Oliver and Swanhild together.

"We must be just even to ourselves. The men brought this on themselves. In three hours Swanhild shall let their women know they will be released; but I, who am morally responsible for this arrest, demand three hours' delay; If only on my own account; for I have risked so much—even my professional reputation and personal good name—in the matter."

"I don't understand," said Oliver, bewildered. Swanhild hurried to him, clasped her hands over his arm and looked in his face wistfully. He contrived to smile at her desultorily. "I shan't commit suicide, at least, Swan," he said. "It was the only decent thing grandfather and the Warlock could do, as they were responsible for the presence of the victims. For me it's different—"

"Luna told me that from the beginning."

"I'm glad she reassured you. My course is to face life—and disgrace. At least you are the same always, Swan. God knew what He was about when He made sisters who *are* sisters. You'll always be the same. And you, Goddard—?"

He glanced at the other man. "Always the same, naturally. Even more so when I'm 'Mr. Swanhild Hammand,' and officially qualified to stand beside you before the world. You might know it without hinting a question."

Oliver's stark eyes softened a little. "I think. I could get my bearings if I knew how much you all know—"

He looked at Madame Yorke. She answered quickly:

"You knew I'm Luna's confidante. She's told me every step from the beginning."

"Luna told me all last Monday night, when she feared she had got to a dead end, and I urged her—ordered her—to keep the secret and search further," Swanhild said in her turn.

Goddard chimed in. "Of course it wouldn't have been cricket for Miss Bartendale to tell me anything while you were in ignorance. I found out the missing word last night. I was investigating off my own bat because I distrusted Miss Bartendale's secrecy; Swanhild explained more while she tied me up, and now I know she has been preparing for the final step."

"The final step?" Oliver repeated.

"One hour's experiment in the hidden room," said Luna. "Oh, don't hope, for heaven's sake! I have practically no hope myself, but we must try if the one weak link of my chain proves unexpectedly strong."

"There can be no cure for hereditary madness until Judgment Day," said Oliver, "and every man's Judgment Day is the day he dies—"

"For hereditary hallucination there may be a cure; if one can find the absolute cause." Luna switched to her professional manner, so strong is the hold of training. "Like most of the general public, you have never considered that any hereditary peculiarity must have a beginning. A beginning and a cause. Some things only God Himself can alter or cure, by such revolutionary miracles as He does not often work lest mankind should depend on miracles and cease to use its gift of reasoning. But in other cases He decrees that the power some of His creatures acquire by study shall culminate in what is a miracle slowly worked. I have told you the

Fifth Dimension is the human brain: the lump of material grey matter which has the power to comprehend all the other dimensions. The solid Third Dimension of our material world; the nebulous Fourth Dimension of ghosts and fairies—all are enclosed in the human brain. But there's Dimensions beyond the Fifth, and one beyond it—far beyond it, though short of the Dimension that is God—is the Mind beyond the brain, the power of abstract thought that animates the brain. I have studied; I have investigated; God's grace has afforded unusual clues to the origin of this Monster mania; and it may be my portion of Mind outside the Fifth Dimension can mould and alter your Fifth Dimensional twist."

He shook his head. "Dear, you forget. Even if you should kill the hallucination I cannot have you linked to our disgraced name—"

"Oh, you man, you stupid man!" she exclaimed in exasperation. "That's what I've been searching for from the Bronze Age to Judgment Day!—the right to share your outward disgrace, if our consciences approve it!"

She had evidently forgotten the others for the moment. "Why, in any case I am involved already," she went on. "I must give evidence of what I have learnt in support of your confession. I may even land in the dock, for all I know."

"Luna!" he exclaimed. Madame Yorke supplemented bitterly:

"She may. She told us to-day. She will have to explain how she destroyed certain proofs, and that she knew the truth from the first day here and let suspicion rest on innocent men in order to shield you."

Oliver had stared at her while she spoke. He turned his eyes to Luna again. "Yes," she answered defiantly. "There was a scrap of your silk muffler in the dog's mouth. Also some hairs that had evidently come from your moustache on its wounds. Any detective would have started to make deductions if he found them. You had bitten the dog, which had *not* done the assault on the girl—a man of your size could have torn the beast as it was torn, if he were in a state of dementia—the family history would become significant. Oh, I definitely gambled my reputation and all on the chance of those poachers not being arrested, when I hid those hairs and the scrap of silk and finally flung them out of the railway carriage."

"It was a desperate risk," he said. She looked round defiantly and went on; her cheeks hotly pink and her eyes like wintry stars in the shadows upcast by the firelight round them. "I could never have a peaceful hour in life if I had not risked all I value on the chance of averting the scandal. I should have gone mad—I know I should—if I had left you to your undeserved fate without risking my all on the infinitesimal chance I saw of either averting the exposure or—making you a normal man."

"You think there is a way of stopping the Monster manifestations; of doing away with the inherited wolf-mania, short of my death?" he said. "That an hour's experiment will settle if I am to live disgraced and alone in the same world with you, Luna; or face and bear the disgrace with you always with me to comfort me and the right to comfort you in the disgrace you have brought on yourself for my sake? Oh, it's no time for pretence! We five understand one another. It is as I have said?

"It is." Her voice was unfaltering.

"Then for heaven's sake let us have the experiment at once!"

The point gained she spoke very quietly, with the quietude of one facing a task that requires complete mental control. "We must have an explanation first, and certain preparations—"

"But the men?"

"They can stand it for my three hours. We will have the experiment before you surrender yourself to justice."

Her personality dominated them all, as it always did when she chose. In Oliver's eyes the red light was rising, it was the light of anxious hope, but it was fierce as that of the lycanthropy had been as he began to realise that the ruin of his life—and Luna's—had a slender chance of averting totality. The shocks of the evening had been so many that his brain was still a little numbed, and the dawning hope of snatching something from the wreck dominated the horrors for a time.

"We will now make ourselves comfortable," said Luna, settling in her chair again. "We cannot be overheard in this waste of room, and I will explain briefly all about the Hammand Monster from the Bronze Age to the Norse Judgment Day."

6

THE VOW OF SIGMUND THE VOLSUNG

Oliver posted himself in the shadow by one side of the fireplace, Luna sat full in the glow. Swanhild sat on a stool beside her brother and clasped one of his hands as they lay on his knees. Madame Yorke and Goddard were to Luna's other side.

"First," began Luna, "I must impress on you that a man's earlier ancestors matter to his history as powerfully as do his childish impressions. Sub-consciously, the more striking incidents of our first years affect us to the end of our lives, and in the same way the more impressive experiences of those who lived in the world's childhood were bound to subconsciously affect their descendants to the end of time.

"Moreover, modern people are not so powerful, as a rule, either mentally or physically, as those of early times. Then, rough living weeded out all but the fittest and, in a sentence, there were giants on earth in those days. The men and women of early ages, also, did not addle their heads by incessant cursory reading and impotent worry over all the affairs of all the world. Therefore they had tremendous stores of vivid mental energy to devote to brooding; for good or ill; over the few thoughts that really concerned them, with a force that affected the structure of their brains and has sent echoes of their thoughts to us along the ages.

"Remember also, that Western mankind now can scarcely realise what religion was to those of far-back days. To the bulk of us in this age it is a mere subject for speculation; to our forbears in the Bronze Age it was as real a thing as love and hate, fear and hunger. Yes, and even more powerful, for love and hate, hunger and fear could be overcome at the command of religious belief.

"Now to begin. Towards the close of the Scandinavian Bronze Age, about 700 B.C., the time of Hezekiah and Sennacherib in the East; you Hammands had an ancestor named Sigmund of the Volsung line, a great prince of the north. It happened, the Volsung race was hounded down until only two members of it were left alive, Sigmund and his sister Signy. And Sigmund only survived by fighting, tooth to tooth, with a wolf."

Oliver started. She nodded gravely to him. "I relate the tale baldly. Sigmund survived, but, maddened for the time by a share of grief, pain, and starvation beyond human bearing; he broke down in nerve and soul. He did what other men have done—cursed his god. Others have done it, but his curse took a specific form. He made a solemn vow that in the Final Warring, the Norse Day of Judgment, when all heroes shall come to life and ride behind the Asa Gods to the Final War with the Powers of Evil, instead of having him—Sigmund the human hero—to help them, they should find him opposing them; as a wolf on the side of the Evil Powers.

"Pray remember again how hard it is for us, in these days of Higher Criticism and Hyde Park oratory, to realise what blasphemy meant in older times. Remember, too, there was no shriving for sin; he who sinned must reap his condemnation. When he came to his right mind memory of his blasphemy never left Sigmund. Rather it increased in force, always lurking in the background of all his other thoughts.

"It was in a wood of firs and pines, on a frosty starlit night, that he fought the wolf and made the vow. Afterwards, when his fortunes were mended, he chanced to be in a starlit pinewood with one of his sons. The associations of time and place brought his long brooding to a head: lycanthropy was a common mania at the time, and he imagined the curse of his god Odin had come on him. In short, he had a fit of wolf-mania. Through heredity and suggestion combined, his son had a similar attack. They remained in that state, imagining they were wolves and behaving as hungry wolves would to all they met, until the daylight came and their senses returned.

"To make the story short: the impression on Sigmund's brain was so acute that it passed on to his descendants, and to this time at uncertain intervals a man has been born in his line liable to turn, mentally, into a wolf in this combination of circumstances:—A wood with pines and firs in it, a cold starlit night, and only one human companion. Do you understand?"

Swanhild answered. "As the smell of hot tar reminds us unconsciously of when our ancestor was at Derek Carver's burning, so the pines and the rest of the combination wake the older recollection."

"Exactly. When the Carver test was so successful I knew I was on the right track. Sigmund doubtless consulted his priests, and they told him the mania was a curse from Odin that would haunt his family for ever. In consequence Sigmund's male descendants were liable to turn werewolves; both because they inherited the brain-convulution made by the vow and *because they were told they had it*. Please note that last clause.

"One of Sigmund's sons was named Hamandr, and he had the wolf-mania and also he had a specially beautiful bronze sword, which he left to his son and heir. From father to son that sword passed for over a thousand years, until the Bronze Age Hamandr's descendant in the Viking Age went buccaneering to England. His name was Magnus, called Fairlocks, and he surnamed himself Hamandr's Son, to boast his descent from a far-off, distinguished ancestor. Iron weapons had long been in use by his date; it is probable the bronze blade was then a sort of sign of headship amongst the descendants of Hamandr. Pretty much as the lordship of the manor of Poynings went with a ruby ring in later times. Anyhow, Magnus Fairlocks was so proud of it that he had new hilt plates put on it, with his name on in runes.

"He came to England, as I said, buccaneering, on a ship with a golden dragon figurehead, married a Saxon lady, and settled down in Sussex. Duly he died, and his longship was dragged ashore and buried with him in it, in a mound on a mount where he had cut a turf and chalk image of the Danes' favourite god, Vingi Thor. His heirloom sword was broken and buried with him because, I gather, he remained a pagan while his children turned Christian, like their

Saxon mother. And on top of the mound they erected a memorial stone with his name and descent on it in runes. In later times this stone was regarded as an accursed Druid relic, thrown down, and buried. Just as the Hove Goldstone was treated a hundred years ago.

"Now the descendants of Magnus—who named themselves 'Hammand' when surnames came in fashion—had the curse of the wolf in them. The origin had been utterly forgotten. Lycanthropy was very common in the Middle Ages, therefore it was not considered so outrageous as in our time. It came to be regarded as a demon who had power to possess the head of the Hammands—"

"One minute," Oliver put in. "Didn't it extend to other branches of Magnus's descendants?"

"No, for we are none of us the sheer victims of heredity. We make our ancestral curses better or worse, because *suggestion is as powerful as heredity*. It was an article of belief that the Undying Monster which represented the medieval idea of the mania could only possess the owner of Dannow, and every successive owner was told that, and *subconsciously expected it to happen*. Unless a Hammand owned Dannow he never expected to be possessed by the Monster; if he owned the place he was always expecting it subconsciously. Also, they knew it could only have power in cold and starlit pinewoods; and with the best intentions they inaugurated a most deplorable practice.

"I mean the ritual. They composed a warning rhyme, describing the conditions, and when each heir came of age he was solemnly conducted to an obscure chamber, taught the rhyme and its meaning, and tested—"

"Tested?" said Oliver.

"There are pines outside the hidden room window. With the shutters open in starlight the conditions are fulfilled. I have proved it. This is the ritual I deduced; the heir was solemnly warned and exposed to starlight in the room. In the circumstances he would be certain to have an attack of lycanthropy. Those in the secret knew how to check it—by showing a light. This would warn the youth to avoid starlit pinewoods—"

"But why didn't my ancestors remove all the pines on the estate?" Oliver asked. Luna smiled.

"Because they were not cowards. They did their best, and if it failed reckoned it God's will. It would have been unmanly timidity to avoid in their own ground what they were bound to encounter anywhere else; as two of them did on the way to Rocamadour. They did all contemporary science could suggest until God chose to arrange a way in which the mania might have died out, if it had not been for the Warlock's unhallowed studies. I mean the Anchorite, of course; he sought to deliver his race by sacrificing himself, giving up his family and his worldly prospects for the life of a recluse and prayers and penances by which he sought power to 'lay' the Monster forever. That he did 'lay' it, compelling it to lie helpless in the Barrow, was firmly believed: *and so the power of the mania was weakened.* Then came the final dispensation of providence; during the Wars of the Roses everyone who knew the ritual met a sudden end, and Dannow came into the hands of a Hammand who had never been initiated into the secret, and who understood the Monster had been chained for ever in the Barrow.

"That was the turning point. For the mental impression that the head of the Hammands was liable to attacks of lycanthropy in certain circumstances, was substituted the conviction that the Monster was chained in the Barrow. In a few generations the cure would have been complete, and the Monster have become a dim memory of something in the past tense.

"Most unfortunately Magnus the Warlock undid the good providence had planned for him, by his occult dabbling. You have heard his version of the opening of the Barrow; I'll elucidate it from the point of exact mental science. He worked by artificial light, with one helper; unluckily he pitched on cold and starlight nights for the operations. When he reached the figurehead his ancestral memory began to stir—as it did with you, Oliver. At sight of his golden-plaited ancestor's bones and Danish harness it woke violently, and he was in a perfect state of nervous tension when the artificial light failed: extinguished by the gases from the open ship, no doubt. He automatically thought it was the Monster, broken free and triumphing over the Hand of Glory, and the mania came on him. He killed his dog in the cutting, flinging its body out, and sprang out to attack his assistant. Fortunately the lantern was alight, and in its rays the mania ceased.

"He knew what he had done, thinking he was possessed by the Monster, but prudently did not tell Slinfold that. Convinced he had released the Monster he recklessly took the inscribed sword hilt, taking his ancestor's runes for a mystic spell. He kept it safe with the Hand of Glory, and some years later tragedy overtook him. He had sunk low enough to use his own child as assistant in his black magical experiments, and during the course of one in the hidden room he must by accident have lit on the fatal combination of star-light, cold and pines. The wolf fit came on him and he destroyed the child. Lady Hammand must have come with a light in the middle of the horror, she died of shock, while he came to his senses and realised what he had done. He had nerve enough not to let the public know he had been the Monster's instrument, as he would suppose; but he probably told his father confessor. We know he killed himself, after buying the incredible pardon and making a cryptic remark about the hidden room. This reference I rightly understood to mean he merely attributed the disaster to his forbidden studies in it.

"After that the course of the mania was plain. The Warlock's evil doing had undone the Anchorite's sacrificed, destroyed the idea that the Monster was chained. The Warlock's son killed his own wife; through shame and horror he would not say what had happened, and pined to death. You will be able to explain every case to yourselves now. When the patient came to himself he saw no reason to explain he had been the Monster's instrument, and the truth was never found out; for the reason that the mania only came on with but one other person present, and that person was invariably killed, being taken unawares. Only in two cases the patient's own dogs must have killed him when he attacked them."

"Grandfather killed two people," said Swanhild.

"He was meeting a woman secretly," answered Luna, drily. "She had met her fate before the blackmailer showed up and met his in turn. So you have the story from the Bronze Age to now."

"Only for my part." Oliver looked up, staring straight before him. "I understand it now. Poor Holder gave no warning because the Monster's approach was only my brain waking, the rage I felt was a wolf's hate for a human being and dog. The poor old tyke must have run off until— until I was done with—oh, I can't say it!—and attacked him. Only the blow on the head; I don't quite understand that."

"You slipped as you threw the dog's body away. Other Hammands came out of the fit naturally, and knew by their own state what they had done. The blow utterly confused your memory. When I broke up the fit by bringing in the motor lamp this evening you woke naturally and understood, confusedly, what you had done."

"Totally ruining my beautiful bought-and-paid-for arm!" said the irrepressible Goddard. "I was in a stew while I didn't know what was keeping you in check, old man! Of course it was the presence of more than one person. I believe we are to learn how you learnt all this, Miss Bartendale?"

"Yes, I must explain my investigation in order that you may all understand the last experiment."

7

JUDGMENT DAY ON THE HORIZON

"When Swanhild told me the traditions I saw there was something at the back of them, something nobody suspected," Luna resumed. "The Shaw at once settled all question of a Fourth Dimensional being. I must tell you that in my professional work I have not yet met with a case of ghostly interference that would stand investigation, but I have established that anything outside of the normal Third Dimension is always perceptible to a dog or cat or human Sensitive. I followed the track of the only abnormality in the wood—that of spilt blood where you were carried, Oliver. I had a suspicion already by that time, knowing you had been cut up a good deal in the war and were in a highly-strung state—"

"You seemed to suspect me of this enormity pretty quickly," said Oliver.

She returned in quite her old patronising way: "Such things are not so uncommon as the laity suppose! I warned you of the Fifth Dimension, but shelved the idea for my subconscious mind to ruminate on while we tried the church. There I looked at the Monster's alleged portraits and found no enlightenment at first. The Pardon gave me my first starting point. A man who was bold enough to practice forbidden arts in Tudor days must have committed some abnormal sin before he would fly to the lowest superstition of his time—the bought absolution—and that of the most gigantic proportions. For the time I wondered if the Monster really started with him, and tradition had fathered it on his forbears.

"As we left the church another glance at the brass brought illumination. The body of the brass 'Monster' is roughly human, while the head might be anything from a dog's to a dragon's, and the paws are short-toed dog paws. The Monster always tore with grappling, hand-like paws; this could not be a literal representation of it, it must be allegorical. A human body; hands and head; the seats of impulse and action; animal. Human body and animal thoughts and acts—I saw the meaning of the rhyme at once:

> 'Hammond Monster, do ye wit,
>   With the race is firmly knit.'

"It explained all, in the Anchorite's day it was known it was something *inherent in the race* which woke and possessed the victim. The dog's not giving any warning was finally explained.

"Remember I have peculiar knowledge, and cases of people who have apparently been possessed by animal spirits are not unusual in my experience. 'Lycanthropy' was what I said to myself as I left the church. Only the hereditary character is unique—in the modern West at least—and that feature engaged my attention at once. Of the origin of wolf-mania nothing is known; with the earliest records it is already an established form of madness. Yet it must have had an origin. A man can go insane through shock or physical accident, but he doesn't imagine he is a particular animal without some mental prompting, and some crime against nature is at the root of all abnormal heredity mania. Crime committed by a single person sometimes extends its punishment to the guiltless through long ages. Might it be possible to find the origin through your hereditary memory?

"You see, even at that early stage the hope of doing away with the Bane had come to me. I had learnt it was a creation of the Fifth Dimension, an impression of the brain that obsessed the brain's owner in specific conditions. Like cures like, if I could find the exact origin might I not be able to banish it by a counter-impression? So I kept my own counsel, the matter was so long-established that only the exact truth of its origin would serve, and I had to keep you in ignorance, Oliver, lest you should unconsciously start to invent particulars. I had to test your recollection by association alone, and see what light archaeology and the family history would shed on what I elicited.

"At that stage all was a chaos of disconnected data, but the hidden room at once afforded something to start from, in the shape of the Scandinavian sword. I had noticed that the family features, like the family name, pointed to a Danish origin; the north was the home of wehrwolves, and the Danish sword and the runes on it might prove the clue to the Monster's origin. The connection with the hand I did not then understand, beyond its proving the nature of the Warlock's work. It will be obvious now how I deduced the ritual, and that it was extinct before the Warlock's time. This extinction was explained by the pedigree, also how providence had enabled him to start life with the entail of the curse broken, and that in some way he must have ruined this advantage through his occult studies.

"While my learned friends wrestled with the runes I tested your memory in the way you know. When the Danish sword suggested golden pigtails and the fylfot I wondered if the Warlock had taken it from some Danish grave, in which case the use of the hand was evident. I had already surmised the Monstrous Man was a Danish creation, as was the corrupt name 'Thunder's Barrow.' The legend of the hidden gold was another step, and my friend's reading the name of your ancestor clinched matters. Then your persistence about the inscription on the bronze blade made me certain that inscription contained the secret: since memory of it had survived when the ritual was forgotten.

"I was right and wrong in the Barrow matter. Right as to the Warlock's digging, wrong as to his motive; as I realised when the gold-plated figurehead appeared. The excavation was an apparent failure, but it was not utterly so, for in the course of it I learnt how strong your dormant memory of old Danish matters is, Oliver, and that encouraged me to persevere.

"I decided to try a serious experiment. You remember that night I hypnotised you in the drawing-room? And that when you were waked two hours later we simply told you we had elicited nothing fresh? Well, during those two hours Swanhild and I took you into the hidden room, bringing you back before you waked—"

"By Jove!" exclaimed Goddard. "Pardon the interruption. I'll tell you about it later, Oliver."

"I had told Swanhild the truth as soon as you were asleep. She could not believe it without evidence; therefore, leaving Auntic in the drawing-room for fear a servant might come on some errand and be puzzled by our disappearance, we took you to the room. There I made you stand inside a chalked pentacle, impressing on you that you could not move outside it, placed the hand, sword, and golden plates, in your view, turned the light low and hit it, and made you believe you were alone with Swanhild in the starlit night with pines near. The effect was overwhelming, the wehrwolf fit coming on at once. You were unable to get out of the pentacle, however; which told me the strong power of suggestion I had acquired. While you were in that state I summoned Hamandr your ancestor to appear, calling him by his proper designation of Skinturner, and hoping to get further information from you; but you were incapable of coherent human speech—to all intents you were a mere animal for the time. It grew too painful for Swanhild to bear, so I conducted you back to the drawing-room, leaving her to recover a little—oh, I'll tell you that in detail later. Next day Slinfold's narrative turned up, we secured the inscribed stone, and it proved to be the final clue. On Thursday my professor read the runic inscription on it, and this is how it runs—"

She unfolded a paper, Oliver held it to the light and read: "*Edith his wife, and Olafr, Rognwaldr, and Swanhild his children, raised this memorial to Magnus, that was named Fairlocks, that was of the blood of Hamandr Sigmund's Son the Volsung.*"

"It was quite enough," Luna resumed. "It linked you with the Volsung tale, as told in the Elder Edda. Now pray attend carefully, that you may understand my weak link. On getting the translation I applied to the British Museum, and had a summary of the Volsung tale prepared from different versions of the Edda. One point eluded me; there must have been some exact connection between the fight with the wolf and the lycanthropy, but that connection was not apparent. The mere fight with the wolf was not enough to induce the abiding mania. At last my Museum assistant, at his wits' end, was reduced to consulting poetry. He produced William Morris's metrical version of the Volsung epic. And in it is Sigmund's vow; which was not introduced in any of the prose translations at my command. This vow idea offers such a convincing and logical reason for the mania that I related it to you in its proper place. Still, it is the weak link, an explanation is not necessarily the true one simply because it is plausible. On the other hand a true poet can so enter into the thoughts of others, even of the dead, that he can often explain a motive of which no tangible record is available.

"That is the history of the Undying Monster. Its cause, blasphemy when men believed with heart and soul and—*brain*. Its agency, a kink in the brain and the unfortunate heirs of that kink. Its effects past summing, ramifying from homicidal mania (to put it scientifically) to a crop of disgraceful legends. Now I shall lay before you the feeble hope I have of ending the history; for the Monster may be Undying in itself, but liable to be killed—if my weak link holds."

Oliver raised his head and looked full at her as she went on: "I came down to-day with the intention of making the experiment; I have only had to hurry owing to these arrests. What I purpose to do is, in a sentence, to make the wolf mania work itself out."

"The mania work itself out? How?" he asked hoarsely,

"By working backward through your memory right to the Bronze Age, until I persuade you you are your own ancestor, Sigmund the Volsung. There was much method in my putting you through your paces at our different sittings! Your memory for ancient Danish religion is very powerful—as I proved apropos of the Last Warring two days ago—I shall wake all recollections connected with Sigmund, then carry it further by suggesting that you—as Sigmund—die, that the Final Warring comes, that the wolf mania has worked itself out, in accordance with the terms of the vow, and that Sigmund has been forgiven by the gods, and taken into the company of the gods and the risen dead at the re-creation of the world. In this way the convolution of the brain that harboured the wolf mania will be altered and henceforth only hold a vague, complacent sense of something done with. Do you understand?"

"I do now. If it succeeds—"

"Oh, do not hope!" she begged. "The weak link—no more than the idea of a poet three thousand years after your ancestor's time— is so very doubtful! But we will try. I shall rouse the wolf mania in the hidden room, put you in hypnosis, and do as I have described. After that we shall repeat the conditions for rousing the mania. If it does not wake, then you are a normal man for ever; but if it wakes the vow idea is wrong and—the problem of the future is for you to settle."

8

THE HOUR OF THREE THOUSAND YEARS

At seven o'clock Luna and Oliver were at the end of a short conversation alone in the Holbein room. "It's time," said Luna. "You quite understand, Oliver? You must not hope, for fear of the—the—"

She hesitated, her eyes seeking his miserably. "For fear of the disappointment if the link fails?" he completed.

"If it fails. But I must hope, for if the link does not fail the whole may yet fail if I do not do my work well. And one cannot work convincingly without hope. It rests on the link—and on me equally."

"It is cruelly hard on you, Luna. It hurts me that you should stand such a strain."

"Oh, I have to consider my own feelings as well as yours!" She saw he was weakening, and braced herself back to her usual manner. "Our assistants should be done now. There was not much to do. Swanhild and Goddard only had to put pine boughs round the hidden room window; anything to accentuate the circumstances, and Auntie to superintend the transport of the piano—"

"Eh? The piano?"

"To the corridor outside the spring cellar. Your reference to Wagner gave me the idea. Anything to accentuate the Norse atmosphere. Besides, it pleases Auntie to be useful to one of her beloved boys. I hear her coming."

They stood up. "The hour that will settle if I must shoulder the curse of the dead"; he looked up at the Warlock's portrait; "or—or—oh Luna!"

"Oh Oliver!" Her voice was unsteady, she stepped close to him and held out her hands. He bent his head, but again ingrained discipline asserted itself and his kiss merely touched her forehead. Only he pressed her chilled hands to his own burning face for a moment.

"That's right," she said. "We can't afford to be unmanned. We must be captains of our own souls; and pray God the link holds!"

Two cool and steady young people accompanied Madame Yorke to the disused complex. The piano stood by the open door over the water; in the hidden room Swanhild and Goddard were adjusting the last big pine bough beside the open shutters. All the party wore their thickest coats, for it was very cold in the stone room with the wind pouring through the window. Madame Yorke remained at the piano, able to hear but not to see what went on in the room. The four young people were very quiet. Three pairs of eyes followed Luna's every movement. With the hush and the blowing air, branches, and gurgle of water, it was suggestive at once of out-of-doors and an impending operation.

The Warlock's table was at the foot of the stairs, the free space beyond it was still filled by the chalked pentacle, now somewhat blurred. Between the chalked line and the window were heaped the gold plates of the figurehead, the hand and bronze sword lay on the table beside a lamp that could be shrouded in an impromptu screen. Luna nodded to Oliver.

He stepped into the pentacle where a chair waited. She took a stick of chalk and re-marked the lines: "Remember, you cannot step beyond these lines," she told him, her eyes holding his. "Look—pines, and stars to be seen outside the window, and cold wind, and—" she gave a gesture and the other two ran up to the niche—"and only one person with you; *garoul Hammand!*"

She slid the screen round the lamp. The room was black to Goddard and Swanhild, as they peered down the stairs, and quite still for a minute. Luna stood with teeth clenched and palms damp; her eyes became adjusted to the dark and as she discerned a star or two through the grille two red sparks lit at the top of the vague black bulk that was Oliver in his chair. The demoniac barking howl that Goddard and Swanhild had heard before broke out. In the corridor Madame Yorke clutched her ears, simultaneously Luna swept the screen aside and the room was lit again. The howl stopped half-way.

The two in the niche returned to their posts at the table. Oliver stood, shaking convulsively, in the pentacle, his face just losing the appearance it had worn in the Shaw. Before he could speak Luna flicked a hand commandingly towards him, "Sit, and sleep!" she ordered.

He sat down, his lids drooping. She closed the shutters and then commenced the process to which all were now used. She led him back through history, shewed him at the proper stages the hand and golden plates, and finally gave him the bronze sword to hold while she explained he was Sigmund Volsung's Son. At that he recognised the blade at once. He had owned it as Hamandr, but it was first made for Sigmund. She spoke of old Danish gods and beliefs, and finally carried him through Sigmund's history, from the fight with the wolf and the vow, to his death. Completely under her mental control he lived over every detail she suggested, as he had lived over the horror of Carver's martydom at the first sitting.

Then she seemed to wake to life. Her voice took on a fervid cadence that seemed to fill the whole room with a thin, hushed mass of sound. "Sigmund Volsungsson—vower of the wolf vow, I speak to you!" she began.

"I hear, whom am Sigmund the king, son of Volsung the king and the vower of the wolf vow," he answered, tonelessly.

"Sigmund, you are dying on the strand of a strange country," she went on. "Dying after a battle wherein Odin's self came to slay thee."

"The old man in cloud-grey raiment, who smote me down with a strained twi-bill, was truly Odin himself," he quietly assented. He sat rigidly at attention, his eyes following her every movement.

"Do you know who it is that bends over you as you die, Sigmund?" she asked. "It is your queen."

He turned his head to the right, but his eyes remained directed to her. "My queen—Hiordis!" he said, and staggered to his feet and

stood swaying. "Let me die standing, as a Volsung should, Hiordis."
he cried in a voice gone suddenly feeble.

"Alas, now is the life gone from you, Sigmund," exclaimed Luna.
Immediately he collapsed into the chair, but ere he well fell back
her voice changed and clanged out ringingly. "Sigmund, awake!"
she called. "Hear the call to Godhome, Volsung soul!—arise and
come away!"

"I come, Chooser of the Slain!"

He sat up as though galvanised. "*Die Walkure!*" she called, turning her head to the stairs; and from the corridor, made mystically
impersonal from the invisibility of its source, the "Ride of the
Valkyrs" swelled through the room. Through what followed it made
a background of swooping, galloping melody, with the gurgle of
the spring running behind it, through which Luna's voice pierced,
thin and clear, in a steady thread of recitative.

"Mount and come, Sigmund, thou Sunlit Hill of Battles! Mount
and ride with the Valkyrs; the Choosers of the Heroic Slain! Hear
the clatter of our horsehooves on the stars as we gallop through
the sky! See, Volsung's son, the stormclouds fleeting past us like
wisps of mist; see the world wax small and ever smaller beneath
us—and hold fast lest you fall!"

The blankness of Oliver's face was gone. It was flushed, his eyes
flamed red. His hands were held in a way that suggested the grip
of an imaginary bridle, at her warning his knees crooked and stiffened as though calves and thighs gripped a horse's sides.

"Onward—ever onward!" she proceeded. "The earth is past; the
stars are past; the firmament's very rim has felt the last touch of
our horsehooves! Winter and summer are outraced—we reach
Valhalla, Sigmund Volsung's son! Enter Godhome, son of Volsung,
enter and rest and feast until the Day of Odin's Need. You are in
Valhalla, Sigmund, feasting, wrestling, fencing, with your peers the
Einheirar, everliving through the short years of unwearying days.
The centuries are sweeping past on midearth, Volsung Sigmund;
long wars there are, and short times of peace, but they pass unno-
ticed in Valhalla, in the fair companionship of the Einheirar. With
the leaves of Yggdrasil, the Holy Ash, ever soughing overhead, and

Odin's self in the shade of it. The peace of Valhalla—and now wake, Volsung's son, for the ages have passed like a night's dream, and it is the Fimbulveter-tide! The Day of Odin's Need—of the Need of the Asa gods—son of Volsung!"

Her voice had risen gradually. It dropped now to a thin thread. The music ceased, and the pianist began an improvisation of her own in a minor key that barely seconded the gurgle of the spring and formed a flat, nebulous background to the flexible voice. "Look down and abroad from Valhalla's golden wall, Sigmund," it exhorted. "Look, as the Asa gods and your fellows the Einheirar look, to earth in the Fimbulveter-tide. The fated three winters of war are overpast, the torn and tangled nations would fain be at truce to till the ground fattened with three years of shed blood, but the judgment of the Norns is upon them. They have spun and carded, and sheared; the Norns of Past and Present and Yet to Be; and the latter days of Fimbulveter-tide follow the first. One—two—three winters—year-long winters of cold—and mankind is spun out and carded and sheared by the sixfold winter of war and cold. As wool is spun and carded and cut by mankind, so is their fate dealt with on the distaff and spindle of the Norns. It is the time of Regnarok; the sun and moon are darkened; the stars vanish in the shrivelling arch of Ymer's Skull—It is THE DAY!

"The Day—the Day of Regnarok, Sigmund son of Volsung! The earth is quaking—Valhalla's self trembles—" Her voice had become a steady, toneless chant. Oliver sat upright, quivering in every limb. "The earth trembles, Volsung's son—look, how Fenrir Lokisson, Fenrir the Wolf, has burst his bonds and rages over the shrinking land. Yes, and behold how Jormundgandr the serpent no longer reposes, tail in mouth, to hold the waters steady around the world, but strives to climb aland and lashes the troubled waters, wave on wave, so that they overwhelm the shore! See the waves writhing upwards even to the shrivelling sky, son of Volsung; and see what creeps forward on the lashed welter of them! Nagelfare it is, son of Volsung; ship Nagelfare, builded through the ages of dead men's nails, and launched now and sailing with a crew of hell's legions to the wreck of Godhome!

"Look, too, to West. Look to the blazing mountain of Muspell-heim—to the flaming mount where bide Surtur and the Sons of the Flame! It is Regnarok Day, son of Volsung, and they arise—they saddle their flaming horses—behind Surtur their lord they ride through the splitting heavens to the wrecking of Midearth and Valhalla!

"See, too, how hell's own jaws open, and Hela its ruler and Asa Lok emerge and range beside the flaming chargers. From Mus-pellheim they advance, and the flames and gledes of it follow them like hounds of fire.

"And wake now, Volsung's son; for Heimdall has climbed the highest height of Valhalla and—hear it now! he has sounded the Gjaller horn! Lo, the Asa gods and Einheirar rouse them. Hear how it drowns the very blast of the Gjaller horn—the clangour as the Asa and Einheirar fling on helm and cuirass and snatch their weap-ons—and hear the sound of the peace strings snapping—"

Oliver sprang to his feet. His face was transfigured, shining with a radiance from within as he towered before her, staring right over her head at some imaginary sight, chin up, eyes flaming and flick-ering under tautened brows. "*Heysa-a-a!*" A long, snarling call rippled from his throat. "A Volsung! A Volsung!"

She made a little gesture to the chair he had left. "Cuirass, and belt, sword, and helm, and shield," she said.

He went through a rapid pantomime. Taking an invisible ob-ject from the chair he went through the movements of dragging it on over one arm and his head, pulling it down round waist and hips, and buckling it down the side, his hands moving with fever-ish haste. Round his waist an invisible belt went, then a helmet on his head, with some adjustment of it over the ears. Something was lifted with reverence from the chair and slung to the belt, some-thing else slung on the left arm and hitched over the shoulder. It was intelligible enough. As he shifted the imaginary shield into place Luna spoke again: "*Die Walkure* once more!" she called up the stairs, and again the tremendous music surged forth and filled the room.

Very coolly and gently her voice took up the thread of recitative.
"The Choosers of the Slain and now the Leaders of the Slain to the
Unshapen Isle and the Last Warring of the Gods and the Sons of
the Flame. Look how the hordes of Muspellheim reach Bifrost—
Bifrost Bridge which mortals name the rainbow! See them crowd
it, rank on rank, and the flames and gledes behind them. See, see—
Bifrost bends—Bifrost breaks beneath them! It comes apart: see
its splinters falling to the foamy sea below, where rides Nagelfare—
opalescent splinters mixed with the gledes and sparks of the flame!

"See, Surtur and his legions are in the wallowing flood. Their
steeds strike out. But the gods are on the strand of Valhalla—their
snowy chargers breast the waves as do the flaming steeds of hell—
the Einheirar are streaming down from the gates of Valhalla—
*Volsung Sigmund—Vower of the Wolf Vow, why do you alone
delay?*"

A look of the most blank and abject horror came to Oliver's
face. The clear battle-light in his eyes altered to an unfocussed glare
of dismay. He stopped in the first movement of a rush forward,
and hung awkwardly on one foot.

"Vower of the vow—you who swore to be a wolf on THE DAY!"
she said quietly. He stayed as he was, glaring before him. "Sigmund,
you cannot join the Einheirar," she went on. "You restrain yourself with difficulty—you know, who vowed the wolf vow, that no
beast nor bestial man can smite upon the side of the gods in THAT
DAY. If you join the strife your place will be with Wolf Fenrir and
the horde of Surtur; and you will tear the throat of Odin's self even
as you blasphemed him in your despair The vow is coming to its
fulfilment, son of Volsung!"

As she spoke the word Oliver went on all fours within the pentacle. The inhuman wehrwolf call crackled and roared out, and so
he crouched, propped on his palms and writhing in every muscle.

9

THE LAST TWILIGHT–AND AFTER

"The Einheirar ride, and you may not ride with them, Sigmund son of Volsung!" Luna went on, intoning now in a species of level chant. "Shall not he who blasphemes Odin Allfather reap the harvest of his tongue; though it be not until THE DAY? You restrain yourself, even as the Einheirar ride in your sight, who would have been their peer and comrade in THE DAY, but for the sin of your brain and voice! See they pass—your father Volsung the king and your brothers with him; there your forefathers; there the Niblung brethren; dark in the blue Niblung mail. There ride your sons, Helgi and Hamandr. There Sinfjotli Signysson who was a wolf with you in your life. There, all golden in dwarf-wrought helm and harness, is Sigurd Fafnir's Bane. Your sons, Sigmund of the wolf vow: for the sin of your lips you must stand aside on THE DAY, yet, by Odin's dear grace, your flesh is battling by the side of the Asa gods in this tide whereto all Time has led."

She ticked off each name with a finger in the air, and Oliver's eyes followed the gesture as though he saw what she described. His face was completely wolf-like, he strained the upper part of his body forward, as he writhed on all fours, with his hands on the chalk line of the pentacle; precisely as though it were a concrete barrier he could not pass. Cold as the room was his face ran with perspiration, as though a rainstorm were beating on it. Swanhild gave a little cry, Goddard slipped one arm round her and placed his hand over her eyes.

"There ride the kings of the North, of Denmark and Norway and Sweden. There Olaf Tryggvesson, for all he brought the White Christ to northern lands, and with him Elinar Tamberskilver, and Kolbiorn, and even Hakon, too, of Lade. There is Canute, lord of all the North; there Sigurd Jorsalafarer, there—stream on stream of them, the Byzantine incense-fumes still in their helmet-plumes—come the Varangers! There they come, one and all, the heroes of the North. Only you; Sigmund of the wolf vow, must stand aside on THE DAY!"

Oliver was alternately straining against the pentacle's line, and rolling on one side and the other, like a rabid dog; writhing all the time, barking, snarling, and panting loudly between the paroxysms. The chant picked up speed.

"They ride the sea; look, Sigmund, you who must stand inactive on THE DAY! Asa gods and Einheirar, ghost-crew of Nagelfare, horde of Hela's realm and Sons of the Flame—they ride the sea! See Odin lay about him with his twi-bill, see Thor's Hammer rise and fall and rise bloodied, see the Einheirar smite! It is vain"; she lowered her voice still further and the music died off until she was speaking, with increasing hushedness, to the mere accompaniment of the gurgling water and the sough of wind between the grilles: "Wolf Fenrir seizes the throat of Odin—Where is the Allfather? Dead—Allfather Odin is dead; and, for the sin of his mind and lips, Sigmund could deal no blow in his defence! Look—look! Asa-god Tyr is down, Garmer the Dog has him—the Sons of Flame win— they win! The Asa gods are slain, the Einheirar drop one by one— Surtar is calling to Muspellheim! He orders—the Mountain of the Flame answers; it pours its fires, stream on stream, over the earth.

"The sea vanishes in a spurt of steam. The streams of fire rush, splashing wave on wave, they overwhelm dead gods and dead Einheirar—they beat against the golden walls of Valhalla's self, as waves beat the seaside rocks: the wall of Valhalla melts, the flame-waves overflow Valhalla, the earth reels, the sky shrivels, the sun and moon alike drop into the sea of rocking flame. Only Yggdrasil the Ash, stands, quivering, amidst the wrack. The gods are dead!"

Then *"Die Gotterdamerung!"* she called, and the sombre cadence of the funeral march of the gods rolled forth. In the pentacle Oliver cowered, half exhausted and foaming at the mouth. Luna's voice sank even lower as she proceeded, and the words came slower and slower. Swanhild, seeing nothing with her actual eyes, beheld all the other woman put into words, in the recesses of her brain inherited memory would have responded, in that hour of highly-strung emotion, to the mere thunder of the ancient Northern names. The images briefly sketched with Luna's magnetic voice made a magic reality of it all. In the dark behind Goddard's soothing hand Swanhild forgot even her brother as she lived through the twilight of the gods and the death of the Universe, as her ancestors had foreseen it for thousands of years.

"All are dead, Asa gods, Earth, and Valhalla, and Time. Only Sigmund son of Volsung lives on in an unliving life: he who for his tongue's sin stood aside on THE DAY. He who did penance for his sin by standing aside on THE DAY. Look upon creation, Volsung Sigmund—a fire-scorched Nothing it lies in your sight, only Ash Yggdrasil stands firm over the wreck. Earth is but an icy-cold wilderness now that the sun is dead. The Sons of the Flame, they who won, died as all powers of evil must die in time. The ages pass, age after age—unreckoned in this eternity after the death of Time. Muspellheim's fires die, the ice of the Gaping Gap, whence came the universe, crawls over their slaked ashes. Only Yggdrasil stands in a dead creation.

"But Volsung, look!" Her voice rose with electrifying sharpness, and the music ceased. "What is happening to the Tree, and what is toward on the earth? The ice is warming, turning to rivers, as a new sun glides up into the new forming firmament. They cut themselves channels in the earth's surface—they rim—greenness is creeping over the dead world—trees are budding from the clefts of the barren rocks. It is spring; Time is born again!"

Oliver cowered in a quivering heap, his scarlet beast's eyes fixed on her. "Look!" she cried. "Who ride forth on the new-born earth? Whence did they come? Horses trampling joyously, harness chiming, voices calling—friend greeting friend. The Einheirar are risen! Who rides at their head? Odin arisen! Who ride amidst them?—the Asa gods arisen! Oden, and Thor, and Tyr, and Baldur—the gods are risen!"

She rapped an order aside to the stairway, and the commanding clamour of the Song of Awakening rang out. Penetratingly clear her voice chimed in with it: "Odin calls—Odin calls his chosen heroes by name to the glory of the new heaven and earth! Rise, rise, Volsung Sigmund, for the first name Odin calls is the name of him who vowed the wolf vow and expiated it by his self-made agony of remaining aloof on THE DAY! Rise, forgiven Sigmund; wolf vow worked out and atoned; rise and join the Asa gods and Einheirar in the newborn Valhalla for ever!"

As her voice ceased so did the music. Goddard gave a little cry and snatched his hand from Swanhild's eyes. She blinked for a few moments, dazed by the change from tremendous melody to silence intensified by the blurred sounds of wind and water, and at the waking from cosmic myth to the concrete, lamplit room. "Look at Oliver!" Goddard whispered.

Oliver was on his feet in the pentacle, almost on tiptoes with the gush of alert energy that had straightened him upright, chest out, chin up, hands raised in what Swanhild somehow knew was the root-attitude of worship in all humanity. His fare was the wolf face, only the eyes were not red. They were human eyes, Oliver Hammand's normal eyes set in the wolf mask, and no sooner had his sister realised that than the wolf features changed. They did not fade gradually, as in the Shaw, into his natural features; rather they vanished between two flicks of the watcher's eyelids, and Oliver was there in his pleasant human entirety. Only he seemed bigger and more splendid than he had ever been before, and his eyes blazed with a steady, ecstatic scintillation, as though they reflected the light from a world beyond ours.

"Worked out—and forgiven—I thank you, Odin Allfather!" he cried. "Forgiven for ever—wolf nevermore!"

Luna, before him, seemed almost tiny and insignificant by contrast with his radiant, magnificent manhood. She trembled and shrank back, then pulled herself together. "Wake, *Oliver Hammand!*" she ordered.

He shut his eyes a moment, gave a little sigh, and opened them. "Why—what—" he began, looking round confusedly. "You were going to hypnotise me, weren't you?"

"In a minute," Luna snapped. "Up the stairs!" she called to Goddard and Swanhild. They obeyed without a word. It was the final minute. "I want to try you again, with pines and starlight, and only myself present," she said to Oliver. Then she swung the shutters open and shrouded the lamp. There was a long pause in the darkness. Swanhild clutched Goddard's arm, and found she was trying to pray with half her mind.

"The stars are very clear," said Oliver quietly, at last. "I don't quite understand. I thought you tested me for—oh, for the wolf mania you told me about. And I thought you were going to mesmerise me. I'm sure I remember sitting down, and I was standing up just now. I'm quite muddled."

He stopped vaguely. The pine branches smelt powerfully on the wind through the grille, by that time Luna's eyes were adjusted to discern the points of peaceful light beyond the ironwork. "Pines, stars, cold, and one companion—*Garoul Hammand!*" she said.

"Good Lord, I remember!" he cried sharply. "You told me I go mad, turn to a wolf in such conditions—didn't you make me do it just now? I—I'm all confused. Only it really doesn't affect me at all—makes me feel rather pleasant, it's all so fresh, and nice-smelling, and quiet. Luna—does it mean you were mistaken about it. But I remember—the Shaw! I feel all confused—am I crazy?

"Not crazy—cured!" She flashed the light on again and confronted him, her eyes almost wild, her breast heaving as she half-sobbed: "Not crazy—cured! You are a normal man for the first time."

"Normal?" he repeated. "Good Lord, I remember fully—I am to tell the police—"

"You are to remember fully that though you must tell the police you are a normal man," she answered.

10
A NIGHT OF UNCLOUDED STARS

Swanhild and Goddard came down into the room and after them Madame Yorke. Oliver hid his face in his hands for a minute. Then he raised it again and squared his shoulders while he regarded his surroundings. The grey of the room, black shadows dancing in it a little as the draught rustled the pine boughs round the grille. The gold plates, Hand of Glory and bronze sword, on the floor outside the pentacle. The others very quiet, as people are after a climax. His look came to anchor on Luna as she leant against the window-sill, the breeze-drifting tendrils of golden curls round the wide, haggard eyes that stared, all pupil, at him.

"I'm rather confused, you know," he said at last. "You've all had more or less time to understand the business; I've only had to-night. But two things I do comprehend—that I'm normal, and that I must ring up the police at once. And, somehow, I don't feel either sorry or glad, afraid or hopeful. It's all been so sudden, and the idea that I was to lose you, Luna, had not time to get a grip of me before you found that the link held. That it held," he repeated, "that God has allowed you to give me hope of a future in spite of disgrace—"

He ended indecisively, and in a different, kindly tone. "You are used up, dear," he said. "We'd better get out of this." He offered his arm, she linked her hands round it, and for a moment elation sparkled fiercely in his eyes. "I'm normal—a sane man—whatever disgrace comes is inevitable, and not our fault. We are equals, you and I!" he exclaimed in a voice for her ears alone.

"Not equals, dear," she whispered back. "My work is done, now you are the man, the strong one, and must shield me."

The plea was what would rouse and steady the best in him. A great calm came to his face, and with it he seemed to grow more vital and virile. He would fail at times, but from thence onward he would always be in his normal mood what he was then; a strong man who had thrust the hopeless past aside and turned all his powers of soul and brain to moulding the future for the comfort of the woman who had earned him the right to mould it. They both forgot the others as they climbed the stairs without further words, their arms linked for the first time.

Swanhild took the lamp, and Goddard closed the shutters.

"Of all this crowd I'm the most upset," observed Madame Yorke. "Presumably because I have the least concern in the matter."

"That," said Goddard, "is sound psychology."

Outside the gallery door Walton hovered. So he had hovered during the first investigation, only now, at night, he was the more abjectly terrified. "Thank heaven, sir!" he quavered.

Luna would have drawn away from Oliver, but his big right hand shut down on both of hers, and held them on his arm. "Well, Walton, what is it?" he asked.

"Inspector Burrell, sir. Just ring you up, sir. I told him your orders were you were not to be disturbed, but I'd tell you when I could."

Luna's hands twitched on Oliver's arm. He smiled down reassuringly into the agony of her eyes. "Very good, Walton. Tell the Inspector I expected the call and will have a few words with him immediately."

Walton hurried away. "It's as well it has come at once, both for the two fellows and our own sakes," said Oliver quietly. "Swanhild, you'll get your motor things to run round to the Ades. Goddard, you'll come with me. No, Luna, dear, I'd rather you went into the Holbein room a minute."

She obeyed without protest. Swanhild ran upstairs, glad of something active to do. Within a few minutes she would be helping to bring the family name down in eternal ruin. What would they do to Oliver? Put him somewhere as a dangerous maniac? And poor Luna—poor Luna who had risked all to save him. In her room two photographs caught her eye; she found herself thanking God silently her father and mother were dead.

When she reached the door of the Holbein room the men were still at the telephone, across the dusky hall. Oliver dropped the receiver and stared at Goddard. Goddard stared back. The whiteness of their faces showed in the dim light. She heard him say: "Goddard!" and Goddard took him hurriedly by the arm. They walked quickly across to the stairs and up them. She waited, to take Oliver's other elbow. Both men had eyes that stared and faces expressionless with too much emotion. Oliver was almost panting. Goddard began to make little sounds that would have suggested incipient hysterics in a woman.

Luna turned from the lire to face them. Her lips worked and her eyebrows almost met with agony, but she smiled at Oliver. "You have told him, dear?" she asked.

He crossed the room and bunched her hands in his. "I haven't—oh, thank God, Luna! Thank God!" was all he could reply.

Goddard shut the door. "Let me tell!" he cried. "It's bathos—and bathos suits me. It's not the Shaw—that's absolutely napoo. Those two men took a bit of brimstone, or sulphur, or something, into old Hudson's preserves last night. Six brace of pheasants—sold to a Steyning poulterer. They were drunk when the boys in blue came for them, and waxed disorderly. It must have been a rural Sydney Street, less the Home Secretary and Maxims. The village flocked to the show while we gambolled undisturbed with the spiritualists; hence exaggerated accounts of the cause of arrest. The family name's saved, all is saved, and the Monster's laid for ever!"

Luna's eyes sought Oliver's. "All saved!" he said. "Only—oh, Luna, the poor girl!"

When Goddard took his departure Swanhild walked with him as far as the moat bridge, and they leant on the parapet a little while. The night world was cold and illimitable under its roofing of translucent black sky and quivering stars. The dark water rippled gently, the wind stirred a million little voices in the ivy round the house.

"Night is the only really peaceful thing in life," Swanhild whispered. "And, though it is not two weeks since—since the Shaw, I feel as though I'd never felt the peace of it before. First the idea of the Monster as a spirit lurking in clear darkness—then the worse horror of the truth! Oh, I never seem to have seen the stars without a cloud near them before."

ENVOI

The inquest came to an end with the second adjournment. The police had to admit they were unable to solve the puzzle of the Shaw, and Kate Stringer's fate was added to the list of Dannow's unsolved mysteries. It seemed that the Ades had never been seriously considered by the official investigators, in spite of Warren's frantic efforts to fix the guilt on them.

"I have given up the Dannow Mystery in despair, and have consequently abandoned my profession in chagrin. At least that's what all the enemies and dear friends I own are saying. They don't know I started the tale myself."

So Luna spoke as she sat with Oliver in the little Chelsea drawing-room a fortnight after the finale in the hidden room. "It tickles my North Country sense of humour to end my career with a failure engineered by myself," she added.

"On the other hand it's held in the Dannow district that you laid the Monster in the Red Sea, on the strength of the servants' tales of our preparations for the last sitting in the room," said Oliver. "Well, laid it is. Ten times since, on frosty, starlit nights, I have been through the Shaw or in the room alone with Swanhild or Goddard."

"Laid it is," she assented. "And it will remain a mystery to the outer world to the end of time."

"Thanks to what you did over poor Holder, dear."

"Under Providence. Providence and I can do wonders when we give our minds seriously to a problem."

She tried to laugh. "Even at that time—the first day—you made up your mind to involve yourself in the family crash," he went on.

"It was impulse, when I worked over the dog. We didn't know an inquest would be necessary, and I felt it was worth the risk of holding back evidence for the sake of an innocent family. I only destroyed the evidence after our drive to Hassocks. It was then I felt the virtue go out of me—in the car—and decided to lie and run risks, sink or swim, for you, Oliver."

"But what virtue, dear?"

"My Sixth Sensitiveness. That sense clung to me long enough to find the hand, but when next I was in the room I felt no discomfort over handling the thing—as Goddard noticed. That's all; I am no longer a trained Supersensitive, but a perfectly ordinary person."

"And I, thanks to you, am also an ordinary person. We can start life afresh, and together, unburdened by the past—" Oliver stopped. "Oh Luna—poor Kate!" he cried. "I dream of her—I don't seem to have realised till now the incredible horror of what I did—"

"Oliver, dear," she interrupted gravely. "You know what I risked for the right to start life with you. Don't make it too hard for me to make that start hopefully and cheerfully."

COACHWHIP PUBLICATIONS

ALSO AVAILABLE

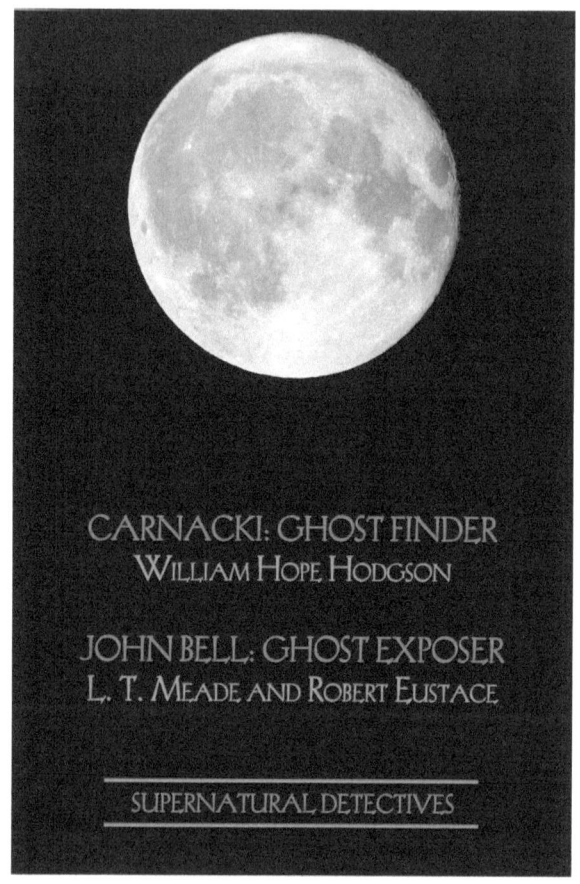

CARNACKI: GHOST FINDER
WILLIAM HOPE HODGSON

JOHN BELL: GHOST EXPOSER
L. T. MEADE AND ROBERT EUSTACE

SUPERNATURAL DETECTIVES

Supernatural Detectives 1:
Carnacki / John Bell
ISBN 1-61646-086-5

COACHWHIP PUBLICATIONS

ALSO AVAILABLE

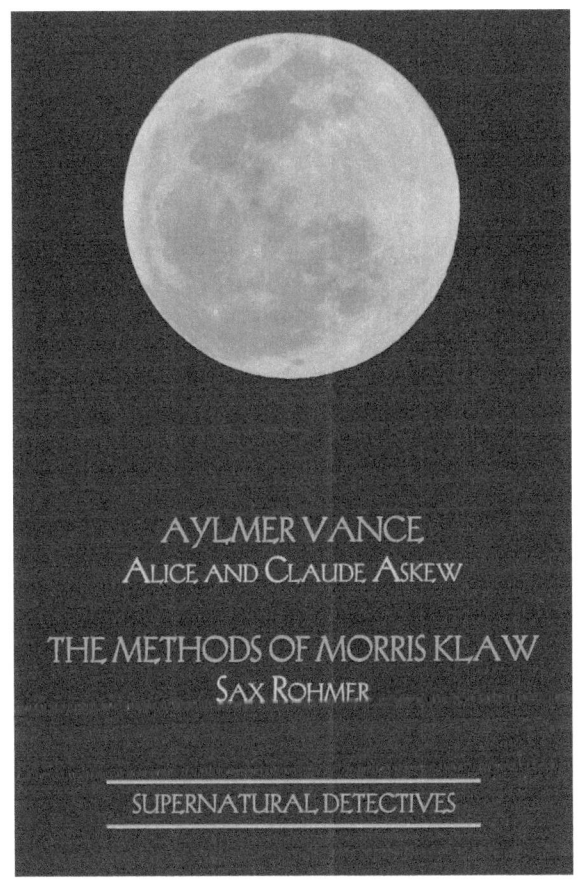

AYLMER VANCE
ALICE AND CLAUDE ASKEW

THE METHODS OF MORRIS KLAW
SAX ROHMER

SUPERNATURAL DETECTIVES

Supernatural Detectives 2:
Aylmer Vance / Morris Klaw
ISBN 1-61646-086-5

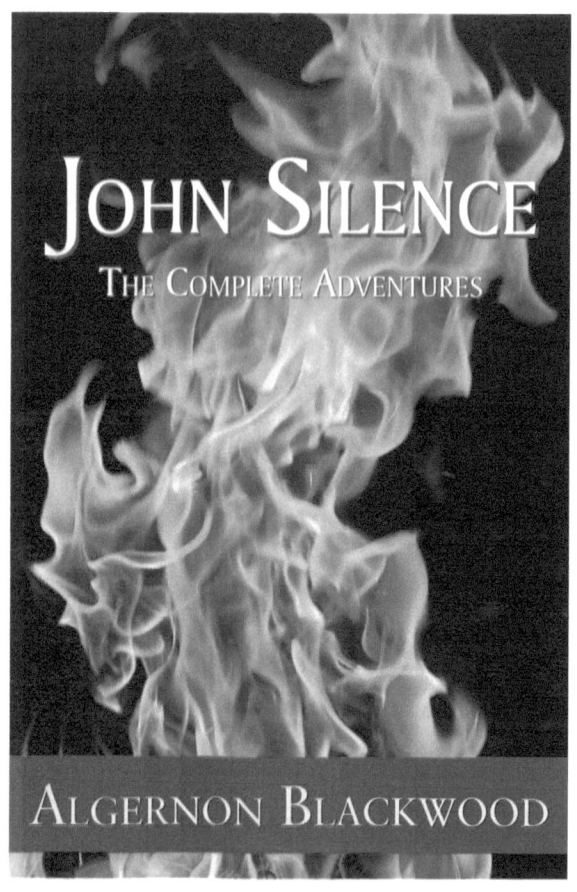

John Silence: The Complete Adventures
ISBN 1-930585-90-X

COACHWHIP PUBLICATIONS

ALSO AVAILABLE

Ancient Haunts
ISBN 1-61646-005-9

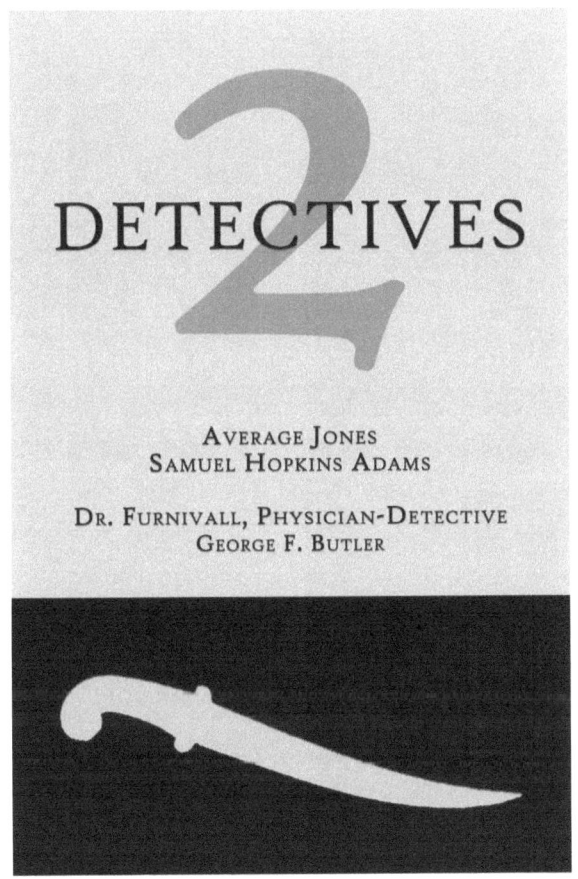

DETECTIVES
2

AVERAGE JONES
SAMUEL HOPKINS ADAMS

DR. FURNIVALL, PHYSICIAN-DETECTIVE
GEORGE F. BUTLER

2 Detectives:
Average Jones / Dr. Furnivall
ISBN 1-61646-098-9

'

www.ingramcontent.com/pod-product-compliance
Lightning Source LLC
Chambersburg PA
CBHW020529020726
47494CB00006B/1683